PAST PARTICIPLE

Longlisted for the Bath Novel Prize 2022

Jane Labous is an award-winning author, journalist and broadcaster known for her work covering human rights and gender issues, always telling the powerful human stories behind the headlines. Jane's debut novel, *The Chameleon Girl*, was published in Nigeria by Farafina Books in 2022. Her credits span a vista of international outlets, including The Times, Voice of America, the UN and Radio 4's flagship programme, From Our Own Correspondent. She has won the BBC Radio 4 and Royal Geographical Society Documentary Award; the Merck More than a Mother Media Recognition & Film Award for Francophone African Countries; and a European Journalism Centre Development Reporting Grant. Her fiction has been longlisted for the Bath Novel Prize and the Santa Fé Writers' Project Literary Award. As a devoted single parent, Jane often writes stories, characters and locations to honour her daughter, who is half-Senegalese, reflecting their own diverse family experience.

For more information, you can visit Jane's website:
www.janelabous.com

'An original and truly gripping read. There are so many strands, twist and turns. Lily is a beautiful and courageous character. Her nurturing attitude to her children together with her courage and determination to uncover the truth at whatever cost, makes us want to be with her every step of the way. A love story and an exposé. It will be on someone's shortlist for sure.'

Jane Teverson, author

'*Past Participle* is a captivating story of murder and imperialist corruption, of friendship and motherhood and of the past haunting the present, told through the interlinking stories of two women. The novel tackles an important subject matter, but in a way that doesn't feel hectoring or didactic. It recognises the nuances of power dynamics, personal desires and social and political realities in framing how people act and why. The novel offers a strong critique of western imperialism, attentive to the macro and micro applications of that, alongside a dynamic and moving story.'

Kieran Devaney, author & literary editor

'The past is another country you can never entirely escape, a feeling shared by Vivienne and Lily, two women a generation and a continent apart. They should have nothing in common; they should certainly never become friends. Past Participle is a love story full of psychological suspense, evoking life in Dakar, Senegal, and Dorset, England, in equal measure. It explores friendship, history, and what happens when good deeds lead to bad outcomes. Vivienne and Lily are strong, independent women, but their success comes at a cost. In describing their colliding worlds is where Jane Labous excels. She has an eye for detail, beautifully creating the thick heat of Dakar alongside the cold seascapes of the Dorset coast. A sweeping story that pulls you in, *Past Participle* leaves you constantly wondering: what would I have done?'

Anne Hamilton, author & literary editor

PAST PARTICIPLE

Jane Labous

Afsana Press
London

First published in 2023
by Afsana Press Ltd, London
www.afsanapress.uk

Past Participle is a work of fiction. All names, characters and events are
the products of the author's imagination, and while certain long-standing
organisations and institutions are mentioned, the characters involved are
wholly imaginary. Any resemblance to actual persons, living or dead, is
purely coincidental. Places and time may have been rearranged to suit the
purposes of the book. The opinions expressed are those of the characters,
and should not be confused with the author's.

Typeset by Afsana Press Ltd
Printed and bound in Great Britain by Clays Ltd, Elcograf S.p.A.

A CIP catalogue record for this book
is available from the British Library

ISBN: 978-1-7399824-7-8

For my parents,
and for Bella,
with all my love.

past participle

noun

GRAMMAR

1. the form of a verb, typically ending in -ed in English and é in French, which is used in forming perfect and passive tenses and sometimes as an adjective, e.g. loved in *he was loved*; aimé, in *il était aimé*.

participe passé

nom

GRAMMAIRE

1. la forme d'un verbe, se terminant généralement par -ed en anglais, qui est utilisée pour former des temps parfaits et passifs et parfois comme adjectif, par ex. *aimé*, dans *il était aimé*.

RESTRICTED

Police Force of Senegal
Witness statement
Date: 25 October 1987
Name of witness: Mr Musa Tunkara

I don't know what you want me to say? However it happened, the boy is dead, isn't he?
Okay, then.
████████████

I'm riding my motorbike along Mutsaka Road, past the Tuli Club, when I hear a commotion. I don't know the exact time, but it must be two am.

My nephew, Aimé Tunkara, may he rest in peace, is lying on the ground in an unnatural way. His arms are folded, like he's praying. I think to myself, the boy is dead.

The funeral takes place within three days. I tell my sister not to attend. It will bring bad luck to the family, this most evil of things that a parent could ever see. Though my sister begs me, I do not even tell her where the burial spot is.

I watch his body put in the ground under the trees. I throw earth over it. I do not allow myself to shed a tear.

Police Force of Senegal
Witness statement (Extract)
Date: 25 October 1987
Name of witness: Mme Rose Tunkara

In the morning, the police came. I had no reason to open the door. I was occupied with giving my small daughter breakfast, and I had no inclination to pay attention. But they insisted, and informed me that my firstborn son, Papa Aimé, was dead. I screamed and buried my head in my dress.

Court Document

PRESS RELEASE ON NGOR INCIDENT

The Office of The Inspector General of Police wishes to bring to the attention of the General Public that in the early hours of 25 October 1987, residents of Ngor and personnel of the Police Force of Senegal were involved in a clash that led to the regrettable injury and arrest of Mr Bakary Ba and Mr Musa Tunkara.

The Office of the Inspector General of Police wishes to make it clear that it did not authorise the use of firearms and will investigate the circumstances that led to this unfortunate incident.

The community of Ngor is hereby urged to keep the peace, be law abiding, and refrain from violence while investigations are launched.

Thank you.

Inspector General of Police

CHAPTER ONE

Lily

It begins with a photograph, discovered by Lily one glaringly hot afternoon while sorting through her mother's old things. As an abridgement of a life, there isn't much. An amulet or two: the first, a bracelet fashioned from goatskin, furry and soft; the other, a stitched leather parcel on string which Lily is aware will contain miniscule prayers sewn inside, for good luck. There are two wax-cotton wrappers, never used by the look of them, carefully folded into plump rectangles. A few decades-old medicine packets and other miscellany. And a Koran, of course.

Then photographs, lots of them. All are crumpled, some damaged beyond repair by damp and age. They show generations of family members posing self-consciously for the camera. Lily spots a bride in white chiffon against a village background, and a great aunt resplendent in a grand *boubou*. There's Papa next to his painted fishing boat, followed by a sepia-toned baby dressed head-to-toe in patterned frills, no doubt a grandmother herself by now.

Lily flips through the stack of pictures until a particular image catches her attention. It is wrinkled around the edges, colours blanched to the sort of artsy retro fade her eldest daughter uses to spruce up her selfies (Face Swap, the app was called, somewhat disturbingly, when Lily checked it out). Lily holds the picture delicately up to the light, scrutinising the faces. It shows a man of around twenty, his left arm draped around the shoulders of a girl who must be nineteen, twenty at a push. The man is black; the girl is white. The two of them pose a few yards from a glittering blue sea, which delineates the figures in sharp contrast. Both are grinning broadly, squinting in the glare of the sun. The girl, barefoot, wears a swimming costume, wetsuit dripping over one arm, and she is slim, with wavy hair of the palest white blonde reaching almost to her waist. The man is bare-chested in a rolled-down diver's wetsuit, and holds a speargun.

Aimé. Lily knows the diver is her brother. But the white girl?

With an eagle-eye, Lily pores over the picture. No. Surely not?

The photograph stays in Lily's mind because the following Tuesday is 25 October, a day Lily finds difficult to bear, a day that is an anniversary of sadness. Not least this year, of all years, because this October is exactly three decades since Aimé died. Thirty years. The idea takes Lily's breath away.

Yet life must go on. Lily drops her daughters off at school and takes the main road out of Ngor, cacophonous now with morning traffic, then turns off and parks her Citroën C-Elysée on the square of reddish dust that serves as the office car park. Inside, the lift creaks and bears her upwards. Behind the aircon-ditioned reception area, a newly hired young secretary is already seated behind her desk, scrolling on a mobile phone with long, fluorescent coral-painted fingernails.

Lily feels a rush of disapproval. What is she – twenty-four, twenty-five, perhaps? Pssht, if Mia or Piretta were to ask for such frivolities, she'd say no, not on your life – of that Lily is sure. When they become young women, her girls, she hopes to goodness, will concentrate on their books, not their talons.

The secretary's name, Lily seems to recall, has something to do with horoscopes. Fortune? Or Karma, like that series her daughters are watching on Netflix? Evangeline? Lily racks her brains, thinking back to the single time she has met the girl previously, at a colleague's *baptême* party a couple of months ago, memorable only because her husband Demba had mysteriously turned up out of the blue. *alhamdulillah* to that, when he never attends her work dos!

Déstine. She remembers now. The secretary's name is Déstine Fall.

'Yo, Madame Tunkara.' The girl sits up straight, stashing the phone. She appears to be chewing gum. 'What's popping?'

'Good morning to you, Déstine.'

A grin. 'Cool dress, Madame Tunkara, love the fabric.'

'Thank you, Déstine!' Lily smooths her hands across the marinière patterned with psychedelic swirls in shades of palest ultramarine. Presumably the girl is at pains to be friendly only because she is new, and keen to impress. 'I do, too,' Lily adds, primly.

The clock on the wall says twenty past ten. Lily makes her way to her desk, setting aside her handbag and briefcase next to her chair, slotting her laptop into a computer dock. She scans her email inbox, then, with brisk clicks of her mouse, launches herself with concentration into the working day. But after an hour or two, she finds herself distracted, and meanders over to the large office window, where she stands gazing out at the miasmas of red dust kicked up by the highway traffic. The dust lends to the scene a soft focus, cinematic feel which suits Lily's pensive mood. After all, it's hard today not to think about the past.

Lily has worked at Ida D. Drameh & Associates LP for over ten years, ever since she qualified as a lawyer. She can still remember the first time she ever set eyes on the impressive façade of the green glass office, rising majestically from the edges of the Serekunda Highway. On the other side of the interview table, Ida was formidable in heavy gold jewellery and flowing robes. Aside from the success of her business, Ida Drameh is a long-standing Dakar legend, a phenomenon in her own right. Ida is a feminist – a pioneer for women's rights and gender equality. She believes Senegalese women must be twice as smart, competent, and resilient as any man to succeed. Also, she detests weakness, marriage ('prison', Ida calls it), male chauvinism.

Lily can still remember her jubilation at Ida's phone call after the interview: *I'd like you to join me, Lily, I need clever women like you.*

Lily Tunkara of all people, a village girl from a family of fisherfolk! Although, Lily thinks with the usual bitter, guilty aftertaste that always springs from such reflections, without Aimé's death, none of it would have been possible. Not the education, or the law degree, or the career. No, about this Lily is under no illusions. In normal circumstances, such aspirations for a village girl like her would have been utterly inconceivable.

Lily closes her eyes, trying to build a memory of her beloved brother, but the fragments she can muster are gathered only from photographs, as far off as dreams. Nevertheless she holds these

8

fragments of Aimé in her mind, flat and voiceless and perpetually smiling, like a jigsaw puzzle with the most important pieces missing. If Aimé was here, would he be proud of his little sister? The idea stirs a familiar sadness. Aimé died when she was just a child, yet sometimes it feels as if she'll never stop grieving him.

Lily sighs and goes back to her desk, extracting an official looking folder from her briefcase. A label on the front reads: COURT DOCUMENTS. It has taken a week, and several white lies, but she has managed to get her hands on the photocopied case files of Aimé's accident, with some sheets removed, the archivist had pointed out, claiming not to know why. Now, driven by an odd feeling of urgency that took hold the moment she discovered the old photograph of Aimé and the white girl, Lily can't seem to stop thinking about the files' contents.

Seating herself, donning spectacles, she takes out the sheaf of papers, which are yellowing from the ravages of time, and flicks through them. There is a toxicology report and an independent analysis from a pathologist, as well as several statements – vague at best – from witnesses. Over the past days, she must have read them a thousand times.

From her handbag, Lily brings out the photograph from her mother's things and stares at it. For the umpteenth time, she scrutinises the two smiling figures. If she's right about this – if the white girl is, indeed, *her*, doesn't it change everything?

With a sense of anxious indecision, Lily stashes the picture back in her bag, bangs the papers together on the desk, and replaces them in the folder. Leaning back in her chair, she takes off her glasses and chews on the wing. At the end of the day, is there any point dwelling on the matter, when it was all done and dusted thirty years ago? More than ever she finds herself toying with the idea of reopening the case, but… The last thing she wants to do is open a can of worms. She must not allow her own grief to influence legal matters.

Still, Lily is deep in thought as she makes her way to the office kitchen, where she helps herself to a cup of strong coffee from the jug brewing on the sideboard percolator. She glances at the clock. It is close to one, and lunchtime already. The spicy smell of rice and fish wafts from the staff canteen downstairs. Belly rumbling, Lily forces herself to concentrate on her work, answering a few emails from clients, jotting a list of tasks for the afternoon. She types quickly, sipping her coffee and focusing her mind. After an hour or two, she makes her way down to the lunchroom, where she finds Ida already installed alone at a table, eating a piled-up plate of *thieboudienne*. Ida taps the chair next to her, smiling.

'How are you, my dear? Not working too hard, I trust?'

'Never,' jokes Lily, answering Ida's questions about her current case, then about the girls, about Demba. 'I think he's having an affair,' she adds casually, spooning rice into her mouth.

Ida kisses her teeth disapprovingly, shooting Lily a maternal look. 'My God!' she exclaims, waving her fork in the air as if to stab a few imagined male adulterers. 'Men! If only they could learn not to reason only with their stomachs and their penises, then maybe the world might be a better place!'

CHAPTER TWO

Lily

Four-thirty. A cool sun through the trees. It is harmattan season, and a haze of dust hangs over the village of Ngor, an outlying coastal district some five kilometres west of central Dakar.

At her home in the newest residential area of the village, Lily drops the car and changes quickly into Lycra leggings and trainers, then speed walks over to the private school attended by her daughters. At this time of day, the quiet, unpaved back streets are dappled with long, feathery shadows from the palms. While she walks, Lily breathes and stretches, as is her habit, circling her arms, wiggling her fingers. Occasionally, she breaks into a jog. To her mind, the al-fresco exercise, not to mention the calorie burn, is much-needed after the stresses of the day.

If only she hadn't eaten a second helping of rice when she's *supposed* to be on a diet. To make things worse, she hasn't done her skipping today. It seems she has no self-control. Still. Lily consults the smart watch around her wrist – a birthday present from Demba when he was still bothering to remember her birthday – which says her heart rate is a hundred and twenty-five, in the fat-burn zone, and she's well on the way to fifty active zone minutes, which can't be bad, she muses. Not for a working

11

day, anyway.

The pavement outside school is crowded with parents laughing, gossiping, scrolling on cell phones. She greets a couple of them, mothers of children in Piretta's class, but for some reason both women turn away, heads together, ignoring her. One dons her sunglasses. Puzzled, Lily stands alone, feeling awkward. From the other side of the gates, another mother of one of Piretta's friends waves and smiles, and Lily waves back gratefully. Two traders pass through the crowd carrying dishes of wares – packaged macaroons, oranges, *bissap*. Another offers peanut brittle. Cars idle on the pavement, sunlight flashing off windscreens, their drivers disguised in sunglasses while they wait for their precious cargoes to emerge.

When Piretta and Mia appear, twelve and six years old, scuffing the sand and dragging their school bags, Lily greets them with a kiss and a hug. Once the three of them are away from the masses, Lily listens with pleasure to their sibling chatter, voices bubbling like waterfalls. As far as Lily is concerned, these tranquil hours, when work is done and she can spend time with her girls, are the best part of the day.

'So, *chérie*,' Lily asks her younger daughter, 'what did you do at school today?'

'Can't remember,' Mia says, predictably.

'I got ten class Dojo points,' Piretta offers after a moment of reluctant sullenness, a near-teenager still childishly in need of praise.

'Oh good. What for?

'I won the weekly spelling bee, for *handkerchief*,' Piretta grins. With the hand gestures of a rap artist, she spells out letters:

12

'H-A-N—'

'Nice work, *ma chérie*,' Lily says as Mia slips one hand into hers, pulling and dancing along.

'Mummy, Fatou said her daddy told her not to play with me.'

'Oh?' Lily looks down at the top of Mia's head. 'Did Fatou say why her daddy said that?'

'Nope.'

'No reason at all?'

'No, Mummy.' Mia hops ahead, the matter over. 'Samba found a worm,' she calls. 'Did you know worms are boys on one side and girls on the other?'

'No, *ma chérie*,' says Lily, letting out a quiet sigh, her mind dwelling on the mothers turning their backs by the school gates. 'No, I didn't.'

In the distance, a man waves. Lily sees that the man is Uncle Musa, of all people, and her heart drops. Is he on his way to pray, she wonders, her thoughts running to the gossipy world of the mosque. Oh well, she tells herself, at least she can ask him about the photograph.

'*Asalaam alaykum*,' she greets Musa when he comes up.

'*Alaykum salaam*. How are things?'

Musa draws from his pocket a small, open plastic bag of peanuts which he begins popping into his mouth. He has close-shaven hair and a well-trimmed beard, flecked now with traces of grey. Today his very black skin contrasts with a pure white robe inset with intricate green-and-gold embroidery – a mosque outfit, that much is certain.

What age is Musa now, Lily wonders, sixty-five, seventy, even – though with his smooth skin and high cheekbones, he looks hardly different than he did when she was a child. Tallish – taller than Lily anyway – he is a good-looking man, and only his decaying teeth in varying shades of brown and black spoil his looks when he smiles, which is rare.

'Good, thanks, Uncle, *alhamdulillah*.'

'Beautiful evening,' Musa comments, drawing closer, shelling a nut with his fingers. He turns to the girls. 'Yo, *les filles*.'

'Yo, Uncle,' her daughters chorus obediently, high-fiving, then fist-bumping Musa's other outstretched fist.

He is sweating, drops of perspiration descending the skin rolls of his neck like the European slalom skiers on the TV sports channel. Lily stares at a flash of brown-and-white teeth. Musa is play-acting the nice guy, she thinks. A wolf in sheep's clothing.

'As a matter of fact, I've been meaning to call you.' She fishes the photograph from her bag. 'I found this in Mum's things. Do you know who this girl is, with Aimé, may he rest in peace?'

Musa peers at the photograph, shaking his head, and continues to pop the nuts one by one into his mouth.

'No,' he says after a moment, 'no, I don't.'

'You've no idea at all?' Lily says, 'I just thought—'

'I've no idea,' Musa interrupts. He crunches slowly, then speaks, 'You know what day it is today?'

'Of course. How could I forget, Uncle.'

'Well, then you'll be aware that it's thirty years since your brother died. You'd do well to leave all that alone, you know. No one around here wants to dig up the past.'

'But it's strange, don't you think – Aimé with a white girl?'

'Nothing strange about it.' Musa shrugs, kissing his teeth. 'Look, the British compensation payments meant you got an education, didn't you? You, a simple village girl! You'd be selling *buye* in the market right now if Aimé hadn't died. So don't go turning over stones three decades later, when it's all finished with, *inshallah*.' Beneath hooded lids, Musa's eyes are riveted on hers. 'Snakes live under stones, and all sorts of other nasty creatures.'

Lily squeezes the girls' hands tight, one on her right, one on her left. Of her uncle's intimidation she is not afraid.

'My situation's by the by,' she replies, tight lipped, 'I'm a lawyer; it's my job, surely, to turn over stones.'

'There are people in this town who won't like it.'

'Is that a threat?'

Another shrug. Lily watches the last of the peanuts churn in Musa's mouth. He swallows, kisses his teeth, and eventually speaks, 'God knows, that business broke our family, especially your Ma, may she rest in peace. She was never the same after Aimé died.' He pauses, crumpling the empty plastic peanut bag in his fist. 'Remember your loyalties, Lily. You're first and foremost a villager. This is something you should not chase up, and I say that as your own flesh and blood. I wouldn't want something to happen to you.'

'Then it *is* a threat?' Lily frowns, putting the photograph back in her handbag. 'But why?' She gives him a quizzical look. 'It's only a picture.'

Silence. Musa kisses his teeth and turns on his heels, stomping off towards the square where a handful of kids are pumping hip hop from a speaker. *Changes*, by Tupac.

'Hey, Musa!' Lily calls after him. 'What in the name of God…!'

Lily watches her uncle go in a fury. Then, feeling mystified, she tugs on the two girls' hands, turning back towards home.

For teatime, Lily puts rice to boil on the stove, then helps Piretta with her homework – a 250-word letter in French to world leaders about climate change – while Mia watches Disney cartoons. There are the school bags to prepare for tomorrow – water bottles, a note for the teacher about Mia's dentist appointment – and so little time in the evenings. She needs an assistant, Lily thinks as she slips the note into Mia's school bag. *Une femme de menage.* Such women are easy to come by, yet she holds off. There's no one she trusts enough to allow into the sacred privacy of her home.

'Finished, Mum.' Seated at the table, Piretta is reading through her exercise book with an intense expression, biro held between her teeth.

'Okaaay,' Lily says, scanning Piretta's book, where the essay is written out over two lined pages in neat, curly handwriting, forcing herself to refrain from correcting her daughter's slang, her lack of correct sentence structure. Teenagers, honestly. 'Did you do an introduction, middle, and conclusion?' she asks.

'Yeah. I addressed it to the American President, I said that the world should stop ignoring Africa.'

'Good.'

At the countertop, Lily slides onions and peppers from a chopping board into a pan of hot oil, flicking the mixture with a spatula while she regales Piretta with a rant about the lack of academic papers from African scientists, all of which the girl adds to the exercise book with slow scratches of her cartridge pen.

Our understanding of climate change, Lily adds, is biased towards cooler climates, because all the scientists are from those regions. Patiently, Lily explains the meaning of 'global south' as

16

she coats chunks of goat meat with flour and adds them to the pan to brown.

'Don't forget,' she adds, 'women scientists on our continent contend with all sorts of sexism, which prevents them from pursuing science in the way men do. I mean, I used to have to do the washing up *and* the household cleaning before your grandmother would allow me to get to class in the morning, just because I was a girl. See how lucky you are!'

Piretta groans, rolling her eyes. 'I know, mummy, I know—' She plonks a full stop on the page. 'Killed it! Can I watch TV now?'

'Yes, alright.'

Lily's mind is still on Musa's puzzling behaviour. She breaks off from cooking to send a text to Bakary Ba, a family acquaintance who goes back years, decades, even.

Salut, frère. You around to talk this week?

If anyone has recollections of the night Aimé died, surely Bakary will.

Later on, once the girls are in bed, the house is quiet and dark. In the kitchen, Lily brews a strong cup of mint tea and sits on the veranda. The moon is full. She can hear the swish of the waves at the shore beyond the courtyard walls, and the further hum of the village – a car horn, the faint roll of a drumbeat. Evening sounds. From somewhere, a dog whines. Lily toys with the idea of sending Demba a text. Yet again, her husband has not come home, not even on *this* day, when he must surely know she will be sad. Earlier, there was a message she scanned, then ignored. *I'm working late*, Demba said, *don't save dinner x*.

Lily sighs, pushing away the idea of getting in touch, along with the thought of Demba's intermittent absences and the other signs she must continue to ignore for the sake of her own sanity. The scent of *thioraye* on Demba's shirt the other night, for example. Not to mention the hair that was not Lily's but a stranger's – another person's, another woman's.

This Lily had sniffed like a dog or a wild cat, searching for a scent of something. Perfume? Sex? Suddenly she was overcome with an animalistic instinct to chase down her rival, and, for the hours that followed, she had allowed her imagination to run wild over the other woman's possible identity and characteristics. Obviously, her husband's lover is younger, she imagines, tall and slim. Pssht...

Lily shudders, returning to her phone. Anything to dispel the thought of this cursed phantom stranger-woman with arms around her husband.

Lily takes a sip of her mint tea, then another. It's all because she told Demba she doesn't want another baby. Whether Demba is genuine in wanting another child, or his male ego is dented – more likely – she does not know. Whatever the reason, now her husband thinks Lily's declaration is a free ticket to play around, and Lily can sense his ideas about a second wife, even if he hasn't voiced them yet.

Lily flaps away a mosquito, gazing out into the darkness at the English-style lawn which she takes great pride in, not least because Mia and Piretta can play within the compound rather than in the streets, like the other village children. From a number of how-to articles on the internet published by British gardening magazines – 'the secrets to a lush lawn' and suchlike – she has taught herself the art of lawn care. She uses a sprinkler to keep the grass hydrated beneath the hot sun; employs a man from the village to trim the grass. Only in the height of the dry season do the sharp green spikes begin to suffer, and then she sends away for more little packets of grass seed from England, sprinkling clouds of seeds into the yellow patches.

The rest of the courtyard is sketched through with red earth pathways where the girls play hopscotch. There are areas of shrubs and flowering trees; a moringa, a flame tree, an avocado. A showy scarlet bougainvillea drapes the far wall of the courtyard, its vivid colour visible even through the dark, and there is her favourite date palm in the furthest corner of the garden, tall and skinny-trunked against the moonlit sky, cascading like an unlit firework into arcing fountains of fronds. After the rainy season ends, the palm occasionally flowers, bearing clumps of sweet sticky fruits that she and the girls use to make drinks and pastes. Her mother once told her that dates are the bread of the desert, mixed up with camel's milk by the nomadic peoples up north for nourishment and strength. And here in Senegal, a traditional way to break the Ramadan fast at dusk. Demba always insisted upon it. In fact, they once had a huge row about dates, when Lily forgot, shock horror, to buy his favourite variety, and he accused her of being a bad wife…

Demba.

Lily surveys the single palm silhouette rising against the moonlit sky, her thoughts turning to the bright blue day she married Demba at City Hall. The truth was that her new husband had made no bones about ticking the 'polygamy' option on their marriage certificate, and if Lily noticed, aged eighteen, innocent, virginal, and somewhat scared, she didn't dare comment.

Now the memory fills her with regret, at her silence, at,

19

through no fault of her own, her lack of *agency*. She wishes she could talk to her mother, who'd have admonished her gently with the air of matter-of-fact resignation so typical of her generation, before muttering something more controversial about men, about Demba, about how husbands, curse them, take it for granted that they can swap an unsatisfactory wife for a second.

'Several wives are their God-given right,' Rose would have said, kissing her teeth disapprovingly, in such a way as to indicate that, however awful, this was a wife's load to bear, for the sake of marital happiness. 'It's in the Koran.'

And who could argue with the Koran?

Even so, one thing's for sure, Lily is not that eighteen year-old girl anymore. She is a grown woman, of a new, modern generation, and she will never accept a relegation to second wife. She'd rather divorce, *inshallah*, than accept this coarse old marriage rule of the middle ages, and she'll tell Demba that when he asks. In truth, Lily wishes this would happen sooner rather than later. What point prolonging the pain? Pssht, how she fears the day her daughters find boyfriends…

The moon is covered over with cloud, the night suddenly dark. She ought to go to bed. Nevertheless, her mind is agitated. Without thinking, Lily leans into the bag left on a chair, retrieves the photograph of her brother and the mysterious *toubab* woman. On the laptop, Lily googles the former British ambassador to Senegal and finds a brief Wikipedia page about John Hughes. There is a rundown of John's early life and education – a BA in Modern Languages from the University of Oxford, an MA in International Politics from London – followed by a lengthy diplomatic career. Now John Hughes is retired and lives in south-west

England, Lily notes with interest, along with his wife, Vivienne.

On further investigation – Lily is well-used to case research of this kind – she discovers Vivienne Hughes's email address on the well-hidden donor webpage of a minor European NGO, though there is no picture of Vivienne there or anywhere, even when Lily searches the image-only section of the search engine, Facebook, and Twitter.

Lily sighs. Technically, she's only researching, not actually making real enquiries. She brews another hot drink, then brings up her Outlook account. In English, she composes an email to Vivienne Hughes, checking the paragraphs for correct grammar and punctuation, as is her habit. Maybe a little more precisely in this case, overcome as she is with a somewhat irrational need to impress this as-yet-faceless Englishwoman, when it should, surely, be the other way around?

Lily leans back in her chair, watching a cloud slide across the moon. Who'd have thought that, all these years since finishing her studies, grammar would still be her thing? Before completing a law conversion course, she was an honours student in French and English, and were she to choose a favourite academic discipline from that era, it would be grammar. She can still remember the cardboard conjugation table she'd discovered in a grubby corner of a classroom at lycée and learned by heart; present, past, future, past perfect, present perfect, continuous perfect, pluperfect…

Subject + have + past participle.

Lily sips the last of her tea. In such combinations – the mechanics of language, so to speak – she finds a kind of soothing alchemy, is fascinated by the way a fine-spun modification of tenses back and forth involves such subtle but important nuances of feeling, of action. An exquisite precision, as it were. An almost poetry. To grammatise, Lily thinks fondly, is to control a disorderly world. Now, that ancient conjugation board hangs in the girls' bedroom. Though scuffed at the corners, the time-old formulations are intact down the generations, a testament to her own passions, her own aspirations for her daughters.

Briskly, Lily turns back to the computer and signs her name at the bottom of the email – *best wishes, I do hope to hear from you* – then hesitates, conviction failing. She saves the message in the drafts section of her inbox, and logs out.

CHAPTER THREE

Lily

It is the hottest part of the afternoon. Lily drives quickly, working the brake and accelerator pedals with heeled sandals, humming to herself. With one hand, she holds the steering wheel, with the other, a baguette sandwich containing sliced boiled eggs, mayonnaise, circles of ripe tomato. In the rear-view mirror, her chiffon headscarf reflects back, strawberry-pink today to match her marinière, and majestically folded into a shape resembling an upturned ice-cream cone.

It is just after two o'clock. Lily has managed to leave early from work for her rendezvous with Bakary Ba, and has dropped the girls off for tea at Aminata Deye's on the other side of town. Her intolerable mother-in-law may be a miserable old crone at the best of times, but the woman has her uses. Aminata Deye doesn't have much time for Lily but, *alhamdulillah*, she happens to idolise her granddaughters.

Bakary Ba's house is in the original part of Ngor, where a coastal settlement of fishing shacks open to the sea has, over the decades, evolved into houses built by the increasingly affluent children of the original Ngor fisher families. Eschewing the snaring of *thiof* in favour of the field of business, the children have established beach cafés, fish restaurants, and a trendy surf school sponsored by a European snowboarding brand which is now the best-known aquatics centre in West Africa.

Lily negotiates the roundabout, then bounces the Citroën onto a patch of shady sand near a red-painted grocery kiosk, and comes to a halt. As Lily turns off the engine, a village woman carrying a cloth-covered dish on her head appears in front of the car. With a direct look at Lily, the woman spits on the bonnet.

Shocked, Lily stares back through the windscreen. First the snub from the mothers at school, then this harridan… Once the woman is gone, Lily climbs out of the car, perusing the little mound of drying spittle on the yellow metal bonnet of the Citroën. Maybe Musa is right, she realises, feeling suddenly boiling despite the shade. People won't like her sniffing around about her brother's death. And no doubt, thanks to Musa, the village already know she's doing just that. Pssht, what a thing to be at odds with one's own people!

Lily wipes her sweaty forehead with her sleeve. It's just as Musa warned. Still, there can be no good reason for such rude behaviour, she thinks, outraged.

Though Ngor has a complex, map-defying layout, Lily knows the maze of passageways leading between the houses like the back of her hand. In familiar territory, she makes her way along a passageway of uneven sand wide enough for one person only, stopping continually to allow others to pass – gaggles of children and wandering sheep, more women carrying cloth-covered bowls, cooking instruments, other paraphernalia. There are smells of fish, diesel oil, sweat, and incense. Chickens peck in corners. Outside the mosque, a collection of old men gossip and stare.

In front of a house, a woman sweeps up clouds of dust that swirl momentarily and descend again.

Eventually, Lily glimpses the sea shining through a gap between the dwellings, then the beach, diamond-bright. Hoisting her handbag higher on her shoulder, she ventures through another passageway. In the sunlight, the bay is aquamarine and inviting. Two boys play football on the sand. Opposite, Lily notes the palm-dotted island a short boat-ride away, where she often takes the girls on Saturdays. Half a dozen surfers float out beyond the swell, waiting for a wave to break.

Lily picks her way along the foreshore, which is puddled with rubbish. There are fish heads and thrown-out drifts of rice, debris washed in on the tide from the island. Into a miniscule dark passageway, she turns left, and from there into an inner doorway. Though Bakary's house was once a mud-brick shack with a corrugated roof, like most dwellings in the village centre, it has grown upwards like a well-watered plant over the decades. The family adds storey after storey whenever there's enough money to buy sand, cement, a few hours of a labourer's time.

'*Asalaam alaykum*,' Lily murmurs, peering into a room where an elderly woman – Bakary's mother, Lily wonders, or sister? – reclines on a leather sofa. The woman holds a can of Coke in one hand, worry beads in the other, and is staring at a giant TV showing the soap opera, *Pod et Marichou*. She glances at Lily only momentarily to return the greeting. On screen, a girl of twenty-something, fashionably dressed, is admonishing two trendy-looking young men, one young, one older. The scene: a sitting room of swish modern décor. The three of them wear solemn expressions; the girl waggles her forefinger.

Lily is familiar with the show; it seems to be obsessing the whole of Dakar right now. She has heard the plotlines discussed in the supermarket, spotted the characters' faces on numerous billboard adverts. Piretta, for one, is keen on the drama, which features two young people who fall in love in the face of *la maraboutage* and illicit parental marriage deals. *If* Lily lets Piretta watch, that is. In Lily's opinion, such matters are far too grown-up for a twelve-year-old!

With a perfunctory *alaykum salaam*, the old woman continues to stare at the soap opera. She sips at the Coke, trundling the worry beads through her fingers.

'Is Bakary here?' asks Lily, venturing further into the doorway.

'No idea.'

'I'll call him then?'

'Let me.'

The woman kisses her teeth, plonks the Coke can on the floor. With movements that couldn't be more languid, she withdraws a cell phone from the slip of her wrapper and scrolls through the numbers with wrinkled fingers, then holds the phone to her ear.

'He's coming,' she announces after a second or two, clicking off.

The space is airless and hot, so hot! Sweat trickles down Lily's neck and down her spine. A couple of children wander in, then out again, one of them sucking on a bag of yoghurt. Lily extracts a handkerchief from a fold in her marinière and fans herself with the cloth, welcoming the miniscule breeze it generates.

Bakary Ba appears, a tall man in his sixties, still rather monumental-looking, Lily appraises, with bloodshot eyes and hair greying around his ears, a squarish jaw and a statuesque nose. Bakary is wearing fading jeans, flip-flops and a woolly hat,

26

his T-shirt emblazoned in English: *We Should All Be Feminists.* Does he even know what that means, Lily wonders with an inner smile of amusement. She hadn't realised the male population of the village were so enlightened. Perhaps Demba should join up…

'W–w–w–why do you want to see me?'

As Lily recalls, Bakary's stammer is a lifelong ailment. When she was growing up, everyone knew of the poor young man down the street with a speech impediment. Now Bakary observes her with a sullen expression. A chewing stick protrudes from his mouth and, with a violent up and down motion, he pushes the slender sprig of wood against his teeth so that the fine strands of heartwood fray across pale pink gums.

'I'm just here to talk,' Lily says. 'About Aimé.'

A silence, accompanied by more teeth cleaning. Avoiding Lily's eye, Bakary kisses his teeth and scrutinises the soap opera on which the old woman appears transfixed.

'Is there,' Lily asks, 'somewhere more private we can go?'

Still looking at the TV, Bakary mutters, 'It's so long ago, there's no point digging up the past. None of us want – want – want to bring up *les mauvaises anges.*'

'I don't know about bad angels,' Lily replies in a matter-of-fact voice, registering Bakary's mixed metaphor, flapping her handkerchief around her face, 'but perhaps all this was never dug over properly in the first place.'

Bakary gestures reluctantly to the stairs. Lily follows him up to the roof open to the sky, where a strong sea breeze squalls around a washing line of fluttering laundry. Bakary goes over to the parapet and stares out at the sea.

'Why,' says Lily, 'did you get arrested after Aimé died, Bakary?

Did you know something, and they wanted to make sure you didn't speak out?'

Bakary's head snaps round. 'Why would you think that?'

'The court documents say you and Musa were arrested the night Aimé died, for causing trouble. Why were you causing trouble?'

Bakary is silent, face set. He turns away, exuding a stubborn indignation. Pssht, she should have known this would be an uphill battle. Out to sea, a bird swoops on the wind currents. The washing flaps with a loud slapping sound.

'It's n–n–none of your business,' Bakary stammers, still with his back to her.

'I just want to get to the bottom of what happened. Did you see Aimé that night, before he was killed?'

'N–no.' Bakary turns and shrugs, hesitating. 'Maybe.'

'You did then? When? Before? Where?'

'Before?' Bakary stares skyward, evidently rattled. 'No, not before.'

'Was Aimé at the party that night, Bakary? Earlier? Earlier than the accident?'

Silence. For a short while, Bakary stares into the distance, frowning, as if considering his answer. Across his face flits a transitory set of emotions that appear and disappear like shadows on a wall. After a moment, he looks over; his eyes meet Lily's and in a flash she sees suspicion and… might that be fear, Lily asks herself, holding Bakary's gaze.

He kisses his teeth, drops his eyes. 'You know, they didn't even come to the funeral.'

'Who didn't?'

'The *tou–tou–toubabs*. That ambassador and his wife. They killed Aimé, may he rest in peace, and they didn't even bother to come to the funeral. It was like he didn't matter.'

'Then tell me what you saw, Bakary. Please?'

'No.' Bakary waves a forefinger close to Lily's face, raising his voice to a shout that is half lost in the wind, 'No, I w–w–w–will not do this, Madame Tunkara!' Continuing to wave his finger, Bakary steps back. He turns at the top of the stairs. 'Talk to Musa,' he spits, 'not me!'

'Bakary, please?'

But he storms away down the staircase.

Lily does not say anything, or try to stop him. Before the force of the wind and the azure sky, she stands upright, watching him go.

Lily walks back through the tranquil passageways of the village, where the earth and plaster walls are burnished gold now in the setting sun. How to persuade Bakary Ba to talk, if he ever will? No doubt he is scared, but of what and of whom? And why does the death of a man killed thirty years ago, seemingly unrelated to Bakary, and when he himself was only a teenager, still prey on a grown man's mind?

Lily's own mind wanders to Aimé, dead now for thirty years. *Thirty years.* She sees him in the photograph again, broad and handsome, sunlight glinting from his wet skin. How vital he was then, how athletic and alive! Her big brother would have been a man of fifty-four right now, a grown adult who would have already lived a whole life – a job, a wife, a batch of children probably, and a bunch of mistakes, like any normal human being.

Instead, Aimé Tunkara is in the ground, bones and earth beneath the whispering acacia trees of the village cemetery.

The savage thought upsets Lily; she does not want to dwell on the morbid image, but her mind insists. *J'aime, j'ai aimé*: I love, I loved. Aimé would never, could never be more than a past participle. Now that was tragic. Doesn't her brother deserve justice, even *ad memorium*?

There again, maybe she should let sleeping dogs lie, as the British would say. Aimé is dead, an entire life wasted, but should it really fall to her, the sister, to make up for the wrongdoings of the past?

Lily shakes her head with a perplexed expression, turning off down a back alley towards the car. As she does, she glimpses a familiar male figure – at least, he looks very familiar – back turned, swerving off with a furtive bearing. Like a stray dog, thinks Lily, sloping off with a prize chicken in its jaws. He turns left, into a tapering pathway leading to one of the dwellings on this side of the village.

Forgetting Bakary Ba for a second, Lily hesitates, her mind abuzz, then carries on with cautious steps to the opening to the pathway, where she peers tentatively around the corner. How ridiculous to behave like a detective, she thinks, leaning with an awkward bend of her neck, and adjusting her focus to the dim shade of the back street enclosed on both sides by other buildings. Is it? Surely she is imagining…

Good God, it can't be!

Her heart jumps; she misses a breath, then gasps for air with the next. Demba stands in the doorway, broad shoulders bent frontwards. He wears a smart, European-style shirt and jeans with his best open leather sandals.

Lily can hardly breathe. Dry-mouthed, her heartbeat slows and thumps. From the interior, another person, a female, extends bright-painted hands – coral, if Lily isn't mistaken – and puts her arms around her husband's waist. In a flash, Demba is pulled inside, as if the dog himself has been drawn into the jaws of a hungry crocodile.

CHAPTER FOUR

Lily

Lily is crying. She lies still on her back staring at the whirring arms of the ceiling fan which jar and buzz like some giant primordial insect. It is seven in the morning and she is huddled in bed while the girls sleep on. Already the sun is a fierce white glare behind the blinds. Though it is Saturday and normally a precious time to relax, centre herself, and spend time with her daughters after the long working week, there seems to be no point, Lily stews, because here she is teetering on a precipice of utter despair.

At this thought a tiny moan spills from a soft, wounded epicentre somewhere in her chest, a place of softest tissue punctured for the first time yesterday and now, slowly, being stabbed into again and again with slow, exquisite cruelty. The effect, she imagines, is like an earthquake diagram – seismic shockwaves diffusing in an ever expanding red shaded circle.

And Lily has no defence, at this point in time, with which to armour herself against the waves of pain.

'Oh, you bastard!' she whispers under her breath, turning face to pillow, letting the feathers muffle her heaving sobs. 'You bastard, bastard, bastard!'

Lily finds her mind locked like a faulty cinema reel on the

vision of Demba, *her husband*, being pulled into the other woman's house. The image loops over and over, technicolour. She sees the slender arms slinking around Demba's back. Demba pushing his face forwards, tenderly, Lily realises now, to meet those cushiony upturned lips.

The *other* woman.

A spasm clenches Lily's stomach and she groans, clutching at her belly. In her mind she can perfectly conjure the other woman's nails, her long talons painted that peculiarly dramatic shade of orange. What do they call it on the nail varnish bottles: Coral or Flamingo? Hollywood gold? Malibu sunrise? Orange Parisienne? No doubt the blasted woman is young enough to wear such annoyingly chirpy, tacky, pop star colours. The reality is so much more painful than all Lily's previous imaginings of the matter.

Wallowing, Lily snuffles into the pillow. Her chest heaves with a fresh sob. To make matters worse, it seems that Demba is quite blatant now about his extra-marital affair, because he's no longer bothering to come home at all – not last night, nor the night before. No more conciliatory, excuse-making texts from her husband.

The girls are stirring in the next room. Lily hears them get up and clatter noisily downstairs. In turn, she hauls herself up and sits hugging the bedsheet over her knees and chest. Physically, she is weak, tearful, and depleted. Eventually she groans and dries her eyes on the bedsheet, gathering it around herself, hauling her body out of bed. At the bathroom mirror, she runs a hand over her braids, frizzy this morning – adding insult to injury – after the humid, sleepless night. Her eyes, scratchy and swollen, weep with unbidden tears.

'Get a grip, get a grip,' she tells herself, cupping her hands and splashing her face with coldish water from the tap. She must pull herself together, because the last thing she wants is for the girls to know she's upset and ask why.

In the shower, Lily closes her eyes and turns her face to the stream of cold water, soaping herself with a mint-scented shower gel that makes her skin tingle. She tries to control the intrusive thoughts that come and go – that if she's no longer a wife, what in the world is left? She does not want to be alone, a single mother, a divorcée, while her husband gallivants off with a fresh, young beauty. God knows, Demba might well be a pain, oh yes indeed, but over the years, before the cheating started, she grew to love him.

She loved him. Past tense.

Lily dries herself, dressing slowly in a wrapper of printed cloth, flip-flops and an ancient T-shirt she uses only for housework. She blows her nose, then inhales, in and out again several times until she feels her heart grow calm. Nevertheless, she feels a slackness deep inside, a lack of motivation, a creeping lack of worth.

On her watch, Lily taps through to the mindfulness app she uses sometimes to meditate and switch off from work matters. The icon is a purple heart with a tracker running across like a heart line on an ECG monitor.

Be still, says the watch companionably. *Take deep breaths. Now follow the circle*. With the slow dilation and contraction of the circle, Lily inhales and exhales.

You are okay, she tells herself. *You are going to be okay, Lily Tunkara*.

The girls are sprawled on the sofa watching Netflix, eating Coco Pops. Whatever they're watching, it looks unsuitable, Lily thinks, but she doesn't have the energy... She leaves them to it.

In the kitchen, Lily makes a cup of coffee. She checks in on the girls again, then, feeling like a naughty child, clambers up on a chair and finds the packet of Marlboro Lights she keeps in a kitchen cupboard for emergencies. Taking out a single cigarette, she sneaks outside, lights up, and puffs furtively, tapping the ash onto the ground. The sun is already hot. At the end of the garden, the blue-green sea already dazzles. The morning breeze brings with it smells of rancid fish and sewage. When the cigarette is finished, she squashes the butt and throws it with guilt in a border of low fan palms, registering the midday call to prayer ring out from the village mosque.

Back inside, Lily is soothed somewhat by the unfamiliar rush of nicotine through her system. After she has prayed, she turns on her laptop and sits staring blankly at the screen, then recovers herself. Justice, she is thinking, overcome suddenly with a euphoric sort of restlessness. Isn't this about justice, no matter how much time has passed – thirty, forty, fifty years even, it doesn't matter? After all, justice in an unjust world is why she does what she does. She is sworn to do right by all manner of people, without fear or favour, affection or ill will. She is a *lawyer*. Aimé was her *brother*. Isn't this reason enough?

Lily takes a deep breath and logs into her email account. With quick movements of her fingers, she retrieves the already-drafted message to Vivienne Hughes, and presses send.

CHAPTER FIVE

Vivienne

At five o'clock exactly, Vivienne Hughes – or Viv, as most people call her – is driving back along the mud track up to Moon Manor, experiencing the usual lifting of her spirits at the sight of her home, square and solid and ever so slightly mystical today, here in the middle of nowhere, against the chilly backdrop of the sea.

'Aah,' she sighs to herself out loud, because there is no one around to hear. It has been a long day.

Moon Manor is at a dead end leading down to a pocket of water behind Chesil Beach, so far in the back of beyond that it was once used by smugglers and by soldiers embarking for D-Day. Viv always has the impression that the house of Dorset stone floats here amid the hilly arable pastures dotted with cows, and the brackish lagoon where flights of swans cross and gather in flocks. Its isolation suits her personality to a T, Viv is aware, because she is solitary by nature, antisocial even.

It was John who bought the place in the eighties, just before they got married. John had grown up in Fleet, had always admired the local manor. When it suddenly came on the market for a snap, run down and needing complete refurbishment, he jumped to buy it.

'You'll think it's gorgeous,' John told Viv. 'Somewhere safe for us to grow old in. You can do the garden, pet.'

'For heaven's sake, I don't want to be old just yet,' she replied, at pains to hide her tinge of irritation beneath a smile, but when she saw the place, she understood.

From savings, John cobbled together the money for the deposit. They moved in one late August day with the sum of their belongings crammed into a pantechnicon.

Viv remembers her feeling of joy at the sight of the ramshackle old house, at its big airy rooms, its front meadow stretching down to the sea and the fields. And her elation at the thought of the children she and John would have there, lots of children whom she'd bring up in a *Swallows and Amazons*-style idyll of early morning swims and rambling walks through the yellow summer corn. As it happened, Viv had not fallen pregnant, not then, not in the years that followed. But, Lord, she was so hopelessly idealistic in those days, enamoured with her new life and its brand-new possibilities as the newly wed spouse of this successful man – not handsome but *solid* – who seemed so desperate to look after her.

Through the windscreen, Viv observes the swallows fluttering restlessly on the roof gutter. She ought to get the gutters cleared, of leaves, of bird shit, of summer debris, but she'll resist until all the swallows have flown. Viv leans forwards in her seat, watching the creatures flit and dive. *Hirundinidae*, or passerine birds, migratory by nature, needing warmth and light to survive, just like humans. It is true to say that she loves them, and always has, these fearless little birds who journey across sea and savannah, forests and farmland down to the Sahara. Every year she notes in her diary the exact dates the birds disappear, then re-appear in the last days of March, bringing the new season along with them.

Where had she heard that swallows can cover up to two hundred miles a day, at speeds of up to twenty miles an hour? A radio documentary, she seems to remember, on Radio 4. People used to think swallows wintered on the moon, she also learned from the same programme. And there were other theories, too: that for the coldest months of the year, the enigmatic birds transformed into field mice, or fell asleep on riverbeds. Only in the middle of the nineteenth century did a savvy scientist rubbish all these theories. The tiny-winged swallows flew south, the scientist revealed, chasing the sun.

Viv pulls up in front of the house, turns off the engine, gathers her things off the passenger seat. For some reason – now the funeral is finally over – she feels exactly like the swallows, restless and longing for the sun, for light, for warmth. Longing for *change*, for heaven's sake. These things she needs too. Perhaps it's the impending arrival of spring, ruffling her feathers, or perhaps just John's death, so unexpected in the end. Suicide, of all things, when she'd have expected him to die of another longer-term ailment – alcohol poisoning, most likely, given that any GP worth their salt would have diagnosed him as a functioning alcoholic. Then the expensive tedium of the funeral arrangements and the sudden realisation of his absence after thirty years of marriage, so finite, so complete. It has been a difficult business. Yet Viv cannot deny the sense of freedom John's death brings, the possibilities.

She shivers audibly, getting out of the car. Yes, possibilities. Already in the back of her mind, the idea of a holiday is forming – somewhere warm and foreign, yet familiar enough to feel at ease.

Somewhere *away*. Somewhere she knows is good for her soul.

Inside, Viv takes off her coat and goes upstairs, where she changes from the dark funeral trouser suit and heels she has worn all day into something more comfortable, a velour tracksuit and thick cashmere socks. She ties her expertly dyed ash-blonde hair – the lighter shade made possible now she's grey – Lord, she's getting old! – into a ponytail, puts the kettle on and, with a mug of strong tea, sits down at the table with a sigh.

Through the window, to the horizon, a cloudy sea blends monotonously with a rain-darkened sky. Closer in, the garden is lush and rain-washed, hardy palms bending in the wind. After they moved in in the eighties, John had embarked on an expensive refurb of the house and exterior, giving Viv free rein to purchase whatever shrubs she fancied to make the place pretty, and nowadays the garden is a flourishing paradise of established sub-tropical varieties that thrive in the south-west. There is a *Trachycarpus* rising now in spiky silhouette, a large date palm, and several high-reaching cordylines flanked by borders featuring echiums and a spreading fatsia, several stunning tree ferns, red cannas, and a grey-green pineapple guava that, cosseted by the coastal micro-climate of the garden, has grown against the odds.

Viv sips the tea, thinking about the wake that afternoon, where old friends swarmed to offer their condolences. *So sorry, old thing. Lovely chap, lovely chap.* There were Fuzz and Miles McFlannery, a few others from London and the embassy days, all the old lot from Senegal. She'd been half expecting Harris to turn up out of the blue, but in the end, to her great relief, he'd stayed away. So she'd smiled dutifully and kissed cheeks, offered smoked salmon blinis and cups of tea, trying to achieve the required funereal balance between grieving widow and sociable hostess holding it all together in the face of extreme difficulty. The guests in their dark suits joked and bantered in a way she found aggravating, distasteful. Yet when she failed to cry at the sight of John's coffin lowered into the earth, the same individuals' disingenuous stares were hot as flames.

Now she is alone, thank *God*. It is over.

Viv finishes the tea and turns on her laptop, which pings with an influx of emails. She puts on reading glasses, leaning in with curiosity to read a message near the top of the stack, entitled: *Making contact*. She registers the name of the sender, and her heart stutters.

Dear Vivienne, she reads.

My name is Lily Tunkara, and I am a lawyer based in Dakar, Senegal. You can find my credentials here: www.idadramehlaw. co.sn

Years ago, my older brother, Aimé Tunkara, was killed in a car accident. I am keen to talk to you and your husband, John, about what happened that night.

I wondered if I could give you a ring on the telephone?

Best wishes, I do hope to hear from you,

Lily Tunkara L.L.B

Oh Lord, thinks Viv.

*

Viv wakes early the next morning from a fitful sleep interrupted by thoughts of the funeral, of John, of Harris and Senegal and

Lily Tunkara tangling confusingly through her dreams. On the balcony, Viv stands in her dressing gown staring out at the mirror-like surface of the sea, rose pink now as the rising sun makes its way above the horizon. She mulls over the email from Lily Tunkara – of all people! – and picks at the cuticle of her right forefinger, biting savagely at the skin, wincing with pain as it rips away, leaving a bloodied flap. *I am keen to talk about what happened that night.*

'Well, aren't we all, love,' Viv mutters to herself, sucking at her stinging finger to stop the bleeding. 'Aren't we all.'

For a few minutes, Viv watches the strip of land opposite transform from a humped silhouette to its usual daytime shade of gravel gold. In daylight, she finds the beach has the look of a surreal moonscape dotted with low-lying fishing huts. Now a pure blue sliver of morning sky reflects so clearly in the still water that the world might have tipped on its head. One might fall into the sky through that water, Viv broods, tightening the belt of her dressing gown around her waist, imagining the freezing depths engulfing her body, her head, then her mouth, gasping for breath to no avail. For God's *sake*. Then the darkness.

She sucks on her finger. The great Atlantic, she is thinking, running all the way down from the UK to Europe to West Africa. For a second she ponders this, imagining the sun down there with its pounding strength, a living thing with its own special moods and whims. On the wake of this thought comes another, more surreal. If only she could fly the air currents like a sea bird, all the way down for her holiday to a Senegalese beach, where she would lie in the sun for a week and do nothing. Oh, the very thought!

41

In the icy cold, Viv's breaths emerge in clouds. There is deep silence, except for the quiet hoots of the Canada geese interspersed with the snappy calls of gulls and egrets, familiar bird sounds that punctuate her days in this quiet place. As she watches, a flight of swans takes off against the gold ball of the sun. With her gaze, she follows the creatures' path as they fly low along the coast, necks stretched forwards like Concordes, wings slapping the water so violently every few seconds, it sounds like the clapping of an audience. John used to say that their swans were so powerful, they could break a human arm. He always used that strange possessive, *their*, as if the two of them owned this piece of coast. As if in his arrogant mind he christened them gods of this place. Over and over he said it whenever the swans took off, a habit Viv secretly found tiresome.

Let's face it, Viv thinks, she found John tiresome. Fucking tiresome, full stop.

The other day, on a whim, she had looked up this well-worn swan fact and found it to be an urban myth, after all those years of believing John's word as gospel! Swan bones were smaller and hollower than a man's, it turned out, and no single swan had so far ever been known to break a human limb. Nevertheless, the myth brought to mind the muscular swan-men of the ballet. You could set the swans out here to music, some sort of wildly dramatic montage to Bach or Beethoven as the majestic birds winged past.

Viv's mind veers off on another tangent, to a Russian ballet dancer – Elmira? Ilmira? And a surname that escapes her now, but containing the ever-glamorous Russian 'nova' at the end. According to the BBC news, the dancer staged an environmental protest by performing *Swan Lake* in minus fifteen degrees on a frozen lake in St Petersburg, with the aim of saving the real swans nesting in the bay from pollution. During the broadcast, Viv was mesmerised by the pale-skinned girl in her silvery tutu pirouetting on the snowy ice.

And wouldn't she do the same, if these swans were at risk? Of course, Viv thinks with sudden fierceness. Of course she bloody well would. Bring on the tutu!

Viv looks down at her stinging finger, where the blood still blooms from the ugly jag of broken skin she has caused. Excoriation disorder, it is called, this ugly habit of picking one's fingers, a habit into which she relapses only during times of exceptional stress. Or, as classified in the 'repetitive behaviours' section of the medical textbooks, *dermotillomania*, which, for heaven's sake, sounds even worse, caused by stress, anxiety, or negative emotions such as guilt or shame.

Viv winces and sucks on the finger, looking around for a tissue to stem the bleeding. In the bathroom cabinet, she scrabbles for a plaster, then stares for a second into the mirror.

'I am a widow,' she says theatrically, out loud to her reflection. 'Yes, yes, my husband is dead. Oh, that's okay, that's okay. It was a blessing, really, all things considered. He didn't suffer—'

The truisms of grief. Viv reaches out and runs a fingernail down the face of her reflection. What is a widow supposed to look like, and how long is one supposed to pretend to be sad?

She makes her way down to the kitchen. Each morning, the same routine. A cup of strong Yorkshire tea and a squeezed lemon in mineral water to kick-start her system. A warm then cold shower (good for the skin, good for the hair). A breakfast

43

of porridge swirled with two spoonsful of full-fat Greek yoghurt (Viv despises the half-fat variety), a handful of blueberries, and a sprinkling of sesame seeds for their zinc, calcium, and magnesium content. Two more cups of tea followed by a single coffee, then a collagen drink made with Brazilian acai and fish eggs. And, this morning, on an afterthought, because all hell is letting loose, a spliff that fills the kitchen with its earthy, herbal smell.

Though who knows, Viv thinks: her anxiety might, in the long run, be for nothing.

Vivienne wears leopard-print exercise leggings and an off-the-shoulder sweatshirt. She unlocks the French doors and wanders onto the concrete, where she spreads out a yoga mat and checks the wall barometer, which says two degrees Celsius. Still in her socks Viv kneels and scrolls to a webpage on her phone, then warms up with a series of arm and neck stretches. The free video from YouTube features a vigorous Californian woman with long blonde hair and a variety of trendy exercise outfits.

'When you arise in the morning,' instructs the yoga teacher in a low, husky voice that sounds, counterintuitively, as if she smokes a hundred a day, 'think of what a precious privilege it is to be alive, to think, to enjoy, to love.'

In a slow circle, Viv rotates her head and reaches her arms first to the left, then to the right, then raises her face to the bright sun which is warm on her upturned skin, despite the bitter temperature.

'Keep your face in the sun and you will never see shadows. Let us be thankful for the day, for our health, for our ability to take time to ourselves—'

Trying to keep her mind focused on the workout, Viv goes through the forty-five-minute class known as 'Awaken', beginning with sun salutations and progressing to downward dog, Warrior two, Warrior three, mountain pose, bridge pose.

'Deep breath in and then exhale, forward fold. Be gentle with your body, be loving with your body.'

But even with the marijuana lingering in her system, even after a final five-minute *shavasana* in the warm sun, Viv cannot calm her brain enough to relax.

'Namaste.'

Viv sits cross-legged and bows at the phone screen with her hands in a prayer position, then turns the video off. Down at the bottom of the garden, she collects kindling for the fire later, bundling it in her arms. Inside, suddenly chilly, she dons a woolly cardigan and puts on the kettle, then the radio, turning the dial to BBC Radio Six and glancing at the clock. Seven am, the day has barely begun.

The kitchen is sunny and silent. Viv brews a cup of herbal tea named Tranquillity. She stands drinking the hot liquid, which tastes of rose mixed with a vaguely tingly menthol undertone. John hated her herbal teas, complaining they reminded him of incense shops in Weymouth, just as he said her rice cakes were like eating cardboard and her yoga was 'a hippy fad'. And she always felt like throwing the bloody yoga mat at him. It occurs to Viv that she's exceptionally happy John is gone. No complaints, no criticism. Just glorious freedom at long bloody last!

On the radio, a Diana Ross song from the seventies comes on, one she remembers from her London life. Viv shifts and moves her hips along to the music, mood lifting. The song reminds her

45

of being young; of dancing all night in Soho discotheques; of laughter and *fun*. She can see her younger self there beneath the glittery lights, hair swinging, feeling the rhythm in her fingers and toes, in her blood. She always was a great dancer.

Then another flashback like the bitter salt chaser to sweet tequila, of Harris...

Dr Harris. The memory is not at all pleasant. Should she get in touch, now there's nothing stopping her? Imagine, after all these years... Viv cannot imagine Harris as an old man; he was the sort of bloke who you'd assume would stay forever young, a handsome Peter Pan always in search of his next thrill or pleasure, whatever that might be – women, drugs, alcohol. Curious that Harris should be a highbrow Oxford don now, doubtless in a tweedy suit and moustaches, all intellect, all scholarly respectability.

Viv slows her bopping and stares out of the window at the palms stirring beneath the morning sun, at the cool backdrop of sea and sky, deep blue. Here she is in this peaceful place, yet she is not at peace; perhaps she has never been.

Wandering to the kitchen table, Viv opens her computer and logs on, clicking into email – where Lily Tunkara's message of yesterday still sits unanswered at the top of the inbox. Turning the screen away from an intruding shaft of sunlight through the window, Viv finds herself staring into space, mind elsewhere.

After a moment, she abandons her emails and shuts the laptop with a bang.

'Alexa,' she announces into the empty space of the kitchen. 'Look up flights to Senegal.'

'Heathrow to Dakar,' comes a pleasant electronic voice after a moment, from a blue-lit, black sphere on the counter, 'with Expedia on Tuesday the eighth—'

'Look up Saly,' Viv says. 'Beach resorts in Saly—'

'Sorry, Alexa did not understand—'

'Saly, Senegal—' Viv waits, then smiles because she imagines herself for a second as the mad widow pouring her heart out to Alexa. *Alexa, is it normal not to feel sad at your husband's death? Alexa, when can I go on holiday?* 'No, on second thoughts,' she adds, 'Alexa, turn off.'

What would people think if she buggered off to the winter sun three weeks after John died? Lord, they'd all be so shocked. People were so judgemental until it came to their own lives. Still...

Forcing herself to concentrate, she turns back to the email and begins to type:

Dear Lily, she writes.

I must say, your note took me by surprise, to say the least.

I'd be happy to talk. My number is 00 44 (0)7983 456784, and I'm on Skype: Viviennerocks, if you'd like to call me on there to save the international costs of a phone call.

Very best wishes,

Vivienne Hughes

The answer comes quickly, with a short preamble. *I'll ring you at eight, Best, Lily*, and Vivienne has a strong impression of the other woman at the end of the electronic system, all the way over in Senegal, connected by whatever invisible satellite is hovering over them both in space. That such a device should allow two strangers to dispatch messages across oceans, across continents and borders via their respective computers strikes Viv as bordering on miraculous – as wondrous as the invention of penicillin or steam power. Wondrous and bothersome, perhaps, bearing in mind the circumstances.

Cup of tea in hand, Viv wanders outside to the patio, lost in thought. The sun is warm despite the freezing temperature. From the water, a flight of geese takes off noisily, flying low, then lands a little way along the spit. Viv watches them.

The easel is in her studio, a glass-walled extension of the living room set up with a canvas pegged on with bulldog clips to face the sea. For weeks – or rather, ever since the day John died – Viv has been afflicted by a strange restlessness in her soul, uninspired to paint anything, yet now suddenly she has a stirring somewhere in her chest and her hands, a visceral need to create.

Viv takes off her sweatshirt and slips on an old shirt, blotched with paint, she keeps to hand for such a purpose. She squeezes oil paints onto a palette, bright spirals of cadmium red, phthalo green, burnt umber and pure cerulean blue that she mixes with white into softer shades of pink and tan and sky. With free movements of a large, squarish brush, she applies a background wash to the canvas, roughing out faint slivers of landscape, then a sea, a sky, and a line of horizon.

Only when the light through the window changes and darkens does Viv rise from her stool, holding the brushes and the palette under the kitchen tap, where in rivulets of vivid colour, the wet paint runs off, turning shades of sunset and sage to muddy brown into the plughole.

CHAPTER SIX

Vivienne

A light supper of salmon with steamed kale and broccoli. Curtains pulled closed. A fire lit with the kindling she collected earlier. In front of the mirror, Viv applies some light make-up and brushes her hair. By seven-thirty, she is sitting in one corner of the sofa reading – or trying to read – a new thriller she ordered on Amazon a couple of weeks ago. It is called *The Hotel; 'a totally unputdownable psychological thriller'*, the critics gush. So far, however, it is anything but gripping, muses Viv. There is a cup of hot chocolate by her side. The living room door is shut to keep in the warmth.

Yet again Viv is restless, unable to concentrate on the printed words of the novel. She gets up and throws another log onto the fire where the damp wood crackles and spits. She sips the warm drink and folds her legs beneath her, staring into the flames engulfing the fresh fuel.

On the table beside her the laptop is open and ready. She has logged into Skype, marked herself as available. Viv leans over and clicks the mouse to refresh the page, then sits back again cradling the mug, finishing up the milky drink which has failed to soothe her properly. For some reason, tonight's call feels important, almost momentous. Partly she wants to cancel; partly she is curious. Partly, she muses, she is quite desperate to find out what the hell the woman wants.

Because, well, *Lily Tunkara*, of all people. Who would have thought...

Filled with nervous energy, Viv sighs and rises from the chair, wandering to the kitchen where she rinses the mug in the sink and returns to the living room. Willing herself to be calm, she stokes the flames of the fire with a poker, then rearranges the ornaments and other paraphernalia on the mantelpiece – photographs, invitations, postcards dating back years. What she feels is a sense of latent dread, a sense that something is about to happen, and she is helpless to stop it, and part of her doesn't even want to. Part of her is saying, bring it on.

A photograph of her and John. Viv picks it up, running her eyes over the two posing figures. It must have been an August sometime in the late eighties, she guesses, after they got back from Senegal for good, because John is wearing a short-sleeved shirt and sandals, and she is so young, with big bouffant hair, Lady Diana-style, a royal blue T-shirt, tanned legs, shiny red lipstick. Her picture-self stares half-smiling at the camera. Likely it was the summer the Sandersons came to stay, when there were daily walks and sea swimming in the rockpool, aperitifs at four pm, and a succession of boozy suppers lasting long into the evening, after which, too many times, John was so drunk she was obliged to put him into the recovery position to ensure he didn't choke on his own vomit. Lord...

Viv picks up the photograph and stares into John's face and her own, then turns the picture face down and returns to the chair, closing her eyes. She slows her breathing to calm herself: *In through the nose for ten, out through the mouth in a light stream, for ten…*

A ring sounds from the computer. Viv opens her eyes. On screen, a thumbnail of a pretty black woman vibrates to and fro. In the picture, Lily Tunkara appears young, mid-twenties by Vivienne's guess, early thirties tops. Lord, how extraordinary to be so high-flying at such a young age.

'Hello,' says Vivienne dubiously, clicking the green button to answer via video. 'Hello there.'

'Allo?' The video pops on as the connection buffers and catches up. 'Allo?'

'Oh,' Viv murmurs under her breath when the other woman's face comes on screen. 'Oh Lord.'

Viv takes a breath and swallows, picking anxiously at the cuticle of her left thumb and feeling entirely at a loss. Even virtually, Lily Tunkara is a beautiful young woman, with a roundish face whose striking features are made more intellectual by fashionable dark-rimmed spectacles, hair in thick braids, smooth, shiny skin. But it's Lily's uncanny resemblance to her brother that's really quite breathtaking. Viv stares at the screen with a strange shocked feeling somewhere in her chest. The two of them could be identical twins, she is thinking, as if time has melted away and this girl, this bright-eyed, educated young woman, has somehow brought her older brother back to life.

Viv swallows and continues to gawk at the screen, pondering the likeness, the familiar features of Lily's face around which memories gather and hustle, wondering how this young woman could manage to bring the past flooding back with such sudden and surprising clarity.

'You are Mrs Vivienne Hughes?' the other woman says.

'Indeed.' Viv clears her throat, forcing her mind back to the matter at hand. 'Call me Viv, please.'

'Thank you,' says Lily Tunkara, 'for agreeing to this call.'

'No problem,' says Viv, leaning forwards at the screen. 'Though I have to say, this is a surprise, to say the least. I'm not really sure how I can help.'

'Certainly you can.'

'I suppose it's about John and me, about—' She trails off.

'About my brother, Aimé Tunkara, yes,' Lily Tunkara nods, continuing the sentence, 'exactly!'

Lily's voice is cool and perfectly enunciated, with the elegant lilt of a Francophone accent. Where on earth, Viv wonders, has Lily learned her English? Viv is fairly certain that none of the graduates of Dakar's British Institute – even those who attended the British Council courses she herself once taught – ever graduated speaking English with such clarity and refinement.

'You must have seen the police reports,' Viv says with a shrug.

'I would argue that the reports are not – forgive me if I use one of your wonderful English idioms – worth the paper they are written on.'

'Oh,' says Viv, taken aback. She hadn't expected the Senegalese woman to be so… *articulate*. But there again, wasn't Aimé astonishingly articulate, intelligent… Suddenly, Viv has the feeling that she wants to cry, and there is an awkward pause, during which she can glimpse herself peering with a gormless expression on the screen. Whereas Lily Tunkara, totally focused apparently, is shuffling papers around with a professional air.

'So, Mrs Hughes, let's say you were a main witness,' the other woman says, 'some would venture, *the* main witness.'

'Please, call me Viv.'

A memory. The doctor, not breathing; the hellish rain; the red mud. Even after three decades, the vision is as clear as yesterday. Viv can feel her pulse quicken and her heart begin to pound, threatening to engulf her words. A grey mist fills her chest, swirling up to her throat, and she looks away to the fire, to the television, anywhere but her interlocuter. She wants to turn the call off and run away, far from here, from this. Eventually she forces her gaze back to the computer screen.

'Look,' she just about manages to say, 'I don't actually think this is a very good idea.'

On the other end, Lily looks up from her papers. Oh Lord, thinks Viv, picking savagely at a cuticle, no doubt the lawyer has in her mind that she is a murderer, a killer, a cold-hearted white woman who crashed a car into an African doctor. Jesus Christ…

'I'm so sorry for what happened,' Viv adds. She takes a breath, blinking back a burgeoning tear as the other woman listens in silence. 'I still replay that night in my head,' Viv adds, 'over and over. I don't know how it all went so wrong. It was truly a tragedy.'

A long pause.

'Well, how it happened is exactly what I intend to find out,' Lily says, clearing her throat. 'I'm gathering new evidence,' she continues, not coldly exactly, but matter-of-factly. Business-like.

In the other woman's eyes there is a neutral affability that brings to mind a detective attending the scene of a crime, just like, thinks Viv, in one of those ITV police dramas. Inspector Jack Frost, for example, or Miss Marple. Presumably Lily Tunkara is like this at work, *Marple-esque*, one might say.

Viv looks solidly back at the screen, affecting the same neutral expression as her counterpart though her mind is buzzing in all directions.

'I'm not here for recriminations on a personal level,' says Lily in a cool voice. 'That's not it at all. I just need to see justice done, as a lawyer, as a sister. I don't believe we – the family, I mean – were ever given the full story about how my brother died, and it's finally time that this happens.'

'I see.'

Viv looks straight back, considering the nature of the other woman's self-portrait. First a lawyer, then a sister. Unintentional, perhaps, but telling. So is Lily Tunkara doing all this in the name of justice or grief, of ambition or love?

'I've contacted the Senegalese Court of Human Rights.'

In silence Viv listens. Oh Lord. She swallows hard. What in heaven's name?

'I'm planning to submit evidence for a new trial,' Lily adds, 'so I'd like it if we could talk properly. Obviously I'd prefer that to be in person, but by the nature of things, with us on different continents, it will have to be done remotely. Does that suit you?'

Lily pronounces 'continents' with a slight accusatory emphasis – or is Viv imagining things? In her mind, a fissure opens between them like a crack in the earth. She sees the two of them standing there, stark figures balanced on the precipices of their respective continents, Africa v Europe, metres above boiling red lava below. Who will win, who will fall?

Viv stares, thoughts in turmoil. New evidence. The case reopening. What does it mean? More importantly, what does it mean for her?

'Well, this is a shock,' she says. 'I didn't expect this.'

'No,' comes the reply. 'I can imagine you didn't.'

Viv looks down at her hands, fingering the wedding ring on the left index finger. She circles the ring of faded gold, as is her habit, and looks up again at the screen, frowning.

'You know my husband is dead? Did you know that?'

'No.' A pause. 'No, I wasn't aware—'

'He died a month ago; his funeral was yesterday.'

Of the details of her husband's death, Viv says nothing, not wanting to reveal too much, or elicit any forced sympathy.

'I'm sorry,' comes the succinct reply.

'So then,' Viv enquires with a new precision, 'what do you need me to do, Ms Tunkara?'

Why did she call her 'Ms'? Chances are this intelligent young lawyer has a husband, children, a lover perhaps…

'Tell me about that night,' says Lily, leaning towards the screen. 'Can you?'

Can I? *The question is, should I*, Viv would like to say.

'No,' she responds with honesty. 'Especially on screen.'

'I see,' Lily says, her face without expression.

Heavens above, thinks Viv, Lily Tunkara is a formidable adversary. Quiet, with the stealth of a tiger. The two of them are circling each other, two beasts in a circus ring, and she has to admire Lily's skills of distraction and delay. No wonder the woman's a lawyer!

'Perhaps you'll take some time to think about it,' says Lily with a question in her voice. 'Would it be possible to have another Skype call tomorrow? We could chat further?'

'I don't—'

'Well then, that's great.' Lily Tunkara shuffles her papers and gives, for the first time, a smile. A dazzling smile, Viv thinks, that somehow in the course of a single second transforms this officious lawyer into a woman, a person, a *sister*. 'I appreciate it.'

Viv inclines her head.

'Well.' The smile remains on the lawyer's face. 'In that case, I look forward to talking further tomorrow, *inshallah*.'

'*Inshallah*.' Vivienne smiles, raises a hand. 'Good—'

But the screen goes dark. Lily Tunkara is gone.

In the morning, it is raining, heavy drops hurling themselves at the windows. Viv wakes dreaming of Aimé Tunkara, a dream she does not wish to escape so soon. Perhaps she has been crying in her sleep because the shadows of tears prick her eyes, a deep, sickening heaviness fills her chest. Beneath the duvet she turns over, refusing the daylight, willing her mind to keep hold of the vivid dream images for a few more seconds. But the raindrops are hammering so loudly on the glass roof of the sunroom downstairs that she can hear the sound all the way from the bedroom. Gradually the dream slips away. She gets up and stares through the window at the rain, at the huddled swans, at the grey sea merging with the sky. She braces herself for the day to come.

When the rain eases off, Viv puts the bins out, brings in a load of washing left out on the line, hangs the soaking garments on radiators and a clothes airer in the upstairs bathroom. Beyond these manual tasks, she cannot seem to concentrate on anything, or shake off the gloomy tendrils of the dream. After several strong cups of tea and a spliff – twice in one week, heavens, she must control herself – she wanders upstairs.

The loft of Moon Manor stretches the length of the house, reached via a folding ladder stored above a trap door in the bathroom ceiling. Given the unspoken gender division of household chores that prevailed in her marriage to John – as, Viv imagines, is common in many other matrimonial couplings of her generation – she has been in the loft only once, perhaps twice in as many decades. And so, it occurs to her as she slips the metal safety latches of the ladder into place and begins to climb the steps, she has no idea what's actually up there.

The vastness of the roof space surprises her. Compressed air, dense and warm, steals her breath, congealing thickly on her skin. Viv coughs, her eyes adjusting to the dimness. A thin ray of sunshine through the dormer windows throws a pattern of light into the shadowy corners. Stooping, she makes her way over to a large boarded area where boxes are piled up, a familiar array of junk and miscellany – old clothes, ornaments, boxes and boxes of books and papers. She should probably clear everything and sell some stuff. What use is all this up here, anyway?

Viv has an idea what she is looking for. She kneels on the roofboards and rifles in the boxes, turning over papers and documents, old bank statements from the eighties, the house purchase file, a shoebox containing ancient birthday and Christmas cards. Nothing of interest.

Then, a folder containing decades of expired passports belonging to her and John, and a few out-of-date yellow fever certificates, diplomatic passes and paperwork, travel visas and their related documents, newspaper cuttings. Most are in French, though there is one from *The Times*, dated 10 June 1987 – only two short editorial columns without a photograph in the foreign news section, its paper yellowing and crumpled now with age. Viv holds it out, reading long-sightedly without her glasses:

'British diplomat and wife flee Senegal after crash scandal,' it reads.

'Ambassador John Hughes and his wife, Vivienne Hughes, fled Dakar this week claiming diplomatic immunity,' says the report, *'leaving Aimé Tunkara's grieving family with many unanswered questions. Mrs Hughes collided with the twenty-four-year-old Senegalese student last month as she drove out of a party in a diplomatic car,'* the reporter continues.

Viv shifts on her knees, pins and needles fizzing in her right foot.

'Asked to comment, spokesperson Miles McFlannery of the British Embassy in Dakar offered no official statement on the student's death, saying only that it was a civil matter being handled in-country.'

'Oh, God,' Viv whispers to herself.

She wiggles her foot about until sensation returns, and settles back in a more comfortable cross-legged position. Outside, it is raining again in earnest and she can hear the whistling of the storm through the rafters, the rain hitting the dormer glass. For a few seconds she holds the article in her fingers, scanning the words again and again with a strange sensation in the pit of her stomach, as if she were falling, falling into a swirling flood of memories.

The weather had been similar that night, she remembers, but with all the force of a tropical storm pounding on the car roof. In her mind's eye she can still see Aimé lying there on the ground by the car, rain ricocheting around his motionless body. Blood, blood everywhere, blood and petrol intermingling in puddles of red mud. John's face, blank of emotion – or was it shock? – as he stood staring at the dead man.

A shadow of fear passes through her and she bends double, retching over and over against the loft rafters. For a minute or two afterwards, she sits huddled, breathing heavily, trying to stem the waves of emotion passing through her body. When she is recovered, she takes the newspaper cutting and slips it in her pocket. She gets to her feet and replaces the boxes, climbs down the ladder and goes downstairs.

At the kitchen table, Viv puts on reading glasses, opens her Apple MacBook with the other hand, and logs in. On the desktop is a single folder labelled 'Memoir' which, when she clicks on it, contains a dozen or so Word documents dated and labelled, running from 2006 – halfway through her marriage to John, when, for her sins, she first began trying to write things down – to the present day.

Viv surveys the folder, surprised to find herself hesitating. She had thought she was just uneasy at the news of Lily Tunkara's investigation, but now she knows that action is needed. God knows why the bloody woman has to dig all this up again! Viv mutters a swearword under her breath. How much does Lily know already, she wonders, and how much can she afford to tell her?

Viv sighs. She will have to buy time while she works out what Lily Tunkara wants.

For so long now, she has worked on this document; and it is all there; dates, names, places, all the random jottings and notes she's made through the years as a way of processing her own private demons. *And* to curate the past, thinks Viv, clicking the mouse. Because, by telling this story, she has been able to tinker and bury and conceal the truth in the time-honoured way of narrators throughout time. Presumably now, for the first time, her endless attempts at writing things down are to come in handy – at least, her own version of the way matters unfolded.

Viv sits straight-backed, staring at the folder containing the past, *her* past, in all its versions, and finds herself at a loss. She *was* hoping to finish this damn memoir now that John is dead and the conclusion looms, as it were, here in real life just as in the written word.

She had it planned out, that ending.

Now... Lord, how things have changed! Out of the blue, there is Lily Tunkara.

But how much is she really willing to tell?

'Shit,' Viv swears out loud, staring out the window. She recalls Lily's peculiarly precise way of talking, *your wonderful English idiom*, the lawyer's words tinkling from her pretty mouth like beads of glass. A bright spark, just like the rest of her family. There'll be no pulling the wool over *her* eyes. Lord knows what she's like in court; truly terrifying, she can imagine!

Viv lets out a groan. She has an inkling that Aimé Tunkara's razor-sharp little sister is going to represent a bona fide spanner in the works.

Viv runs a fingernail over the yellowing newspaper article from the loft, smoothing the paper against the woodgrain of the table. Lord, how can there be so much to say, and therefore so much to hide: about that year, about the crash, about Harris and

John and Aimé. She will have to be so careful. At the same time, she almost feels an irrational urge to tell this Lily everything, no holds barred.

Viv grimaces, shaking her head as if to shake away the notion. True, there would be catharsis, but…

'Don't be so bloody stupid, Vivienne Hughes,' she whispers into the still air of the kitchen. Telling the truth would only get her into more hot water.

She takes her spectacles off and sits staring into space, preoccupied, fingers fiddling nervously with the frames. After a moment or two, she gathers herself back to the present and scrolls down through the folder of Word documents, clicking open the latest iteration of the memoir, relating to her recent past.

With a small sigh, she bends her head to the keyboard and begins to doctor the earliest part, fingernails clacking on the keys as she types.

CHAPTER SEVEN

Lily

A Sunday. Lily sleeps late after several more exhausting bouts of tears that enveloped her after the Vivienne Hughes call. She wakes feeling depleted. Right now, she's like some sort of clam. Every time she takes off her hard lawyer shell, she's just a pathetic beating muscle of unprotected emotion, vulnerable and soft.

'Mum!'

It is Piretta calling from the kitchen. Lily's mood lifts at the sprightly sound of her eldest daughter's voice.

'Yes, *ma chérie*,' she calls back in a weak, tear-choked voice, 'what is it?'

Lily rubs her eyes, exhales and hauls herself up, feeling drained. With slow motions, she ties the dressing gown tight around her waist as though the fabric belt will somehow keep her soul intact.

'You got a text!'

Lily treads downstairs, willing herself to buck her ideas up. The girls need their breakfast. If she is no longer a real wife, then she's still a mother, isn't she, above all else!

'Thank you, *ma chérie*,' Lily says, taking the phone from Piretta's tight-gripped fingers, typing in the lock code. From an unknown number, the text says:

QUIT POKING YOUR NOSE INTO JUDICIAL MATTERS. ITS' NONE OF YOUR BUSINESS!

Lily experiences a peculiar loose feeling in her stomach, forgetting Demba for a moment. Pssht, who in God's name has sent this? In shock, she stares at the stark capital letters of the text, running her mind over possible senders and their motives. Musa? Bakary Ba? Surely not?

Though it seems odd that such a missive would arrive the day after their somewhat disagreeable meeting, Lily cannot imagine such behaviour from mild-mannered Bakary. The man might be stubborn, but he isn't vindictive, and never has been. Besides, she isn't certain Bakary is capable of spelling 'judicial', let alone knowing what it means.

No. So is it Musa? Doubtless Musa is angry about her ever increasing investigations, but is her troublesome uncle really nasty enough to threaten her in this way?

Whoever her new pen pal might be, Lily notes, they do not understand the correct use of an apostrophe.

Who is this? she types back.

In the kitchen Lily turns on the coffee machine. It is the first day of November, the beginning of this year's Ramadan month, but she will not fast, not this year, she has decided. She is already feeling too fragile, without adding starvation to the mix. With hens' eggs from the fridge, she cooks up a breakfast omelette for the girls. She butters two lengths of baguette, whisks and peppers the egg mixture, adds cubes of tomato and onion, then fries the mixture on the stove.

Afterwards, Lily makes herself a coffee, adds hot milk and two sugars, and opens the door to the garden to let in some air. It is eight am. Outside, the cloudless sky gleams azure blue, the sun already hot and, by the looks of it, only getting hotter. Beyond the compound wall, the sea gleams deep topaz. It's going to be a scorcher.

'So,' says Lily, taking a sip of the hot drink, then another as she serves the plates of food to Mia and Piretta. 'What shall we do today? Do you want to go swimming?'

'Yes please, Mummy!'

'We can have lunch at the Madrague if you like, like the tourists.'

'Ooh, ooh ooh—' Mia does a little pirouette.

'Ace!' Piretta cheers.

'Can we have ice cream?' asks Mia.

'Please, Mum?' adds Piretta. 'We haven't had ice cream for *ages*!'

'Yes, *mes chéries*,' Lily agrees, plonking knives and forks on the table, guiltily registering the call to prayer drifting from outside like an admonishment. She probably shouldn't be offering her daughters ice-cream on the first day of Ramadan. 'But only if you come and eat this,' she adds, sternly.

Her daughters tuck into the meal with gusto, and Lily feels better.

Isn't she, when all is said and done, a fighter? The sort of strong woman who has climbed from village girl to top Dakar lawyer? Surely, if she can do that, she can be a single mother, too, a lone parent, a divorcée… Besides, for so long she's managed life alone, because Demba is never at home. So, logic dictates that her husband's sordid affair sets her free, surely?

Lily draws a deep breath and stands up tall, straightening her shoulders. After all, she mustn't forget that she's an independent woman of means, with money in her own bank account, her own house and income, her own car. How relieved she is never to have compromised on this particular aspect of their marriage.

The girls race from the table, and Lily washes their plates with a new, raw sort of energy. She does not need Demba – perhaps she never has.

'Mummy,' says Mia, coming up, 'my tooth is wobbly.' With a thumb and forefinger the child jiggles her front baby tooth. 'The teacher said that if it falls out, the tooth mouse will bring me a new one?'

'Only if you're good, and you brush your teeth every single day.' Lily bends to examine the tooth, smiling. She puts an arm around Mia, dropping kisses on her cheeks and forehead.

Lily brews another coffee and stares out of the window, reflecting again on last night's conversation. When the coffee is ready, she goes over to the table where the old photograph lies in the same place she left it the night before.

Lily picks it up, staring at the faces of the young black man and the white girl. She sips her drink, pondering them. Last night, she'd been in two minds whether to say something there and then, because the minute Vivienne came on screen, Lily knew. Close at hand, there was no mistaking *that* beautiful face, *that* white-blonde hair. The Englishwoman's roundish face and high cheekbones, her luscious blonde hair and big, blue eyes. Without any shadow of a doubt, Vivienne Hughes was the toubab girl with Aimé in the photograph from her mother's things.

And in the event, Mrs Hughes had been pleasant, more than pleasant, a long way from the cold, coarse diplomatic wife of Lily's imagining. Though of Vivienne's real character, of her actual life, Lily has no real idea, and can conjure only the image of a luxurious, European-style house in a cold landscape, and plenty of money. A solitary life, Lily assumes for some reason, because there's something deeply solitary about Vivienne, something lonely even, if Lily can call it that. Had Vivienne and John had children? Lily does not know.

She sighs and peers closer at the photograph. So Aimé knew Vivienne Hughes – and rather well, by the looks of things. But what does that mean?

Lily puts the photograph down and sips her drink. During the call, she'd surprised herself with her own somewhat dramatic declaration, because the truth was, she'd not been planning to submit new evidence about Aimé's case, or apply to re-open the trial. No, nothing so drastic! Until yesterday, Lily's casual enquiries about her older brother's death had been simply that – casual. And then, in a split second of conversation, everything seemed to crystallise. Lily has effectively stated her intent, an intent that in the light of day seems increasingly necessary, the more she thinks about it.

Because now, more than ever, isn't it the time to fight on all fronts? She knows Demba will try to stop her in her tracks. Oh yes! Were it not for the money, Demba would have persuaded her to quit her job long ago, because secretly he detests the fact that his wife is a successful working woman on double his own salary – that of a civil servant at the lower end of government.

In fact, whenever she talked about work – in those early years when they *actually* communicated – her husband's face used to take on that amused, vaguely indulgent look that certain men get when women dare to show their brains, as if she were Mia spinning princess stories, or some adorable little lady twittering on about hairstyles.

That's how the look made her feel, anyway. And then his avuncular response, always a cut-down out of the blue, like one of those colonial explorers slashing his machete about; a challenge that made her question herself, or an unsought explanation – *mansplaining*, they called it on the internet. *But I'm a qualified lawyer*, she'd tell herself, *I spent two entire semesters writing a dissertation about this.*

And then, unnecessarily: *And I'm not an airhead!*

At the sink, Lily vigorously scrubs egg off the plates. Pssht, if there is such a thing as a threatened male, Demba is it, she muses: insecure, arrogant, possessed with a need to be right all the time.

She scrubs harder, filled with a hysterical urge to cry or shout out. Presumably Demba thinks taking another wife will reduce her to a helpless little house servant, but he is wrong, so wrong! Lily Tunkara is a hard nut to crack, that she can guarantee, and she has no intention of becoming a second wife, nor a third, nor a fourth for that matter... In fact...

On impulse, Lily grasps one of the clean plates with soapy hands and marches to the open door. With a cry she chucks the dripping china plate straight at the concrete wall, where it smashes in an arc of frothy dish water with a loud, reverberating crash of breaking crockery. In fact, she'll wipe that self-satisfied smile off Demba's face, if it's the last thing she does.

Silence.

Lily goes slack, observing the wreckage of fragments fall onto the shady reddish earth, and lets out another sharp sigh of satisfaction. To hell, she thinks, with Demba.

Piretta runs in, followed by Mia, eyes wide with expressions halfway between surprise and admiration.

'Mum, what *on earth*,' exclaims Piretta with vague disapproval, 'are you doing?'

'*Mes chéries*, we girls have to be strong,' Lily announces firmly, hands on hips, turning from the doorway. 'You know what Viviane said?'

'No, Mummy?' Mia says.

'Power,' replies Lily. 'We have the power, darlings.'

'You mean,' says Piretta dubiously, 'Viviane the singer?'

'I do indeed, *chérie*. Don't ever let a man patronise you, my darlings, or make you question yourselves, because that's what men like to do. We must not give men our power!'

'So is Viviane a feminist, mum?'

'Yes, and so are we, *ma chérie*.'

'Men don't like feminists, do they?'

'No, darling, they don't tend to be our biggest fans.'

Lily wipes her soaking hands on her wrapper and begins to laugh. For a minute, she stands bent double, unable to control the eruptions of mirth rising in waves from her chest and throat. 'We,' she adds, waggling her forefinger, 'we girls have the power, don't forget it—'

Her daughters stare back with bemused smiles hovering on their lips. Eventually, they too start to giggle. They repeat the mantra in comedy voices, wiggling and dancing, twirling with excitement.

Then, 'Go and get ready, for goodness' sake,' Lily chortles, eyes blurry with tears – of laughter this time, not grief or despair. To hell with that!

In a flurry of activity and merriment the three of them make their way through the house to the bottom of the stairs.

Because, Lily resolves once and for all, recovering herself slightly as she ushers her daughters to get their swimming things, if there's one thing as sure as night follows day, Lily Tunkara becoming a helpless little housewife is the last thing on earth that's ever going to happen…

CHAPTER EIGHT

Lily

Half past seven in the evening. Lily reads Mia and Piretta a bedtime story and remains perched on the bed while they fall asleep, within minutes as it happens, exhausted by the day's sea swimming.

For a few moments afterwards, Lily hovers at the bedroom door, marvelling at the peaceful ups-and-downs of her daughters' chests as they breathe, synchronised in twin single beds placed at opposite ends of the room. Mia's mouth is open, arms flung above her face on the garish Disney princess pillow she had pleaded for during a trip to the central market.

How marvellous to fall asleep so easily, from wakefulness to dreams in a finger click, Lily thinks with a surge of love so physical it takes her breath away. She goes over to the bed and presses a kiss on Mia's forehead, then Piretta's.

'Love you,' she murmurs under her breath, then gently closes the door and goes downstairs.

Out in the garden, a sea breeze stirs the tall date palm. The evening air is soft on Lily's skin, the warmth almost touchable. She drinks a glass of water containing several cubes of ice, savouring the sensation of the cold stream of liquid penetrating her throat and stomach, and sits still.

Music is coming from somewhere down the street. As it happens, it is a song by Viviane, then a random burst of drumming. Lily hums along to the music.

Against the outside lamp, a gang of mosquitoes swarm with lanky silhouettes, but when she reaches for her laptop and turns it on, the insects migrate busily to her glowing computer screen. Lily sighs and picks the machine up, goes inside. In the kitchen, she leaves the light off and the door open, appreciating the stream of cool air in the warm darkness, unwilling to allow the nocturnal bugs to invade. She pours herself another glass of water, then another.

Now Lily waits for Vivienne to come online. For some reason, her stomach lurches when she spots the little blonde avatar appear. Lily postpones answering the call and rushes to the loo, emptying her bowels with a nausea that rises from her stomach, burning her throat.

Back at the kitchen table, Lily presses the small blue telephone icon button. It does not do to be emotionally unstable in this way, she thinks, realising that she hasn't tidied her hair – which is wrapped up this evening after the effects of the sun and sea – or applied make-up as she normally would for any social or professional occasion. Is she losing her sense of pride now that she has a cheating husband?

No, Lily tells herself firmly. It is *Demba* who is wrong, *Demba* who is betraying her: so why should she lose herself, then? If anything, she will be prouder and more successful now, *inshallah*. After all, doesn't she tell the girls that nothing comes easy, that nothing is won without a fight? She must practise what she preaches.

In the empty room, the computer rings loudly for a second time. There is the added advantage of thinness too, Lily reflects as she watches the screen pulse back and forth. She might not be officially fasting, but already she's experiencing the welcome thinning effects of this dreadful crisis – a dry mouth and lack of an appetite. The stress-induced bout of diarrhoea just now. Quite literally, she can feel the kilos dropping off, *alhamdulillah*. Today on the beach in her swimsuit she felt, well, positively lithe.

No! If she will be obliged to divorce Demba, then she must seize the opportunities this presents – a stronger spirit, greater financial independence, and extreme levels of weight loss. Plus there seems no reason, *now*, not to purchase the pretty and very expensive bikini she's had her eye on from that village boutique, for when she reaches her target weight. Just in case she encounters Demba's mistress on the beach… All this is possible now that she's to be a divorcée not a wife, a term which somehow sounds so plodding, now, so *lumpish* and unexciting. And who wants to be that?

'Hello, are you there?'

It is Vivienne on the other end. The Englishwoman's voice is smooth as glass. There is a smile on her face that doesn't reach her eyes.

'Here I am.' Lily forces herself to concentrate. 'Mrs Hughes, Viv, hi there, good evening.'

Vivienne reminds Lily of one of those news presenters on the European TV channels, or the model Elle Macpherson, or that other woman, Cindy someone, the same name as Piretta's dolls. Or is it Sindy with an 's'? No matter…

At any rate, Lily has never met a white person quite like

Vivienne Hughes, who seems – even within the virtual strictures of Skype – to possess all the composure of an African woman. It surprises her how Vivienne is most unlike other *toubabs*, who are generally rather unappealing, with their dumpy figures and unattractive clothes, their distinct lack of posture and poise.

'You wanted to talk further,' says Vivienne Hughes, 'but having thought about it, my answer is still no.'

The Englishwoman's voice is cool and without emotion. Lily hears the television in the background, the sound of English being spoken, and is aware of her adversary watching expectantly, probably appraising her in the same way. And what does she see? An exhausted single mother with dusty eye circles? Lily pushes the thought away.

'Have you frozen?'

This time it is Vivienne taking the lead, Lily notes. She coughs, then clears her throat, shaking her head, forcing herself to concentrate.

'My apologies, no,' says Lily. 'I've been out all day in the sun with my daughters, and I haven't prepared.'

'Well, it *is* Saturday,' Vivienne says, seeming to thaw. 'How old are your daughters?'

'Mia is six. And Piretta's twelve.'

'Oh, how lovely.'

Lily finds herself describing the girls, Mia's reading progress, Piretta's love of drawing and maths. All the time, Vivienne listens and nods with a look of genuine interest.

'My apologies,' Lily adds. 'Let's get back to business.'

Yet strangely, despite herself, she feels buoyed up by the conversation, by the company. Lily has few local female friends in whom she can confide unguarded, without fear of gossip. On the whole, the mothers at the school are vicious creatures; they swoop on the slightest nugget of intrigue like gulls playing with a juicy piece of fish, throwing it around among themselves. She dreads to think what will happen when they find out about the Demba situation.

'Well,' Lily says. 'If it's a no, I'm not sure how to proceed. Your evidence is pivotal to the case, of course.'

'Of course.' Vivienne takes a sip from a wine glass. There is an awkward silence during which Lily's mind turns over, searching for a solution, but the fact is, she is tired, too distracted to analyse the situation. Not her usual self.

'I understand,' Lily offers eventually. 'Look, it's not the right evening for me, either. We can talk another time?'

'Another time?'

'Perhaps it might be easier?'

'I don't see how that will help—' Vivienne says dubiously. 'I can't promise—'

'Of course, if you don't consent to a chat, I'd have to take a legal course of action.' Lily pauses, thinking, then adds, 'I don't want to play games, Mrs Hughes. We can do this as decently as possible, but I *will* need to get your side of the story, and you know it.'

Vivienne Hughes drops her gaze, frowning, then looks up again, raising a hand with a small smile on her face. 'Hold your horses,' she says. 'As it happens, I *am* writing a memoir. I've been writing it for many years. I suppose you could read that.'

'Well then, that's great news.' Lily nods, glad of a resolution. 'Absolutely,' she adds, 'that is an option.'

She has no interest in open conflict with Vivienne Hughes if she can help it.

There is a long pause.

'On second thoughts,' Vivienne meets her gaze, questioning with blue eyes clear as glass, 'will it become a legal testimony? Because I'm really not sure that would be a good idea—'

'Well, yes,' says Lily after a pause, 'it would be a testimony, legal or otherwise, and admissible in court if you provide it.' She pauses, then gives a matter-of-fact smile: 'Would that suit?'

'Okay,' concedes Vivienne. 'Okay then, if it's helpful.'

'Right,' says Lily, fiddling with the mouse. 'That's settled then, Mrs Hughes.'

For some reason, she finds herself reverting to the more formal greeting. After all, in French they would continue to call each other by the respectful *vous* salutation, not the more familiar *tu*. So not Vivienne, then, or even Viv. Surnames only.

'Please,' Lily adds, 'send that over as soon as you can.'

Vivienne nods, then raises a hand in goodbye and rings off. Lily stays still, staring at the blank screen. The conversation has not gone as she had expected; is it her imagination, or did Vivienne Hughes just bamboozle her into avoiding a conversation?

In the bathroom Lily washes her face, brushes her teeth. She takes a paracetamol for a burgeoning headache, and goes to bed earlier than usual.

In the early hours of the morning, Lily is woken by the sound of shattering glass. Then a sound downstairs, a thud of sorts, or so she imagines.

75

Is there someone in the house? Lily's stomach lurches at the thought of an intruder, her worst nightmare. Or was it just a dream? She lies still and hyper alert, heart pounding, trying to quell the intrusive thoughts rampaging through her sleepless brain.

She is hot, too hot. Does she have a touch of sunstroke, she wonders, after the long hours in the sun? After all, sunstroke can cause hallucinations... On the island, it was boiling hot, topping thirty-five degrees, and Lily and the girls had struggled to find shade beneath the midday shadows of the palms.

The girls! Lily tiptoes through to their room and stands guard in the doorway, brain racing. She is sure everything is locked up. Did she check the bolt on the kitchen door before going to bed, as she usually does?

The menacing text of the other day is hard to forget. Could it be that her antagonist is willing to take things further? Lily has heard of atrocious burglaries in other parts of Africa, Johannesburg and Nairobi, in which the dwelling is raided by men with machetes, parents and children murdered in their beds. In her head, she's run a thousand times through the sorts of martial arts movements she'd pull off to protect her family in this situation.

Now, though, all her bravado is gone, and Lily's heart leaps from her chest. A superhero, Lily decidedly is not.

'Hello!' Lily calls, eventually. 'Anyone there!'

Silence. She needs a gun, a knife. Where on earth does one acquire such a thing? Now that she is a single mother and this is a female-only house, it looks like she will have to invest in protective weaponry for herself and her daughters.

Lily glances down at the doorstop of the girls' bedroom door, which is a heavy granite rock collected on a honeymoon boat trip with Demba to a tiny desert island off La Petite Côte. The island is inhabited by giant red crabs. Blasted Demba… Lily wishes she'd thrown him to the crabs now…

Rock in hand, Lily creeps downstairs. First she inspects the hall, then the living room. But she must have been imagining things, because there is no one there. Yet Lily is spooked by the rooms' looming shadows and her own lingering fears. Something is wrong; she can feel it.

'Hello!' she calls again into the dark, straining to listen. 'Hello?'

Lily's heart thuds so hard in her chest it takes her breath away. She is covered with perspiration. She inhales, then opens the kitchen door and creeps in.

Shards of glass litter the tiled floor. The front window is smashed. Through the jagged glass, a stream of coolish night air passes into the quiet room. So someone was prowling out there, Lily thinks in a panic; some malevolent stranger creeping about while they slept.

Now that the imagined horror is real, Lily is overcome. Her limbs go loose and shaky. She is helpless, useless. Were this shadowy criminal in front of her right now, she would be powerless to fight.

There is a brick on the floor, wound with a rubber band. Underneath is attached a piece of paper. In shock, Lily takes a deep breath then another, trying to calm her pounding heart. She reaches for the light switch, flooding the kitchen with light, then picks up the brick with trembling fingers and extracts the note.

LEAVE WELL ALONE, it says.

For a while Lily sits weeping on the sofa in the other room, arms wrapped around herself. She is shivery, as if a fever is coming. She will have to get the window fixed tomorrow, she tells herself, but for now, the house is not secure. Anyone could jump the wall from the passageway or the beach, as the attacker had done, and climb through.

How easy it is to take for granted one's own security, yet, in actual fact glass is just a thin illusory layer of manmade material. Oh, too much to bear!

But it is two am. She has no choice but to leave the broken window gaping open in the dark. It dawns on Lily that, in the course of the last two hours, she hasn't even once thought of calling Demba. Upstairs, she crawls into bed with Mia and holds the child tight, too tight. Why ascending a flight of stairs should import a feeling of safety, Lily does not understand. She snoozes fitfully, refusing to allow herself to sleep.

Every ten minutes or so, Lily opens her eyes with a jerky motion to check – for *him*, she supposes, in case whoever he is returns to murder them under their blankets. He, him, his. Of course he is male. What other pronoun could shoulder such violence, such savagery?

In the other bed, Piretta slumbers on. In Lily's mind, the letters of the threatening note form and repeat, *leave well alone*, and she doesn't just see the words, but feels them, touches them. Lumbering and neon-lit, the consonants and vowels are menacingly alive.

Eventually, Lily falls into a heavy, dreamless sleep.

'Mummy, what are you doing here?' Mia whispers with a pleased smile at five am, before the light has risen. The little girl turns and nestles into Lily, sweet-smelling of soap and sleep and a trace of yesterday's sun cream. A million miles, thinks Lily, from the terrors of the night before.

'Just keeping you safe, *ma chérie*.'

'Mummy,' the child says in a sleepy voice, warm breath on Lily's cheek. 'If I ate a thousand carrots, would I be able to see in the dark?'

Piretta stirs but sleeps on. Lily yawns, considering the question as she stares at the square of sunrise slowly appearing around the blackout window blind. Her preoccupied brain turns to the smashed window downstairs. She will have to find a handyman to fix the damage.

Doubtless someone from the village can do it, she thinks, but who to ask? She does not want to advertise the fact that the three of them, three helpless females all alone, have been attacked. That her home is a sitting duck for any old burglar – indeed, for any individual with murderous intentions – who fancies a night-time raid, a daytime one, even.

'One hundred million thousand?' Mia insists.

'Possibly, *ma chérie*,' Lily murmurs. How to think up, at this hour of the morning, with the house suddenly transformed into a hostile environment, a suitably intelligent answer for the cognitive challenges of Mia's whirring imagination? Such things are more exacting than the toughest of high court appearances.

'Apparently, the tooth mouse eats trillions of carrots,' Lily offers, pulling her daughter close, planting a kiss softly on her forehead.

CHAPTER NINE

Vivienne

'Well, here goes nothing,' murmurs Viv, drawing a breath as she pulls up outside the ivy-clad country hotel in Dorchester where she's agreed to meet Miles McFlannery – or M, as they all used to call him, some jokey reference to James Bond they must have all thought hilarious at the time. In the embassy days, there was a lot of that – larking around over evening gin and tonics. Ex-pats living the good life in the sun, not a care in the world. Lord, all that seems a world away now. Perhaps she shouldn't have come. What a risk, after all! And what's the point in stirring up trouble?

Viv turns off the engine and sits watching a couple arguing as they unpack their Volvo Estate with two children in tow, then a forty-something woman in sunglasses and a dress in a fabric too floaty for the time of year, descend the front steps of the hotel, talking on her mobile phone. The sight of the woman's pasty-white limbs emerging from the fabric – is it silk, Viv wonders, or some sort of fine cotton? – makes her shiver. There's something so sad about those thin arms, like flimsy branches about to snap.

Viv hates winter with a passion. The thought of leaving home beneath grey skies in the bone-chilling damp leaves her drained, and she inevitably tends to cancel social events at this time of year, the rare lunches or *quick cuppas* – how she hates that expression, it's so unbearably bourgeois – with the few local friends in Fleet she's made over the years.

Of course, summer's another story. When the heat comes something almost magical happens to her, and she likes to go outside and lift her face to the sun, take off her clothes and soak it through her pores until her skin glows gold. A sun bath, Viv always thinks, of the kind taken by birds, as if the warm rays will top up her body like fuel, heat flowing through her veins like lava through a frozen landscape.

But today couldn't be further from the summer of Viv's imaginings. What with the shortening autumn afternoons and the increasing chill in the air, Viv can feel herself beginning to hibernate like a dormouse, or a bear.

Even her *clothes* are different in winter. In the cold, Viv's wardrobe comes down to a selection of fashionable leisure wear – vertiginously expensive cashmere tracksuits she finds in the postal catalogues that pop through the letterbox of Moon Manor. Thermal base layers sewn from sustainable bamboo. Merino hats and thick woollen socks with Nordic patterns – she has a recent thing for Scandinavian fair isle – from small clothing companies in Wales, which she generally tucks into hiking boots.

All this rather than any form of proper clothing, which has no real place in her life now she is alone and spends her time in the fresh air, the garden, or walking the coast path in the wind and rain with only the seabirds for company. Whereas in summer, well, she feels younger and fitter. Her outfits involve expensive linens, pure white cotton, designer swimwear…

Viv sighs. She's only venturing out because meeting Miles McFlannery feels, since John's death, suddenly urgent. Before the funeral, she hadn't seen M since... Oh, it must have been 1987, when she and John left Dakar in a rush, *under a cloud*, as it were. As Third Secretary and John's right-hand man, M was the one who sorted everything out.

Thank God, in fact, for M.

M always had a crush on her, and at the time Viv quite fancied him back, though he must have been a good ten years younger. Viv remembers the frisson of electricity running between the two of them, the way it always cheered her up to see this young officer, fresh to the diplomatic service from the higher ranks of the British army – and so fabulously easy on the eye – staring at her with his puppy-dog look when John was being particularly horrible.

She seems to recall that M married a nice girl from the London typing pool. She has an inkling they'd settled in Surrey, had a couple of children, moved at some point down to Dorset. The usual story.

What a shame, Viv muses. She'd have enjoyed a good flirt, even though she's such a dried-up old bag these days. This despite all the yoga, the collagen shakes, and half lemons squeezed into boiling water every morning. That trick she'd learned from a fellow model back in the day. What was her name? Delphine le somebody... She was French, certainly, and claimed the lemon flushed all the toxins out, whatever *they* were. Viv can always imagine the disgusting acid lemon flowing through her veins, zapping anything in its way – floating parasites, bad thoughts, past sins, pow, pow, pow.

This, and the leafy greens Viv consumes with a dedication bordering on obsession, plus the twice-weekly face masks laced with turmeric and other antioxidants... And she read somewhere – was it a medical textbook? – that good marijuana has youth-giving properties, too.

Though it must be said she's beginning to feel she can no longer disguise her age. The other day after a restless night she discovered, to her horror, a wrinkle neighbouring her left nostril, the sort of line some might say was caused by smiling, but towards which she is anything but sympathetic.

For heaven's sake, is that damn thing still there?

'Oh *shit*,' Viv says, grimacing.

She leans up on the steering wheel, peering in the rear-view mirror, but her skin is china-pale and smooth as ever, thanks – and Lord, she thanks her lucky stars! – to the litres and litres of Evian water she knocks back every single day, and a mere smidgen of Chanel make-up.

Viv sits back down, willing herself to keep calm, and takes a deep breath. *One, two three...* She counts to ten, *and breathe.* Perhaps she's imagined the wrinkle; perhaps old age isn't quite knocking on her door just yet. Perhaps she's still got it.

Besides, flirting aside, Viv reminds herself, she must talk to M about what happened back then, because for too long... Well, for too long, John had stopped her finding out what people actually knew and thought.

And now John is gone.

In the hotel lounge, all expensive tweeds and natural fibres, Viv finds Miles ensconced in an armchair near the fire, which is lit, flickering cheerfully as if winter has already come. Straight away, Viv finds herself slipping into her usual smiley, breathless blonde act, all designed by her subconscious – this, she has long realised – to hide her nerves.

'Morning, Viv,' M says, standing up with a straight back, saluting with a wry smile. 'Seen the enemy?'

Viv smiles back, recalling Miles's signature greeting, ever the ex-Army man.

'Hello, hello, gosh, chilly isn't it!' Two kisses on opposite cheeks, an awkward hug. They are two half strangers, she thinks to herself, not knowing exactly how to act now they are one-to-one, away from the alcoholic hubbub of John's wake. 'Thanks for coming, M.'

'My absolute pleasure,' M says, eyes wrinkling, scrutinising her. 'Bloody hell, Viv, I know I said it last week, but I'll say it again. You've hardly aged at all. What's your secret?'

'Age cannot wither her,' she says, falling easily into the old ex-pat banter, 'and all that.'

She laughs, anxious to avoid having to admit that M *has* aged, that the handsome young officer she once made eyes at now resembles a middle-aged accountant with his paunch and bad complexion, his puffy chin reaching to his checked shirt collar.

How did that happen to someone? Too much booze? Too much fast food? Too much unhappiness, she wonders, glancing at his left hand devoid of a wedding ring, telling herself not to ask what happened.

'Shall we get some tea?' she suggests instead, sitting down in the opposite armchair. She tells herself not to tease him, not to flirt, always her default position with men, as if by turning on the charm she can hide her nerves, the crippling shyness that overtakes her sometimes.

'I ordered some wine – hope that wasn't taking a liberty—'

'Oh, I'm driving,' Viv says. 'Sorry. Besides, I don't drink. I mean, very rarely, anyway. I suppose the odd glass of Sauvignon Blanc never goes amiss, but—'

She is babbling, and lying.

'Must be why you look so young.'

M winks awkwardly, gesticulating to the waitress, and Viv cringes inside. Does he think this is some sort of date? To make clear that it is not, she retrieves a notepad and pen from her handbag, and begins to scribble somewhat aimlessly. She writes a title – 'Miles M' – then the date, and underlines it several times.

When the waitress comes, she orders a cup of tea and a glass of mineral water, sparkling, with ice and lemon.

'So,' M says with a question in his look. 'This is a surprise. You wanted to see me?'

Viv meets his eyes, which are watery brown and ringed with fatigue. Does he normally wear glasses, and has taken them off? For her?

'Yes.' She clears her throat. 'It's about Aimé Tunkara.'

'I suspected that. Why didn't you say anything at the funeral? We could have talked then.'

'I guess it didn't seem appropriate. You can't have two deaths in the limelight, can you?'

Viv shoots M a wry smile and pauses while the waitress loads the table with drinks. When the girl is gone, Viv stirs the tea pot, pours out a cup, stirs in milk with agitated hands.

'I've always felt the whole business wasn't finished,' she

continues, sipping the tea, which is hot and restorative. 'That there was no closure.'

'Closure?'

'For us, for Aimé and his family. I mean, what happened to them? It was all so bloody awful.'

'Christ almighty, you can say that again.' M adds sugar to his tea, and Viv watches him stir the drink with a faint tinkling sound, then drink, little finger extended. In turn, she stirs her own cup and sips, chasing with a sip of the sparkling water. 'An awful business,' M adds, thoughtfully.

'Did John ever tell you exactly what happened that night? He'd never speak about it. I used to want to discuss things, but he got angry—'

'John wasn't very nice to you, was he?'

M stares with a serious look and Viv feels her cheeks reddening, mortified. In her bag, her cell phone buzzes and she scrabbles for it, grateful for the distraction.

'Just the grocery order,' Viv says, checking the text, diverting the conversation. 'I'll have to rush back after this. Amazing you can get it delivered, isn't it? It's been such a blessing, out in the wilds as we are, as I am, I mean—'

'Anyway, you had Harris, didn't you?'

'Harris?' It is her turn to stare. How could he get it so wrong? 'Yes, yes, I suppose I did.'

'It's a long time ago, but there was something,' says M musingly, ignoring her answer. 'Something I thought was strange, though I didn't tell the police.'

'Strange?'

'John used to have an appointment every week out in Ngor.

Marked "L" in his diary, but without any details. He used to tell me not to worry about it.'

'Just "L", nothing else?'

'Yes.'

There is a pause as they both consider this.

'Any idea,' she asks eventually, pencil poised, 'who the appointment was with?'

M shakes his head, eyes wandering to the fire, to the door, back to her. 'Not a dicky bird, I'm afraid.' He takes a sip of tea.

'Don't you think it could have been a—' Viv hesitates, searching for the word. 'An *assignation*?'

M smirks. 'Christ, Viv, you're so polite. Might well have been, knowing John.'

A silence.

'To be frank, I always thought it was strange that you were driving that night,' M says. 'You never used to drive anywhere.'

Viv stares, holding his look. 'John made me drive,' she says, flatly.

'I figured.'

There is an awkward silence before the conversation rears back from such loaded territory. Viv finds herself chit-chatting on lighter matters, and, for several minutes, the two of them reminisce about the past, about Senegal, about the delights of the hot weather there. Nothing of significance.

It is not possible to address this now, thinks Viv. There's a bloody great elephant in the room, an elephant about to crash in and break up their sedate little tea party.

'Well,' she says, stashing the notepad in her bag and taking a last sip of her drink. There is more in the pot, but she is keen to go now, has had enough of the false sociability that comes with such a rendezvous. 'It's been lovely to catch up, M.'

Just then, a woman wanders over, the woman from the steps, Viv realises. Close too she is youngish-looking for her age but heavily made-up, pretty perhaps, under all that foundation. What a shame. She could do with some sort of base illuminator, and a shade-match from one of those helpful women in Boots…

'My girlfriend,' says M awkwardly. 'Sonia. This is Vivienne Hughes.'

'*Enchanté*,' Viv says.

Girlfriend. What a strange word for a nearly middle-aged person, redolent of cinema dates and snogging rather than a mature adult relationship. Viv is not sure she could ever be a girlfriend to anybody, now.

Making herself concentrate, Viv shakes hands with Sonia, emitting the appropriate sounds and small talk. Then, using the excuse of the imminent Tesco delivery, Viv gathers her belongings and makes her way to the car, grateful to be alone once more. She should feel relieved, but instead she feels shivery and anxious. M doesn't appear to know anything dicey, but on the other hand, wasn't it his job to keep secrets? Is he holding back, then? And what was that about Harris? Why mention him at all? Somehow the meeting has only stirred up more worries, as though she has unwittingly revealed her hand.

When night comes, Viv cannot sleep. The bedside clock says two sixteen am. In the past, she has suffered from insomnia; now, she finds herself lying on her back in bed staring into the noiseless dark. Here in the countryside, there is hardly a sound at night, hardly more than the occasional whoop of a bird to break the deep silence of the lightless landscape.

Eventually, Viv gives in to her wakefulness and goes downstairs. She sits at the kitchen table with a drink of water. In the lull of night, the heavy tick tock of the grandfather clock comes loud, marking three am, then four.

She thinks of M politely drinking tea that afternoon, the way that with such diplomatic aplomb he neither revealed nor queried anything. Never complain, never explain, who was it who said that? John? One of the other ambassadors? Or was it something to do with the Queen? Anyway, that was the attitude – old-school British stiff upper lip, on *everything*. She could have questioned him harder, of course, could have pushed him more. But M is old school, she thinks; bright but not that bright. She wonders what he actually knows, she suspects he doesn't know the half of it.

No, it is Lily Tunkara she really has to worry about.

Viv goes over to the dresser where she keeps her stash of weed in a drawer. She opens the silver tin and rolls a spliff. Sitting down at the table again, she lights it up and puffs deeply, tapping the end on the ashtray, then opens her laptop and brings up the latest memoir document.

Frowning, puffing on the spliff, she puts on her reading glasses. Lord, there are so many edits needed to cover her tracks, almost too many to get her head around in the time afforded by Lily Tunkara!

Viv shakes her head, balancing the spliff on the edge of the ashtray. She dreads the memories gathered there at the fringes of her mind, like a baying crowd. Bad enough are the flashbacks, the nightmares that wake her, sweating and crying out, in the middle of the night. And the deep inner panic that grips her sometimes, just like now. She can feel her heart fluttering too fast, a winged creature in her chest trying to break free. She takes a long breath, then another, trying to calm herself down. She drags at the spliff, imagining the weed curling through her bloodstream, her heart and lungs, giving her strength, or is it courage?

Taking a sip of water, Viv begins to type.

CHAPTER TEN

Lily

A Thursday morning. Lily delivers the girls to school, then drops into Ngor village, where she arranges for a local handyman to repair the broken window. The negotiation is easily achieved via family friends of friends, and the practical necessities of the transaction serve to soothe Lily's distress about the intrusion. When a cousin, then a cousin-in-law, pries as to the causes of the breakage, Lily palms them off with a story about her daughters and a miscreant tennis ball. To a mason known for his neat work, Lily pays twenty thousand CFAs in cash, is assured the glass will be replaced that day, *inshallah*.

Back at home, Lily checks over the locks a second time, taking a deep breath. By the evening, she tells herself, everything will be back to normal, God willing. She glances in the mirror, adjusting her hair, and is just about to gather her belongings for work when she hears a key turn in the front door.

'Lily?' It is Demba in the hallway, out of breath, brows drawn together. 'They said a window was broken? With a brick?'

He has put on weight, remarks Lily, all that rich lovers' food after sunset'... 'They?' she says.

'Your cousins, said it happened in the night?'

Drat the village gossips! Impossible to keep secrets in Ngor…

'I've fixed it. Everything's fine.'

'For God's sake, Lily.' Demba glares, pushing his lips out with a belligerent expression. 'You're putting us in danger, you know, with all your snooping about. The girls. Me. You really have to pull yourself together—'

Lily stares at her husband while he rants further, feeling a rush of annoyance at his belated concern. How useless he is, turning up after the event. As if that helps anyone.

'You know what's putting us in danger,' she says in a cool voice when he has finished. 'What's putting us in danger, Demba, is that you're never at home. You're too busy screwing some other woman—'

Lily watches her husband storm out, banging the door behind him.

When Lily arrives at the office car park, the sun is already high in the sky. There is what looks like a press conference going on, and a youngish female reporter is talking into a microphone labelled 'Sene-News'. She has relaxed hair and heavy lipstick; she wears heels and a western-style cotton shirt with palazzo pants. Behind her, two cool-looking guys with cameras are both in skinny jeans and T-shirts. One of them, the shorter one, has large, dark-rimmed spectacles, as is the fashion lately in Dakar.

The young woman turns and saunters towards the car. Lily groans. It's happening then. The national broadcasters must have picked up the story about the re-opening of Aimé's case, and soon, Lily thinks, reporters will be dogging her like stray dogs with a bone.

Camera bulbs pop. Out of the car Lily smooths down her skirt and stands up straight, alert to the imminent questioning. The journalist's manner is steely-eyed and impenetrable, as if she imagines herself as a brand new Woodward or Bernstein breaking the Watergate scandal. Lily suppresses a smile. The microphone is thrust in her face.

'Why do you feel it's important to dig up the past?' comes the question. A lens zooms in.

'Justice,' Lily replies firmly. 'Because my beloved brother, Aimé Tunkara, never got justice.'

Lily turns to go, hoisting her handbag over her shoulder, ignoring the questions shouted in her wake:

'Why now! Don't you think it will damage this community?'

'Do you really think you'll get justice?'

As Lily enters the building, the camera crew circles like strays around a fresh carcass, sniffing scandal, gathering for the kill. It'll blow over, Lily tells herself, and the journalists will be running after the next scandal soon enough. There is no reason to be alarmed.

She is just out of the lift when Ida pops out, regal in a boubou and matching headscarf of symmetrical green and yellow flowers.

'Got a minute, Lily?'

Inside her boss's office, the air-conditioning is fierce. Shivering, Lily is waved into the chair in front of the desk. With the wheezing breath of the very overweight, Ida seats herself opposite.

'Lily. We haven't caught up for a while, and I wanted to talk about your brother.'

'Yes, of course.'

'I realise you're doing all this *pro-bono*, and what you do in your spare time is, frankly, entirely your affair, *inshallah*, but I'm worried about the distraction, and the effect on our business, reputation, and all that rubbish, but it's important. We can't be seen to be—' A pause, in which Ida seems to cast around for the right word, narrowing her eyes and skewering Lily's own, 'controversial,' she comes up with, after a second.

Lily feels suddenly exhausted. Not Ida, too. Ida, her hero, her champion.

'I promise,' Lily says, holding Ida's gaze, 'that I won't let this interfere with my work. I give you my word.'

Ida sighs. 'It's not just the work, Lily. It's the business, the long-term consequences.'

'I know it's a big ask—' Lily hesitates. 'I won't let it affect our clients. I believe, well—'

Ida widens her eyes. 'Yes, Lily?'

'That Aimé deserves justice, Ida. I'd rather resign than—'

Ida holds up a hand. 'Stop.' Her voice is hard. She wags her finger. 'You're an excellent lawyer, Lily, and an even better human being. But I can't let your personal affairs affect my business.' Ida smiles, eyes now twinkling. 'Deal with your brother's case, then come back to work. As from now, you're suspended on half-pay.'

'What? Ida! Please—'

Ida shakes her head. 'Sorry, Lily, I'm not changing my mind, and I'm doing you a favour. I hope you'll see that, *inshallah*. Take time out to do what you have to do.' Ida smiles gently. 'Look, take care of yourself. Aimé's case is ruffling feathers, even now, and it's going to ruffle many more. Be prepared.'

'I know,' Lily says. 'As a matter of fact, I've been getting threats by text.'

94

'Have you now?' Ida's face is full of concern.

'Someone threw a brick through my window.'

'My God!' Ida swears, looking concerned. Poor Ida, Lily thinks. Her boss is caught, she can sense, between her sharp business-mind and her humanitarian instincts.

'Just take care of yourself, my dear.' Ida snaps her fingers in the manner of a headmistress addressing a wayward child. 'Nothing is worth your personal safety, *and* those gorgeous bundles of loveliness that are your girls, remember that. Don't forget we're expecting them to take over my business when I'm dead, *inshallah*!' Ida frowns, her chins wobbling. She claps her fat hands. 'Now then, go, go and find justice for your brother, chop chop chop!'

Lily bows her head, unsure whether she has just been fired or set free to follow her heart. Still, perhaps it is what she needs.

'*Jërëjëf*,' she replies, 'please, I'll be finished in a few weeks.'

As she exits the room, Ida calls after her, 'don't forget I'm hosting the Americans next week, Lily. Judge Souma is coming. We won't mention you're suspended. You're my star lawyer, I need you there!'

Lily exits the office in the bright noonday sun, carrying the witness statements from the original case in her handbag and remembering what Bakary Ba had said – talk to Musa. It is true Lily has an inkling that Musa knows *something*, but what? Her uncle's original police statement taken the night Aimé died was so strangely non-committal; there are no real details as far as Lily can see, and much of it is redacted. So why? And who took her uncle's statement in the first place, a Ngor police official, or

95

someone higher up?

Before starting the car, Lily rummages in her handbag and pulls out the witness statements. She looks over Musa's statement, noting the redaction at the top. She holds the paper up to the sunlight, peering in. But the photocopy holds no clues. There is no chance of deciphering the words underneath, though without doubt they reveal the name of the duty police officer interviewing witnesses that night.

Lily sighs. As much as she doesn't want to have to talk to Musa, pretty much ever, it looks like she'll have to.

The sun is boiling hot. Lily starts the engine, wiping away a sheen of sweat from her forehead. She pulls out of the office car park, trundling back through the traffic to the village. In Ngor, she finds Musa sitting on the steps of the mosque with a few other elders. Like the others, Musa wears a grand boubou and flip-flops, is scrubbing his teeth with a cleaning stick. When Lily approaches, the group of men falls silent.

'Musa, can we talk?' Lily says awkwardly.

Musa observes her with widened eyes. The other men stare. One of them mutters something under his breath, reminding Lily of a Greek chorus in a play, elders poised to offer fatalistic commentary.

'I'm just about to pray,' Musa says. The other men nod.

'It's okay,' Lily shrugs, 'I can wait.'

With languid movements, Musa rises, kicks off his flip-flops, pads barefoot into the mosque entrance, and disappears. In the direction of the remaining elders, Lily offers a smile, then takes out her phone and scrolls through her emails to avoid the awkward silence left by their stubborn lack of response. Every few minutes, men and women exit the mosque, rearranging their robes. She flicks away a fly, then another. After a time, one of the elderly men taps her on the arm.

'*Madame, il est la-bas.*'

With a wizened finger, the man points with telescopic precision. With quick steps, Musa is making his way out of the mosque gates with the furtive demeanour of a man trying to remain unseen. Lily finds herself momentarily baffled by the older man's easy grassing up. '*Merci*,' she murmurs and stashes her phone, walking swiftly after her uncle.

'Musa, wait!' Lily joins pace with him, striding to keep up. 'Look, Uncle, you can't avoid me forever, you know. Once this gets to court, they'll call up witnesses, subpoena them if they have to.'

'I'm not *avoiding* you. Just busy.'

'Can we go somewhere to talk?'

'I've got things to do. Don't you?'

Lily frowns, ignoring his sarcasm. 'Just one question, then. Do you remember the name of the police officer who took your statement on the night of the accident?'

Musa stops and turns to face her. Droplets of sweat are making their way down his face. From his robe, he brings out a cloth and wipes the sweat away. Lily watches in silence.

'No,' Musa says eventually.

'What are you hiding, Musa?' Lily says quietly, holding his gaze. 'It was John or Vivienne Hughes who killed Aimé. There's no reason for you to protect them, so why are you against this?'

'You don't know what you're getting into, Niece.'

'I do.' Lily does not drop her eyes. 'I do.' She sighs. 'Look, if you know something, Musa, tell me. I can do something about this. Who are you protecting?'

Musa kisses his teeth. Then: 'The man's name was Bouba. Bouba Diop.'

'He was a police officer, or an inspector?'

A shrug. 'How should I know?'

'And why were you and Bakary arrested afterwards for making trouble? It doesn't make sense.'

'I can't talk about it.'

'Musa?'

But her uncle is already walking away, shoulders bowed.

It is only two years since the national police archive was transferred online. Lily logs in to the computerised system with a sense of relief that she no longer has to go traipsing down to the labyrinthine paper archive in the city centre, where junior lawyers face the wrath of a grumpy archivist whom everyone reckons sleeps among the rows and rows of brown manila folders.

After inputting a few different search criteria, Lily discovers Bouba Diop under Police Officer, Retired, 1980 to 2015. And there is a home address out in Yoff: 21, Beach Tenement, Yoff Plage.

On the way to the fishing suburb to the east of Ngor, Lily parks near the law courts to grab some lunch at a street-side place open during Ramadan, called The Exclamation Mark. She orders a plastic plate of *yassa poulet* and sits munching on mouthfuls of the spicy chicken and sweet onion, watching a few other customers file in for lunchtime: a pair of executive-looking women in grand *boubous*, evidently not fasting either, followed a short while afterwards by a white man in a western-style business suit.

Lily's eyes fall on the diners, mind wandering despite herself as she considers the grammatical scenario, *elles mangent* to *ils mangent*, abruptly. Once early on, she and Ida had found themselves bonding over the intrinsic sexism of the French language: the fact that as far as French grammar in concerned, as soon as a single man enters a room full of women, the masculine pronoun comes to dominate the feminine one.

Might one simply change the rules, Lily wonders, in one's own conversation? Here in Senegal, isn't there room to play with the language of the colonial invaders – isn't it an African's *right* these days? And Ida, for one, is all for a gender-neutral pronoun; for introducing feminine forms of the words' masculine counterparts; for calling themselves, as women, *une avocate, une ministre, une chef.*

Lily herself is aware that the debate still rages on in France. She's heard somewhere – she forgets where – of a male French MP insisting on calling a female minister *Monsieur* Le Ministre out of pure stubbornness. Pssht, how could it be okay to teach such grammar to our little girls?

Lily turns her mind back to the matter at hand, the conversation with Musa. She pauses her meal to look over the documents again. There is Musa's witness statement, then Bakary Ba's. After that, the coroner's report. With fresh eyes she peruses the exact descriptions handwritten in black ink of Aimé's clothing, his shoes, his skin and facial structure, then the more gruesome particulars of his fatal injuries, which though they make for difficult reading, are listed broadly as trauma to the neck and back.

As far as she can see, everything is correct. The finer points of the description correspond to the trauma caused by the impact of a car. And yet…

'Hey, Lily.'

The voice is male. Lily looks up. It is Lion Savané, the investigator from the office, and an old friend from the village, a Catholic. With a half-full plate of food and a Coca-Cola, Lion is seated at a table opposite.

She has known Lion since childhood; they grew up together in Ngor; played chicken-chicken-goat in the sand; attended primary school then *lycée* and university. Truth be told, Lily recalls, she had a crush on Lion once as an early teenager, though it was nothing but the sugary romanticism of a fourteen-year-old girl. Like two ships on a radar screen, the two of them have circled each other over the years, but these days Lily does not know Lion well, apart from the occasional coffee machine chat at work.

Even so, it dawns on Lily as Lion picks up his plate and his can of drink and comes across, that the two of them share the easy connection of two people who understand each other's pasts.

'You like this place too, then?' Lion grins and, without stopping to ask, slides onto the bench opposite Lily. 'The Yassa's pretty epic.'

Lion's tight T-shirt is emblazoned with the logo of a surf brand, 'Billabong, surf for the soul', and clings to his chest and broad muscles of his upper arms. Lily finds herself noting the line of Lion's bicep running into the strong, principal vein of his forearms…

'Lion,' she says, pulling herself together. 'This is a surprise.'

'Indeed.' He smiles and swigs from the can. 'Do you come here often?'

Lily can't help a small snort of laughter at Lion's easy flirting. 'Sometimes,' she says. 'It's just round the corner from court. I agree, the chicken's delicious.'

For a few minutes, they talk and eat, the conversation swinging easily between them. They talk of Ida and her fearsome brand of kindness, of the trials of practising law in Dakar. Lion tells Lily of a book he is reading, of his love for American thriller writers. In return, Lily imparts her liking for Scrabble. Though Lily mentions her precious daughters, she does not touch on her marriage, or on Demba. Nor does Lion refer to a girlfriend, she notes, or a wife or partner, though he mentions his older sister, Maria. Lily recalls that when they were children, Lion's family had struggled to deal with Maria's disabilities and resulting special needs.

Lion balls the rice with deft fingers, chews the remnants of flesh off the chicken bones. Lily likes his humour, his bright mind which swerves off at energetic tangents, matching her own. Then: 'I heard you're investigating your brother's case?'

'Mm. I'm not exactly in Ida's good books about it. She's suspended me.'

'Hell, really? But good for you.' His expression falls serious. 'Look, if you need any help, just shout. I don't mind facing the wrath of the titan.' He winks, laughing.

'Thank you,' Lily looks across at him, and smiles, 'that means a lot.'

'Well, talking of Ida... I better go, or she'll *eat* me.' Lion pushes away his plate, rises from the bench. 'Keep cool, Lily.' He fist bumps her then pauses, as if weighing up whether to say something else. 'So,' he adds, 'there's this excellent new patisserie down by the roundabout, sells these cream cakes and coffee... I could show you sometime if you like—'

'Pssht, in your dreams.' Lily kisses her teeth, not entirely convinced by her own rebuff. 'I'm a married woman.'

'You know, Lily Tunkara,' Lion says, undeterred, 'maybe you should get your head out of those law books and have a little fun.'

Lily shakes her head with a small smile, watching Lion walk out of the restaurant with the vague hip-hop swagger adopted by most men of his age these days. She has to admit that flirting with handsome Lion brings a certain relief after all the trauma of the last few weeks. How old must he be exactly, she wonders, her age exactly or a year younger? And so refreshing after dull, plodding Demba and the clichés of his middle-aged affairs. Still, there is no getting away from the fact that she is still a married woman!

Lily rises from the table, returning the witness file to her handbag with a sense of unease that lingers even after the somewhat pleasurable interruption by Lion. Something is still niggling at the back of her mind. For the life of her, she can't think what it is about the report that bothers her so much. Then it hits her. The blood reports. Aimé's blood reports are missing.

In Yoff, Bouba Diop's place turns out to be a desolate-looking apartment block directly on the beach, arranged around an open courtyard on the ground floor where a couple of women are hanging out washing on a line. Chickens peck the ground. Lily can smell and hear the sea, the sound of the warm wind whistling beyond the walls. When she asks about Monsieur Diop, the younger woman nods with a nonchalant expression in the direction of a flight of stairs.

At the top, two teenage boys hanging around on mobile

phones eye Lily with suspicion. For some reason Lily feels a stirring of unease somewhere deep in her gut. What if someone finds out she is here? She remembers Musa's words, urging her to stop asking questions. Is she being foolish, putting herself and her family in danger with this relentless unearthing of long-forgotten events?

But not by her, Lily reasons. For her, the past is not forgotten, it's inescapable.

'I'm looking for Bouba Diop,' she says to the teenagers, forcing herself to focus. She is here now, after all. 'Do you know where he lives?'

'In there,' says one of the boys, hooking a thumb in the direction of a shabby, unmarked doorway, where cigarette butts are scattered all over the ground. Lily moves towards the door and knocks cautiously.

'*Oui?*' A head pokes out accompanied by a blast of fresh cigarette smoke.

'Monsieur Diop?' Lily holds out a hand, but the man refuses it silently in the way of the older generation sometimes. 'I wondered if you have a second to talk to me?' Lily adds, dropping her hand. 'It's about the Aimé Tunkara case.'

The door opens and Bouba Diop stands in the doorway. He is very tall and thin in a grey *djellaba* and slippers, a day's stubble shadowing his chin. His eyes are sallow and ill-looking. Deep wrinkles line his face. He observes her with a look of suspicion.

'The Tunkara case?' Bouba says dubiously. 'That was decades ago.'

'I'm Aimé Tunkara's sister,' Lily says. 'My name's Lily Tunkara. I was five when my brother died.'

103

Bouba stares, as if taking Lily in for the first time. 'I see,' he answers, hovering behind the door. Then he inhales deeply, somewhere between a sigh and a groan, with an intake of wheezing breath, 'They told me not to talk to you.'

'They?'

'The powers-that-be.' Bouba kisses his teeth, giving Lily a dull look. 'Thirty-five years I worked for that police department, and what do I get for my troubles? A squalid flat and a miserable retirement, that's what.' He kisses his teeth again, seeming angry. 'Now they want me to do more dirty work for them.'

Lily finds her palms are sweating. Who are these so-called powers-that-be? What dirty work? She glances behind her with that uneasy feeling again, of eyes on her, of being watched, but the loitering teens are gone. There is no one there. She looks back at Bouba, frowning.

'The last thing I want is to get you into trouble, but doesn't it strike you as odd that someone doesn't want this case uncovered?'

Silence. Bouba's expression is still belligerent, though whether in relation to her visit or to his former colleagues, Lily isn't sure.

'My brother's case, I mean,' she adds, 'something isn't right.'

Bouba's fingers fiddle agitatedly with a pocket of his robe. He kisses his teeth several more times, in quick succession. Eventually he gives a wheezing sigh, and gestures with a bony hand into the room.

'You'd better come in.'

The room is neat, with strong smells of incense and tobacco. There is a large wooden bed laid with a blanket, a red and blue woven plastic mat laid across the tiles, a small stove and teapot set in the corner. A single chair is placed by the open window, where a makeshift wooden shutter bangs in the wind. In the silence, the banging sound jars Lily's nerves.

'I must get that fixed,' says Bouba, following her gaze. 'As I said, police pensions don't add up to much these days, even when you've given them your blood, sweat and tears. Anyway,' he adds, fetching some glasses, leaning down with an effort to set a kettle on the stove to boil, 'I'm not sure I can help you. All that's a long time ago, you know.'

Lily seats herself sideways on the bed, crossing her legs. Bouba stands up and extracts a packet of cigarettes from the pocket of his robe.

'Apologies—' He lights up and goes to stand by the window, drawing deeply. 'Ramadan, you know – makes me smoke more, God forgive me. The tea is doctor's orders, my illness...'

Lily smiles, wanting to wince, imagining the nicotine eroding the man's already-damaged lungs. She has an inkling that smoking is not permitted either during the fasting month. Then: 'You worked as a police officer in Ngor?' she asks. 'You were the one who took the statements the night my brother died?'

'Yes, I was. I was just a young police officer then, it was one of my first cases.'

'I'm taking a new look at the evidence.' Lily hands Bouba her work business card, which he turns over in his hand, raising an eyebrow, puffing on the cigarette. 'I believe there was more to it, and I've applied to have my brother's case re-opened at the African Court.'

'Oh?' Bouba takes another puff and exhales slowly. 'You have?'

The shutter bangs insistently, once, twice.

'Can you tell me about the witnesses you spoke to that night.

Specifically Musa Tunkara?'

'Musa was the one who found Aimé.' Bouba picks the kettle off the stove and pours the dark liquid into two tiny glasses. 'I recall he seemed shocked, could hardly formulate a sentence.' Bouba hands her a glass. 'It was a terrible business.'

The glass is very hot to the touch. Lily puts it down on the tiled floor to cool. 'Did Musa seem nervous,' she asks. 'I mean, do you think he was telling the truth?'

'I always wondered. He was certainly holding something back. A few days later, just before the case was closed, I asked to re-interview him, but I was stopped.'

'Who stopped you?'

'The inspector of the time. Rumour was the British got to him. They closed the investigation down pretty quickly. Pinned it on that poor young man smoking *ganja* before he even started out.'

'That was the official story,' Lily says. 'So you think it was a cover-up?'

'I do.' Bouba sips from the glass of tea, shaking his head and looking agitated. 'I don't know what was going on, or who was pulling the strings from above, but I was told to conclude the witness statements fast, and put it to bed.'

'And they also removed the blood reports, so no one could see Aimé's system was clean as a whistle?'

'Sure.' Bouba puffs and drinks. 'From what I remember of your brother, he wasn't the sort of chap to smoke anything—'

From the floor, Lily picks up the glass of tea and takes a sip. It is eye-wateringly sweet. She takes a second sip, then another. A strong gust of wind bangs the shutter particularly violently and Lily jumps, wincing, the glass of tea still held in her hand, then carries on, 'So what do you believe *actually* happened?'

Bouba shakes his head with a pained expression. 'There was something fishy about the death report. I always felt things were missing, that there was misreporting going on, though of course that's nothing unusual in the police, especially back then.' A pause, and Bouba frowns, drawing deeply on his fag, shaking his head with a desolate expression. 'We were always getting interventions.'

'Interventions?'

Bouba nods thoughtfully. 'Sure. The whites, the *toubabs*, pulled the strings. Big cheeses, we used to call them. It was all about money.' He rubs the thumb of his free hand over the tip of his index and middle fingers, and Lily has a sudden vision of hundreds of dirty coins and notes, slipping from hand to hand, from pocket to pocket to pocket.

'There were other cases covered up, then?'

'Sure, sure.' Bouba gives a mirthless little laugh that gives way to a coughing fit. He takes a few small sips of his tea, cigarette glowing in his right hand, then continues, 'Embassy staff, they were the worst. The French, the British. You wouldn't want to know the stuff that went on; those guys thought they were gods, thought they could use us blacks like toys.'

Lily listens with a sort of shocked horror. 'Couldn't you do something, speak out?'

'Who me? Go up against the great colonial powers?' Another dry, mournful laugh. Wheezing, Bouba leans down, balancing his cigarette on an ashtray on the floor, then rises to his feet. 'Look, dear,' he says, standing facing her, 'I was nineteen years old, the most junior policeman in the department, and lucky to

107

be there. Who was I to say anything? I had a family to feed, so I kept my mouth shut and got on with the job.' Bouba shrugs, opening a side door. 'Excuse me one second.'

Lily hears Bouba coughing and pissing in the next room, a roar then a trickle. A toilet flushes. She sighs, her curiosity giving way to a sudden feeling of helplessness. She was just a child during those years, but she remembers the deep confusion she felt about white people; the knowledge, but without detail, undefined, that a white woman had killed her brother, yet the sense she had that the *toubabs* were somehow *better* than them, more sensible, more capable, more worldly, as though the Senegalese were children, and the whites were grown-ups.

By some strange osmosis she had understood, as a small girl, that this was why the *toubabs* made the rules, even twenty or so years since Senghor's independence. How easily they all accepted this! She even seems to recall wishing she were white at one point, aged seven or eight perhaps, because in her immature mind she figured that despite her own privilege, the lives of those with pale skins were in a different league altogether.

And still, Lily thinks now with infuriation, ashamed of the memories, to this day the tendrils of colonialism creep through their lives, unspoken. She would like to go back and shake her eight year-old self, tell that girl to be proud, to be strong, to be confident.

Anyway, it turns out she came to her senses. As a young teenager, once she understood more about Aimé's accident, she became quietly rebellious. She had been brought up with Wolof, had long mastered the French language. Having persuaded her mother to let her sign up for extra English lessons, she spent hours in the British Council library, devouring the dusty collections of British classics, Graham Greene and Shakespeare and Dreyer's English Grammar, discovering the French and British legal textbooks that would set her on a firm path to the law, to justice for all. To use the whites' resources was the only way, as far as she could see, to equal the whites.

For the first time it occurs to Lily that it could have been then, somewhere in her teenage subconscious, that she resolved to find justice for Aimé one day.

Bouba is back in his seat. The tea has cooled. Lily drinks the rest, extending her glass for a refill. With heavy movements, Bouba leans to pick up the pot and pours from a height, a stream of golden liquid. The fresh cup is cooler, sweeter.

'Everyone was at it,' adds Bouba in a low voice, as Lily sips. 'I was no angel, either.'

'I understand,' Lily says. 'Humans follow the pack, they always have.' She watches Bouba draw at the remaining stub of his cigarette. 'Tell me then, what happened after you noticed the missing reports?'

Bouba nods, appearing to focus his mind. 'This student came to see me some weeks after, wanting to talk.'

'Another student?'

'Yes. His name was Ali? Alou? Something like that. Anyway, he must have been much younger than Aimé, still a teenager. Said that he was a friend of Aimé's, and he had some information. Anyway—'

Bouba takes a wheezing breath and throws the still-lit end of his cigarette out the window. Lily watches the glowing stub catch the sea wind and float away.

'Yes?'

'I agreed to go and talk to him, but when I turned up, the family told me he'd drowned.'

'Drowned?'

Bouba inhales, rattling breaths coming faster with the agitation, Lily wonders, of the memory. He leans on the window frame for support.

'Yes. Just after he came to see me. It seems he went diving with friends out in the bay and got caught in the current.'

'Said who?'

'Well, that's the thing… It was his father who informed me. And when I asked if I could speak to the mother, he wouldn't allow it. Stopped me in my tracks. And, well, drowning is so commonplace isn't it, around here, there wasn't a police report, or even a file recorded on the incident.'

'Do you have the family's name?' Lily asks, bringing out a pen and notepad. 'Any details?'

'Yes, I remember it distinctly because it was my brother's name.' He draws another deep breath, and pulls out another cigarette. 'The boy's father was a man called Jawara. Jawara Niang. He was a teacher, I think, secondary school.' Bouba lights up, puffs on the end and exhales the smokes through his mouth and nostrils. 'I wondered at the time—'

'What did you wonder?' asks Lily, scribbling down the name.

'Whether Niang had been your brother's teacher, too. It seemed, well, a coincidence that it was Aimé who died, then his own son. It's all connected; it must be. Anyway, I suppose I'll never know. I knew I had to stop there. It was more than my job was worth at the time, you understand.'

'I do.' Lily nods, jotting the name, putting the pen and paper away. 'Thank you, you've been very helpful. One last question. Did the family live in Ngor?'

Bouba nods. 'Yes. In the rundown district next to the bakers – at least it *used* to be rundown. Ngor is rather swish nowadays, so I've heard. Anyway, it was a long time ago, who knows if the family's still there.'

Lily gets to her feet, swigging the last of the tea, and gathers her things. With the cigarette still between his fingers, Bouba shows her to the door.

'Be careful, Miss Tunkara.' Bouba stares her in the eyes. 'Something always seemed to me to be off about the Tunkara case.' He pauses, staring somewhere into the mid-distance. 'Dangerous people, you know.'

'Funny,' Lily says, a chill running down her spine, 'you're the second person to say that to me today.'

In the distance comes the call of the mosque for afternoon prayers. From her bag, Lily's cell phone buzzes. She steps down the stairs, waving to Bouba Diop, who gazes after her, seemingly deep in thought. Lily takes her phone out of her bag. On it, a single text message: YOU NEED TO STOP.

She shudders and walks on, glancing around her with a hunted feeling. Not until the end of the road does her heart stop hammering in her chest.

That evening there is an email waiting for Lily from Vivienne Hughes, containing a Word attachment labelled: 'Memoir: Part 1'. For a brief moment Lily comes up in goosebumps, bracing herself to read whatever the message might bring. When she interrogates how she feels, the sensation is not dread exactly, but rather a stressful sort of trepidation as to the truths or half-truths written therein.

Or whatever constitutes the other woman's truth, Lily corrects herself. Given that Vivienne Hughes, so cagey in person, has so much to lose in the course of any investigation into Aimé's death, her words must be treated with scepticism.

To Lily's mind, Vivienne Hughes is only a single eyewitness of many. If anything, Lily will read and take notes of whatever she has to say.

So, once the girls' bedtime is complete, Lily settles down to read Vivienne's memoir:

Memoir, Part One

Soho, 1986: I wake earlier than usual to a commotion of rowdy partygoers bailing out from Gerry's downstairs. The light's just beginning to break, sounds filtering through the grubby glass of my bedroom window. I lie beneath the blanket with my eyes closed, half-listening as a reveller groans and vomits onto the pavement before trailing away behind the others. Then there's the swish of the street cleaners moments later, and the growing rumble of traffic down Regent Street.

Exhausted but wide awake, I get up and wander barefoot through to the kitchen, where Ruby – Ruby Brown, my flatmate, who's twenty-three like me – must have been drunk or high the night before, because she's left a hell of a mess. I survey a rancid pool of what looks like tea and baked beans oozing from an abandoned plate. *Ugh*, I think.

Heavens, that bedsit was awful. Allow me to describe it for you. Mould spots the upper corners of the walls, and a murky smell of damp and weed pervades the flat, even the sheets of my bed, no matter how much I open the windows to let in the air.

There's a *teeny tiny* living room with peeling anaglypta walls, which I've furnished with a decrepit yellow velvet settee from a junk shop in Camden, which I bargained down to £2.50. A record player with vinyl stacked alongside: Earth, Wind & Fire, Sister Sledge, Led Zeppelin, that sort of thing. Ruby's illegal collection of marijuana plants lined along the skirting board in the hall. A metal rail to hold our clothes, and a full-length mirror leaning sideways against the wall with make-up scattered next to it.

Then there's the kitchen with its temperamental old gas hob, a sink, a grotty Formica table that wobbles when you sit down, and the two miniscule bedrooms, Ruby's and mine, where we hang sheets at the windows as curtains, beds covered with blankets.

I consider the mess in a daze, then wipe the surfaces with a cloth, scooping food into the bin. I boil water in a pan on the hob and help myself to a glass of tap water, then another, before preparing an instant coffee with several sugars. I sit shivering on the sofa, coffee in hand, brooding over my situation.

It's the middle of winter and the bedsit's bloody freezing. God knows, I've been plotting my escape route for a while, but for now, any sort of breakout seems nigh on impossible, especially if I want to keep on volunteering at the lab. The modelling agency pays a pittance. As for the escort job… Well, it's good money, but there's a reason for that! The male clients, big and lecherous, the way their faces break into expectant smiles when I turn up, make me feel physically sick.

As it happens I'm booked that night for a *rendezvous*, as the agency likes to call it – somewhat ridiculously, I think, presumably because the French word's less sleazy. In reality, most of the men are married, which means – logically – that I'm one step away from a hooker.

You can imagine how that makes me feel. Fact is, I'm so broke, you understand? It's a few months since Mum died, leaving me no money to finish the final part of my studies. Despite the best efforts of my tutors, I've had to leave Oxford halfway through the fourth year of my medical degree. I'm qualified, but not fully. Even all these months later, it's hard to accept that I won't ever become a proper doctor.

The only chink of light in all this misery is that I'm just about managing to keep my intellectual brain intact, by volunteering at a research lab in London, under one of my former supervisors, Dr Harris Burns. He's a high-flyer, researching anti-malarial drugs, and because I'm already qualified as a junior, I'm helping him, as well as sleeping with him.

Well, that's obvious, isn't it… Harris is handsome and clever and extremely slippery, plus a total player when it comes to women. I don't trust him as far as I can screw him – excuse my French – and I'm well aware he's using me for sex.

But that's okay, because I'm using him, too.

Anyway, according to the agency girl, tonight's bloke is 'a nice one', in inverted commas. I cringe at the way she says it, *lasciviously*, as if I'm in the market for a house or a new cooker, for heaven's sake. Okay, okay, I know she's just trying to be kind. There are so many bad apples around, so a *nice one*'s a rare find.

John, his name is. In the photo, he looks a mild-mannered

114

sort, good-looking even, in a staid, conservative sort of way, with pleasant green eyes. But perhaps it's his clothes – jacket and tie; or the way he wears his brown hair – so neat! I know he isn't my type.

John is forty-one, the agency girl informs me, though he looks younger, and his work is something high-up to do with the diplomatic service. He wants dinner and conversation, but don't they all. It's why they like me, I s'pose; and why the escort agency jumped to get me on their books, because I'm sexy *and* brainy. An Oxford medical grad, *no less*. I reckon most men, idiots that they are, will refuse the brains without the body, but they'll always take the body *with* the brains. Until you start expressing actual opinions, that is. Then, oh, then, Lord, they wish they'd never bothered.

Later on in the day, when the streets are loud with traffic and crowds, I pour one gin and tonic after another. I kneel in the bathtub and wash with cold water because I can't be bothered to warm a pan on the stove, then select a tight-fitting top, jeans, and platforms. I backcomb my hair, buzz it with spray, line my eyes with thick black kohl and mascara.

In the mirror, the make-up brings out the blue-green of my irises, my freckles and high cheekbones. I look thin and cool and slightly wild; it's a good look. Five minutes later, Ruby comes in while I'm leaning out of the window, smoking a joint.

'Hey, man, you look pretty. Got a date?'

She's naked, high again.

'Some guy called John,' I reply flatly. 'Dinner, drinks. Ten quid an hour.'

'Be careful won't you, babe.'

Ruby puts some clothes and the record player on and we bop about to Led Zeppelin, drinking more gin until the alcohol blurs my senses. Some more girls drop by. They pass a joint or two around while we drink and dance. Outside, the sky turns from grey to blue-black. After a while, I smoke another spliff. The pleasant numbness it brings on will, I know, arm me well for the night ahead.

At five past five, I put on my fur coat and step outside into the rainy evening. At that time of night, the city's settling in for an evening of revelry. The restaurants are already filling with people. Music drifts from a couple of bars. There are people everywhere, students, teenagers, couples, shopping and wandering about.

I look up at the bright window of the bedsit where one of the girls is leaning out, totally stoned. A strong smell of weed wafts down. I envy her, wishing I could stay at the party and never have to do another rendezvous with a random stranger ever again.

I cut along the back streets, smoking, taking my time. According to the agency instructions, the client's waiting at Sloane Square tube station, where – standard procedure – he'll take me to a restaurant of his choice.

The thought depresses me. Despite the weed, I've no appetite. John, I think. Just another faceless man who'll look at my breasts, not my eyes. There again, it's a business transaction, I tell myself. I'll use my posh voice, smile sweetly and sexily in the way that men love. I'll be all ears to John's stories without expressing too many of my own opinions, or revealing my own education, my ambitions.

I draw on my cigarette. Then, with the heel of my shoe, I grind the still-burning stub into the pavement, and descend the steps to Oxford Circus tube station.

Part one, as defined by Vivienne, ends there. There is nothing else, at least not for now. Lily lifts her head from the computer,

116

pondering what she has read. She finds herself intrigued, wanting more, though she has to wonder why Vivienne Hughes is telling her all this when all she had originally requested was information about the accident itself. This so-called memoir, well, it seems rambling at best, though well written – perhaps too well-written? Is Vivienne Hughes simply trying to distract her?

For all Lily knows, the white woman's memoir is all lies. It reminds her of the literary and women's fiction she has read widely in both French and English. As a matter of fact, the image offered by the narrator jars with the white woman she met the other night on video, who struck her as so refined, almost royal. So, instead of a straight statement, Lily wonders, is this to be some rags-to-riches tale of a forlorn Cinderella rescued by a handsome prince, in the form of who? This John Hughes person mentioned by Vivienne? Really?

In Lily's mind's eye lingers the image of this beaten-down young woman presented by Vivienne, and the awful dinginess of London. Such dreary winter cold, Lily reflects. Not to mention the drugs. Lily has never been to Europe, and has never thought of visualising the European world in this way – so poor and so squalid.

Anyhow, Lily wishes Vivienne would just get to the point. As far as Lily knows from the police reports, it had been Vivienne Hughes driving the night Aimé was killed, and not her husband. So will Vivienne say differently? That's all Lily wants to know, as well as what came before. Because whoever the driver really was, they are a murderer.

Later in the day, Lily takes the time to bring out the box of her mother's belongings from where she has stored them under the bed. Lily arranges the items – her mother's precious things – with precision on the bed cover. For a few minutes, she finds herself fascinated by a picture of her parents. By the look of it, Lily thinks, it was taken before Papa died in the pirogue accident, three months before she herself was born. Rose looks happy and holds a child by the hand. Aimé?

There are more photographs of Aimé as a chubby-cheeked toddler, then a gangly teenage boy. One shot, the only one that's framed, Lily has seen before. It used to hang in her mother's room, and captures Aimé's portrait against hazy sunlight. Her brother must have been swimming in the sea, thinks Lily, because water drops sparkle like crystals against his dark skin. With shining eyes, he smiles straight into the flare of the sun.

Aimé. Now the image brings a sudden single memory; of a kind boy swooping her up in his big arms, of the sun in her eyes, of paddling in warm, shallow water, of the same boy beside her, large hand holding hers, reassuringly solid. Yet the memory is nebulous, elusive and half-formed, slipping out of reach as quickly as it comes.

Lily exhales, overcome with a sense of grief that grips her throat and brings tears pricking her eyes. Curious that the memory should come today, out of the blue. She had not realised she remembered anything at all.

With tenderness, Lily runs her forefinger over her brother's face in the photograph.

'What happened to you, big brother?' she whispers. 'How on earth did we manage to lose you?

CHAPTER ELEVEN

Vivienne

At Kew Gardens, Viv turns right down a side road and comes up quickly to the blockish modern building backing onto the Thames, which houses the National Archives. Viv hadn't heard of the place before Saturday, but, inspired by another sleepless night plagued with thoughts of Lily Tunkara's imminent investigation, *blast the woman*, she emailed David Beauman.

David B, or Fuzz, as he was known to all his peers, had been John's civil service colleague back in Morocco, and he later joined them as an embassy posting in Dakar. The nickname, John had explained to Viv once in the course of a conversation about the intricacies of male-nicknaming protocols, came about because when David was young, his neck hair always grew back within a few hours of a haircut.

In later years Fuzz went bald, said John, but the name stuck.

As Viv remembers, Fuzz had always been helpful, and because he had worked for the British government for forty years, the man was an excellent source of information. *Did there exist an official Foreign Office report about the Aimé Tunkara affair*, Viv asks in the message, getting straight to the point. *And if so, where can I find it?*

An hour later, the answer wings its way back: *'I don't remember, though any document like that would be available in the National Archives. The difficulty is where to start searching and in which subject files. It can take months of research at Kew, plus it might be classified. Don't wade in too deep for your own good, will you, Viv! Sorry I'm not much help – and hope you're okay. We all miss the old chap. Fuzz.'*

Now it's Tuesday, and through the swing doors of the building, Viv fills in a badge at the front desk, receives her plastic-covered clip-pass, and follows the receptionist's directions to the lift. On the third floor, she makes her way along the corridor to the reading room, where some of the documents she ordered over the phone have already been laid out for her. A personable young man with exceptionally well-groomed eyebrows and a soothing voice shows her the computer, explaining how to access the archive, and Viv thanks him warmly.

'What an interesting job you have,' she comments. 'Are you a history graduate, or politics?'

'Medicine, actually,' the young man answers.

'Oh,' says Viv, interest piqued, 'med school or post-grad?'

'Six years in. Are you a doctor, then?'

'Oh no!' Viv is flustered, 'No, no, nothing like that.'

'Well, ask me whatever you need.' With an affable smile, he leaves her alone.

First, Viv searches the electronic library, entering the dates and details of the case: *Aimé Tunkara, 1987, Senegal, John Hughes*, working the sluggish mouse to access the links. Various country policy papers come up featuring John's name, then a series of benign-looking files concerning Senegal's diplomatic relations with neighbouring countries in the region, and a detailed missive on British foreign policy in Senegal at the time, authored by her late husband, Viv notes with a strange flash of nostalgia.

Viv turns to two manilla folders and a box file laid out neatly on the desk beside the computer, but at first glance the folders detail only the red tape of foreign aid policies of the time, and contain nothing of interest. Interestingly, there seems to be no record at all of the Tunkara incident. That would be M, thinks Viv – tidying everything up with supreme efficiency. Dear old M, if only he knew...

Opening the box file, Viv experiences a jolt of adrenalin.

'Oh,' she says out loud, perusing the title of the document with interest, pertaining as it does to a series of visits to Senegal made by Dr Harris Burns of the London School of Tropical Medicine. 'Oh,' she says again under her breath.

Viv scans the record: as a guest of the British High Commission, Dr Burns presented the British Embassy's Queen's Birthday Lecture in 1987.

Viv leans back in her chair and takes off her reading glasses, staring into space. Deep in thought, she walks over to the photocopier and copies the most relevant pages of the file. These, she stashes in her bag. With a thank you to the helpful assistant, she leaves the reading room.

In the Orangery at Kew, Viv orders a cheese toastie and skinny latté. Then, because the sun is out and she is craving the fresh air after the windowless reading room, she chooses a table for one on the terrace.

There Viv shivers and wraps her sable cashmere scarf tighter around her neck, pulling her coffee towards her and wrapping her cold hands around the tall glass. She adds sugar, and sips the lukewarm drink. Bought coffee is *never* hot enough, she is thinking with a sense of exasperation; as if these café people are afraid the general public will burn their mouths. Talk about health-and-safety gone mad, for God's sake! Treating us like *toddlers…*

She casts her eye over the botanical gardens, where a horticulturalist in a miniature tractor is pulling a trailer of heaped-up leaves across the close-cropped lawn. A border of *Acer Palmatum* glows all the shades of sunset against a red-brown oak and the cones of a giant Lebanese cedar scatter the grass. She takes a second sip of the lukewarm coffee, then another. The café terrace is crowded and humming with the clink of china cups, children and their mums on coffee dates. It must be half term, Viv realises, glad suddenly of the human company and the buzz. She doesn't want to be alone, at least for now. The morning's discovery is no surprise, yet it nudges at her deepest fears. At worst… Well, she really doesn't dare imagine the disturbing revelations this blasted business of Lily Tunkara's might lead her into.

The waitress brings the toastie, hot and melting with cheddar, to which Viv adds ketchup and a sprinkling of pepper, grateful for the sustenance. Hypoglycaemic shock, she thinks, recognising the symptoms – shivering, fatigue, a raised heartbeat – brought on by the idea that her fears, buried so far that they're no longer even memories, might be resurrected.

Of course, she thinks, biting into the toastie, she ought to leave the past well alone, get on with her usual daily routine as if nothing has happened. Her yoga, her coastal walks, her painting and onerous attempts at a memoir. But now that she's opened the door, as it were, and now that Lily Tunkara, too, is looming on the horizon, she is seemingly compelled to follow the path beyond, no matter what dark directions it may lead in.

Nothing to it, Viv decides, than to go and see Harris.

Lord.

Dr Harris Burns, who these days is Emeritus Professor of Medicine at Oxford University, no less. What was it M had said at the funeral? *Did you hear about Harris?* But for the life of her, she can't remember if he'd said any more. She must have been so distracted, trying to field people's condolences, so M never got around to telling her *what* about Harris in the end. Strange that he hadn't mentioned it at their coffee meeting either.

No, she'll just have to go to Oxford and find Harris.

Really, Viv?! she exclaims in her head. Lord, after all this time. She groans out loud at the thought, nearly spitting out a mouthful of coffee, and glances around in embarrassment, hoping no-one has noticed.

Harris and his chaos, the trail of destruction he always seemed to leave in his wake. Over the years she's heard via their circle of friends about Harris' scrapes and scandals, and for this and other obvious reasons has purposefully kept her distance. So, she broods, fingering the tassels of her scarf, she does not care to return to those times even in her head, or offer refuge to these rising memories. Lord, no. Not now, not ever.

Viv shivers, chilled to the bone now that the lunchtime sun has slipped behind a cloud. The cold air is suddenly raw, biting at her fingers and cheeks. She pushes the remainder of the toastie to the side of her plate, and finishes the last of the coffee.

As a matter of fact, she thinks, carrying her plate and cup inside and placing them on the trolley reserved for people's empty trays, ever since John died, she's been trying not to think much, and has attempted to bury herself in trivia – because, let's face it, her life is chock full of trivia – so as not to have to confront old sorrows, old regrets.

If anything, she's blocked out her emotions about John's death, about the past in general. For thirty years she's been a trapped bird, unable to sing or see the sun. She leaves the café through the shop, reminded suddenly of the Indian folktale about a skylark captured and put in a golden cage for the emperor's pleasure. Her own cage was golden too, yet all she wanted was to fly away.

Viv retrieves a pink cashmere beanie from her bag and adjusts it over her hair, patting it into place, before making her way through the café vestibule to the street, and along to the tube station.

It's a tedious journey home on the underground to Waterloo, then the South Coast express train back to Weymouth. She leans back in her seat, overcome with exhaustion, head jam-packed with intrusive thoughts. Of John and Senegal. Of Lily and her questions. Of Aimé Tunkara and Harris. Now that the time has come for the past to rear its head, it is uglier than ever. Is she strong enough, capable enough, now that all hell is letting loose, to get through this, too?

Evening comes, and Viv is glad to be home, though she is too tired to paint or write, or do anything much but sit and brood. On her computer she googles Harris Burns but finds nothing – not even an academic bio. She no longer has his number; does not know his email address. It's as if he doesn't exist, she thinks.

Then, using other search criteria, she finds a news article from the Oxford Mail, dated six months previous: *A professor at Oxford University is being investigated after ethical irregularities were uncovered in recent tuberculosis trials. The professor in question cannot be named for legal reasons.*

Viv stares at the screen, then shuts the laptop with a snap. The wind is squalling outside the manor windows, rattling the frames. Viv closes the curtains, battens down the hatches. Storm Anthea, they're calling it on the weather forecast, like the girl in *Five Children and It*. Lord, she could do with E. Nesbit's Psammead right now, popping up to grant her wishes. She'd ask for an enormous glass of gin and tonic, please…

And why not, Viv thinks; it's been a long, exhausting day. She goes through to the kitchen, where she pours herself a gin and tonic from the cupboard, adds ice and a slice of lemon. On an afterthought, she rolls a spliff, then sits back on the sofa curled up, idly perusing *The One Show* and letting the weed and the alcohol tranquillise her over-active mind. She wears thick socks and slippers, a dressing gown over tracksuit bottoms and a sweater, yet she is still cold. Around her shoulders, she pulls a blanket, gathering it up like a cloak.

Bored with the frothy presenters, Viv flicks over to a nature documentary on BBC 2 and lets her brain meander along with the soothing images of David Attenborough's oddball creatures of the deep sea. There is a mantis shrimp of remarkable colours floating through a merry cloud of coral, then a Fantasia jellyfish with outlandish pink tentacles, then an eccentric frilly mollusc known as a flamingo-tongued snail. Combined with the natural effects of getting high *and* drunk, the garish colours of the ocean depths are rather pleasantly relaxing, she finds, like a lava lamp, or some out-there 1970s pop video.

All the while, Viv ponders her day. She is going to have to find Harris, that much is clear, and dig up the snippets of the past they share.

CHAPTER TWELVE

Lily

Lily dreams of Demba in the arms of his girlfriend. In the dream, the other woman's orange-painted fingernails leave red, raw gashes on her husband's skin.

For a few seconds when she wakes, Lily cannot separate reality from the dream. If over the years she hasn't appreciated Demba's physique, her husband is, for all that, so familiar, so comfortable. It strikes Lily that anything other than her husband's body scares her. She cannot imagine another man inside her. She turns her face into the pillow, wracked with sobs, then falls into another fitful sleep.

But when the morning light comes, things seem easier. Lily wakes early and dresses in Lycra training gear, pads downstairs to get some aerobics done before the day starts. With her phone propped up against the settee, she performs air punches, star jumps, and press-ups along with a noisy YouTube video, is pleased to see her heart rate soaring when she consults her wristwatch.

Half an hour later, Piretta appears downstairs with Mia trailing in her wake. Sweating, Lily gives them both a kiss and flicks on the television for them.

'Mummy, I made up a joke,' says Mia. 'What do bees chew?'

'I don't know,' Lily pants. 'What do bees chew, *chérie*?'

'Bumble gum.'

'Very good.' Lily smiles. 'Now what do you two want to drink?'

'Milk please,' says Mia, fiddling with her wobbly tooth.

'Hot chocolate for me,' adds Piretta.

'Hey, where did "please" go?'

'Mummy,' remarks Mia, as if an afterthought. 'When I was born, did I come through your bottom?'

'Yes, *ma chérie*, you did. With great effort, I seem to remember.'

'Ugh, I'm not doing that again!'

Lily laughs, still chuckling as she sets the table for breakfast.

On the hour at seven am, the report appears on the Sene News headlines, accompanied by a picture of Lily in court attire taken from the law firm's website, and a ticker tape headline: 'Dakar law star re-opens dead brother's murder case'.

'The Senegalese Court on Human and People's Rights will press for an "urgent and full" investigation,' pronounces the reporter from yesterday, 'into how a brilliant student doctor died after crashing into the vehicle of a British diplomat in 1987.

'The man's surviving sibling, Lily Tunkara, now a practising bar-qualified lawyer, wants the case reopened. Thirty-four-year-old Tunkara is applying to the Senegalese Court for a hearing, stating an alleged violation of human rights. The hearing was granted yesterday.'

Then Lily's own quote to camera and a run-down of her law degree, her work for the Senegalese Women Lawyers Association (SWLA) and the United Nations Economic Commission for Africa. The report runs shots of Lily emerging from her car, close-ups of her face. Lily winces. Good God, does she really look that tired?

'The Foreign and Commonwealth Office (FCO) has declined to comment on the case,' the reporter concludes.

The girls are spooning chocolate Rice Krispies into their mouths when there is a noise at the back door and Lily spins around, heart hammering. She is on-edge, hyper-alert to intruders after the other night's smashed window.

But it is Demba taking off his shoes. For a second, Lily glimpses her husband as a stranger would, a handsome, wide-chested man with smooth skin and a big, close-shaved face. He's in good shape, she must admit, his mid-section still slim for a man of his years – approaching forty.

Demba's expensive cotton work shirt is ironed, Lily notices, the trousers of his formal business suit perfectly creased. He wears cuff links and a tangy aftershave she doesn't recognise. There is a new sleekness about him today, like an otter, all fresh-groomed and shiny.

'Demba?'

'Good morning, my ladies, good morning.' Demba kisses the girls, flings his jacket over the edge of a chair. 'Is there any coffee left for Papa?'

'Where have you been?' Lily stands, hands on hips, still sweating from the workout, aware that she smells faintly of sweat. She can feel little bubbles of perspiration breaking out on her forehead and top lip, which she wipes away with a forearm. 'You've been gone for days.'

'Work, *ma chérie*, work. It's really crazy at the moment.'

Lily kisses her teeth, and sniffs. Beyond the aftershave, another scent lingers around her husband. A waft of something floral, of cheap perfume, the sort of rip-off designer scent you could pick up in the market for a few CFAs. No class then, this fancy new woman.

In silence, Lily pours coffee from the jug into two mugs, slams one in front of Demba.

'Are you staying?'

'For breakfast? No, I'm fasting.'

Demba's eyes meet hers. Is there a challenge in them, as if he is tempting her to make some reproachful comment? The whites of his eyes are bloodshot, Lily notices, from the heat and dust and hunger – or another sort of fatigue, she wonders. All the late nights, all the great sex. If the woman is younger, there's no doubt she'll have Demba's big cassava root working hard. Lily cannot help smirking to herself at the thought.

'You're tired?' she says smoothly.

At her question and her scrutiny, Demba's eyes shift about, perusing the table, scanning the view into the garden, anywhere but her. He kisses his teeth, as is his habit, Lily is aware, when he is nervous.

'I'm on night duty this week, all week,' Demba says. 'I just came home to see my girls.' He grins. 'Got to see my princesses, right, my ladies?'

'Oui, Papa,' the girls chorus.

'Fine,' Lily says, crashing about with the washing up. Never has she felt so angry! Night duty work, she wants to say, or night duty with *her*? But she is not ready for a showdown, not just yet.

'I'm busy, too,' Lily says instead, in the coolest voice possible.

Half-past eight. Lily wears a wax cotton dress with bubble sleeves, in shades of sky blue and apricot. Her bright lipstick matches pleasingly with the cloth. In the mirror, she smacks her lips together, thinking of Demba. Pssht. Then, despite herself, of Lion.

Outside, the heat hits Lily like a weight. She ushers the girls into the car for the school run, ducks into the village centre on the way back from dropping them off, and parks in a backstreet. This early in the day, the village is sleepy and deserted. There are just the sounds of daily life: a cockerel crowing, workmen hammering, music coming from a radio somewhere. A stray dog scavenges in the dust, then curls up and goes to sleep near the front wheel of the car.

The bakery is already open, but a surly young woman behind the counter wearing an elasticated head wrap of red-and-white gingham plastic knows nothing of a Jawara Niang, nor anything about a family by that name.

Turning away, the woman shakes her head huffily, heaves a metal tray off the counter, and begins wiping the surface, ignoring Lily's presence. From the queue, Lily notices a teenage girl in jeans, flip-flops, and a tight T-shirt eavesdropping without embarrassment. Her T-shirt reads *Princess* in silver letters. She chews gum.

When Lily and the woman finish talking, the girl puts headphones back in her ears, jigs her hips to the music. In two minds whether to ask the girl, too, about the Niang family, Lily decides against it, and turns to go.

It is baking time, and the smell of fresh bread floats onto the street. On a whim Lily stops and waits with the other bystanders for the trays of golden baguettes to emerge from the back. How on earth can she find Jawara, she wonders, as the counter girl wraps three baguettes in folds of paper. The trail is dry. There's simply no sign of him or the Niang family, unusual in Ngor, where someone usually knows someone who knows someone. That's the way village life works.

The surly woman shoves the bread into Lily's hands, and, her mouth watering, she carries the baguettes to the car, resisting the urge to tear off a piece. What was it one of her classmates in law class used to say: *A moment on the lips, a lifetime on the hips.* One thing's for sure. Now more than ever, there can be no relaxing of the rules – absolutely none – now she's about to become a single woman.

And she must do something about it, pronto, Lily decides, pushing the keys into the ignition but not starting the engine. The sooner they divorce, the better, what with Demba's absences, his blatant infidelity, his absolute lack of any *shame*. Why should she wait or delay when he continues to behave like such a devil? But a divorce won't be granted without proof, especially to a woman.

This, Lily knows from numerous court cases for which she's presented evidence. In Senegal the woman is always on the backfoot…

On a whim, Lily takes out her mobile phone, brings up Lion Savané's number.

'Lion,' Lily says when Lion answers. 'Yesterday when you offered to help, were you serious?'

'Sure thing.'

'There's a guy—' Lily starts, then stops. How has it come to this? She ought to forget about her husband, get on with her life. There were so many other wives experiencing similar

132

distress without complaint. But she can't help herself. Lily gives Lion their married name, though Lion will twig eventually, she thinks. It's only a matter of time. 'His name's Demba Dow, and he's seeing a woman, in Ngor.' She offers the address from the other day, describes the woman's height and ebullient shade of fingernails. 'I was wondering—'

'Whether I can dig the dirt?' Lion finishes her sentence. 'I can find anything, Lily. I'm the *king* of investigations. But you have to promise to have cake with me after Ramadan.'

'What if I don't like cake?' Lily finds herself smiling.

'Everyone likes cake.' She can hear Lion grinning. 'As I said, you need to have a little fun, Lily Tunkara.'

A knock on the car window. It is the teenage girl from the bakery.

'Gotta go,' Lily says hastily and hangs up, winding down her window. 'Can I help you?'

Still chewing, the teenager takes her headphones out of her ears.

'I heard what you asked in there.' The girl twiddles her fingers in and out of the headphone cord. 'I'm Marine Niang. Jawara's my great-grandfather.'

'Oh, yes.' Lily takes a breath, then scrambles for her handbag and gets out of the car. 'I mean, thanks, Marine, for catching up with me. Do you still live around here, then?'

'Yeah.' Marine's manner is casual. She points down a street off to the right. 'Just down there.'

'I'm sorry to ask, but did you have a relative called Alou? He died a long time ago—'

'You mean Al?'

'Yes!' says Lily. 'Yes, Al. He drowned?'

'My family don't talk about him.' Marine shrugs. 'The subject of Alou is taboo in my family—' She makes a cut-throat gesture.

'I need to talk to your grandfather, Marine,' Lily says. 'Can you show me where he lives?'

Another shrug. 'Sure.'

The girl turns towards the sand backstreet and leads the way at a casual pace, humming to herself. Lily follows as the way ahead becomes narrower and pitted with puddles, opening out into a smarter area where a number of painted brick buildings in different shades of pink and yellow sport smart wooden doors and balconies.

A building of several storeys on the left side of the street, painted burnished orange. Marine pushes open the door, shows Lily into a vast open-plan area that is tiled and cooled by air-conditioning. A spiral staircase leads upstairs. Lily glimpses an enormous kitchen lined with shiny black fitted cupboards. Someone has money, then, she thinks.

Marine leads Lily into an expanse of neatly swept courtyard with a mango tree in the centre, where a heavily made-up woman in tight designer jeans comes out breastfeeding a baby swaddled in a printed wrapper.

'*Maman*,' says Marine, stopping and nodding at a screen door, 'this lady's looking for Pape Jawara.'

'Pape?' The woman hoists the baby higher up her bosom. 'He's at the mosque.'

'Good morning!' says Lily. 'Gorgeous baby. What's her name?'

The woman gives a thin smile, confides that the baby's name is Awa, her own, Sylva.

'Do you know when he'll be back?' asks Lily.

Sylva shakes her head. 'In an hour, *inshallah*. What do you want him for?'

'It's about Alou.'

Sylva's eyes shift about. With slow movements, she shifts the baby from her left nipple to her right, then stares back at Lily.

'Why do you want to know about *him*?'

'I'm a lawyer. I'm looking into a case that happened a long time ago, and Alou's name came up.'

'A lawyer?'

Marine has disappeared. Sylva gestures at Lily to follow, leading her into a living room furnished with two large cream leather sofas. A giant television housed on melamine shelves dominates the space. The only other furniture is a plastic potted cheese plant in the corner.

'I can't talk about Alou.' Sylva jiggles the baby on her shoulder. 'You'll have to speak to Jawara.'

'Can I help you?'

Lily turns. A very tall man in a smart white boubou is standing in the doorway, his face devoid of expression. Presumably this is Jawara, Lily judges, from his height and icy demeanour.

'I'm sorry to trouble you.' Lily holds out her hand, but for the second time that week, finds it ignored. 'My name is Lily Tunkara.'

'And what's that to me?'

'You worked as a school teacher in 1987?'

'I did indeed. I'm retired now. Why do you ask?'

'You remember Aimé Tunkara?'

Jawara's eyes drift. 'Not clearly.'

'That's strange, considering you taught him.'

135

An almost undetectable flinch. Jawara's lips form a thin line. 'How could you possibly know that?'

'A hunch,' Lily says. 'You taught your own son, too, didn't you? Alou and Aimé were in the same school, good friends even; then Aimé went off to university and your son began work as a fisherman.'

Jawara lets out a sigh. He goes to the furthest sofa and slumps into the leather, rubbing his forehead with a palm.

'Yes, I taught them both in various grades. Aimé was a brilliant student, destined for great things, if you ask me.'

'And your son drowned a month after Aimé died.'

Jawara nods, 'Yes, that's true.' Yet she senses the man is lying.

'Monsieur Niang, why don't you just tell me the truth?'

Another sigh, accompanied by a small groan. The baby begins to grumble, and Sylva bounces her up and down, then leaves the room, quietly pulling the door closed behind her.

'Alou was my only son,' says Jawara when Sylva is gone. 'He was good friends with Aimé Tunkara. Alou was younger, seventeen. I'd somehow managed to get Alou through secondary school, and I was proud of that, but the truth is, I was always working.' He gives a sigh. 'Anyway, my son began fishing for a living, but he always seemed to have money, quite a lot of it.' Another sigh. 'Not the salary of a fisherman, you understand. I was so busy working, you understand, and I didn't take any notice, not enough to be alarmed, you understand. There's not a day goes by that I don't regret—' Head bowed, Jawara presses a finger and thumb against the corners of his eyes.

'I'm so sorry for your loss, Monsieur Niang.' Lily pauses, allowing him to recover. 'Please continue.'

'Alou had money, but suddenly he wasn't well. He began to have fits – at first, just the one, then they became more frequent. Eventually, he was having fits every other day. One day, I called the ambulance. But it was too late. Alou—' Jawara puts his head in a palm. 'He died before the paramedics could get to him.'

'So Alou didn't drown?'

'No.' Jawara shakes his head. 'No, he didn't drown.'

'So why did you tell the police he drowned? I'm baffled.'

There is a long silence.

'Tell me,' Lily asks then, 'your son had made an appointment with the inspector on Aimé Tunkara's case. He obviously wanted to tell them something. Do you know what Alou could have wanted to tell the police?'

'You can't prove that. What evidence do you have?'

'I don't.' Lily stops, mind turning. 'I can't prove it, but I believe they got to you, too, didn't they, Monsieur Niang? They – the British, the police, whoever it was – paid you off, so that you wouldn't talk about what happened to your son? Just like my own family were paid off about Aimé?'

Jawara shakes his head with vigour. 'I don't know what Alou wanted to tell the police. That's God's own truth. But I do know that someone didn't want my boy talking. A few days after Alou's death, a man from the British Embassy came to my door offering me money, lots of money.' He waves a hand around. 'Look at this place. How do you think I paid for all this?'

'Who was the man – do you remember his name?'

'No idea.' Jawara shakes his head. 'I just know that Alou was up to something. He seemed to have new possessions, clothes, money in his wallet. Someone was paying him, for something.'

'And you really have no idea who the man was who came? Was he British?'

'Yes, but he spoke excellent French. He was very charming. Sat me down, went through some paperwork, made me sign something.'

'What did he make you sign?'

'He said it was to tie up the ends – that I needed to sign it because once I had the money, I was bound by the document not to talk to anyone about my son's death or the money I received. You see, I really shouldn't be talking to you.' Jawara looks anxious. 'It's so long ago – how can all this still matter?'

'It was what's known as an NDA.'

'A what?'

'A non-disclosure agreement. Basically it's used to shut people up, standard practice of powerful people, I'm afraid.' Lily gives a rueful smile. 'Do you still have that paper?'

'Yes, somewhere.'

Jawara goes away. After a few minutes, he comes back with a document in his hand. Lily takes it from him, scanning the document quickly. On the last page is Jawara Niang's name and a signature. Next to it a British name and another signature: M McFlannery.

'Thank you, Monsieur Niang,' says Lily. 'You've been very helpful.'

As she is leaving, Jawara calls her back. 'There was one more thing. They gave me cash. It was a boy who brought it – younger than my son, he must have only been about fourteen, as I recall.'

Lily frowns. 'What did he look like? Do you remember?'

'Not really. I just remember how young he was. Oh, and he

had a stammer.'

'A stammer?'

'That's right, a bad stutter. Poor little chap. You had to feel sorry for him. They'd do something about that nowadays.'

Two days later. In the office, Lily pulls up the computer's search engine and enters the name: 'M McFlannery'. She tries some forenames: Matthew? Michael? But there is nothing other than an article and backstage pictures of a Toronto-based fashion designer. After a moment, Lily goes into Aimé's original case file and peruses the photocopied documents, but again, there is no mention of the name. It's no good, Lily thinks. She will have to visit the archive in person.

In the city centre, the streets are quiet and hot. Everyone is out at lunch, including the famous archivist. Lily shows her identity card at reception, waits patiently on a straight-backed chair in the anteroom for the man to return.

'I'm looking for an old case file,' Lily says when, after a time, he appears. True to the rumours, he looks ancient, wizened and studious, in spectacles and a brown djellaba. 'The Aimé Tunkara case?' she adds. 'Number 2845.936.'

'That's decades ago, you should look on the computerised files—'

'The photocopies aren't at all clear. I need to see the paper copies. Please?'

'I'm not even sure they'll be intact,' the archivist says. 'It was a very antiquated system, you know. It was me who digitised everything.'

'Oh, well done you.'

The archivist grumbles to himself, 'Everyone seems to be after that file at the moment.'

'What do you mean?'

'There was someone else asking for it the other day.'

'Oh?' Lily says. 'Any idea who they were?'

'None at all. You better come through.'

With reluctance, the archivist gestures Lily to follow him. The airless room is filled with towers of manila folders stacked in rows on metal shelves. There is a heavy smell of paper and mildew. On the wooden desk, otherwise empty, is a giant ledger and a set of three glasses, a silver teapot, a packet of gunpowder tea, as if the old archivist is braced to help himself to *attaya* at any moment. Lily dreads to think where he warms a fire for the kettle; all that paper…

For a few minutes, the archivist disappears. He returns shaking his head with a puzzled expression on his face.

'I'm sorry, Miss, but the file isn't here. It's already been signed out.'

'Oh?' Lily looks mystified. 'By whom?'

'Again, I can't really tell you that.' The archivist shrugs and begins walking back to the desk. 'Must have been the bloke from the other day.'

'Wait,' Lily interrupts. The man turns around, and she sends him a faintly apologetic smile. 'I'd be so grateful—' Sometimes, Lily is thinking, sometimes it doesn't hurt to be a woman, to use a few feminine wiles. 'It's my only lead at the moment, and—' She shrugs, affecting a helpless expression.

Sure enough, the archivist grunts, then consults the ledger, running his finger down the list, murmuring under his breath until he finds what he is looking for. 'It was a Monsieur Lô,' he announces eventually with a touch of reluctance. 'Monsieur Adé Lô, of the British High Commission, the day before yesterday.'

'The British High Commission?'

'That's what it says here, Miss.'

So this Lô person must have come to get the document out the day before yesterday, Lily calculates, thinking fast, when the television news report came out about the reopening of the course. No coincidence, then. People are watching, powerful people who have lots to lose, even now, decades later.

Lily thanks the archivist and leaves.

CHAPTER THIRTEEN

Vivienne

It is nearly eleven by the time Viv refills the car with petrol and sets off for Oxford. Dressed for the cold, she wears jeans, leather boots, and a polo-neck cashmere jumper, her usual beanie hat, fingerless gloves, and a scarf. A touch of make-up. Blow-dried hair because, *obviously*, she'd want any old lover – no matter how much of a bastard he was at the time – to find her attractive still. She ought not to care, but any woman would... Besides, she is nervous, and always she stresses about her looks, her clothes, when she is nervous.

On top, a shapeless khaki puffer coat that transforms her into something resembling a military-trained marshmallow with legs. Nothing worse than freezing your butt off, Viv reasons, peering through the windscreen at the drizzling rain, speeding up as she turns onto the slip road for the A34. And in this weather... Well, it'll be dark again in a few hours. The murkiness of the British winter never fails to amaze her. She indicates and enters the slow lane. She has nothing against Scottish farmers, not really, but their dubious decision to limit everyone's sunlight across the rest of the British Isles seems bloody well churlish, at best.

In a rucksack beside Viv on the passenger seat are rye bread sandwiches wrapped in greaseproof paper, a hunk of eighty-five per cent dark chocolate, two bottles of mineral water and a large thermos of sugar-laced tea, iron rations for what in her head is a mission, no less. Indeed, in usual times Viv would not relish such a journey, detesting motorways as she does – the roads are full of such bloody idiots these days! – but today she feels uncommonly galvanised. Heartened, too, by the familiarity of the destination.

Given that she had nearly completed the first four years of her degree, Viv is still officially classed as an Oxford alumnus, and in this capacity is invited back for gaudies and suchlike, though she never bothers to go. John, on the other hand, an alumnus of St Anne's, used to attend anniversary dinners almost every year, enjoying the buzz and the alcohol at those events, it was no holds barred in terms of drinking. He had invited Viv to the odd gaudy, though always as a showpiece, as she recalls. Always she had the impression her presence made her husband look good, an apparently brainless bauble on his arm rather than an academic in her own right.

Anyway…

Heavens, there's no denying her nerves. Viv grips the steering wheel as a lorry lurches past in the middle lane, then pouts at herself in the rear-view mirror. Harris will be older, yes – *aren't we all* – but Viv cannot imagine he'll be any less handsome. Or any less of an asshole. Lord… Why the hell is she doing this? Wouldn't it be easier to let sleeping dogs lie, as it were. Bury her head? She ought to leave Lily Tunkara to knock herself out with her silly investigations, and sod the consequences.

But how can she? There is too much at stake. Isn't that why she's writing this stupid memoir? Because she's a lost girl, lost one awful rainy night in Dakar in 1987.

Viv grips the steering wheel, biting her lip, aware of her fast breathing above the noise of the engine. It's not just that, she is thinking. The past has never faded, as far as she's concerned. Nothing has gone away, not the pain, not the terrifying feelings of loss and grief and guilt. Still, when she takes her mind back to that night in Dakar, she feels a deep, inner shudder of agony, as though she's being hollowed out inside. For some reason she has long attached an image to these feelings, from where she isn't sure – a horror film perhaps – of a crazed and hysterical ice-cream seller scooping out the wreck of her guts, and dumping them in a waffle cone. *Three scoops, love? Heart, life, future. Here you go, enjoy…*

Often, she dreams of this, of the ice-cream and the pain.

Agitated, Viv speeds up to eighty miles an hour. Before she knows it, she is indicating left from the dual carriageway onto Oxford's ring road. She swears under her breath while negotiating an over-complicated route to a park-and-ride, then stations the car in a vacant space and catches the bus into town.

Five past one. In the thick of Oxford city centre a watery sun beams low above the domes and spires, more rain-soaked than dreamy on this grim November weekday, Viv thinks, though Oxford is far and away one of the most enchanting cities she's ever known. She loves the contrast of the magical golden-stoned silhouettes with the hubbub of daily life: scarf-wrapped students cycling to lectures, a busker outside WH Smith, shoppers spilling out of Tesco, carrier bags in hands.

Then, through a cast-iron railing, the castellated battlements and towering pinnacles of Magdalen College, her old college, where a black-capped don eats a sandwich, gown billowing as she makes her way across the quad. Such is life here, thinks Viv, the highs and the lows, the soaring and the mundane. Once, this place was her world.

In a coffee shop on Cornmarket, Viv orders a pot of tea. She recalls that Harris ended up as a professor at Exeter College, which is just around the corner opposite the Covered Market. A year ago, Harris had written out of the blue asking if they could meet. *'Since that time, I've felt very bad about the way I treated you during my visits to Dakar. It was absolutely unacceptable behaviour. You never deserved to be used like that.'* In the end, Viv couldn't bring herself to reply, and she didn't tell John.

Now, well, she is half looking forward, half dreading seeing Harris. For heaven's sake, after all this time!

Viv pays for the tea and tracks the helpful blue arrow on Google maps past Waterstones and the Radcliffe Camera, where a group of graduates in black-and-white sub-fusc are laughing and chattering like magpies in a field, gathered for some ceremony or another.

Exeter is a small college tucked away on Turl Street. Inside the porter's lodge, Viv takes in the noticeboards clipped with posters advertising social events and charity rag appeals. In front of the rows of pigeonholes, a student with curly ginger hair tears open a letter.

Viv approaches the friendly man at the desk, but the porter frowns and shakes his head at her enquiry. He hasn't heard of a Professor Burns, he muses, donning spectacles and consulting his computer, then extending a visitor's ledger, which she completes with her name, phone number and time of day.

'Are you sure you've got the right college?'

'Professor Burns is a fellow in medicine here,' Viv explains, 'and has been since 1993.'

'Righty-o. I'm new, so I might have got it wrong. Let me have a gander on the system for you.'

Forehead creased, the porter types in silence for a minute or two, then turns back with a smile.

'You've got the wrong college, sweetheart. It says here that Professor H. Burns is a Jesus man; he changed colleges seven years ago.' The porter points helpfully towards the stone walls opposite, visible through the lodge door. 'Just over the road.' He winks. 'Our arch-rival.'

'Oh,' Viv smiles, 'it just shows you can never trust Wikipedia.'

'Too right.' The man laughs. 'Good luck.'

At Jesus, Viv finds the porter's lodge chilly and unmanned. In the pattering rain, she wanders through into the peaceful quad, taking in the well-groomed lawns edged with stonework, the flowerless winter roses whose branches curve around the heavy door of the college chapel. Steps up to an arch, then a cloister-style interior walkway where a drift of lunch being prepared wafts into her nostrils: fish, broccoli, and something like custard.

Viv peeks into the college dining room. There are dark oak benches running the length of the hall, where, Viv knows, generations of professors and students have sat feasting over the centuries, and a majestic oil-painted portrait of Queen Elizabeth 1 gazing down from the furthest wall. She can't place the smell, but it reminds her incongruously of school dinners at her inner-city comprehensive in Romford, of crowded classrooms, of kiss-chase and playground bullies, of a world away from this familiar haven of age-old academia.

'Excuse me, Madam, but can you show me your college pass?'

Viv turns. The missing Jesus porter, no doubt, a grey-haired man of about sixty with a clean-shaven, too-thin face. He wears pin-stripe trousers and shiny shoes teamed with a sweatshirt branded with the college crest featuring capering stags. Clipped to his chest is a plastic badge: *Terry Parker, Head Porter*. With watery brown eyes, the man observes her with the look of a fox eying up a potential prey.

'I'm sorry,' Viv says. 'There was no one to ask, so—'

'No one's allowed in without a pass, I'm afraid.' Her interlocuter's accent is South London, estuary. The man tracks his eyes greedily down the length of Viv's body and back up again, and she lowers her gaze, feeling suddenly exposed – violated, even.

'As I say, there was no one to ask—'

The rain has turned from a drizzle to a downpour, and she pulls her coat closer around her.

'I should chuck you out, love.'

'I'm an alumna,' Viv perseveres, ignoring the man's creepiness, trying a different tack. She knows enough of Oxford from her four years as an undergraduate to understand the way it works. 'I'm having tea with my old tutor.'

'You better come with me, then, love, hadn't you?' The porter gives her an insinuating smile, obviously enjoying the power he can wield over random female visitors, Viv thinks, wishing she could tell the awful Terry Parker where to stick it, then deciding such a course of action would be entirely counter-productive. Still!'

'I'll see what I can do,' the porter adds.

'It's with Professor Burns,' Viv says when the porter is back installed behind his computer and a safe distance away, she judges with relief. She peers through the sliding window. 'Professor Harris Burns, medicine.'

The porter looks up sharply, perusing her face with narrowed eyes that now register curiosity as well as desire. 'Professor Burns?'

'Yes, as I say, he invited me for tea—'

'Well, that's very strange, Miss,' says the porter, sitting back in his chair and folding his arms with a triumphant expression. 'Very strange. Because Professor Burns ain't no longer a fellow at this college, and sure as eggs are eggs, he won't be hosting any tea parties.'

'He won't?'

'It happened in the summer, he left under a cloud too, in point of fact.'

The porter pronounces the word 'clad', she notes distractedly, somehow destroying all the ethereal fluffiness of the celestial themed word.

'I don't understand?'

'He died, massive heart attack, so they say.'

Viv stares. Her breath is gone; she cannot speak, cannot move. Harris? Dead?

Then: 'What on earth do you mean?' She swallows. 'And what sort of cloud?'

'The investigation. Wouldn't surprise me if he popped it from stress.'

'What investigation?'

'Confidential, sorry.' The porter eyes her with a sly expression. 'Funny you've got a tea party with a dead don, isn't it? Very odd, that—'

Viv clears her throat, gathers herself.

'I was trying,' she manages, 'to find out about the professor for a piece of research I'm doing.'

The porter holds her look with a steely leer, in his eyes a veiled innuendo. 'Well, that's just too bad, love, ain't it, because I don't give up information just like that, not for free.'

Viv turns away, murmuring a thanks, though in truth she is repelled by the porter's veiled suggestion. She ought to pursue the matter, but she does not know how, does not care to come up with a strategy right now. For heaven's sake, how silly of her to expect to turn up here and find what she is looking for. How bloody ridiculous!

Her stomach is rumbling. It's been a long morning, and she is shivery cold and depleted. Shock, of that, she is sure – just like the other day. She needs food, and time to process the news, to formulate a new plan.

Outside the college, Viv leans against the wall, hands on knees, inhaling and exhaling to stop herself crying.

'Oh,' she moans under her breath, 'what the hell, what the hell.'

'Are you all right, madam,' says a passer-by, pausing with a concerned look. 'Can I get you some help?'

'I'm fine,' Viv stands up straight and slashes an arm across her eyes. She gives a forced smile. 'Absolutely fine, thank you. No need for concern.'

It is two o'clock. On the corner next to the walls of Jesus College, a cluster of South American musicians – from Peru?

149

Bolivia? – have set up a stall and are busking with loud multi-tubular flutes. The jangling tune shatters the afternoon peace. In a daze, Viv does a turn of the town centre, where numerous posters advertise the Christmas pre-sales. Numb, she purchases a ready meal and a packet of luxury chocolate biscuits in the crowded food hall of Marks and Spencer's, heads back to the park and ride.

For the length of the drive along the dual carriageway out of town, Viv finds it difficult to concentrate. Her mind is full of what she has and has not learned. She indicates, waiting for the traffic to pass, pulling onto the M4 back down towards the coast. Cars slow and overtake, craning to look at the slowcoach in the middle lane refusing to speed up. Someone raises a finger at her.

Oblivious, Viv grips the steering wheel and breathes a sigh of relief when she reaches the slip road for Weymouth. She just about manages to keep it together for the rest of the drive home.

By the time Viv arrives back at Moon Manor it is approaching six o'clock. She fixes supper, picks at the *coquilles St Jacques* from the responsibly sourced collection at M&S, which she finds mysteriously tastier than the so-called fresh scallops they serve up in the Lugger Arms, the pub John was so fond of in the village.

At some point, she pours herself a small glass of Sauvignon Blanc, then a larger one, and retires to the lounge, where she lights a fire with the last of the kindling, and opens her laptop. She urgently needs to do some more work on the memoir, because Part Two needs editing. Blast, she thinks then, realising that Lily

Tunkara has arranged to call. For God's sake, it's the last thing she needs, just when she needs to concentrate!

On television, the news headlines come on: images of Westminster, of grey-suited politicians defending some new policy. The newsreader reappears, introducing a segment about a new anti-malarial drug for children. Viv turns up the volume, all attention. Trials suggests malaria could be cut by seventy per cent in young children, reads the headline ticker. The preventative drugs show 'striking' results, details the reporter, marking a breakthrough in tackling the deadly mosquito-borne disease.

Viv sips her wine, watching the rest of the report with interest. When it is finished she turns to her computer, distracted; the edits are going nowhere. On the Oxford Mail website, Viv again searches for Dr Harris Burns. First, the news article from six months previous that she'd found the other day. She shudders, ignoring it and clicking on another link, to a short obituary she hadn't noticed before: *Dr Harris Burns, Emeritus Professor of Medicine at the University of Oxford, passed away unexpectedly on 28th August, aged 58, from a heart attack.*

Viv turns the TV off, puts the laptop aside and sits staring into the dancing flames. From a side table, she picks up an art pencil and A4 pad and begins to doodle, sketching an eye over and over with the soft graphite: first the almond oval shape, then the pupil with its square light-glare. With small flicks of the pencil, Viv shades in the iris, the brow and eye creases, the skin shades and nose line. Then the thick, curved fringe of eyelashes top and bottom. Gradually she finds herself pencilling the image darker and darker, until the shadows obliterate the eye itself.

August 28, three weeks exactly before John committed suicide in September.

Viv drops the pad, clicks the pencil against her teeth and stares into space. Her eyes fill with tears. If she'd felt disinclined to talk before, now she feels a pressing desire to tell someone, *anyone*. Who knows, Viv thinks, maybe Lily Tunkara can be her ally, if not quite her friend.

CHAPTER FOURTEEN

Lily

Sometime after six o'clock, Lily prepares for Ida's work do, having already dropped off the girls at their grandmother's for the night. Lily puts on a grand boubou with puff sleeves and a towering headscarf, adds lipstick of flaming carmine, then mascara and a touch of powder. Finally, a pair of gold leather sandals with low heels. If in the mirror she looks regal, she also looks older, Lily thinks critically. Grandeur is not a look she enjoys.

When she appears on screen, Lily is aware of Vivienne Hughes's curiosity, and for a moment she feels self-conscious, but the other woman is obviously too polite to enquire why she is so dressed up. For a few minutes, the two of them chat politely, an undercurrent of tension running between them, until the conversation dwindles into nothing.

Lily finds herself asking about Vivienne's written account.

'I read your memoir extract,' Lily says, 'and I wondered why you're telling me all this? Is it relevant?'

Lily is not sure why she is compelled to act as if she were in court with this near-stranger, but she finds herself switching automatically into lawyer-speak.

'To clarify,' she adds, 'I only want to know about the night my brother died.'

Vivienne seems unruffled. 'Well.' She pauses, thinking. 'What I wrote is background, right?'

'Sure,' says Lily, 'though I just need the facts, to be honest. Reading takes time, you know.'

'I was so idealistic—' Vivienne trails off. 'I suppose,' she adds after a second or two, 'I suppose I want you to understand what I was like back then.'

'Fair enough.'

They are both quiet for a few seconds. Lily reaches round and rubs her shoulder, massaging a tight knot in the dip between her shoulder blade and neck.

'My husband's getting a second wife,' Lily blurts out without thinking. 'A younger woman.'

Vivienne blinks. 'He is?' She pauses, frowning. 'I'm sorry, I don't know you enough to ask, but bloody hell, are you all right?'

'Yes.' Lily sips at the glass of water, feeling reckless, suddenly. 'Thank you.'

'What are you going to do?'

'Divorce him, of course. I refuse to be a co-wife.'

'Good for you,' Vivienne smiles.

'The truth is,' Lily says, 'he's a lot older than me, and well, it wasn't ever a love match.'

'An arranged marriage?'

'Not entirely, he was a family friend. My uncle approved, persuaded my mother, you know how it goes—' She trails off.

'Yes, I do.' Vivienne shoots her a sad look. 'Funny how people always want to fiddle about with others' lives.' She shakes her head. 'Anyway, perhaps it's for the best, then. I mean, it'll hurt like hell, but you'll get through it. We women always do, don't we. And your daughters will think you're Wonder Woman—'

'Well, let's hope so, *inshallah*.'

Tentatively, they both laugh. Lily is surprised to find that across thousands of miles something has passed between them: a feeling, a spark. A sudden imperceptible connection bringing a premonition of friendship. Yet such a thing is impossible, of that Lily is certain.

'I had some bad news today, too,' says Vivienne. 'An old friend – well, yes, I suppose he was a friend – anyway, he died. A man called Harris Burns, he came once to Senegal.'

'I'm sorry.'

'It was a shock.'

'I'm sure.' Lily meets Vivienne's eyes on the screen. 'Did Harris have anything to do with what happened?'

'Of course not.' A pause, in which Vivienne's gaze slides away to somewhere beyond the screen. She seems to hesitate. 'Look, I'm too tired to talk; it's been an emotional day. I'm no good for anything. Can we do this another time?'

'Okay,' Lily says, '*inshallah*.'

'*Inshallah*.'

The sense of connection is short-lived. Lily rings off with an awkward goodbye. We are getting nowhere, she thinks. And what is Vivienne Hughes hiding?

The gathering is being held at Ida's luxurious coastal home on the western-most side of the corniche. The garden stretches down to a vast sweep of ocean that seems to blend with the sky, pinkish tonight as the sun drops, burnished with streaks of gold. There are tables set out, and a bar laid with snacks for Muslim guests to break their fast, manned by a waiter in a vivid wax-print shirt. On the terrace a local *mbalax* band is playing staccato beats, the talking drum mixed with the bass guitar and a kora. Lily can smell the salt air and hear the waves, the sound of them crashing onto the beach mingling with the music.

All of a sudden the sun is gone. The night is hot and soft. Crickets scratch noisily in the foliage. In the warm darkness the palm trunks twinkle, wound with fairy lights. Lily stands alone on the pristine lawn watching the crowd of guests dressed in their finery, Ida in the middle surrounded by the great and the good: intellectuals, businesspeople, Dakar's close-knit diplomatic crowd. Lily recognises the current British High Commissioner, Frank Johnson, and his wife, Elise, along with the Senegalese Foreign Minister, Alioune Sarr. From the centre of the group Ida's ebullience emerges in the flamboyant gestures of her arms, her booming, infectious laugh.

Lily holds a stemmed glass of icy *bissap*, scarlet-hued, sugar sweet. After a quarter of an hour or so, Lion comes up. Lily gets the sense that he has been waiting for her to arrive. Lion wears a traditional boubou of interwoven geometric flowers in shades of blue and turquoise and gold, with leather slippers. The garment fits Lion well, Lily notices, giving him a distinguished look, and the primary colours suit his skin. A look, too, of an older man. He smells faintly of vanilla. He sips the same drink of flowers from a tumbler.

'Well, everyone's here tonight.'

'Indeed.'

'To be honest, parties aren't really my thing,' Lion says. 'All the small talk.'

'Me too.'

They watch the crowd together, then: 'I did some digging for you. And I found something.'

'Oh?' Lily's stomach lurches. 'You did?'

'Yeah.' Lion has a puzzled expression. 'Are you sure you want to know?' When Lily confirms with a nod, he takes out his phone, types in a text. 'I've got you a name, and the address.'

'No wonder Ida likes you.' In her bag, Lily feels her phone vibrate. 'Thanks, Lion.'

'So when are we going for this coffee and cake?' Lion smiles and Lily picks up a tinge of shyness. He is definitely sweet on her, she thinks.

'Lion, you know I'm married. My husband is—' Lily sighs, catching her words. She does not want to badmouth Demba to a stranger. So far, she has not told anybody about the affair, about the impending divorce. 'He's having an affair.'

Lion sighs, and frowns. A look passes between them, a deeper look than simply flirting. 'You love him?'

Lily sighs. 'He was older when I married him, it was—' she stops to think, 'more like father and daughter than husband and wife. At first I thought he was a good person, a good father, the sort of man who would always look after me and my daughters.'

'And then?'

'And then he proved himself to be just like all the others.'

'And what is that?'

'A cheater. A liar.'

'You have an extremely cynical view of men.'

'It's only the truth,' Lily says.

'Two things,' Lion holds her eye, 'not all men are like that, Lily. And, well, your husband's a very lucky man.'

He knows, Lily thinks. Lion knows Demba – the man whose mistress he has just investigated – is my husband.

'I only hope he realises it,' Lion adds.

Lily drifts about the party, making polite conversation with clients and work colleagues. Later, she finds Lion at a table.

'Sit with me,' he says.

For an hour or so, Lily finds herself talking to Lion, the conversation flowing as before, in and out of life and work and politics. Lion tells her of his home, his perspective of growing up in Ngor village, and they laugh at numerous mutual memories. Lily tells him about her daughters. At one point, Lily insists she must go, but Lion persuades her to stay. One more drink, he says, and Lily remains despite herself, talking on.

At the car, Lion goes to kiss her.

'Please, I can't.' Lily pushes him away, resting her hand on his chest. 'I'm married. Not happily – but married nevertheless.'

Lion sighs. 'Even when we were kids, I liked you, Lily, Lily Tunkara.'

There is something sexy about the way Lion says her name, something that stirs her. He takes her hand, and for a second Lily holds on. Lion's palm against hers is dry and solid-feeling. Then she lets go.

'I know.' Lily gets in the car. 'And I'm sorry.'

When Lily gets home the house is empty without the girls. She boils the kettle and makes a cup of mint tea to distract herself from the gap left by their absence, then sits at the kitchen table sipping the drink and observing the window, which shows no trace now of the other day's breakage. On her phone she stares at Lion's text with the name and address of the other woman, and sighs, remembering Lion's smile, bright as the sun. Strange how comfortable she feels whenever they talk, as if somewhere deep inside her she lets go, settling down like a person curling sideways into a comfortable armchair. It is a long time since she has talked to a man in such a way, as a friend and an equal, but there is something about Lion that encourages her to open up, that makes her feel she could say anything, and that anything would be okay.

Unlike Demba and his constant criticisms, Lily thinks bitterly, his constant jabs about her looks, her weight, her job. Lily's mind returns to the unpleasant matter of Lion's text message. She doesn't dare open it, not yet. She turns the phone's screen face-down on the table.

Outside, there is a clattering sound and Lily jumps. With the sudden thudding of her heart comes a flutter of panic in her chest and throat, and she stands up shakily, checking the window, unlocking the door and peering outside, but it is just some night creature, she realises, a stray dog or a rat ruffling through the compound bins. Lily shakes her head and takes a deep breath, returning to her laptop. Springing the machine to life, she brings up the latest memoir instalment from Vivienne Hughes:

Memoir, Part Two

By the time I emerge from the tube at Sloane Square, it's fully dark and the usual festivities of a weekend evening in Chelsea are in full swing. Outside the station entrance I stand watching the crowds spill out from The Boar's Head across the road. Music drifts from the pub's interior, mingling with the roar of laughter and beer-fuelled conversation from punters clustered in the drizzle, seemingly unaware, or uncaring, I suppose, of the weather.

Biting my lip and shivering slightly, I scan up and down the street, wondering how I'm to find John, let alone recognise him. As always in these moments, I feel stricken with self-consciousness, there in my glad-rags and heels, the drinkers scrutinising me with laughter in their eyes, sussing out somehow that I'm meeting a man for money. Lord! Shame washes over me. I hug my coat and lower my head, pulling my woollen hat further down over my forehead, hoping no one will notice me.

A second later, a figure across the pavement catches my eye. The stranger's smiling and waving in a friendly way. On a single, cursory glance my client is tallish, well over six foot, with mousy hair and glasses, holding an umbrella in one hand. I watch him check the traffic and step off the pavement, waving his umbrella aloft like some sort of annoying traffic warden through the slow line of cars and taxis. I note squarish shoulders, an expensive-looking overcoat, leather shoes. Not handsome, I think, not by any stretch of the imagination. But at the very least he isn't short, or too old, or deformed, or creepy-looking. As far as I can see John is relatively normal, well-dressed and civilised.

Beggars can't be choosers, I decide.

'You must be Vivienne,' he says breathlessly, coming up. Before I can answer, he lifts my gloved hand and gallantly plants a kiss on it.

160

'And you,' I incline my head, unable to restrain a smile, 'must be John.'

'Indeed. Well, this *is* a rum business, isn't it.' With a low laugh, John drops my hand and looks back at me jovially. He has straight teeth, thank God, and quite a jolly smile that lights tired eyes of a non-descript shade of sage. 'Shall we get a drink and try to forget the fact we're complete strangers?'

'Sure. Where are you taking me?'

'Oh, I have just the place. Would you do me the honour of taking my arm?'

I take it – he's the client after all; he can have whatever he wants, right? – and we walk up the King's Road arm in arm. For a moment, I turn, glad of the distraction, to look at a mannequin in the window of a fashion shop, and there in the lit-up glass our tall and short figures reflect back at me. The idea strikes me that this strange man and I appear just like a married couple: close, domesticated, even in love. People are probably looking at us thinking the same. I stare at the image in the glass for a second, transfixed by the absurdity of the situation.

'All okay?' John says, squeezing my hand. If he notices my infinitesimal hesitation, he does not comment on it.

'Oh, sure,' I reply with a smile, still shivering, turning away from the window. 'I'm dying for a drink though, in this cold.'

'Come on, we can't have you freezing, can we?'

It turns out John wants to take me to Buzzy's, a choice he obviously thinks is highly original, because he informs me in a pleased tone that the restaurant is Ringo Starr's favourite place to eat. I don't have the heart to break it to him that I've been there many times before with different men, both lovers and clients, and it doesn't seem to matter.

While we wait for a table, John makes his way to the bar to fetch us drinks. I take off my coat and sit observing him with an appraising eye as he waits at the bar. In a plain white cotton shirt and slacks, John's back is broad, his legs long. He isn't stylish, exactly, but smart – well turned out, you might have said. In that moment, I judge him to be one of those solid men with good morals and a general sense of sensible practicality. On the back of this thought, I wonder to myself why such a man would possibly feel the need to engage the services of an escort agency. He doesn't seem the type who'd enjoy a rendezvous with a stranger, let alone random sex, or a one-night stand.

It may be, I reason, that he's shy or just socially inept? All the same, if he *is* a diplomat, this hardly makes sense, for isn't it a diplomat's job to be sociable?

Then I catch myself. From what I've learned of human beings by that time – especially men – they are contradictory creatures and rarely what they seem. I tell myself not to trust this new client too easily or make assumptions, good or bad, about his character.

When John returns with a pint of Guinness and a double G&T for me, we chit-chat easily against the hubbub of bar noise. John tells me he works for the Foreign Office, that the previous October he returned from a two-year posting in Morocco, where he was sent because he spoke fluent French. I don't reveal that I, too, speak French, that I grew up speaking it with my mother, that my bilingualism is the reason I occasionally get booked as a model by the Parisian fashion houses. Once in a blue moon, that is, I think, my mind drifting. If only they booked me more, I wouldn't have to bloody well do *this*.

When I re-focus on John, he's in the middle of confiding that he misses being abroad. He struggles with the cold, he tells me, and the loneliness.

'Loneliness?' I reply. 'As a matter of fact, you're not alone. Most men I meet are lonely. It's the name of the game, I suppose.'

'There've been a lot? Of men, I mean?'

'Yes.' I stare at him, for this is familiar territory, and I'm going to have to steer him away from the subject of my questionable career. Yet for some reason I find myself opening up. 'I don't like it, *this*, I mean. But I'm not supposed to tell you that.'

'Why?' John bends his head to sip his drink. 'I mean, why aren't you supposed to tell me?'

'Isn't it obvious?' I pause, unsure why I find myself driven to reveal such confidentialities. Then I carry on: 'You men aren't after emotions, are you...? It sort of spoils the attraction, right?'

John laughs. 'Depends on the man.' He sips again, then puts the pint back on the table as if he's banging a gavel. 'I think you're pretty damn sexy, emotions or otherwise.'

And so we talk, through a dinner of steak and chips at a table with a checked tablecloth and a candle in a straw-covered bottle. Through after-dinner drinks at Angelique & Francoise down the road, where we stand crammed in trying to make conversation. Then we bop in the disco for a while.

To tell you the truth, I'm quite drunk by the time we leave the club. It's pouring and I cling to John's arm, leaning in when he opens his umbrella and braces the sail against the driving rain. With his other hand he deftly lights my cigarette, then his own. We smoke and splash through the puddles, and as we walk, John talks about his hobby of collecting maps. He particularly likes rare antique maps, he reveals, and sea and star charts. One day, he wants to own a house where he will frame them and hang them on the walls, is keen to go in search of more maps on his travels. Finally we reach the tube station, where John hails a taxi and offers to escort me home.

'Your feet are wet. You'll get a chill.'

'Don't fuss,' I tell him, laughing, flirting a little by this time. 'It's not far.'

'I know I'm not supposed to ask, but where do you live?'

The alcohol has loosened my tongue, because I find myself blurting out about the bedsit, about the damp and the mess.

'Sounds grim,' John replies, frowning. 'Will you be all right?'

'Of course,' I say, wondering if he means in that single moment, or just in general. I take a last drag of my cigarette and throw the stub on the ground, grinding it on the pavement with a heel. Then I shove my hands in my pockets. 'Don't worry about me.'

There's a long pause, during which a taxi pulls up beside us. John gives me that soft look that men so specialise in, *that* look meaning they want to kiss you. But in a rush, I turn away, reaching for the handle of the taxi door, and John seems to gather himself. With a note of anxiety in his voice that I recognise from other men, he says, 'I've had such a lovely evening.'

From the pocket of his overcoat he draws out his wallet, fumbling for a moment, then presses a business card into my hand. *John M Hughes*, I read: *Department of Foreign Affairs, Whitehall*. And a phone number.

'Look,' he continues, lowering his voice and giving me a sideways smile that contains a hint of shyness. 'I know this might not be the done thing, but I'm not after sex, Vivienne, or anything

164

sordid. I'd just like to take you out to dinner again, properly, if you know what I mean, without it being some sort of transaction. Would you like that?'

I cram the card into my coat pocket and stare at him, one foot already inside the taxi. My clients are always asking me out, trying to get me to meet them out of hours on this sort of basis. Opportunists they are, to a man, as if somehow persuading me out on a proper date is some sort of bloody conquest.

'Soho, please,' I call to the driver. 'Grain Street.'

'Righty'o, love,' says the driver from the front. 'Hop in.'

I scramble inside, glancing back up at John. 'All right,' I relent. 'I'd like that.'

'Phew.' He grins, stepping back. 'Jeanie is my secretary. Ask her to put you straight through.'

I nod and slam the door closed. As the driver rumbles us away into the darkness, I light another cigarette and peer out of the back window misted with condensation. John is standing very upright on the pavement, his pale face lit up by the cab's tail lights. His hand is raised as a last goodnight, on his face a regretful smile because, I suppose, he hadn't used up the last of his contracted minutes to kiss me there and then.

The cab rounds a corner and John disappears. I drag at my cigarette and sit back in my seat, fingering the card in my pocket with a sense of something new. It's anticipation, I decide, as well as exhilaration brought on by alcohol and a good flirt, mingling with a vague feeling of unease brought on by the fact that somehow I'd let this John Hughes person – John Hughes, *a client* – push through the robust wall I purposely build between my personal and professional life.

Technically, I reflect, rolling down the window and tapping ash into the dark, I should report a client for giving me his card. In the contract, it's very clear: *No propositioning the girls. Strictly no contact beyond the contracted hours.* Yet I wouldn't dream of such a thing. I don't know yet if I'll telephone John's office, but on the other hand, the man is kind, professional, and not unattractive. If anything, I can forgive him for daring to ask me out for real. Were I to choose a man to be with, it would surely be someone like John. Solid, upright, the sort of person who would look after a girl, even a girl like me.

In bed, Lily stops reading and puts the memoir aside. She lies down, pulling the covers over her head. Though she is tired, she cannot fall asleep, her thoughts buzzing from Ida's party and Lion, and now, Vivienne Hughes's story.

But after a time, Lily sleeps. That night, she dreams of Vivienne, then of Lion, their stories mixing up. She dreams of reaching out for John Hughes, who turns into Lion, and then she wakes, as the warm morning light rises through the shutters, with a palpable sense of loss.

Thursday, eleven o'clock. The British Embassy is over on the other side of the corniche in a smart city district that houses most of the foreign embassies. Lily parks in a road nearby and walks around the block. She flashes her identity card at the guard slouched in the small kiosk by the gates, requests to see Monsieur Adé Lô.

With languid hostility, the guard scrutinises the card, asks if

166

Lily has an appointment, and hands it back to her with a vaguely disapproving expression.

'I was hoping to catch him,' Lily replies. 'It's an urgent court matter.'

The guard kisses his teeth. *'Attendez-là, Madame.'*

For a time Lily waits. The leafy street outside the embassy is quiet, sleepy even. Under a tree, a trader sells omelettes from a makeshift tarpaulin stall. The air smells of frying oil and onions. Lily watches a few passers-by come and go, including a few embassy staff, black and white, who enter through the compound gates with their takeaway food. The wind coming off the coast rustles the tops of the trees against a searing blue sky.

Lily peers through the gates and spies the guard talking to a man, short, with a puffy face, dressed in a too big navy-blue suit unsuited to the weather.

The guard returns.

'Desolée, Madame, but Monsieur Lô is very busy. He says you'll have to make an appointment.'

'I can wait. I just need ten minutes. You might want to mention Ida Dramé; she's my colleague. In fact, maybe I should call her—'

That Ida's name will open doors, of this Lily is sure. She extracts her phone from her bag and the guard exclaims hastily, *'Non, attendez, si'l vous plaît,'* the first time he has shown any signs of life, Lily thinks. Again, the guard disappears and reappears seconds later with the same languid movements, opens the side gate.

'Desolée.' He shakes his head and Lily senses his satisfaction. 'Monsieur Lô is busy.'

Lily makes her way across the road, where she purchases

an omelette from the stall and seats herself under the shade of the tarpaulin with a number of other punters, ordering a sweet coffee made with condensed milk as an afterthought. She sits eating and watching the street. After the savoury, the coffee is sweet, like a dessert. She can see the embassy gates, the guard back at his post, cleaning his teeth with a stick. She glances at her watch. Five past twelve. Chances are this Adé Lô, whoever he is, will be out for lunch soon.

In time, Adé Lô appears. He is short for a Senegalese man, Lily notes, shorter than her at least, clean shaven with the slow scuffing shuffle of the perennially unfit. He wears a cotton shirt and ill-fitting, European-style, trousers. He carries a worn leather satchel.

Lily gets to her feet. Outside the embassy gates, Lô stands for a second to light a cigarette then sets off along the street, puffing on the end. After a while, he throws the fag on the pavement near the trunk of a tree. Lily tracks him through the leafy embassy district to a restaurant on the corniche, watches him seat himself and order from the waitress. A plate of *thieboudienne* arrives and he tucks in with gusto. A Catholic, then.

Only then does she approach.

'Monsieur Lô?' Lily says, holding out her hand.

Lô's eyes light then darken as his delight at being approached by an attractive woman gives way to hostility at the intrusion. He ignores her outstretched hand. Lily notices his pockmarked skin caused by too much oily food, she speculates, or the nicotine perhaps. Who knew what it did to your system?

'I hope you don't mind if I sit here.' Lily places her bag on the chair before he can protest. 'I need to talk to you.'

'I'm eating my lunch.' Lô regards her sullenly. 'I don't want to be disturbed.'

'Why did you get the case notes for the Tunkara case out of the archive?'

Lô frowns, rubs his nose. There is something stubborn, thinks Lily, about the way the man sits and the set of his mouth. He takes a mouthful of food and she finds herself vaguely repulsed at his chewing and the spicy smell of the rice and fish mixing with a whiff of cigarettes.

'Who told you that?'

'Your name's in the logbook.'

Lô looks at her, forking a mouthful of rice into his mouth. A few grains scatter on the table. He doesn't bother to clear them up.

'It's none,' he shovels more food into his mouth, 'of your business.'

'You know, Ida Dramé is mates with your boss. I wonder what the High Commissioner would say if he knew you were taking confidential files out of the archive. Or maybe he's in on it?' Lily shoots him a smile. 'Even more scandalous—'

Lô observes her with a flat expression, forehead glistening with sweat.

'So who,' says Lily, 'asked you to get the file, Monsieur Lô?'

He breathes in heavily, almost wheezing.

'No, you can say what you want, but I'm not spilling–'

'Hmm.' Lily extracts her phone from her handbag and taps the screen. 'I don't know many people in this town who'll mess with Ida,' she remarks mildly, fixing her gaze on the man's face. 'And Ida and the press, well...' she crosses her fingers and smiles, 'they're like this—'

Lô sighs with a hunted look, and stops eating.

'Please Monsieur, do the right thing.'

A fly buzzes across Lô's lunch plate and he flaps his hand at it, revealing a spreading semi-circle of sweat under his right armpit.

'Terribly sorry.' Lô's eyes shift about. He is sweating in earnest now, drops rolling down his forehead and onto his nose. He picks up the paper napkin and pats it against his skin with heavy breaths. 'I can't talk.'

Lô pushes the plate away, smacks his lips and wipes grease off fat fingers onto the paper napkin. With a screeching of his chair, he scrambles upright, reaching for his satchel.

'Madame,' he says loudly, causing some other diners to turn their heads, 'will you please stop harassing me!'

Lily sees Lô's eyes flickering from left to right, and she has the distinct impression he wants the rebuke publicly observed, though by whom, she isn't sure.

Lily is walking back to the car when she hears footsteps. She turns around to see Lô trotting towards her, puffing and panting. A couple of his shirt buttons have come undone, revealing an expanse of pudding-like belly. His forehead is sheened with sweat.

'It's a man called McFlannery,' Lô gasps, coming to a halt, bending to rest his hands on his knees like a sprinter after a race. 'Miles McFlannery. It's just that my colleagues go to that restaurant. I couldn't be seen giving you information.'

'I see.' Lily can feel the beginnings of a headache coming on. 'Why not?'

'You never know who's watching.' Still breathing heavily, Lô stands upright, sending wafts of onion breath in Lily's direction. 'One minute you're having your lunch, then...' he gives a strange little laugh and snaps his fingers melodramatically in the air, 'poof, you're gone.'

'And who is this Miles McFlannery?' asks Lily, ignoring the man's supposed attempt at humour. 'I mean, does he work here at the embassy?'

A shake of the head. 'Used to, years ago. He's high up in the UK now.' Lô extracts a tissue from his trouser pocket, wiping sweat from his forehead with tiny dabs. 'London, you know.'

'And how do you know him?'

'Look, I gamble, okay. McFlannery discovered some money I'd... reassigned. Anyway, a couple of weeks ago, he got in touch, told me he wouldn't tell my boss here if I procured this document for him. Said his name couldn't appear on the records, but he needed it, fast. That's all I know.

'I see.' In her head, Lily runs through the facts. Is it possible that Vivienne Hughes knows McFlannery, whoever he is, from their diplomatic days, that she has alerted him and now he is desperate to get his hands on this document? But if so, why? 'And this McFlannery,' she says after a second, 'he has the file now?'

'Not yet, but close.' Lô sniffs, balling the tissue in chubby fingers. 'I put it in yesterday's courier despatch to London.' He stuffs the tissue in a pocket with an air of finality, and clears his throat. 'Now, Madame, will you leave me alone.'

'One last question, please. Where can I find this Mr McFlannery?'

Pushing out his lips with the air of a condemned man, Lô

fishes around for a few seconds in his satchel. He brings out a pen and notepad and scribbles something, then tears out the piece of paper and hands it to Lily. It is a phone number, with the international code for the United Kingdom.

'Thank you,' says Lily, taking the piece of paper and stashing it in her handbag.

CHAPTER FIFTEEN

Vivienne

The beginning of the day. In goggles and a violet-hued swimming hat, Viv is swimming lengths in the sea pool. Her arms slice through the water as morning sunlight ricochets off the shimmering surface. At first Viv had found the water ice cold, so cold her breaths became fast, constricting her chest. Now, after fifty or so turns back and forth, her body has acclimatised and she is energised, renewed even, by the bracing water, like the limpets clinging to the edges of the pool.

The sea pool is hidden in a craggy hollow at the shoreline to the far west of Moon Manor's segment of land, a natural crater hewn out of the granite like a living tidal sculpture – on a par with something by Henry Moore, Viv often thinks, or Barbara Hepworth. Then perfected decades ago by the previous owners of the property. The smooth basin of the pool fills up on high tide, stays full until the sea water gradually seeps away, refreshing again with the tidal wash of the waves. This rhythm, with its pace and its surety as natural as the rising and setting of the sun, Viv finds soothing.

Today, the sea beyond the rocks is ruffled with white horses, contrasting with the still surface of the pool. At either end, Viv takes a racing turn, pushing off and flipping over so that her limbs streamline into a preliminary stretch of front crawl. She's lost count of how many lengths she's done already: fifty-five, sixty even. Now, as she strokes and breathes, Viv lets herself become one with the rhythm of her own body and the cold ocean. With every second stroke, she lifts her head to take in air.

With the pumping of her heart, Viv's mind unwinds, freewheeling in this underwater space. Her thoughts wander to Lily Tunkara, then to John. John. Her husband was never a fellow swimmer, thank God, and so after they moved to the manor, this pool had very quickly become her place to be alone, her sanctuary. Here Viv was able to escape whatever mood overtook her husband on any particular day. Here she had gathered her thoughts and her strength.

On the back of these memories, more come flooding: of the night of the accident, of Aimé Tunkara. Of rain and blood and petrol. Of Aimé dead beneath the wheel of the car, their car.

Viv lifts her head, gasping for air, treading water, pushing her goggles up onto her forehead and wiping her eyes with her fingers. She needs to work up the courage to write *it*. That day, that night. What had that tutor told her, during the one-day writing-a-memoir course she'd signed up for on a whim, years ago, when she first conceived the idea of putting things down on paper? *Write what you're most afraid of.* Now she feels an urgency in her chest like a bubble that needs bursting, a need to get everything down on paper before, what? Before it's too late?

And should she tell the truth, or a version of the truth? She breathes out and ducks underwater, popping up again. Is it her own weakness talking, or is she beginning to think that Aimé Tunkara's sister deserves more than lies? For a second, Viv feels overcome with unease; Lily reopening the case, Viv's own discoveries – or lack of them – in Oxford. It all feels strangely foreboding. Yet Lily – well, Lily Tunkara is a force to be reckoned with, and Viv respects that.

Viv pulls down her goggles again and breaststrokes to the edge of the pool, pushing off into butterfly, aware of her own power surging through her body as she lifts her arms, flips her legs as one like a mermaid's tail. Presently, she climbs the rope ladder up the side, breathing in gasps, and spreads out her towel, lying flat on the dark rocks to dry off, eyes closed.

It is not the season yet for the rocks to absorb the sun, and Viv can feel their hard surface stony-cold beneath the towel. Her skin is flushed pink with the cold. Under her swimming costume, her flat belly rises and falls, and she feels a pleasant satisfaction that her metabolism is fired up for the day after such early exertions. Funny how the more exercise you do, the more you want to do, like an addiction. That's why – she's heard – the outdoors is prescribed for depression nowadays. What a breakthrough. As far as she can remember, the brilliant medical minds of the eighties, when she was a med student, hadn't got there yet.

Viv can feel the warmth of the sun percolating through her body, flowing through her legs, her arms, her chest. She stills her breaths and sits up cross-legged. With her eyes closed, she breathes in and out to a count of ten, letting it come. *Namaste,* she murmurs under her breath, making a prayer motion with her hands.

After a time, Viv drinks mineral water from a litre bottle, wraps herself in a large towel and makes her way in flip-flops along the sea path to the house.

The Skype call comes after Viv has showered and dressed, hair still drying into wavy curls. She is sitting in the kitchen drinking a second coffee. To Viv's surprise, the caller is Lily Tunkara.

'I need you to visit someone,' the other woman announces without preamble. 'In England.'

'You do?' Viv raises an eyebrow. 'Who is it?'

'The name's Miles McFlannery. He worked at the British Embassy, apparently, in 19—'

'Miles?' Viv interrupts, frowning. 'I know Miles well. He was my husband's colleague in Dakar, his right-hand man, you could say.'

Viv listens to the lawyer recount what she has found out – that Miles has somehow got his hands on the Tunkara case file, that the file is being couriered to England as we speak. Viv is all attention. So, she is thinking, Lily Tunkara is using her as an ally – and M is hiding something after all. She should have known, should have suspected that all that puppyish charm the other day was nothing but a cover-up. She has long ceased to believe that people are what they first appear, and now... now M's about-face comes as no bloody surprise.

Viv informs Lily that she saw Miles a week ago, but there was nothing untoward, no hint that he was hiding anything. In fact, hadn't he even offered a clue about that weekly meeting of John's, the one he said he knew nothing about. Or was M lying about that, too?

'I can try and see him again,' Viv suggests in a placid voice, almost as if she doesn't care, 'though I don't know what good it will do. If M is really trying to cover things up from afar, he's hardly going to tell me about it.'

'The courier document is on its way,' says Lily without hesitation. 'If you arrange a meeting, you can ask him about it?'

Viv nods. 'Okay.'

'Ideally we need that document.'

'You want me to get a look at it?'

'Yes, please. Can I trust you?'

'Yes,' says Viv, surprising herself, 'of course you can.'

For the second time, Viv finds herself emailing M. *I need to talk to you again. Sorry.* The answer comes later in the day: '*What about, Viv? There's nothing to discuss… John's gone. Why don't you just enjoy your freedom? M*'

But Viv manages to pin him down to Thursday, two pm, his place, and he texts her an address. Luckily it's not far, she thinks, just down the coast on the border with Devon, somewhere called Mow in the Marsh. She is apprehensive this time; surely the meeting will not be as amicable.

Viv spends the day in the garden, mood lifted by the energising early swim. She weeds and digs the borders, turning over the earth with her fork and her fingers, enjoying the physicality of the movement, the soft feel of the dark soil in her hands. Always when she is physically exhausted, she sleeps well, deeply, without dreams or anxieties.

Viv wears gardening gloves, kneels on a cushiony pink

mat John had bought her once as a birthday present from the garden centre in Bridport. She mows the lawns, prunes the roses with secateurs to encourage new spring growth. As she works, she thinks about M, the fact he has requested the report on Aimé's death. What can he possibly want with it all these years later? What in heaven's name is the bloody man *doing*?

Viv's mobile phone rings.

'Hello, this is Vivienne Hughes.'

'Hello, Mrs Hughes,' says a young, male voice. 'My name's Patrick Brown. I got your number from the porter at Exeter College – he mentioned there was a visitor looking for Dr Harris Burns, and well—'

Patrick trails off, then when prompted informs Viv in a Scots burr that he is a PhD student in Medicine at Exeter College, Oxford, and Dr Burns was his tutor. There's something he needs to talk over, the boy says, about Dr Burns's death.

'I wondered if we could meet?' Against her better judgement, Viv finds herself agreeing to meet the boy in Oxford, the following day, grimacing as she does so at the prospect of another tedious drive.

When the conversation is over, Viv sits outside in the garden chair with a cup of tea. The noonday sun is unseasonably warm for the time of year, and the birds are loud, as if they too have got the month wrong. Only a few months now until the swallows will be back, and she longs in her bones for summer. She takes off her outdoor boots and stretches her feet, rotating her ankles, then falls into a doze with the sun making patterns on the backs of her eyelids.

Later, once the sun has gone in and the afternoon is grey and chilly, she makes her way to the studio. For an hour or so, Vivienne continues the painting she began the other day. She hums to herself. Apart from her humming – Nina Simone, for some reason – and the faint swish of the brush against the canvas, there is no other sound in the room. On the pale layer of background wash Viv deepens the landscape, adding light and shadows, filling in the details of the sky and land from memory.

Around her, the shadows deepen, too, until Viv makes for a straight-backed figure in silhouette before the square light of the window. Viv paints there until the room is in complete darkness.

Later, when it is finally night-time, Viv opens her laptop and logs in the travel website recommended by Alexa. Using her credit card, she books the flights and all-inclusive hotel she has had on hold since the weekend, then checks her email for the reservation confirmation documents.

Afterwards, Viv boils the kettle. Cup of tea in hand, she edits the next part of her memoir:

Memoir, Part three

As I recall, it doesn't take me long to decide to telephone John Hughes. Maybe a day or two at most, just the time it takes to weigh my godawful status quo against the advantages of linking up with a man like John. As I mull over his invitation, I reproach myself for being so hard-hearted. Am I really one of those terrible treasure-seeking girls I used to meet at Oxford, whose sole aim in life was to meet a man with money and become a kept woman? Lord, what have things come to!

And I don't want to give the impression that I'm as calculating as those girls, because, if anything, my motives are more impetuous than premeditated. People say that poverty grinds you down, and in my case this is true. The dreadful food, the dankness and dirt of that flat, the strange men with their hungry eyes who are my only source of income. All this naturally generates in me a wild instinct to escape. That's all. Still, I feel ashamed of myself that life hasn't gone my way, that I'm reduced to destitution when I should have a good degree in medicine and a future career as a doctor.

Yet I've no interest in diamonds, I reason, or fine clothes, or any of the usual assumed luxuries of a kept woman. I just need a place to stay and a reason to live. And though I'm aware that John isn't the sort of man I could ever fall head-over-heels for – he's far too straight for my taste, too grey, too *old* – I do like him.

Plainly, I need to be practical. Mum is dead. I have nothing and no one. If men use women, why shouldn't women use men, in turn? Call it what you will: desperation or survival. There's nothing for it but to find a way out, somehow.

John picks me up in a smart, tomato-red, two-seater MG whose engine rumbles like a jungle beast, and we bumble, top down, along Regent Street and on along the Strand. It's a spring evening and the clocks have gone back the night before. Something about the balmy light and late hour – its novelty perhaps – must be luring people outside, because as the evening fades, there are couples strolling on the riverbank hand-in-hand, a girl reading under a tree, and some sort of party happening on the deck of a ferry moored near the bridge. The disco beat of the Bee Gees drifts over the car as we pass, along with the gabbling voices of the partygoers, high and excitable.

'You're beautiful,' John says several times as we drive. When we pull up along the pavement beneath an apartment block, he squeezes my knee and kisses me on the mouth more forcefully than I expect from such a geeky man: 'You're the most beautiful girl I've ever seen.' He reaches over to the dashboard and draws out a brown leather wallet and a set of keys. 'Here we are; here we are.'

John's apartment is on the fifth floor, spacious and very neat, with impressive floor-to-ceiling windows overlooking the river. I sit down on the sofa while he goes into the kitchen, then wander over to watch the purplish sky settle with subdued streaks of sunset over the city skyline.

In the last of the light, the water of the Thames glints silvery black, the trees and the buildings turning to silhouettes. In the glass, my own reflection – a faceless shadow girl – is transposed on the background of the evening sky.

In the hall, the telephone rings and I listen to John answer it, wondering who might be calling him and what it must be like to live a life like his, where work calls invade even one's home life.

When John returns to the lounge, he brings red wine and two glasses, though no food to speak of. I find out later that he can't cook, won't cook, considering it to be a woman's job. He eats all his meals at the Foreign Office canteen.

By now it's dark. John pulls the curtains, which swish as he manoeuvres them in a smooth motion along their plastic tracks, and I say something about the view, something about how pretty it is, about how it must be good for the soul to live in such a place.

'The job pays for it – this flat, I mean.' John fills up my glass. 'Which means I can save a hell of a lot.' He smiles. 'Lots to spend on my beautiful girl.'

He leans in again as if he wants to kiss me, but at that moment, I notice his lips and teeth are already dark-stained with wine, and I feel a sudden rush of distaste. I turn away in a panic. I feel overwhelmed, if I'm honest, suffocated by the kissing and constant endearments. I know I'm not ready for such displays of… what? Affection, or something like possession?

As I do so, I accidentally catch John's arm with my hand, and his glass of wine goes flying onto the carpet.

'Oh, Lord, I'm so sorry!' I exclaim. 'Heavens, what a klutz I am!'

'Don't worry, don't worry,' he says. If he has noticed my reluctance to kiss him, he does not comment on it. Even so, from the kitchen he brings a cloth and a large tub of salt and spends the next ten minutes cleaning up the mess with a fastidiousness that surprises me, sprinkling salt onto the stain with little jerky movements of his fingers.

'I'll have to call you Little Miss Clumsy from now on,' he jokes. 'My Miss Clumsy.'

I watch the back of him as he kneels scrubbing at the mark which doesn't seem to budge, a slash of blood red on the pristine beige pile. I tell myself to keep my eye on the prize.

Afterwards, John pours himself more wine, then more, though after the second glass, I decline. John seems to drink a lot, I remark to myself. When I mention the incident with the wine, offering another apology, he shrugs, swigging at his drink.

'Look, Viv, in my eyes you can't do much wrong, okay. Other than shagging my boss.' He snorts with laughter. 'So don't worry about it.'

Some weeks later, John proposes. The spring weather has turned into a prolonged dry spell, and April dawns with an early heatwave. On the Saturday, John suggests a lunchtime picnic in Regent's Park, and thus I find myself sat next to him on a bench, my pasty winter legs stretched out to the balmy sun, sharing sandwiches – cheese and ham as I recall – and some cream cakes he's bought us from an expensive patisserie nearby.

Though I decline, John sips champagne – Moët & Chandon– from the bottle. Fleetingly, I'm struck by John's decadence, which I suppose I find surprising considering how straight he is, how square and *ugly*-looking. It sounds ridiculous, but I've never imagined that *those* sort of men – not the hunks, the good-lookers or the dreamboats, but the *others* – could be debauched, or sexual. How bloody wrong I am!

'Mm,' John remarks at one point, nibbling my ear. 'Beautiful woman, beautiful weather. What a lucky man I am.'

It's nearly one o'clock and the sun is scorching, the sky searing blue and cloudless. There are people lying on the grass in shorts, reading and sunbathing. Hungry, I wolf down the sandwiches, then a delicious-looking cake filled with jam and cream. The flowering cherry trees and horse chestnuts dotting the park are just starting to blossom, their little bursts of pink-and-white blooms lending the scene a festive feel.

'Viv,' John says, 'what do you think about getting married?'

It couldn't be more out of the blue. Mouth full of cake, I gulp and turn to look at him, but he's staring straight ahead, still eating.

'Marriage?' I say. 'You mean, marry you?'

'No, the Incredible Hulk.' He turns to look at me, seeming amused. 'I suppose you want me to go down on one knee?' He slides off the bench and kneels in front of me in a way I find slightly comic, taking my hand. 'So, here I am, your knight in shining armour. Viv, will you marry me?'

The proposal is surprisingly flippant, almost mocking, not the way I've ever imagined such a moment would go – which you'd have thought would be somewhat tender, if a little bit corny, leaving both parties rather starry-eyed. But then what do I know about such things…? I'm only twenty-three, and in the field of romance, you could say I'm startlingly ignorant.

Except there's a little voice in my head saying stop, for God's sake, but I don't listen to it. *Of course* I don't. My judgement is off, skewed by my general situation at the bedsit, by my sadness and shame and the hollowness in my stomach most days. There's no point stalling, I tell myself. An offer of marriage from such a man is like gold. And I sense – even if I don't know for sure – that John's not the sort of man to take no for an answer. That, quite frankly, if I refuse his offer now, there'll not be another.

'Um—' I stare at a hippy guy with long hair sitting cross-legged under one of the trees, plucking at a guitar. 'It's only been six weeks.'

'And?' John grins, and kisses me. 'It was love at first sight, Viv. You know that! You're my love, my soulmate. Don't tell me you're going to say no.'

'No, not no—'

'Then it's a yes!'

184

I sit staring ahead. After a few seconds I turn back to him.

'Yes,' I say in spite of myself, a split-second decision that is to change my life forever. 'All right.'

'You will?'

'Yes, of course.'

John kisses me with exuberance again and again, on my lips and cheeks, hugging me close, talking about the diamond ring he intends to buy for me. In my ear he whispers how much he loves sapphires, that he knows a solitaire set with a sapphire will suit me to perfection, and I feel a terrible claustrophobia, as if I'm being pinned down by the throat in a stranglehold. But I tell myself to get it together. John is kind and he is rich. I don't love him, but I'll be a good wife and a good mother, when the time comes. He will give me a good life. I just need to apply myself.

People call these things a whirlwind and they are not wrong. Over the next few weeks, as I pack up my stuff from the bedsit and say my goodbyes to Ruby and the other girls, I feel caught up not in the feeling, but in the *idea* of romance.

'Are you sure about this, babe?' says Ruby, looking surprised when I announce the engagement, but then shrugging with a little smile, resigned, I suppose, to the fact that girls like us must do what we have to do to survive. 'Well, as long as he looks after you,' she adds. 'You take care, babe.'

It's like a rush of madness to think about a ring, a wedding, a house together, all domestic visions so far from my own reality that they seem both breathtaking and also take my breath away.

A life together with John, of all things! The idea washes over me like a tidal wave. Suffocating. Drowning me. No, Ruby, I desperately want to say. No, I'm not sure at all…

Yet John is the ideal man for me, I tell myself once again, and as far as I'm concerned, love doesn't matter as much as survival. What is love, anyway, but a stupid, fanciful idea from the cinema, and not the real world at all?

For God's sake, Viv, I tell myself. *Pull yourself together.*

CHAPTER SIXTEEN

Lily

Lily, still off work, has a rare moment to herself, and because it is not school pick-up time just yet, after lunch she reads Vivienne Hughes's third diary instalment. In time, Lily puts the text aside, reflecting on the story of the marriage proposal from John, the husband and ambassador, his latent air of... what? Frivolity? Threat? Is Lily to understand that the driver was John then, all along, and Vivienne had simply taken the blame by saying she was driving, as per the witness statements? It is not beyond the realms of possibility. But there is something else nagging at Lily, too, the passing mentions – of the medical lab and the other man, the doctor, Harris Burns. Who is this Harris, and is there more to their relationship than Viv is letting on? Curious, thinks Lily, reading on:

The day of the wedding is a Tuesday, and it's raining. The preparations have been stressful, and ever since I've moved in, John has seemed strangely moody, picking at me, finding fault. The previous night, we have a row about something stupid – something about the way I wash up that John isn't happy with. Exhausted, I snap back at the criticism, and after going round and round in circles for a while, arguing, I sleep in the spare bedroom.

Once or twice, I wake up with a start – or am I dreaming? – and think I can hear John still up and boozing, the clink of bottles from the kitchen, the sound of singing and talking.

Today, by contrast, my husband-to-be is nice as pie, all smiles despite a visible hangover that greys his skin and tugs his eyes downwards. He holds an umbrella aloft with all the over-the-top gallantry of our first meeting. As we're about to get in the car, he lets down the umbrella and takes my hand. He twirls me around and kisses me on the lips, breath tinted with sleep and alcohol.

'You,' he says, 'look like an angel.'

For an hour or more, we wait in the lobby of the registry office in Haringey, where the temperature is sticky, and the damp air smells strongly of sweat – mine, possibly, or the men's. I pull at my dress of white cotton – by design, as simple as possible, because after all the pomp and ceremony over the ring, John's made clear he doesn't want a fuss.

I wear hardly any make-up, another thing that John doesn't like. 'You don't need it, pet,' he says if ever I apply blusher, or lipstick. In my hair is pinned a spray of lily of the valley, and a short, fashionable veil covers my face.

If I think it strange that John's declined to invite his family, or friends for that matter, I say nothing. A couple of colleagues from his office turn up as witnesses, persuaded to attend – presumably – with promises of a slap-up meal and lots of booze, all of which happens afterwards. While we wait, the three men laugh and banter, swapping work stories, ignoring my presence entirely. As for me, my head aches. I need a drink of water. Unable to stomach breakfast, I now feel hungry and miserable. When the registrar's assistant calls us into the marriage room, I experience a sudden and unexpected urge to cry.

'Ready, pet?' says John gently.

My heart melts. The recent criticisms and mood swings are surely just a consequence of stress, I tell myself, from John's demanding job, the pressures on a man that a woman like me can't possibly understand. I'm far too sensitive, I reproach myself, just as John says. For a brief moment I allow myself to hope that John, is, after all, a nice man, a good man, the right man. After all, I'm doing all this for a reason, aren't I?

'Ready,' I reply, following him inside.

The weeks pass. I'm about to turn twenty-four years old. I've left my escort job, obviously, but my supervisor, Harris, persuades me to continue my work at the lab on a voluntary basis, because the trials he's working towards are nearing reality – they'll take place somewhere in Africa, probably Senegal on the west coast.

The work occupies my days and gives me a welcome distraction from the fact that my new husband is increasingly bad-tempered, his long silences ever more frequent. Meanwhile, I give Harris a talking to.

'I can't sleep with you,' I tell him primly. 'I'm a married woman now.'

'As if that ever stopped anyone,' he laughs, and carries on flirting and trying to kiss me, until finally I give in to his persuasive charms because it seems easier. No harm, I think, in sleeping with Harris occasionally, bearing in mind I'm not in love with my husband – who, I am beginning to realise, is becoming meaner and meaner.

One day, Harris tells me that the drug trials are confirmed

for Senegal.

'Do you want to work on them, Viv?' he asks. 'It could make your career.'

Meanwhile, John completes the purchase of Moon Manor, and I'm excited about that, though another issue hangs over me – John's been offered a post in Toronto in two months' time. I busy myself with preparations for the two moves, first to Moon Manor, then on to Canada, but my heart's not in it. Over dinner one night, I mention to John that I'd rather we go somewhere in Africa, and I find myself suggesting Senegal. He looks surprised, and says he'll look into it. I leave it at that, and cross my fingers. A fortnight later, he comes home with good news.

'There's a three-year posting in Dakar,' he says with a rare smile. 'Do you want me to take it?'

'Yes,' I reply. When I tell Harris, he's ecstatic.

The first serious sign of trouble comes the day after my birthday, a Friday night, when we're still at the London flat, though most of our stuff is already in boxes by then. We eat at a restaurant where John seems to want to drink a lot, first wine, then whisky shots, one after another. Back at the flat, he drinks more: beer, gin, whatever he can find. It's the first time I've ever seen him snort cocaine.

I dress for bed in knickers and a pretty silk dressing gown John's bought me for my birthday. I sit watching as he uses his own business card to cut the white powder, then snort it off the wood surface. Within minutes, he's high and euphoric, talking too quickly about all sorts of nonsense, declaring that I'm sexy as hell, his angel, his perfect woman. Sweat beads his forehead. Without preamble, he pins me on the sofa and grabs my ankles with one hand, lifting my legs up in the air in a way that reminds me of a butcher manhandling a carcass. Taken aback, I pretend to like what he's doing. Grateful for the attention, perhaps. Without asking he pushes his fist into me, too hard, too fast, so that I cry out in pain.

'Does that hurt you?'

But eyes on mine, he doesn't stop.

I suppose the weirdest thing of all is that when I glance down his body, he isn't hard at all. In fact, he's slack, completely slack.

'Right,' he announces, 'that's your lot.'

As if I have initiated the whole thing.

That night, it dawns on me that John is far from the sweet, boring, kind-hearted man I met on that first date on Kings Road. Not so straight, not so stable. For a start, there's the drink – plus the drugs and the mood swings, which seem ever more extreme. And the sex, of course, or lack of it – cold, when it happens, sometimes bordering on violent. It happens less and less. Though John ogles me often, waxing lyrical about my sexiness and desirability, he never kisses me properly. All talk, no action, I begin to think.

Nevertheless, I don't care to pursue the thought or face my secret fear that my wonderful new fiancé might not in fact be so wonderful. Call me naïve, but I don't *want* to consider whether there might be skeletons in John Hughes's cupboard, or entertain the idea that, in accordance with the age-old rules of the universe, if it's bad now, it can only get worse.

Because I need him, you see.

'Did you switch on that light?'

It must be past midnight on the same evening. John is coming down from his high. I'm on the sofa, my vagina still sore and smarting from earlier, legs curled beneath my dressing gown. I'm drinking a nightcap of warm milk and reading a novel.

John doesn't like me going to bed before him, so I'm getting used to staying up, reading a little blearily by lamplight while I wait for him to come to bed, always past midnight, sometimes even one or two in the morning before he decides to turn in.

'Sure.' I glance up from my book. 'I thought it would be cosier.'

With a frown, John goes over and examines the standard lamp on the sideboard. In a belligerent sort of way, he runs his forefinger over the stalk and base, then examines it with over-dramatic movements for dust, as if he intends to make a point – though I'm unsure what this point might be. Then he switches the lamp off. Without a word, he leaves the room.

In his wake, I experience a strange chill run through me. Of confusion, of dismay. Without the lamp, it's too dark to read. Why would he do that?

But later, when I slide into bed beside him, we speak no more of it. I put my arms around him and snuggle against his chest, kissing his shoulder, wanting the reassurance of physical touch.

'Darling,' I continue to kiss him, 'give me another cuddle.'

But John pushes me off. 'Please,' he says, turning away so that his back is a barrier between us. 'You get turned on at the most peculiar times.'

'Oh,' I say, taken aback, 'do I?'

I lie staring up into the dark, crushed to the core.

For half an hour Lily follows a fitness video in the garden, press-ups, star jumps, a round of burpees. Afterwards, she pours herself a *bissap* drink from the fridge and stretches on her back in a *shavasana* pose to recover. It is a fresh, breezy day. Across the lawn, the date palm makes cool, sharp shadows like sketches on the earth. But the hot season is only going to get hotter. Lily can feel it coming, the deep searing heat that cracks the earth and makes the very city sweat.

Lily lies on her back staring up into the crackling palm fronds, feeling the lawn's needle-like spikes pressing in her back. How rare it is to spend time alone these days, without work or *this*, or her children interrupting. Yet there is nothing she loves more than being with the girls, is always glad of their interruption. The paradox of parenting, they call it. But when did she come to lose herself?

Years ago, Lily could not have imagined being suspended from the law firm. She would not have coped with the idea. Her work and studies are too important. They have always driven her so hard; they have always come first. Now nothing seems as important as finding justice for her dead brother. In spite of herself, she welcomes the break, too, and the chance to take a breath, for once.

Lily sits up, watching a black and white butterfly with a Dada-esque eye-pattern land on a bougainvillea. On the pinkish flower, the creature seems to glow in the sun, faintly trembling. It takes off again, lands, takes off as Lily follows its movements with her eyes, still mulling the events of the day. Of all things, she has never taken for granted the trajectory of her own past. The fact she is educated, the fact she is a *lucky one*. For the compensation payments from the British government which meant she could go to school, then on to *lycée* and university, she has always felt indebted. As a child, then a teenager, Lily was acutely aware of her own unusual privilege when all the other village kids, bar a few, Lion being one of them, were made to leave school – the girls to get married or help in the family home, the boys to find jobs. Fishing, trading, whatever they could drum up to bring in a *sou* and contribute to the family income. Still, Lily does not care to call her situation lucky. To her mind, her big brother died and so she got educated. Such an unhappy twist of fate will forever leave her torn between gratitude and agonising guilt.

Lily sighs, wondering if she is somehow losing her mind over the whole thing. After all, that's what Demba often says. *You're crazy. You're over-sensitive.* A fleeting wish comes to Lily out of nowhere. If Lion were here, he would listen… Hastily, Lily dismisses it. Why on earth *would* Lion be here?

The butterfly takes off again, dancing around the flowering plant, landing on another higher blossom where it quivers and goes still. Lion. Lily inhales, another thought fluttering somewhere in the hinterlands of her brain. But the thought wings away, escaping her for now. She stretches her left leg to the sky and pulls her thigh with her hands, lengthening the muscle, then swaps to the right leg.

Sitting up, Lily bends forward, grasping her ankles and exhaling, feeling her back and calves resist then grow soft with the stretch, somewhere between painful and necessary.

Lily lies down again, closing her eyes, and dozes for a little while, ten minutes, or perhaps longer.

At the school gates, Piretta asks if she can go home with her friend, Aïda, a long-legged girl of the same age with hair scraped into two fluffy pom-poms. The mother is not a stranger; she and Lily have greeted each other with smiles whenever their paths cross. Lily has an inkling the woman is a school governor, or something to do with the board.

The woman – *Ramatoulaye; please, call me Rama* – is very well-dressed; has a distinguished accent in both Wolof and French; is, she informs Lily, Rama Sow, Deputy Head of Disaster Response at the UN headquarters in central Dakar. The family lives in the same section of the corniche as Ida Drameh, Rama tells Lily, and would love to invite Piretta to do her homework together with Aïda.

For a quarter of an hour or so, Lily stands on the pavement chatting with Rama about this and that while the girls huddle with secretive expressions, sharing intimacies. Lily finds herself half-tempted to confide to Rama about the divorce, but stops herself, not wanting to complicate matters by offering the branch of friendship. Instead, she jots down the woman's number and address into her phone, arranges for Rama to drop off Piretta back home at eight o'clock.

'See you later, *chérie*,' Lily says, patting her older daughter's arm, feeling a tug in her chest as she watches her eldest offspring bundle with her friend into Rama's large black Mercedes. Piretta is nearly thirteen, Lily tells herself, almost a teenager. Pssht, how alarming it seems when they're helpless babies, and yet that fear is nothing to this. This *independence*. Now, she must force herself to acclimatise to Piretta's budding autonomy.

Lily and Mia stand waving. Mia's baby tooth is on its way out. At right angles from her mouth, it sticks out above her lower lip.

'You look exceedingly piratical,' says Lily with a smile, taking the little girl's hand, walking with her in the other direction.

'What's piratical?'

'Like that teeny tiny little pirate in your reading book.'

'How do you spell it?'

Laughing, Lily sounds out the phonics: Py-rat-i-cul.

Mia swings her bag around her waist, wobbling the tooth.

'I'm a pirate, I'm a pirate!' Giggling, the child grimaces upwards, tooth bared. 'Arr! Arr!'

CHAPTER SEVENTEEN

Vivienne

Two days later, Viv sits in the garden of Miles's cottage in a village near Lyme Regis. Miles has gone inside to make the tea. Next to the open French windows, garden chairs are arranged so as to use the glass as a windbreak. A shop-bought Victoria sponge cake is set on the outdoor table, as yet without its parasol. M is making an effort, thinks Viv, as if this were any old afternoon tea between two old friends.

It is a fresh, sunny day with more unseasonable mid-winter warmth; clouds scud along in the pale sky and a sea breeze shakes the leafless top of a chestnut. On the still bare branches of a fruit tree – apple or plum? – Viv can see tiny white buds forming, too early. A winter-flowering *Acacia dealbata* at the end of the garden sways in the wind, its yellow bunches of pom-poms contrasting with the blue of the sky, bright flowers wild with motion, as if waved aloft by some invisible troupe of cheerleaders. Mesmerised, Viv pulls her coat closer around her, enjoying the sharp salt air bracing on her skin, the colours, the sunlight.

'Twice in a month, we *are* doing well.'

With a clatter, M sets the tray of tea things on the table: two floral-patterned teacups of bone china, matching plates, a milk jug, a bowl of sugar lumps and two silver teaspoons. Old embassy habits die hard, thinks Viv, watching her companion stir the pot with familiarity and precision, then seat himself on the other garden chair with a small groan, throwing his right leg over his left knee to reveal red socks with a single navy stripe running through them.

'And isn't it glorious weather,' Viv says, as something to say, 'for this time of year?'

'Climate change,' agrees her host, 'who'd knock it?'

In the sunlight, M's hair is noticeably greying at the sides, a small area of brown still visible towards the crown. He wears a grey woollen jumper and slacks, muddy at the knees as if he has been gardening. Viv notices again how old he looks. Old and grey. Soon, she will be like that too.

For a few moments, the two of them continue to make small talk: the weather, the fact that Sonia, M's girlfriend – Lord, that word again – is away on a "girls' do". Cringing, Viv asks about M's children, two grown-up sons, one a banker, one a fund manager. The elder boy is getting married, is obsessed with chair décor and wedding favours: 'Like a woman!' confides M with a grimace. 'And I'm bloody well paying for it. Anyway,' M leans over, pouring the tea. 'I suppose I'm wondering why you wanted to talk again so soon? I assume it's not just because of my riveting conversation. Sugar?'

Viv shakes her head. 'No, thanks.'

'Thing is, Viv,' Miles continues, plopping two lumps into his cup and stirring, then meeting her gaze with a frank look, 'I'm not entirely sure what more I can say on the matter. That appointment I mentioned, of John's – I'm pretty sure it was one of his fancy boys.'

'That make sense.' Viv pauses, allowing herself to dwell for a second on the memory of her late husband's infidelities. 'Disturbing sense,' she adds, 'but sense nevertheless.'

'Well, then,' Miles shrugs, a question in his face, 'is there anything more to say?'

'Have you received a courier delivery from Dakar?' Viv takes a sip of the tea and holds M's gaze. 'This week, I mean.'

'No.' M's eyes shift away, and he stirs the tea again, then raises the cup to his mouth and sips. 'But forgive me, why would you ask that?'

'I have it on good information that the original case file of Aimé Tunkara's death is winging its way to you by courier, if you haven't already received it.'

'What case file? What courier?' M is all charm, all innocent bemusement. 'What in the world would give you that idea?' He leans over to the table. 'Cake?'

Viv shakes her head again, watching M cut a slice of the sponge and place it on a china plate. A memory comes to her, of M all those years ago, of the way he was able to appease the niggles and complaints of the embassy staff. With his nice smile, his British manners and subtle charisma, M was the sort of man who could charm the birds from the trees. She remembers how very good he always was at smoothing over any little domestic rift; from the first secretary over from London to the embassy housekeeper, M was ever the diplomat. She can see him now, back at the residence in Dakar, smooth talking all the kitchen staff.

'Look, how much do you know?' Viv says. 'Tell me the truth,

M, don't you at least owe me that?'

There is a silence during which M appears to be thinking. The cake sits untouched. Viv raises the teacup to her lips and drinks, watching him. He looks suddenly old and very tired, she thinks, exhausted even.

'Don't ask me, Viv,' M says, shaking his head with a look of dismay. 'Not that. I've always been discreet; you must know that.'

He lets out a sigh and drains his teacup, extending his little finger outwards to the right, swallowing then gasping. All the while, Viv stares, waiting for an answer. He places the cup on the saucer with a faint chink. From what she can make out, he is deep in thought. When he speaks, his voice is different, cooler. The jovial tone has disappeared.

'In the mafia, I suppose someone like me is called a cleaner.' M gives a small, unamused laugh. 'Look, Viv, I never knew the details, okay, whatever you think. Christ almighty, that's the last thing I wanted! I just did what John said, cleared up the mess.'

'Did you suspect what was going on?'

'Bloody hell.' Miles puts his head in his hands, lets out a long sigh. 'Look, I need to be careful, Viv.' Again, he shakes his head, frowning. 'I've got kids, grandkids.'

'If you tell me what you know, I might be able to help?' she insists. 'All this happened so long ago, but there's someone who… well, she's unturning stones, as it were.'

'More tea?' M tops up her cup then his own, sits back in the chair, crosses his legs the other way. He buries his chin in his palm with a pained look. Viv takes a sip of the hot drink, and waits.

'Aimé Tunkara wasn't the half of it, was he?' A pause. '*Isn't* the half of it,' adds M with a questioning look. 'I always suspected there was stuff happening at the FO I didn't even want to imagine. And if you ask me, Viv, you were a lamb to the bloody slaughter, given the Lady Bountiful role to play, pulled into things you were too innocent to imagine.'

Innocent. Viv feels the bubble in her chest that has been forming since Lily Tunkara got in touch tighten and expand. M gets up, goes to stand with his back to her, looking out at the trees with his hands on his hips. Considering the situation, it's a strange pose, Viv thinks, almost Roman, bringing to mind Marc Antony or Julius Caesar. A powerful stance when, in actual fact, defeat is nigh. Presumably M is trying to muster his courage.

'For God's sake, M,' Viv says with a mixture of anger and frustration. 'Stop talking nonsense. I'm not a bloody fool! It was my job to *be* Lady Bountiful, wasn't it? That's what embassy wives *do*.' Viv pauses, thinking fast. 'What did John tell you at the time?'

M turns from his position, comes to the table and leans on it with both hands, head bowed. Viv catches a sandalwood whiff of male deodorant. Close to him, she can see notches of stubble around M's jaw, and tired lines around his eyes.

'Just the bare bones. The Senegalese doctor was dead. You were involved, and Harris. We needed to pay people, and fast, and get rid of the police nosing around. I can't say I understand all of it, to be honest.' M gives a weary smile, and shakes his head. 'As I say, I did what I needed to do, and I didn't get involved. I was never able to get to the bottom of it, bloody fool that I am.

201

I *do* know that Aimé Tunkara was just the fall guy, the collateral damage. Aimé found out something, and someone didn't like it. I went in to clean up the mess, as it were.'

For so long Viv has done everything in her power to avoid thinking about this – exactly this, she realises now. She takes M's words and shifts them about in her mind. With the words come half-formed memories, snags of the past dawdling back through years of self-deception: of the fact that it was she who left the club first, she the one in the car.

For the moment, she chooses to make no reference to these things.

'So what are you saying, exactly?' she eventually manages to say. 'Are you telling me that you think Aimé's death wasn't an accident and that someone bumped him off?'

Miles stands straight and nods. 'Sure.' He turns his gaze to hers. 'Sure.'

'So it was all a set-up?'

'From the start, I believe.'

'What in hell was it? Sex? Drugs?' Though she is sussing M out, Viv speaks with genuine passion, taking herself by surprise. 'Something else even more unspeakable? Don't spare me the gory bits, M.'

Without replying, M goes inside. On the table, his mobile buzzes: the screen flashes 'SONIA', then goes dark. M comes back with an envelope in his hand, slaps it down on the table in front of her. Viv casts a sidelong glance at the top, which is marked in thick black pen with M's full name and address.

'Knock yourself out.' M rubs his temple with a thumb and forefinger. 'Another cup of tea?'

Viv refuses and, while he goes back inside, she brings the document file of brown manila out of the envelope. Quickly she sorts through a bundle of witness statements, autopsy details, and a police report stamped in black ink, *Case Closed*.

From the folder Viv brings out a photograph. It shows Aimé Tunkara lying on the ground. He is spattered with blood. Viv draws a slow breath, then another. A deep wave of emotion rises from her stomach in the form of nausea, and for a moment her studied composure is rocked. She gasps, then gathers herself. Placing the photograph face down on the table, she stares at the garden, the trees, the sky, greyish now the sun has gone in, rain clouds looming.

'Tell me the rest of what you know,' Viv says when M comes back and sits down. 'Everything.'

She shows no sign of what she is feeling: rather, she is cool, collected, emotion-free.

But M shakes his head. 'Christ, Viv, they'll know you've been to see me. You need to go home and keep a low profile, lie low at the Manor where you're safe, do yoga or whatever it is you do, otherwise this whole thing will blow up in your face.'

There is a long silence while she ponders his answer. It begins to rain. A single drop lands wetly on her forehead, then another. In unison, she and M stand up, chairs scraping on the concrete as a flurry of rain squalls across the patio.

'Who do you think they are, M?'

'No idea.' M gives her a helpless look, and shrugs, rain settling on his skin like a layer of mist. 'But the bastards are out there, sure as bloody eggs.'

They shake hands. Viv leans in and kisses him on both cheeks with a tender expression, pressing a little too long, squeezing his arm with her right hand.

'And the file?'

'It's safe with me.' M gives a matter-of-fact nod, guiding her inside. 'Whoever your contact is over there, they've done themselves an almighty favour, because if that file gets into the wrong hands now, whoever had it would be in bloody great danger.'

Viv is back at the manor. She feels exhausted but wired, unable to switch off. Around the house she wanders restlessly, picking at her cuticles, running her mind over the conversation with Miles and the terrible photograph in the file. Her thoughts go to the doctor, to their friendship. Who is she to hide what happened from Aimé's sister? Doesn't this young woman who so resembles Aimé deserve the truth at long last?

Viv makes tea, lights a spliff, pours a glass of wine. But not even the combination of alcohol and weed can calm her down. At the laptop she sits down to write, trying to make her rational mind overcome her heart:

Memoir, Part Four
Dakar, Senegal

Night-time in Dakar is like walking under a blanket, disorientating and hot, the sunless heat a soft mantle on my skin. At least so I imagine every time I venture out after dark, for in those days there are no streetlamps in the city, no lights at all other than the dim haze of the few motorised vehicles, or the passing flash of kids riding mopeds along the coast road, torches held in mouths as precarious headlights.

Via the embassy grapevine, I've grown all too used to hearing about horrific crashes in which a boy – it's always a boy – swallows the torch on impact, straight through the windpipe. Notwithstanding my horror at such news, I find myself dwelling on these accidents. Like a vulture picking at a carcass, I turn over the carnage in my mind, conjuring as it does the jeopardy that seems so ever-present in Africa – and so close, as if life on that continent is somehow more precarious and unpredictable than in England.

More disposable, too, though, given my status as the British Ambassador's wife, I'm lucky enough to be swaddled in a layer of diplomatic protection that includes burly embassy guards recruited from the national military, and my own designated driver, Lamin. It's only later, following the events of that terrible June night, that I find myself wondering with appalled dismay why we humans so frequently seem to value one life over another.

In any case, it's about six months into John's posting. Harris is here, and by this time I'm trying to avoid him as much as possible – him and my husband. That day, I hide out in the garden and spend all afternoon helping the groundsman, Ebrima, plant banana palms and frangipanis sourced from a nursery outside the city.

We work until four under the hot sun until I leave Ebrima mowing the lawns and sweep the paths myself, clearing the fallen petals and the crescent pods that tumble from the acacias, splitting their seeds into the shady dust. It's hot, too hot, brewing for a storm. The air smells of flowers and cut grass intermingling with the sea breeze. When I finally walk back through the gardens to the house, I'm exhausted, my head throbbing.

Inside, I make a cup of tea and take an aspirin, then go to find John. That night, we're supposed to be going to Julia and Tom's wedding anniversary party at the Tuli, at which all the high and mighty of Dakar are due to converge. After such a tranquil afternoon, the very thought of such furious socialising makes me feel worn out. I'm dreading it. So I muster my courage and go to find my husband in his office, where he's sat, head bowed, at the desk, writing with a cartridge pen, half silhouetted against the yellowish light filtering through the window blind.

'Darling, sorry to bother you,' I say, knocking on the door before stepping inside, 'but I've got a headache. Would you mind going alone to the party tonight?'

John glances up from the document he's reading and observes me with a look somewhere between confusion and dismay. 'But what about us? I can't do without you, you know.'

'I'm sure you'll enjoy it better without me spoiling your fun,' I reply flatly, aware of a new but familiar tension rising in the atmosphere. In turn, I can feel my own anxiety accelerating as I seek more justifications to back up my plea, 'I think I've got a migraine coming.'

'Viv—' He gives a sigh accompanied by an infinitesimal shake of his head, as if I'm a misbehaving child.

In that moment, I note the bewildering fact that my husband is much more attractive with a touch of sun. He's just back from a field visit to northern Senegal, observing British government-funded projects, as he has told me. His greenish eyes – by and large insipid – stand out against his newly tanned skin.

'There are,' he adds, 'some big names dropping in.'

'The thing is,' I insist, 'you always say I'm not fun enough at parties. Surely, just this once—'

'No, pet.' He drops his gaze, the matter dismissed, his tone failing to match the habitual endearment. 'High Commissioners do not attend parties without their wives.'

Upstairs, I lie still in the bath, eyes closed, letting the cold water cool my skin and contemplating the layer of red earth beneath my fingernails. Though I had been perfectly calm, now I'm filled with frustration at my husband's stubbornness and the way, more often than not these days, I have to tread on eggshells around him. If anything, I want to go back down and confront him, insist on staying at home, but I know such behaviour will only cause more trouble.

We've been married for eighteen months. Gradually it's dawning on me that John is changing his colours, like the slow turning of a leaf in autumn.

Up in the bedroom, I put on a lilac-hued silk dress and stare into the mirror. My skin's flushed from the sun and still hot to the touch. I smooth a hand over my belly in the thin, clingy fabric, pressing its flatness for a few seconds.

Let me make it clear right now that by this time, John and I are *not* having sex anymore. Still, I harbour a tiny flame of what – hope? dread? – of the kind I don't dare contemplate. My monthly period's two weeks late, and I'm filled with a languor that weighs down my very bones. I make an effort to push away any recognition of my fatigue to the edges of my consciousness, savouring the idea that I might finally be pregnant like some sweet forbidden

207

nugget of candy.

Downstairs, John informs me that Lamin's been taken ill. Dengue fever, John says, so we'll have to drive ourselves to the party. It's eight o'clock by this time and raining heavily, mud flowing in torrents past the front gates. The car's headlights, always dim at best, are on the blink. In a blur of pouring rain and darkness, we just about make it to the nightclub compound on Mutsaka Road, where the party's already in full swing.

It's mostly Senegalese glitterati, embassy people, white and black, plus a few government ministers who like fraternising with the British, and the singer, Idris Malika, with his fashionable posse. By midnight, the party gets pretty wild. People are dancing and kissing, smoking in the club and out by the pool. John is drunk in a matter of minutes. I notice with a sinking feeling that he has a spliff in his hand and is passing it around the crowd. Weed always makes him hyper and attention-seeking.

As for me, I'm not drunk or high – I figure I better not risk it. But there can't be any harm in dancing. Somehow Julia's persuaded the Super Diomono to play – they're all the rage in 1987 – and for an hour or so I lose myself in the hearty merengue rhythms.

Later on, I find my husband talking to one of the band members, a tall black man who looks like a model.

'I'm tired, darling,' I say. 'Can we go?'

For a moment John looks affronted, as is his way. His reaction is always to mockingly question my motives, some criticism hovering behind his look like a barbed missile ready to launch.

'Go?' he says. 'The party's just getting started. I'm having a good time.'

The young bloke observes us coolly, then meanders off like a model on a catwalk.

'Please?'

At the anxious look on my face, my husband gazes at me with a half-smile, then glances at his watch.

'We'll go in half an hour.'

'Okay,' I agree, and leave him to it.

I drive, because John's too drunk to take the wheel. We drive out of the compound onto Mutsaka Road at twenty-five to three. There's no traffic, but it's still raining hard, and the windscreen wipers can't keep up with the torrents of water hurling themselves at the glass. As we turn onto the main road, the car headlights flicker and die.

People say life can change in a split second. One solitary second amid all the trillions of mundane moments in a lifetime that changes the course of things forever. This flick from normal to something else, something wrong, happens so quickly, there's no time to understand. And so it happens for me that rainy October night.

I remember the thump of the car impacting against something, the sickening bump of hard metal against something softer, something weaker. In that moment, I have the fleeting illusory thought that whatever *it* is must be a body of some kind, animal or human?

The rain's hammering on the windows. The car brakes, once, twice, and on the third time we're swerving in the mud. The steering wheel's loose and out of control. There's a big bang. It's the kind of thing that happens in films – the rainstorm, the dark, the stoned, boozed-up passengers, the dying headlights.

When I emerge from the car, the ground's stained with blood

and petrol, swirling in the rain. I see something lying in the hellish slimy mud. Someone. With a swiping motion I wipe raindrops out of my eyes. Then I see him.

He lies on his back, arms by his side. His face is scuffed with reddish mud. A beautiful man, and quite still, as though he is asleep.

In the pouring rain I gaze down.

'Please,' I say. 'Can you hear me, please, wake up!'

It seems some seconds, a too-slow tick of time passing, before it dawns on me that the line of his neck is twisted in an unnatural way, and he isn't breathing. For a moment, all is stillness apart from the hammering of my own heart in my chest.

'Jesus. Jesus!' I begin to yell, and sink to the floor. 'John, do something!'

But John's silent, staring and unresponsive, his face a mask that covers all emotion, if there is any there at all. It seems to take an age for the ambulance to arrive, and in that time I sit and hold the man's hand, filled with some sort of numb expectation that he might live.

But the paramedics shake their heads.

'Sorry, madame,' they say to me, meeting my eyes with sorrowful expressions, as if they deem it necessary to be gentle, as if they think I'm somehow the man's relative. 'So sorry.'

When the ambulance draws away, siren wailing, I stand dry-mouthed in its wake, experiencing a familiar cramping and a sensation of dampness in my underwear, then a rush that turns into a torrent. My period.

I clutch my belly and watch the taillights disappear, my flame of hope extinguishing with that dead man and the little bloody ball of dead cells beginning to exit my body.

The man's name, in the witness statements later, is Aimé. It means loved, of course you know that. There's the French noun, *amour*, and its verb, *aimer*: to love, a regular verb, following all the usual grammatical rules. Then its past participle, *aimé*.

The dead man's name is Loved.

CHAPTER EIGHTEEN

Lily

Lily stops reading. *The dead man's name is Loved.* The sentence repeats in her head, over and over. Pushing the laptop away, Lily bows her face to the wood and closes her eyes for a second. She is sure now, sure that Vivienne is lying. If anything, the Englishwoman is an unreliable narrator trying to pull the wool over her eyes. Lying by omission. But she can't quite put her finger on what exactly is missing.

Lily makes breakfast for the girls, manoeuvres them into their uniforms, and drops them at school. Only then does she turn to the text message from Lion he'd sent her at the party. For days, she's been avoiding reading the awful thing, unwilling, if she's honest, to be confronted with the identity of Demba's mistress – though she has her suspicions... Now she goes to open the message, and sighs. No: no, no, no.

With a small grimace, Lily pockets her phone, refusing to face the reality. Not here, not now.

'There was a meningitis outbreak in 1987, in Ngor.'
On the other end of the line, Lion Savané is talking quickly.

Lion is aware, he tells Lily, that she never asked for his help on the matter, but he was curious. He has, he informs Lily, found a snippet of information that she might find useful. He does not, she notes, ask if she has opened the ill-fated text.

'Pssht,' Lily says, 'you could get the sack.'

'This is way bigger than my job,' Lion replies with a serious tone. 'Kids were getting ill, one way or another. Apparently it was put down to an outbreak of meningitis, but that was a lie.'

'How do you know?' replies Lily, in the same moment a fleeting thought strikes her about Lion's sister, Maria, and the cause of her disability. Curious, Lily thinks, that Maria was another ill child at the same time as Alou Niang. Can it be a coincidence that so many Ngor children of the same generation grew ill or died?

'We weren't even born,' Lily adds.

'I asked my parents why my sister Maria ended up in a wheelchair. They never speak about it – I mean, why would you keep secrets from your own children, right? But in the past they've always been adept at changing the subject. They think digging up the past won't change anything.'

'And why did she?'

'There was an outbreak, and Maria was paralysed. It came out of the blue. Before that, Maria was a healthy seven-year-old.'

'So what if it wasn't meningitis, Lion,' Lily says, thinking on her feet, 'but something else? Something more sinister.'

'And record keeping wasn't the same back then,' Lion counters. 'It was easy to cover things up.'

'If children were being hurt, Lion, we need to find out why.' Lily gives a sigh, then exclaims, struck with a brainwave. 'Oh, there's someone who might know. Leave it with me.'

'All right. I'm glad to be useful.'

'I'll give you a call, *inshallah*,' adds Lily, suddenly restless to act, to do something, 'when I have something.'

By the time Lily tracks Bakary Ba down, it is lunchtime, and Ngor village is quiet and sleepy. Cooking smells waft in the air. Out to sea, a few surfers float on the break. Lily's phone buzzes and she checks her messages casually, but her stomach lurches when she opens the new text.

YOU NEED TO STOP, LILY.

She shakes her head and stops in her tracks, jabbing at the phone, but the number comes up as unknown. Vexed, she replies: *Please stop messaging me, whoever you are*, then deletes the message and stashes the phone in her bag. Beneath the sun, she is too hot, suddenly, annoyed and sweating. She stands for a moment breathing out, fanning her face with her hand. Then she takes a breath and crosses the hot sand to find Bakary at the further end of the beach sitting by a cluster of painted fishing boats. Bakary wears surf shorts, a T-shirt, and a woolly hat, and sits on a low wooden stool, repairing a beached pirogue.

When Lily approaches, Bakary appears a vision of concentration; he tucks his head into the painted side of the boat, tapping a hammer on a panel of amber-painted wood with light movements of his wrist. A lone sheep noses the dust. The foreshore is only footsteps away; beneath a cloudless sky the blue

214

bay twinkles in the sunlight. Over on the other side of the stretch of water, the ferry pirogue is just approaching the island's rocky shore, leaning left in the water with the weight of its passengers, leaving a deep foamy V in its wake.

'Bakary. Do you have a second?'

He shakes his head and continues to hammer, more loudly now, tap, tap, tap.

'Please? I won't take much of your time, *inshallah*.'

'*Joge fi.*' Bakary bows his head to rest it on the wood, then half turns to look at Lily. 'Wha–wha–what,' he adds with a sullen expression, 'do you want?'

'Just to talk. Can we go somewhere?'

With reluctance, Bakary drops the hammer on the hard sand and heaves himself up, then stretches out his back with a groan. They walk across to a crumbling concrete structure west of the boats, that must once have formed, Lily wonders, the beginnings of a dwelling place. Nowadays, the old men of the village are in the habit of sitting in the abandoned but pleasantly positioned structure to gossip and take in the ocean views.

Lily can see why. Roughly hewn, open-sided, the random square of concrete frames the panorama of sea and palm-fringed island like a picture frame. Two elderly men drying off after a swim give the briefest of nods and continue talking, casting them sidelong glances. In the corner, a lone dog sniffs at a scattering of litter. Bakary seats himself at the other end, and Lily sits down next to him.

'Well?' says Bakary. And then, 'I'm really not, not sure how I can help you, Mrs Tunkara.'

'Please, call me Lily. God knows, you were around when I

was in nappies!'

For the first time a smile, though reluctant.

'I know it's difficult to talk about that time.' Lily pauses, searching for the words. 'When Aimé died, I mean. But it wasn't just my brother's death, was it? I talked to someone who was given money by you – the father of another student who died.'

Bakary stares out to sea. In profile, his face is expressionless, just a slight twitch of his jaw hinting at some hidden emotion.

'That boy was Alou Niang, one of your mates, too, wasn't he?' Lily ploughs on with a question in her voice. 'Bakary, I know none of it was your fault. You can tell me, honestly, and I'll do my best to protect you. You don't have to keep this secret anymore.'

Bakary turns, frowning. 'H–h–how do you know that was me?' His eyes suddenly brim with tears. 'How could you know that?'

'Your stammer.' Lily places a hand on his arm. 'I'm sorry.'

Bakary brushes his other hand across his eyes, face still turned towards the sea. Then: 'Aimé was a good man, he wanted to ch–ch–change things.' With a thumb he picks with savagery at the cuticle of his index finger. 'It w–w–wasn't Aimé's fault.'

'Did he get you to ask your friends?'

'Y–yes. They wanted kids like us, you know – t–teenagers.'

'Go on.'

'Alou was h–helping, and he brought me in on it, like his wingman, ya know? I was y–y–younger, naïve, I guess. I was only fourteen. W–w–we'd find a kid, tell them they'd get paid, put them in touch. Bang, we both had *dix–dix–dix mille* in our hands. It was easy money.'

Lily glances down at Bakary's hands. The cuticle is ripped

now, and bleeding, scarlet blood bright against black skin.

'And do you have any idea who *they* was?'

'Uh uh.' He shakes his head. 'We were just the middlemen. W–w–we found the kids, passed them on, got paid. Easy peasy.'

'But—'

'But Aimé got w–w–wind of something dodgy. I s'pose we'd both assumed whatever they wanted the kids for was pretty mild – drug running or s–s–something like that.' For a moment Bakary falls silent. Eyes closed, he takes a breath. 'Then this kid got s–s–sick, really sick. And another. One went blind. Alou started having fits.'

'And you never found out why?'

Bakary shakes his head. 'Aimé was the one in charge, he f–f–f–found out, then they killed him. Aimé was smart, man, so smart.'

'Tell me what happened.'

'Aimé got the w–wind up. He didn't like what was going on, and started to investigate. I mean, drugs were fine, but this was something else – more sinister. He didn't tell me much, didn't want me involved, but I knew he–he was worried. He got anxious, ya know, told me he couldn't sleep. He shut me out completely in the end. Wouldn't talk about it.'

'You saw him at the Tuli club that night, didn't you?'

'No, but I s–s–saw him just before, in the v–village. He was g–getting on his motorbike. I asked him where he was g–g–going and he said the T–Tuli. It was the l–l–l–last time I ever spoke to him.'

'Then Alou died. Do you know how?'

'No. It was s–s–strange. I was s–s–sent over there with cash for the family by this English bloke from the embassy. It was the last thing I did after Aimé was killed.'

'And Aimé never revealed what he'd discovered?'

'N–n–no.' Bakary shakes his head. 'Said it would put me in danger. I think he was trying to get them to stop. When he was killed, I knew I couldn't breathe a word to anyone, ever, because the same w–w–w–would happen to me.'

'But you and Musa were arrested?'

'Yes, a f–f–few days afterwards, we got stopped by the police, charged with disrupting the peace. It was a w–w–warning, you know, from them.'

'Them?'

'The people Aimé was involved with, the people h–h–hurting the kids.'

Lily takes a deep breath. 'Can you remember any of the children's names who got ill? Are any of them still alive?'

For a few seconds Bakary thinks hard. 'There was a boy,' he says eventually, 'Oumar S–s–sy. At the time we recruited him, he was only eleven. He went blind; I was given the cash to pay off the family – fifty thousand CFA.'

Lily breathes in, trying to contain her emotion. The scumbags, she is thinking. The scumbags. 'Where,' she asks, 'does Monsieur Sy live?'

'I'll t–t–t–take you.' Bakary sighs. 'He's not far away. Right now if you want.'

'Yes,' Lily says, surprised. 'Is there anything else?'

Bakary turns away, staring once more out at the water. Lily follows his gaze, watching a large pleasure boat motor out of sight behind the curve of the island, fibreglass sides flashing where they catch the sun.

'I've t–t–told you,' Bakary says without looking at her. 'That's everything I know, Lily.'

The two-lane road running out of Ngor village into central Dakar is busy even at this time of day. The whole area is a cacophony – a word, Lily feels, that finds its true definition right here – of jammed-up vehicles hooting their horns and revving exhaust fumes into the atmosphere. The smell of diesel hits her in the throat.

Through the narrow gaps between the cars, traders weave their way, selling an assortment of sundries: biscuits and mosque-shaped alarm clocks, plastic-wrapped peanut brittle and fake designer sunglasses. Off the metal bonnets, the sun boils and radiates, amplified engine heat mingling with choking clouds of dust and exhaust fumes.

'What on earth are we doing here?' Lily calls to Bakary, flummoxed by the noise and heat.

But Bakary nods in the direction of a man with wild dread-locked hair in electric-blue robes who is shambling in circles between the busy traffic. In his fifties, Lily estimates in shock, sixties, even, the man carries a white stick in one hand which he holds outstretched in front of him, gingerly tapping the tarmac.

'That's not Oumar, surely?'

Beside her, Bakary nods. 'At night, his family t–t–tie his wrists with rope. In the day they let him wander.'

'Oh, good God,' Lily murmurs, trying to collect herself. How can he look so old, when she herself is eleven years younger than him! 'And he's been like this since the eighties?'

219

'Since it happened, yes. Before that he–he was a normal kid.'

Lily sees that Oumar Sy has husky, curling fingernails, and represses a shudder. He smells of ingrained sweat and urine. Muttering under his breath, Oumar twitches his hand for money at the drivers and passers-by who ignore his presence, or occasionally press a coin into his palm. Lily has seen these troubled souls before, but never paid attention. They are part of life, part of the city landscape. Are we really this used, she thinks with sadness, to these mentally unwell fellow humans lost on Dakar's streets? She has never thought to consider their stories.

'Oumar.' Bakary puts a hand on the man's arm. 'It's m–me, brother. Bakary.'

The man nods and gives a cheery smile, showing black, broken teeth, waving the stick, turning sightlessly in their direction. With gentle pressure, Bakary moves him to the side of the road, presses a coin into his spare hand. All the while, his stick tap taps on the tarmac.

'Oumar, I brought someone to see you.'

'*Asalaam alaykum*.' Lily takes Oumar's hand. 'Come, monsieur, drink some water with us.'

In a roadside café nearby, Lily buys *attaya* tea and bottles of filtered water. The three of them sit together on benches under the tarpaulin shelter. Oumar continues to mutter an unintelligible string of French and Wolof.

'She w–w–w–wants to ask you about the past,' says Bakary, 'about the *toubabs*, the white doctors.'

Oumar smiles and nods, takes the bottle of water and swigs from it with loud slurping sounds.

'Oumar,' Lily says, 'can you tell me what happened to you?'

With unexpected force, Oumar lets out a piercing howl and jumps up from the bench, waving the water bottle so that some of the liquid sprays out. A few passers-by turn to look. The other patrons of the stall leave in haste. Oumar flails his arms, still crying out. His eyes stare blankly in Lily's direction. His suffering is almost unbearable, she thinks.

Bakary strokes his hand, Lily takes the other.

'It's okay,' she says in a soothing voice, 'it's okay.'

'I'm sorry,' Bakary says, 'he's unwell.'

To leave Oumar would be, she thinks with rising guilt, an abandonment. As if reading her thoughts, Bakary takes the blind man's arm, guides him back along the road to the family dwelling situated on the edge of the smaller village roundabout.

A beaded curtain hangs at the door. Inside, a woman in a T-shirt and floral wrap is bent double over a small stove. The distinctive smell of *thieboudienne* fills the room, of *netetou* and roasting *thiof*. The woman straightens up, seemingly unsurprised to see Bakary there. At her son, the woman smiles, reaches over, squeezes his arm. Without responding, Oumar shuffles through another door and disappears. For a second or two, Lily is momentarily blindsided by the tenderness of the woman's gesture. She clears her throat, offering the usual Wolof greeting.

'*Alaykum salaam,*' replies the woman. '*Naga def?*'

'This is Bibi,' says Bakary, 'Oumar's ma.'

On the plain plastered wall there is a single photograph hung on a nail. Lily stretches up to look, recognising Bibi holding Oumar's hand. The boy must be six or seven, a grinning lad in shorts and T-shirt holding a lethal-looking spear gun and largish tuna by its lower jaw.

'That was before he got ill,' says Bibi quickly. 'He used to love diving with the men.'

'What happened?' asks Lily.

Bibi eyes her suspiciously, but at an encouraging nod from Bakary, she speaks, 'Doctors came to the house. They said it was an important mission and Oumar was chosen to be part of it. We'd be paid a lot of money, they said. Of course, we said yes.'

Bibi turns back towards the cooking pot. Lily clenches her fingers, repressing a rising anger. The power of money, and a child's life ruined. How dare they!

'What did they do to him?' she asks.

'They had needles and a chart with green writing on it. They took Oumar's temperature, blood samples, everything. Made me and his father sign forms, but they were in English, and we didn't understand them. The next day, they injected my son.'

'Do you know what they injected him with?'

'After the money stopped, I threw away the forms.' Bibi shrugs, stirring the pot, stony-faced. 'Oumar told me he felt ill. He was shaking, sweating; he had a fit. We thought it was malaria. They told us it was meningitis. Then he began to lose his sight.' Bibi's voice quivers. 'When the money ran out, we didn't have anything for the medical bills. That's why Oumar's like he is. We have to tie him up to keep him safe.' Bibi turns her face, frowning. 'You'll think me cruel, but how do you think I feel watching my son like that, and there's nothing I can do!'

Lily is silent. She is late, too late to this, decades behind time, when something should have been done before. The injustice takes her breath away, the injustice and sheer cruelty.

'Bibi,' Lily says, trying to control the emotion in her voice.

Still, she can hear the edge of anger present as she speaks. 'You won't have heard of informed consent, but what those people did was illegal. Oumar was the innocent victim of an illegal clinical trial.

'Such things have been going on for years in other parts of Africa,' Lily carries on, 'in Nigeria, Kenya – but never here, or so we all thought.' Lily takes a breath. 'Tell me, is there anyone else I can talk to? With more testimonies from families like yours, I believe we can build a strong lawsuit, get you the compensation you deserve.' Lily takes Bibi's hand, meets her eyes, which as they look into hers are flat with something like defeat. 'You, your son... Your family should not have to live like this.'

*

The sun is hot and hard on the car roof. Still feeling agitated, Lily goes back a different way than she normally does. The road winds to the left, continuing via the Mutsaka Road into Ngor village. Out of the blue, Lily spots the long-abandoned site of the Tuli Club. She slows the car and cranes her neck to look, glancing first at her watch – which shows half-past two – then into the rear-view mirror. She isn't due to pick the girls up until half-past four today, and, even then, they'll probably be late out, God willing. They usually are after the multi-sports clubs run by the teachers every week: soccer, tennis, basketball. Her girls' privilege does not escape her, a world away from the lives of Bakary Ba, of poor Oumar and his family.

Dropping down a gear, Lily parks one wheel up on the verge and peers out of the car windscreen.

Further back along the highway, the roadside had been

223

teeming with people and small businesses: Ma Sow's Salon de Tresses, Graine D'Or Patisserie with the usual queue outside for afternoon baking time, an Orange mobile phone shop and the new Tropical Dream ice-cream parlour that the girls are dying to try, attracted like butterflies to nectar by the myriad of bright, sweet flavours displayed in the window.

By contrast, this section of Mutsaka Road is empty and seemingly dedicated to construction. A half-built, glass-clad apartment block gleams in the scorching sun, overshadowed by the ungainly arms of a looming crane. Lily is fleetingly reminded of a video she and her fellow students watched during her university days called *The Tripods*, which featured tall, metal-clawed aliens snatching humans from the earth's surface. Lily has a clear recollection of the English vocabulary list: Sci-fi, dystopia, capping… Such things are hard to forget.

The Tuli appears to be a building site now, Lily assesses, forcing her thoughts back to the issue at hand. She adjusts her headscarf in the mirror, touches up her lipstick, and gets out of the car, her mind turning to what she knows of *that* night.

By all accounts, the famous Tuli Club was all the rage in the early eighties. People said it was the only nightclub in Dakar for the young and beautiful to see and be seen, but afterwards, well… The place never recovered from the Aimé Tunkara scandal in 1987. A dead young man – a brilliant medical student, no less – discovered outside ruined the Tuli's image, and, as far as Lily knows, its trendy clientele gradually faded away after a time, migrating to the newer, unblemished disco venues that sprang up throughout the nineties in the city centre.

The gate is open. Apart from the faint scratching of insects and the sound of the wind off the coast, the building site is silent. God willing, there is no one around to see her poking her nose about. Handbag held tightly under one arm, Lily sets off through the courtyard where a patch of building sand is marked with the ghost of wheel tracks, a bulldozer by the looks of things. To the right is an enormous pile of rubble and other rubbish. She takes in the twisted limbs of several disfigured chairs, a smashed mirror, and what appear to be a few dozen broken chandeliers. At the back of the plot, the skeleton of the Tuli building is nevertheless still intact, an unprepossessing one-storey construction that seems very retro nowadays, Lily thinks, among so many new buildings. A skip stands chock full of more rubble.

So someone has been here recently – to knock it down, Lily speculates, to build more apartments or houses? Filled with a sense of intrigue, she follows that thought. In the field of property development, there are only three main companies dominating the market in Dakar: Afric Housing Ltd, Aquasun Real Estate and… Lily searches her brain for the last, and the biggest… Sky High Group Senegal. If she's not mistaken, the company is owned by the brother of the Tuli's former owner. Now that, she tells herself, cannot be a coincidence. The truth is that Dakar's still a village, though it seems to grow outwards and upwards by the hour.

The door to the building hangs ajar on its hinges. Lily pushes it open and pokes her head inside, taking in the silent space where a few gilt-armed red velvet banquettes languish like ageing movie stars. She casts her eyes along the bar, a mess of disintegrating white plaster frescoes – broken-faced cherubs, wingless angels, the collapsing remains of a mythical dragon. Dust particles dance in the static rays of sunlight penetrating the windows.

Kenopsia, Lily thinks, picking her way further inside, mind veering off at a tangent. The word is one of the rather intriguing neologisms she has learned through a recent court case involving an internet tycoon, and means, Lily had discovered with interest, the forlorn atmosphere of a once-busy place that now stands empty. Like a school classroom in the holidays, the man had explained to the court, or a shut-down airport devoid of queues and crowds. Or an abandoned nightclub, thinks Lily. Not just empty, but the sensation of a negative, a loss, even. *Une absence.*

Lily scans her eyes to where a dirty, dusty cocktail glass still adorns the bar, as if its drinker simply upped and left in the middle of a party, Lily thinks, abandoning his or her Pina Colada for whoever might care to find it! From the floor, she picks up a torn drinks mat, *Bière La Gazelle*, and turns it over in her hand, then places it carefully on the wooden surface, squaring it with precision.

Outside, Lily crosses what used to be the patio terrace to an abandoned swimming pool. Cracked concrete edges disintegrate into a dry rectangle that must have once been filled with sparkling water. Scattering the site are broken tiles, hundreds of them, in a blue mosaic pattern.

Lily leans down and picks at a triangle of tile, loosening it from the ground, crumbling the fired clay between her fingers. It is true that in its time, the Tuli had a reputation for debauchery, for wild parties and alcohol, drugs and sex. How many revellers had stood right in this spot, drinking and snorting cocaine, kissing strangers in the pool beneath the floodlights? There is that feeling again, of their absence and the empty spaces left behind.

From Lily's fingers, the dust falls onto the dry earth. She stands upright. What secrets are buried here, and what lies? What did the guests see that rainy night when Aimé died? And what on earth was Aimé, of all people, a straightlaced, hard-working young doctor, doing outside a nightclub at four o'clock in the morning in the first place?

Bakary Ba must know *something*, Lily thinks, filled with a sudden determination. She marches back to the car, clambers into the driving seat. Why else were Musa and Bakary arrested the night of Aimé's death and interrogated by the police, apparently for no reason? Then – silence. Scanty, highly redacted witness statements. No arrest report. *Rien de tout!* And then there was Musa's peculiar reaction to the photograph. No, the whole thing was fishy from the start, of that Lily is certain now.

Lily starts the ignition and drives away.

CHAPTER NINETEEN

Vivienne

In Costa Coffee, back in Oxford after another early start and exhausting drive, Viv purchases a gingerbread latté with two sugars, at Patrick's request, and a medium breakfast tea for herself. While they wait for the young girl behind the counter to hand over the drinks, Patrick talks about his home in St Andrews, his post-graduate studies reading medicine at Exeter College, Oxford.

'That's how I knew Professor Burns,' he adds. 'I got assigned to him at Jesus, for my tutorials in Michaelmas Term last year.'

On closer look, the boy (Viv can't help considering him a boy – he can't be more than twenty-one, by her estimation, twenty-two at a push) is very slender, in a scruffy Shetland jumper that bags around his shoulders. He has a pleasant, almost pretty face framed by vivid curls and adorned with a scrappy, half-grown ginger goatee.

The coffee shop is buzzing and jolly. Viv can smell coffee and damp coats mingling with the cosiness of a trendy chill-out music track featuring trumpets and the rich tones of a female vocalist. She steers Patrick towards a pair of comfy-looking leather sofas by the window.

When they sit down, Viv takes her coat off and cups her own hot drink in its cardboard takeaway cup, feeling fortified by the caffeine. She leans forwards to Patrick with a reassuring smile, though inside she feels a pressure of growing concern that is almost parental, accompanied by a nebulous sort of dread. With the premonition of what is to come, she feels half afraid. How easy it would be to get up now, she is thinking, and walk away from this child and his dangerous revelations. God knows, she does not want to have to do anything drastic.

'So you knew Professor Burns quite well?' Viv says, nevertheless compelled by necessity to stay.

'As much as anyone knows their tutor, I guess,' answers Patrick, 'I was so pleased to be taught by a world expert, you know.'

'But something happened?'

Patrick takes a sip of the coffee, then another. While Viv waits for him to speak, she takes out her sandwiches and unwraps them. Extending the pack to the boy, who takes one of the triangular sandwiches with a thankful look, Viv selects another. Together they munch in silence, until: 'Professor Burns took me under his wing, you might say,' Patrick says, finishing a mouthful of sandwich and gulping at the coffee. 'He was heading up a research project sponsored by a big pharmaceutical company – a partnership between the company and the university. He said it was taking all his time and he needed my help.'

'Yes, go on?'

'I was flattered.' Patrick shrugs, selecting another sandwich. 'Also, he said he'd give me money for the work. I'm broke, so I felt pretty lucky.'

'So you went the extra mile?'

'Yeah.' Patrick smiles and nods, pausing to munch and swallow. 'I did. I spent a lot of time down at his department on the Banbury Road, going through findings and collating the results.'

A few raindrops still nestle, jewel-bright, on the reddish strands of Patrick's curls and the rough wool of the jumper. It strikes Viv that Patrick is not an average young man. There is a delicacy about him that is bordering on angelic, she determines, and not just because he looks undernourished. He reminds her of a pre-Raphaelite redhead, *une âme trop sensible*. Evidently one of those delicate, brilliant, sensitive souls one always finds in places like Oxford, heads stuffed full of facts and dreams and poetry.

'Go on,' Viv says in a soft voice.

'One day I was looking for something. Information post-2000 was all documented on the computer system – but the old stuff, pre-millennium, from clinical trials done years ago, was filed in cabinets down in the basement.'

A pause. Patrick seems to have finished eating. Through the glass reflections he considers the street outside, where the rain is hurling onto the pavement, causing a river to form in the gutter. Hunched pedestrians file pass the window under an assortment of umbrellas. In a rush of spray a bus pulls up, collects a line of passengers and pulls away again.

'What happened then?' Viv prompts in a gentle voice. Patrick stares at her, clear blue eyes stark against alabaster skin sprinkled with freckles.

'I spent several days down there, going through the files. The professor was away. There were hundreds of them, it was a labyrinth.' He frowns. 'Well, anyway, on the second day, I discovered this file labelled confidential, all a bit secret service, you know—'

'Yes.'

'It was from a clinical trial the doctor had carried out in the eighties somewhere in Senegal, in West Africa. There was all the paperwork, names of kids, consent forms. As far as I could see, they were trialling a drug called Aspiximal.' Silence, then Patrick carries on, 'I took a look at the consent forms, because I'd done an essay about patient consent and the difference between informed and uninformed consent.'

Viv takes a breath. 'Oh?'

'Yeah, and these forms. Well, the people in the trials can't have given informed consent. Because all the forms were in English, and Senegal is a former French colony. I looked it up. They speak French and Wolof there, not English. There's no way village people of that time would have spoken another language.'

Viv looks at Patrick's face, round and animated. 'Where is this file now?'

'I took it home, because I wanted to have a closer look.'

'And did you?'

'Yeah. This was a few months ago. I was going to confront Burns about it, but then, well, he died.'

Viv offers Patrick the piece of dark chocolate she has been keeping for later. He accepts it and eats, slowly this time, with a frown. A second or two later, he says, 'Mrs Hughes, I think I should go to the press with it. What do you think?' He holds Viv's gaze with a wide-eyed, searching look, then covers his hands with his face, and groans. 'What a responsibility.'

'It shouldn't be your responsibility. It's too big. Did you tell anyone about this file?' she probes. 'Your friends, anyone else?'

Patrick shakes his head. 'No, not a soul.' He crosses his arms. 'Not a soul.'

'I have one question,' Viv says. 'How did you find me?'

'On the paperwork – during the time Burns spent in Senegal, it says he visited the High Commission.' A pause. 'Then the porter at Exeter mentioned there was a woman looking for Dr Burns. I put two and two together and got your number off the college ledger. I thought you might know something.'

'Oh, you clever child,' Viv says again in a soft voice when Patrick has finished, extending a hand and patting his knee, then withdrawing it again with the vague worry that this might be inappropriate behaviour; one never knew nowadays. 'I need to see the file,' she adds. 'I've a friend, a lawyer, who's looking into this case. This might be exactly the evidence she needs. I could accompany you back to college now, to get it?'

But Patrick shakes his head. 'I took it home to St Andrews for the holidays. It's still there.'

Viv sighs, extracting a promise from the boy that he will get his parents to courier it down immediately, scribbles her address on the back of the napkin. After they have said goodbye, she watches the boy's small figure wander off down Ship Street.

The following day, a swim, then yoga, a shower, then dressed and breakfast and the preoccupying matters of the day. The room used by John for his work in the north wing of Moon Manor is less like an office, more like a mausoleum. Viv can smell the musty aroma of stale air, of the rising damp affecting this side of the house. Since his death, Viv has purposefully left the room untouched, unsure how to even begin sorting through the decades-old piles of paperwork that even in retirement John seemed compelled to work on. The files and folders piled on shelves running the perimeter of the walls, papers he was forever glued to night and day. Viv would hear him on the telephone sometimes, his hectoring voice informing some poor soul how busy he was, how in demand: 'I do sixteen-hour days every day and articles published every two weeks,' Viv would hear John announcing pompously, presumably to the admiring students who wrote often, via snail-mail or email, asking for work experience or advice about entering the diplomatic service, or sometimes for John to look over their theses. 'I'm afraid I don't have time to read drafts, except for the thousands of pages of legal submissions I'm involved with.'

Now the ghost of her husband lingers – a cartridge pen left uncapped on the desk, as if John were caught in the middle of writing something when he decided to kill himself. Viv picks it up, feeling shellshocked, turning it over in her fingers and trying to imagine what could possibly have been running through John's mind as he sat here that day. She sighs, slotting the cap on the pen, placing it back on the desk. There are several plastic trays he always used to organise correspondence. And his laptop closed on the desk. But her husband preferred paperwork to computers, condemning all the later forms of technology as new-fangled, over-complicated.

Viv sits down at the desk and turns to the trays, sorting through the reams of letters, of bank and visa card statements, of faxes, printouts, notes and other miscellany, scanning down the summaries of John's accounts, of his outgoings and his payments in. In the desk drawer, his latest passport and diplomatic papers, his bank cards, his recent yellow fever certificate, his wallet.

Afterwards, Viv plugs in the laptop and turns it on, keying in John's password. In the inbox of John's Outlook account emails appear one by one. Peculiar, Viv thinks, considering that whomever they are from, they're now messages to the dead.

Viv scrolls through, noting the senders, reading and filing the messages of importance. After a short while she sits in silence, overcome by oddly mixed feeling of loss, of gratitude, of finality. She will never know why John killed himself when he did, but she is grateful for his legacy, however unfinished. Whether he intended to or not, he has set her free.

Downstairs Viv cracks an egg into a pan of boiling water, then another, watching the liquid whites solidify around the yolks, as if by magic, into perfect floating spheres like tiny spaceships. She adds chia seeds and avocado to the plate of poached eggs, followed by two slices of rye toast. From the cupboard, she retrieves a bottle of ketchup and adds a dollop. She sits eating at the kitchen table with a glass of Evian water.

'Alexa,' she says, finishing her mouthful, 'turn on.'

'How can I help you?'

'Look up my flight to Dakar on the sixteenth.'

Viv makes notes with a biro as the soft electronic voice reels off the flight time and scheduled gate, plus other pre-departure details.

CHAPTER TWENTY

Lily

Another Saturday, and a game of Mamadou Diop is underway. Lily can hear her daughters yelling at either end of the courtyard. They throw the name back and forth as they hunt for each other among the low ornamental palms.

Lily has risen late, but is still exhausted after, according to her smart watch, six hours, nine minutes of sleep, of which only fifty-one minutes constituted deep sleep, Lily's phone informs her when it syncs, while ten per cent was REM, the best kind. For some reason, such statistical information, testifying so precisely as to the quality of her rest, makes Lily feel better.

So it's all in the mind, Lily thinks, after all.

She stands at the sink washing up the breakfast things, bent over the foaming water. Afterwards, she takes her laptop outside, ready for the call she has arranged, sits sipping a sugared coffee, watching the girls play. A moment of relaxation before – what? Allowing all that she has learned the day before to enter her thoughts again? From this, her mind wanders to Bibi, then to Oumar, the appalling memories of yesterday inciting a gasp of apprehension.

'There was a death in another village too,' Bibi had told Lily just before she left. 'In Keur Samma. A child, the mother was called Aminata Fall, she was the local midwife.'

Lily feels her stomach churn. Suddenly she does not fancy the sweet, indulgent coffee, and pushes it away. All at once she feels anxious at the thought of what she might undoubtedly discover in Keur Samma: more pain, more tragedy.

Lily logs into Skype, scans the screen for the invite from Renata Bell at the Pavos Foundation in Amsterdam. Renata's status already reads online. Lily clicks call. On the other end, Renata has a matter-of-fact German accent, wears a headscarf and nose ring, and looks intensely at the camera from a strange sideways position, which Lily presumes has something to do with the positioning of her computer. When Lily mentions the drug trials, Renata nods.

'Sure, illegal clinical trials have been going on in sub-Saharan Africa for decades. It's the old story – dodgy trials, secret deaths. Big pharma are just as bad as arms dealers or tobacco companies, and it's the sad truth that Africa is still used as a testing ground, with a complete disregard for ethics or patient safety.'

'African lives are disposable lives, you mean,' Lily says, 'and we the Africans get screwed over every single time.'

'Sadly, yes.'

'Do you have any record of a medical trial out here in 1987?'

'I had a look for you, but there's nothing recorded from that time. We were less established back then, just a bunch of disorganised hippies raging against the machine! And a country like Senegal was the Wild West for clinical trials.'

'Is there anything at all that might be relevant?'

Renata nods. 'I did find something interesting. There's a

company, Sedaxo, the Senegalese partner of a British pharmaceutical company called Atlantis Pharmaceuticals – they've been researching anti-malarial drugs for the last two decades, funded by the British government, interestingly. Atlantis also produces one of the highest selling malaria medicines for adults, Timberulone, marketed as Durastan 1. Global sales of Durastan 1 amount to around three billion euros a year.'

Mia and Piretta come up, laughing and panting. Together, they troop inside the house to find water, spilling out again still laughing to continue their game.

'Sorry,' says Lily to the screen. 'Go on.'

'You don't need to apologise,' Renata says. 'Over twenty years ago, Atlantis created a drug that's been in phase two trials for years, called Aspiximal, registered under the name Byotec in the UK – an anti-malarial using elements of Durastan 1 that was developed originally by medical researchers at the London School of Tropical Medicine, and sponsored by Atlantis. We got a report in 2009 that clinical trials were being conducted by Sedaxo on children aged up to ten years old in rural and urban Senegal.'

'What happened?'

'The children in the trials were showing terrible side effects – loss of nails, eye problems, bleeding, inflammation of the airways. A child died. Others must have been simply terrified. The trials were hushed up, people were told their children got ill from meningitis. Everything went quiet for a while. Then they went big. You might have seen the reports in the press recently – look them up – heralding a game-changer drug for preventing malarial sickness in children. And it *is* a breakthrough – if it weren't for the years of hidden human cost behind the scenes.'

Lily sighs. Children like her own, dead for nothing but a quest for power and money. Such a casual waste of human life, as if those small lives hadn't mattered at all.

'So you think it could have been the same drug being tested in Ngor thirty years ago?'

Renata nods. 'It could have been, yes. Sedaxo's been on our radar for a while. Aspiximal was always Atlantis's baby, and it's making them billions now, as well as defining them as the world's new humanitarians – which will only get them tons more business. No wonder they were willing to kill kids.'

'Scumbags.' Lily draws in a breath. 'Criminals.'

'And it's still happening, Lily, no doubt of that,' adds Renata. 'Whether the world gives a shit is an entirely different matter.'

In Lily's email inbox looms another message from Vivienne Hughes. For some reason, Lily finds herself dreading what's inside. So she reads hesitantly, wondering what she will find:

Memoir, Part Five

Dakar Dakar Dakar! That rolling cry of a *car rapide* barrelling down the road, its teenage bus conductor hanging out the back and chanting like a prayer, *cent francs, cent francs, cent francs*, is one of my first memories of that hot, dusty, wonderful city.

Imagine.

Scrambling into the back of a battered old minibus and handing over my hundred CFA coin. I'm not the British ambassador's wife but a young girl of twenty-four, adventuring in an African city, having the time of her life. No one has any idea.

But that happens only after a few months, once I've found my feet and persuaded John that it's safe for me to take public transport. Before that, I travel by chauffeured car, as becomes the wife of the British Ambassador, and this is how I arrive in Ngor village for the very first time, on a Wednesday afternoon in early January, the middle of the dry season – in a shiny, silver-grey Citroën DS with diplomatic plates and a small English flag waving on the bonnet, driven by Lamin, my personal embassy driver.

You may laugh, because yes, I'm conspicuous, and no, I'm not comfortable with it. I feel ridiculous. This life of diplomatic pomp and circumstance is something it will take me a very, very long time to get used to.

And then the section ends abruptly. Lily scrolls down, searching for more, but there's nothing – and anyway, why on earth would Vivienne send her a section of memoir, randomly it seems, that's dated before the accident? Puzzled, Lily checks the email again – perhaps the file is corrupted? – but the attachment is the same, a few paragraphs on a blank page. Lily gets up from the table and goes outside. At the end of the courtyard, Mia and Piretta are flopped in the shadow of the tall palm, reading.

'Come on,' Lily says, wiping her eyes with a hand, 'get yourselves ready.'

The girls grumble and get up. The sky is overcast, the city's humidity higher than usual as the season is beginning to change. Beads of sweat spring up on Lily's forehead and upper lip. She can hear the sounds of the village outside, where a cockerel crows with insistence. Beyond the wall, a gaggle of kids chatter as they pass the compound, and the ever-present hammering of ongoing construction in the village.

On Lily's phone comes a text message. It is from Vivienne Hughes: *Let me know what you found out. Speak later x.*

But to Vivienne, Lily makes no mention of her discovery the day before. Not yet, she tells herself. Besides, what's with the kiss?

Vivienne Hughes, Lily is convinced, is still hiding something. So far she has failed to get to the bottom of the other woman's side of the story. Lily mulls over what Renata has told her. Aspiximal. The name rings a bell, niggling at the back of her brain. Where has she heard it before?

To the girls, Lily calls out again, 'Five minutes, and we're out of here!'

'Oh, Mummy,' Mia calls back regretfully, 'we're playing!' After a minute she comes running, draping her arms around Lily's neck.

'Where we going, Mummy?'

'On an adventure.'

'An adventure?' Mia comes up. 'What sort, Mummy?'

'A spy adventure,' Lily says. 'We're the spies, and we have to find something out.'

'Can I bring my magnifying glass?'

'Better do,' says Lily with a wink. 'You may need it.'

The village of Keur Samma is an hour and a half out of Dakar. While the girls bicker in the backseat Lily hums along to the radio – Viviane's new release, then the reggae beats of Jah Moko – and negotiates the many potholes of the bush road inland that goes up to St Prince. She keeps the car windows down, an influx of air that freshens the burgeoning heat as the coastal road turns into rust-hued plains edged with forest and swampy ponds. Eventually, a somewhat ramshackle settlement straggling along the edges of the road comes into view.

What a God-forsaken place, thinks Lily, staring through the windscreen, yet Bibi's tip-off is enough to merit the journey.

Lily parks the Citroën up in the reddish dust, turns off the engine, climbs out of the car where the heat hits her with a punch, taking her breath away. Here inland, the heat is more intense, and Lily is unused to its weight, its force and stillness after the refreshing maritime climate of Dakar. Out here, in the hot season, there is a complete absence of breeze to cool things down. In the rainy season, everything turns to mud. How on earth do country people bear it?

Lily ushers the girls out of the back of the car, and from her backpack issues them with litre bottles of water, sunhats, factor-fifty sun cream. A series of low buildings line the road. Outside one, dozens of packets of Kirène mineral water are stacked high in the hot sun outside. A boutique advertises mobile phone equipment. A fruit stall shaded with a stripy umbrella is piled with variably sized orange papayas. A mosque. In the near distance, a brand-new looking Esso petrol station.

'I'm too hot,' says Piretta miserably, taking Lily's hand. Mia clasps the other. Together the three of them trudge towards the grocery store as a motorcycle roars past, kicking up a cloud of dust.

In the coolish interior of the shop, a shopkeeper in a blue *djellaba* and skullcap skulks in the dark space behind the counter. Lily buys three bread rolls from the glass vessel on the counter, counts out four thousand notes, and gives them to the man, who fumbles about for change with all the dismay and bafflement, thinks Lily as she watches him, of a drowning man searching for the nearest land. His expression turns to blankness when Lily enquires about Aminata Fall.

'Can't help you,' he shrugs, flicking away a fly with a plastic flyswat. 'Ask around. Someone might know, *inshallah*.'

'Come on,' Lily says to the girls, abandoning the quest for change, handing out the rolls, 'let's walk up here.'

But Mia wrenches her hand away, holding the roll with her teeth, extracting a colouring pen and notepad from a Barbie-patterned bag strapped across her chest.

'What's up, *chérie*?'

'You said to take notes of our location,' Mia says with her mouth full. 'Silly! That's what all spies do.'

'Oh, come *on*, Mi,' exclaims Piretta in an exasperated voice, 'it's really hot and Mummy's in a hurry!'

A cluster of motorbikes beneath a tarpaulin shelter strung between two trees. A boy in blue overalls is crouched by one of them, tapping at the exhaust pipe with a spanner. When they approach, he looks up, wiping oily hands on his overalls. Lily specifies the name, mentions the midwife, and the boy gestures towards the mosque.

'Over there,' he says, pointing with his head, 'past the petrol station.' He goes back to his fixing.

'*Merci*,' chorus the girls.

Some way past the Esso garage, the shack is brick-built with a corrugated-iron roof. Three or four skinny chickens peck the dust. The compound has a dirty feel of rank poverty, thinks Lily, of abjection, of hardship. Patches of oily sand are scattered with bits of discarded food, grains of rice, a stray fish head. There is the spiky buzzing sound of horseflies. Mia and Piretta have gone quiet, staring. Lily grips their small, sweaty hands, sweat pouring down her own back, feeling all of a sudden boiling hot, and overwhelmed. But in truth, isn't this reality? While her own children live a life of so much privilege, of readily available food and private school, this world remains, this Senegal of poor people surviving against the odds.

Why in God's name has she brought them here? Even so, it is good for her daughters to see this other existence, Lily is thinking, which is, in its own way, an education. Good for them to see how lucky they are and where hard study and hard work can get them, can get all women!

A teenage girl in a tight T-shirt and patterned wrapper, baby tied to her back, sweeps the sand with languid movements. The girl stops sweeping and puts her hand on hip, eying them with suspicion. When Lily asks about Aminata Fall, the girl kisses her teeth and throws them a sullen look. Then, with slow steps of her rubber flip-flops leads them around the back of the dwelling, where a woman in a shabby cloth wrap is chopping potatoes into a metal cooking pot. A cooking fire crackles nearby.

The girl flicks her hand, sauntering away as the brown-eyed baby stares.

'You're Aminata Fall?' says Lily.

The woman shakes her head. 'Ami isn't here. She's at the hospital.'

'Where's that?

'No hospital here,' says the woman. 'The next town. Bambara.'

It takes fifteen minutes to reach the hospital. Lily drives

quickly, using the accelerator to overtake an overloaded bus straining with passengers and livestock. As they pass, it jangles its horn, whether to congratulate or admonish her, Lily isn't sure. From the backseat comes the peaceful swish swish of Mia's colouring pens. Piretta is listening to music on her phone through headphones, which emit a low, tuneless hum. The moving air through the windows is pleasurably welcome. Lily flaps her top, feeling the freshness of the moving air soothe her overheated skin.

The hospital is a shabby, white-plastered building fenced with barbed wire. Outside, a decrepit sign reads: *Clinique Pasteur de Bambara*. Inside a foyer, a woman seated at a desk behind glass shakes her head, tutting and waving her finger at the two girls.

'You'll have to stay here, my sweets,' Lily says to the girls, dropping her backpack on the floor. 'Water and snacks are in there. I won't be long.'

Lily asks for chairs, sends the girls to help the receptionist shift them nearer the desk. She instructs her daughters to wait, at which they sit nicely with a vague look of disorientation, clutching at their water bottles.

'I'll be ten minutes max,' Lily reassures them. 'Here, have some biscuits. Piretta, why don't you help Mia write her notes about the journey?'

Piretta groans. 'It's too hot to do anything, Mummy. When can we go home?'

'Be good, darlings.'

The receptionist waves at Lily to follow. They wind their way through the corridors; Lily notes the rough concrete walls stained with age and other inexplicable fluids, extending into wards labelled *Emergences, Chirurgie, Maternité.*

The maternity ward is a low, dingy, stiflingly hot building at the far end of the hospital site. Around fifteen women occupy beds without curtains. Some of them are curled asleep or breast-feeding; some of them sit up, holding their babies. Two women have drips attached to their arms. One stares, following Lily with her gaze. There is a hush and bustle of a women's world about the place, the intimate warfare of childbirth and new life. A baby begins to cry and the high, sharp shrill cry of a newborn child fills the ward.

'Can I help you?' says a woman in neat blue scrubs and a plastic head wrap standing by one of the occupied beds, perusing a clipboard of notes. She is in her sixties, Lily estimates, with a distinct air of authority, large-bosomed and pleasingly maternal, with an appealing round face and shiny skin, wearing an old-fashioned white nurse's apron embroidered with a red cross, fob watch clipped to the pocket. Lily notices how clean the woman's hands are, nails pristine and pink, uniform spotless. She seems to radiate a serene sense of calm.

'*Asalaam alaykum,*' Lily says, offering her name and a brief explanation of who she is. Aminata says nothing, but hands the notes to her colleague and murmurs something in Wolof. The other nurse nods, then begins attaching a blood pressure band to the arm of the woman in the bed.

'Five minutes,' Aminata says abruptly to Lily. 'That's all I've got.' At the open ward she waves a hand. 'These babies don't feed themselves.'

As they pass through reception, Mia and Piretta are still sitting obediently in the provided chairs, munching from mini packets of biscuits.

'These are your daughters?' says Aminata in a warmer voice than before.

'Yes.'

'Come,' says the midwife to the girls, 'you should be near your mama.'

Outside they seat themselves on a low brick wall in the shade of a mango tree. Lily glances at her watch: half-past one. In the relative cool, the raging midday heat is less intense, less searing. From the backpack, Lily distributes water and peanuts. The two girls crouch in the sand in the deep shade near the tree trunk, devising a game of *kapo* with the nuts.

'You lost a child, years ago,' asks Lily. 'Aminata, do you mind telling me about it?'

'It's Ami,' she says, unscrewing the lid of the water bottle, and swigging from it. 'Why do you want to know about such things? It's a time I try to forget.'

'My brother died in an accident – or so they say. I'm trying to find out the truth. Someone told me there were children who died too, other kids who died.'

Ami sighs. 'I see.' She puts down the water bottle and reaches into the pocket of her apron, extracts an ageing leather purse, draws out a small passport-sized photograph and hands it to Lily.

'Her name was Coco.' Ami smiles. 'Like the fruit.'

'She's so beautiful.'

A pause, but Lily does not speak further, letting Ami talk. 'People thought I was crazy,' continues Ami. 'Too modern, they said, calling your little one after a coconut! Now all the mums want new-fangled names for their babies.'

246

'It was a few days after Coco's first birthday. The British came to visit us at the hospital, asking for volunteers.' Ami falls silent, then exhales before continuing. 'They offered money, more than I'd ever imagined existed. I was a poor girl, a young widow with a newborn baby. What else could I do?'

'What happened then?' says Lily softly.

'Coco died three weeks after they gave her the drug. They told me it was meningitis.'

'Was there any record of this, any sort of report?'

'Not even a death certificate.' Ami turns to face Lily, eyes bright with anger. 'It was like my baby never existed.'

'Do you remember the name of the drug they gave Coco?'

Ami shakes her head. 'It must have been on the paperwork, but as I say, I threw it away.'

'Does Aspiximal ring any bells?

'I'm sorry.' Ami thinks, then shakes her head. 'It was a long time ago.'

The two women are silent. In the leaves above, a group of miniscule birds emit high-pitched, noisy chirps as they swoop in and out. In the kerfuffle, the moving branches of the tree send dappled sun shadows dancing across the two children, who have moved on from the peanut game and are restlessly making shapes in the sand with the toes of their trainers, a circle, a square, a heart. Then their own two forenames: MIA, PIRETTA.

With their feet, they swipe the letters away and start again. Lily watches her daughters and the sand drawings come and go, stretches out her legs, gathers her thoughts.

'Do you remember anything,' Lily asks, 'about the British people who came that day? What they looked like? Any details?'

Ami thinks for a few seconds. 'There were three of them. There was a white man, a white doctor. The other man was black, a doctor, I think; he wore a white coat.'

'Okay,' Lily takes notes in her head. 'Anyone else?'

'There was a woman.'

'A woman?'

'Yes,' Ami nods. 'Very young, very pretty – like a model. I've never seen a white woman like that before.'

A slow dawning.

'Who administered the drug?'

'The white doctor. Afterwards, the woman helped soothe my baby. She was kind, I remember.'

Lily gives a sharp intake of breath, and stands up, pacing the sand.

'Would you be willing to stand in court and say this?' Lily looks at Ami's face. All trace of Ami's previous emotion is gone, replaced by cool serenity.

'Of course,' says Ami. 'There were other children, other babies. We were *des cobayes*. That's what people said.'

'Your babies were human guinea pigs,' says Lily firmly, 'and what those people did was evil.'

Hands on her hips, she stands still, gazing up into the dark and light underbelly of the tree. So it was Vivienne Hughes, then, with her husband, John Hughes, or the doctor guy, Harris? And Aimé, Lily's brother. But why? Aimé was a good man, a good doctor. Of this, Lily is certain.

Lily sits down again on the wall. 'Did no one do anything?'

Ami shakes her head. 'I went to the police, but they threatened to arrest me. Told me to shut up, and that was it. The doctors gave money to the village, you see. People profited. So I've grieved in silence all these years.'

Lily can feel Ami's eyes on her, can feel the woman's flourishing hope that someone, finally, will hear her pain. She takes a deep breath to cool down her own anger and glances over at Mia and Piretta, now sitting with backs against the tree trunk. The knees of their stretched-out legs are dusted with red earth. Here, Lily thinks, here in this God forsaken place, it is as though nothing ever happened. As if here in the back of beyond of Africa, a single lost human life doesn't even matter. A baby girl's name swiped away, just like that. Past wrongs, past tragedy, smoothed over and buried like shapes in the sand. How could that be tolerable by any normal human morality?

Is she foolish to take all this on? Is the idea that she can finally get justice for these wronged mothers and children simple recklessness?

'You'll go to court, then?' says Ami.

'It's dangerous, but yes, that's the plan.' Lily swigs at the water, gestures at her daughters about their imminent departure, stands up, and hoists her backpack over one shoulder. 'This should never be allowed to happen to another child.'

The girls trudge over, looking tired and hot. Lily slips her other arm through the second strap of the bag and takes their hands, one in her right, one in her left, feeling the familiar sensation of her children's small, warm palms in her own. A sensation of safety, of love, that gives rise to a fierce, almost painful urge to protect them, at all costs. How unimaginable, to lose a child.

As Ami gets up, Lily glimpses an amulet on her wrist, just like her own mother's. In a flash, it comes to her, the thought that has been niggling at her since the morning.

Lily recalls now that in Rose's belongings there was a drugs packet, random, as she'd thought then, a piece of rubbish somehow caught up with her mother's memorabilia. But Rose had the packet saved on purpose, it dawns on Lily now with a flush of realisation. She's certain, too, that if she looks at it, the name of the packet will be Aspiximal.

'Come,' Lily says to Ami, 'you need to get back to your babies.'

CHAPTER TWENTY-ONE

Vivienne

Patrick Brown is as good as his word. Two days later, a package from Scotland arrives at Moon Manor by next-day delivery, just as the boy had promised. Slitting open the sellotaped envelope with a kitchen knife, Viv almost feels sorry. Bless, she thinks; such blind good faith the boy has, and all for nothing. *Tant pis*, as the French would say. Life could be cruel, that's for sure.

And later, Viv stands at the window of the lounge with the contents of the envelope in her hand, listening to Big Ben's bongs from the kitchen radio announce the nine o'clock morning news. The day has dawned reluctantly, the sun invisible behind greyish skies.

Quite unlike the skies of Africa, Viv broods, struck by a memory of Dakar's bright blue coastal vistas. Of the flat-roofed, white-painted buildings spilling down to the jagged curves of the city's corniche. Of the piercing blue of the restless ocean matching the hot sky. For a moment, Viv is transported. She used to love peering down as the plane circled above the city, wondering what creatures caused the cascades of white foam on the ocean's surface, for all the world as though some dolphin or shark or porpoise played beneath.

How Viv had loved Dakar from the very minute she laid eyes on that westernmost fragment of Africa jutting into the great Atlantic. January 1986, and everything slotted into place, thank goodness. At that point, John had no idea that, as far as Viv was concerned, his diplomatic status had sealed the deal. She'd known she must get a wedding ring on her finger ASAP, given that the field of tropical diseases had long been her passion. Without John, well – it would've all gone tits up. But what a mistake it turned out to be…

Tuberculosis, Ebola, malaria, these were Viv's specialisms. In the third year of her Oxford degree, a secondment had taken her to the London School of Tropical Medicine, where a project in the field of malaria was focusing on new routes to developing a vaccine.

Back then, Dr Harris Burns was just plain old Harris, fresh from his PhD. Six years older than her, attractive, seemingly kind.

For those few short months, they were together in the lab almost constantly, during which time Harris took the opportunity to flirt outrageously until she succumbed to his charms. Later, Harris became terribly eminent, a malaria specialist heading up the tropical medicine department at Oxford, but when she first met him in 1983, oh heavens, Harris Burns was just a horny young doctor with a whip smart wit that made her laugh – and a raging sex addiction, or so she suspected.

Harris.

'Ugh,' Viv groans out loud. In some ways he'd been the most awful creep. She remembers the way he confused her with his own particular brand of humour, kindness, cleverness, and cruelty. A narcissist, by all accounts, just like John. At first, Harris couldn't do enough for her, and then… She was too sensitive, too boring, too apologetic. Too everything. She was like a frog being slowly boiled, as she recalls; at least that's how she understands it now after researching the matter on various internet forums. If you put a frog straight in boiling water, it would jump straight out, explain the online experts. But slowly increase the temperature, and the frog will passively stay there, to the point of death.

No wonder John had seemed another angel – at first.

Viv shivers. Who was it who told her recently that the internet frog theory isn't true? Frogs will try to jump out – or simply die right away in boiling water.

'Bastards!' she exclaims out loud.

She goes to the kitchen, switches off the radio, boils the kettle. Outside, a darkening sky heralds rain. A few drops patter on the window glass. Viv selects a herbal teabag called Serenity – with liquorice root and chamomile, the paper cover declares, for calmness and purity. Ha! While she waits for the kettle, she takes a packet of rice cakes from the cupboard. One by one, she butters four rounds of the dehydrated grains, then puts them on a plate. Into a mug, she pours water and stirs the hot drink, letting it brew, lost in thought as she carries her elevenses to the table.

She was so young, so naïve. As clear as yesterday, she remembers Harris's hard, athletic body, the way his roughish hands explored her skin – he was a good lover, methodical and focused, though she sensed the darkness in him, whether depression or a personality disorder, she wasn't sure. He seemed to veer between a sort of giddy flippancy and black desolation; after the first few times they went to bed, he showed himself to be cruel, heartless even, and she considered walking away. But she enjoyed the work. Despite herself, she continued to sleep with him.

Viv munches on a rice cake, but finds she has no appetite, so instead she sips the herbal tea, and sighs. That was all before disaster struck, and boom, when it came, it really didn't hold back, as she remembers. Poverty was quick and without sugar-coating. Mum's inheritance was needed to pay off the soaring debts she had acquired in old-age, and Viv was left with nothing.

She left Oxford, but Harris, in a burst of emotion, said he didn't want to lose her.

'Sod all those boring old academics, Viv,' he'd joked when she finally told him what had happened. 'Come and work for me in the real world. That's where we make real changes happen. Besides,' he'd added, grinning and straying his hand round her waist, twirling her around, squeezing her backside, 'you make my lab look infinitely prettier.'

So she volunteered at his lab while he was trying to get the drug side of his malaria research funded – in which case he'd give her a job, he promised. The pharmaceuticals company was called Atlantis. It was her one chance to continue in medicine. Presumably Harris knew she had the brains, and what was a degree but a piece of paper, after all?

'We're nearly there with it, Viv,' he used to tell her. 'If I can get this off the ground, it'll be a fucking breakthrough! A vaccine for malaria, Viv, just imagine!'

Anyway, according to Harris, Viv was five times more intel-ligent than any of his actual tutorial students. What did he used to say, in his kinder moments? Your eyes of blue steel... Brains and beauty, the whole package. Cheesy, but in those days she was all too flattered, all too easily manipulated with empty compliments.

And his offer? Well, it was a no-brainer, or so she thought.

Viv sips her tea and munches a rice cake, her mind returning to those days before Senegal.

In desperation, she'd taken the escort gig for a few months to make some cash, and lo and behold, John popped up with an offer of marriage, thank God.

And Harris stuck to his word. The funding for Aspiximal finally came through from Atlantis, and Senegal was suggested for the field trials, so that Viv could run the operation *sotto voce*, as it were.

She even went with Harris to the final meeting with the bigwigs at Atlantis, as his research assistant, or so he told them.

'The people are hungry,' Viv remembers the CEO, Charles somebody, saying in a grave voice during their face-to-face. 'The harvest's failing, and people need money, which sure as hell makes our job easier.'

Another memory on the back of the last. Harris ranting, over and over, about changing the world and making a difference.

'We're saving lives!' he'd lecture her. 'We're these people's saviours! Who else is going to help the poor sods? I'm not going to let anyone stand in my fucking way!'

She hadn't thought to question Harris's assurances that the drug trials were for the greater good, or that Aspiximal only needed to jump the last hurdle to approval.

And so in Ngor, she and Aimé had been carried away on a wave of idealism. Together, they'd busied themselves finding families and organising numerous junior subjects for the trials, convinced they were taking part in something big, something *important*.

It's why Viv persuaded John to get Harris out to Senegal quick-sharp when, out of the blue, the LSTM stopped funding the other branches of the doctor's research – something about ethical standards not being met.

Lord, she remembers as clear as yesterday how she pleaded with John, how she lectured him about their duty as white people to save the children of Senegal.

Caught up in the passion of what had by then become *her fight*, it was she who had introduced Aimé to Harris, she who had pushed to make sure the trials for Aspiximal got off the ground.

It was she herself who had made sure Aimé got involved in the trials from the beginning, so as to help him further his career as a doctor.

By that time, John had no choice but to get on board. As the British ambassador, he was the last person who could be seen to be blocking important medical advancements.

And Harris, in his customary way, made it clear that he'd oust John as a child molester if he said anything against the trials. In fact, Harris asked John for money. It wasn't blackmail exactly, as much as a backhander.

An amuse bouche, as Harris put it.

When, thanks to John's diplomatic status and her own strategic proposals, Atlantis signed off funding for the full costs of Harris's clinical trial of Aspiximal in the villages of Ngor and Keur Samma, Viv found herself hugging nearly-doctor Aimé Tunkara, the two of them caught up in their own idealistic dreams of eliminating malaria altogether, in Senegal and all of Africa.

Viv pushes away the plate of rice cakes, appetite gone. She feels a small explosion of fury somewhere in her chest. If she hadn't married John, if she hadn't gone to Senegal, Aimé Tunkara would be alive now. Why the fuck hasn't she done something before?

She takes a breath and closes her eyes. Lies. Conspiracy. Now, all she needs is the truth, however hard it is to confront.

'Alexa,' Viv says a short while later, 'find taxis to Heathrow for Sunday.'

'Taxis to Heathrow,' comes the smooth electronic voice, seemingly unfazed by any request. 'Sundale Cars, Abbotsbury—'

'Alexa, should I stay or should I go?' Viv smiles, cocking an ear to listen. It amuses her, to play like this with the machine, whose response is quite unruffled.

'Alexa does not understand—'

'Oh, fuck off Alexa,' Viv retorts.

Into the taxi's website, Viv enters her debit card, then the details of her diplomatic passport. The flight ticket, she prints and files. She goes upstairs to pack a suitcase, which is quickly done: a few hot weather outfits, make-up, swimwear, sun cream.

Upstairs, she calls M from her mobile.

'Please,' she says when he answers. She can hear him drawing breath, calculating consequences in his head. 'Tell me what you know, M, and I promise I'll never bother you again.'

In the sunroom studio, suffused this afternoon with light despite the dreary weather, Viv wets a brush and squeezes paints to the palette, adding turpentine, absorbing herself in applying colour to the canvas she started weeks ago. For an hour or two she sits filling in the detail, but when she stands and moves back several paces from her creation, she feels as if she is waking from a dream.

For the finished painting on the easel is not Moon Manor, nor the surrounding coast; in fact it is not even England. No, not at all. The canvas Viv has painted depicts quite a different scene: of a bay, purest blue-green, of a curve of sand the shade of palest sugar. Of changing light and heat and sunshine that brings to mind the tropics. And with blurry brushstrokes of an impressionistic style, a pair of figures who challenge the perceptions; are they a man and a woman, black or white? Whatever, they are smiling.

Vivienne stands by the bonfire watching a curl of smoke rise into the dingy afternoon sky. The rain has stopped, though it is the wrong weather for a fire and the kindling she collected earlier is damp, creating flames that sputter, pop and smoke. Beyond the rectangle of exposed shore opposite, the sea horizon blends with the sky. All around is never-ending flatness, broken only by the swans taking off and landing at intervals on the unstirring expanse of water between the mainland and the spit.

Viv begins throwing pages on the flames, first messages and faxes dating back decades; records fastidiously filed away, page by page, of names, of dates, of medical details. Of the exact doses of Aspiximal that were administered to children aged newborn to eighteen years old in 1987. Of the so-called consent forms in English, ticked and signed – in their way – by parents who, if not illiterate, did not speak, let alone read English. Of the gradual trickle of the clinical trial results, data showing numerous debilitating side-effects including fits, stuttering, blindness, paralysis – and death.

After all, thinks Viv with a heavy heart, isn't she only doing what is right?

The papers curl and go brown, rearing up before falling to ash. Viv's thoughts wander to their source, to the village of Ngor and the children there. How she was pushed and pulled between Aimé with his high ideals and Harris, blasted Harris, who she knew by then would stop at nothing. Nothing.

Aimé had searched out the kids and their families to take part in the trials, and Viv organised the forms. She or Harris administered the drug. Simple.

They'd thought they were doing good. Aimé was her *friend*. Viv ponders this for a few moments, feeling a sort of spiky pain in her chest where the bubble is as she allows the memory to rise and take shape once and for all. She exhales, closing her eyes and lifting her face to the sky. For so long, she has suppressed the memory.

'Aimé,' Viv whispers.

She feels tears prick at her eyes, and blinks them away.

The first time one of the trial children showed a minor side effect that was a bit off, Viv could sense Aimé's brain mulling over the information, forming questions and suspicions which he brought to Harris with a sort of blind innocent faith that the English doctor would do something about it. Truth be told, she'd had the same questions, but the trouble was, questions put everyone in danger.

'Lord,' says Viv aloud.

How is Viv, then, to look into Lily Tunkara's beautiful brown eyes and tell her the truth about herself? What will Lily say once she knows how inhumane she is, how cold, how calculating?

The fire sputters. Onto the flames, Viv throws the rest of the papers, the bank statements recording years of regular payments between John Hughes and Harris Burns, payments running from the eighties to the present day.

'Ugh,' Viv exclaims, chucking the papers on to the flames with wide motions of her hands. 'Good riddance, good *riddance*!'

Thank God, she is thinking, because this is everything that John covered up so well, with M's help, of course. John panicking, running around, making sure everything was watertight. Acting like a weasel running from a trap.

Poor John: for once, it wasn't his fault.

Finally, Viv takes the envelope sent by Patrick Brown and extracts the file from the interior. She thinks of the loose threads she still needs to tie up if she is to cover her tracks completely. Just a couple to deal with now. Just a couple and then it will be over. Viv flings the file on the flames and watches it shrivel to ash.

All of a sudden, the wind gets up. The fire dwindles and cringes. Viv stands tall and straight against the grey sky, as poised as a ballet dancer. As if on cue, it begins to rain. The dying flames crackle and pop. The last shreds of paper curl red then yellow then brown, and disappear.

Back inside, Viv watches from the sunroom as rain thunders on the windows, sending rivulets of water streaming down the glass. She observes her painting drying on the easel, its summery colours vivid against the stormy skies, considering all the aspects of the scene that she cannot paint, but which are, in her memory, as vivid as yesterday: the safe feeling of his arm around her shoulders, the salt streaking his skin, the tiny crinkles around his eyes as he collapsed into full-throated laughter. And his teasing: *you'll be the first ambassador's wife in history ever to use a spear gun...*

Another life, another time, bright as the sun, before reality came and ripped them apart.

'Aimé,' Viv whispers, feeling a huge, terrible starburst of grief erupt in her chest.

CHAPTER TWENTY-TWO

Lily

In the Tropical Dream ice-cream parlour on Mutsaka Road, the girls have persuaded Lily to buy them sundaes. 'A reward for being good, Mummy,' they had pestered in the car on the way back, 'because waiting for you was soooo boring!'

'One mango surprise, two hot fudges,' Lily says to the waitress, her mind veering off at a tangent as to the correct grammatical use of fudge – singular, plural? The construction bothers her.

She extracts a packet of baby wipes from her bag, wipes the girls' palms of accumulated dust and sweat. A soccer match is playing on TV. The score is two-nil, according to the ticker: Guinea v Cameroon. A goal is scored. A player in an acid-green kit does a turn of the pitch, arm thrust in a superhero stance. Another forms a heart gesture with his fingers at the camera.

'Why,' says Mia, chin in hand as she squirms in her chair, 'are people made?'

Adjusting her chair, Lily draws a breath, recalling a parenting article she read online about the importance of being honest when it came to one's offspring's natural curiosity about reproductive matters. 'Because, darling, their mummies and daddies love each other,' Lily offers, brushing the child's cheek with her fingers, 'and want a baby.'

'By kissing,' Piretta adds, giggling, pursing her lips and making smoochy sounds.

'Don't confuse your sister,' says Lily, flapping her hand at the older girl. 'Think of it as people are created from love,' continues Lily, refusing to be blindsided. 'Why do *you* think they're made, *ma chérie*?' A pause. Lily watches Mia's face as her childish brain processes the information at hand.

'Because they're wanted,' the child says eventually. 'Like you wanted me, and Pi, soooo much.'

Lily laughs at the echo of her own much-used endearment. 'Yes, just like that,' she agrees.

When the ice creams arrive, lemon-bright, dripping with canned cream and synthetic-looking cherries, fudge sauce and chunks of fruit, Lily sits watching her children hungrily scoop the sweet concoctions into their mouths. How such small human beings are capable of eating so much, she really does not know! Lily's mind drifts elsewhere, to Aminata Fall and the story of her dead baby, to all the broken parents and their lost children who would never know the pleasures of ice cream or spy adventures. Parents for whom the easy-come happiness of her own privileged life is beyond comprehension.

Given that Lily herself has been fortunate, more than fortunate, she has to remind herself of her roots sometimes. As a successful woman now defined by the benefits of an education and a high-flying career in law, it's too easy to forget that her own mother sold powdered baobab and dried *bissap* flowers in the market. That Papa fished for a living before he died in a pirogue accident at sea. That the Tunkaras, too, were a family who struggled – until, that is, a son died.

Their son.

If it hadn't been for Aimé, Lily herself would be no better off than any Senegalese parent struggling to pay their child's secondary school fees, food, uniforms, bus fare. She does not care to call that luck. The awful reality is that her whole life has been fuelled by white money, white mistakes, and *toubab* privilege. The thought is humbling. Despite her children's easy chatter, a cloud falls over Lily, at the wrong of it, at the injustice, at the helplessness of her own people in the face of a bunch of powerful foreign doctors.

In her line of vision, Lily sees a young woman approach the counter. She is slim in a traditionally patterned dress, shapely ankles emerging from expensive-looking heels. Familiar-looking, even from behind. When the woman turns, she is holding a pistachio cone in dazzlingly manicured fingers.

The new secretary from work, Déstine Fall.

Lily's heart stutters as the young woman nods and smiles in her direction, a strange smile, thinks Lily, like a cat who got the cream. She watches Déstine leave the shop, and pushes her ice cream away, appetite gone. When she thinks back to that day she saw Demba with his mistress it seems unreal, like some sort of apocalyptic dream. And now, and now… She pushes the thought away. Dry-mouthed, she feels a fury rise from her belly, more profound than ever before, a deep-seated anger telling her that now it is time to fight this fight – for the parents of Ngor, for Senegal, for Africa that has been screwed over by the West for

264

far too long. She is set, clear-sighted.

Collate the evidence, Lily tells herself, and go to war.

When they get home, Mia and Piretta, sugar-dazed, glue themselves to Netflix and a programme featuring a strange boy-man dressed in clown clothes called Blippi. Lily makes her way upstairs and brings down the box of Rose's belongings from the top of the wardrobe. She rummages through for the medication packet, knowing what the brand name on the front will say even before she finds it: Aspiximal.

Lily stares at the name, running over the facts in her mind. Was it possible that Aimé had confided in Rose, then? Why else would their mother have kept this particular box of medicine? Her brother was getting close, that much is certain, and presumably he was on the point of going to who – the authorities, some sort of responsible European NGO? – but decided the possibility of a bit more cash was worth a try. Aimé, Lily imagines, no, she *knows*, was a man of high ideals – a clever man weighing up his options, walking the tightrope between a desire for the medical prowess of launching a new malaria breakthrough and his own steady sense of morality. For God's sake, why hadn't someone thought to protect him!

Downstairs Lily adds the medicine packet, now hard evidence, into the file of her documents on Aimé's case. While the girls are quiet, she fetches a pen and spends the best part of an hour writing notes in a hardback pad she uses for work, detailing by hand her interviews with Aminata Fall, with Renata, with the family of Oumar Sy.

After a time, Lily keys Lion's number into her cell phone. Lion answers with a smile in his voice. If he is surprised at Lily's call, he does not give a hint of it.

'Want to go for that coffee?' he says, hopefully.

'Not exactly.' Lily fills him in briefly as to what she has found. 'Do you think your parents would give evidence about what happened to Maria,' she asks, 'if there was a possibility of compensation?'

'Sure,' Lion says. 'If there was money involved, then yes, of course.'

'Okay, I'll come round later, *inshallah*, to talk to them.' Then: 'You should prepare them,' she adds, as an afterthought, 'I don't want them to be upset by my questions.'

'Sure.' Lion sounds hesitant. 'Sure I will, Lily.'

Lily rings off, turns back to the notepad, deep in thought. After a while, she leafs through the pages, reading back the scribblings she has recorded.

Late in the afternoon, nearly half-past five, and there is a knock at the front door. It is Uncle Musa.

'*Asalaam alaykum*,' he greets, '*naga def.*'

Lily is aware of the case notes lying open on the kitchen table. She does not want her uncle to see them, and she tries not to look surprised.

'*Mangi ferek*,' she says. 'Come in. Do you want some water?'

'No thanks,' Musa shakes his head. 'I'm fasting.'

'Oh sure, sorry.'

Leading Musa into the kitchen, Lily turns the notebook on its front. In silence, she sits down at the table. Musa draws up a chair and sits down.

'So what do you want?' Lily says. 'Forgive me, but it's not

like you to visit.'

'I heard you spoke to Jawara Niang, and Bibi Sy.'

'How did you find out?'

Musa gives a thin smile. 'People talk.'

'I've been getting threats, texts. Is it you?'

Musa kisses his teeth. 'I told you the village wouldn't like you lifting up old stones.'

Mia comes in asking for a drink, climbs onto Musa's lap. For a few minutes, the uncle and his great niece talk about nothing in particular. Mia picks up the notepad from the table.

'What's As… As-pix-i-mal?' Mia says, spelling out the phonics.

Hurriedly, Lily takes the notepad from her and puts it on the side.

'That's mummy's.'

'Is it,' Mia adds, 'to do with the lady you talk to on the computer?'

Musa's face is without expression.

'It's none of your business, cheeky,' says Lily, making a joke of it.

'But you told me we were spies, Mummy. I made notes.'

Lily picks Mia up, nuzzles her face with kisses. The child clings to her, wrapping her legs around Lily's waist, pressing her cheek against her right shoulder.

'Good girl, *ma chérie*, my little spy.'

Musa still does not speak, but gazes at the two of them as if fascinated by their easy physical affection.

'You found out, didn't you,' says Lily to Musa, plonking Mia down and shooing her off into the other room, 'about Aimé being mixed up with Vivienne Hughes and the doctor – Dr

Harris Burns. Were you trying to protect Aimé?'

Musa switches his gaze out through the kitchen door to the garden, then back to Lily. 'Sure,' he says. 'They were dangerous people, and your brother was just an idealistic student with his head in the clouds. A clever man, but a naïve one. I think Aimé thought he could get some sort of justice for our people.' Musa shakes his head. 'The naivety of youth. I think we were all idealistic like that when we were young, weren't we, until we realised that the world fucks around with Africa – no questions asked.'

'You went to the Tuli that night, to try to stop Aimé threatening to go to the authorities. Because it was Vivienne and Harris, wasn't it? The woman with the doctors – that was Vivienne Hughes?'

Lily waits for Musa to speak, but he does not. He stands up and crosses the room to stare, in profile, out of the open kitchen door. Outside, it is nearly dusk. Musa closes his eyes, pressing the palm of his hand to his forehead, and kisses his teeth just once. His big shoulders seem bowed with emotion.

For a moment, Lily wonders if her uncle is about to cry. It dawns on her that Musa buried his emotions, his pain, his anger, when Aimé's dead body was put in the earth. There his grief has lain, all these years. How indescribably painful it must have been for a man like Musa to feel so powerless to help his young nephew.

'Yes. Yes, it was her.' Musa takes a long breath. 'She was the mastermind, as far as I could work out. People thought she was some kind of angel, a white woman who came to save us all, and I swear at one point they thought we'd all be rich because of her.' With slow steps, Musa comes to sit again at the table. 'But she orchestrated the whole thing! Honestly, people are such fools. Fools.'

Lily begins to prepare for supper, a dish filled with greens to offset the sugar rush of the earlier ice cream binge. She chops onions, slices tomatoes, then aubergine into cubes. She puts everything in a pan where the mixture begins to sizzle. The sweet scent of frying vegetables rises into the air. 'You think Vivienne Hughes killed Aimé?'

'One way or another, yes. But I can't prove it. The woman's clever, I'll give her that – word is she was a medical student at a famous university, but people say she never qualified. I've wracked my brains for years how she pulled it off. And I made a fuss at first, me and Bakary Ba. But they arrested us, the police – powerful strings were being pulled. Then I thought it best to leave it be.'

'Let sleeping dogs lie,' Lily says in English.

'What's that?'

Lily stirs the pan, adding chunks of raw fish then a tin of tomatoes, a teaspoon of mustard and a Maggi cube, crumbling the bright yellow spice between her fingers into the pan. 'It's an English idiom. It came from the fact that dogs are unpredictable when they are suddenly disturbed.'

'You always were too clever for your own good.' Musa gives a small laugh, then looks thoughtful. 'Vivienne Hughes always struck me as very clever, too; she was just so single-minded about everything.' He taps his palm on the table. 'You were foolish to open this up, Lily. They were dangerous people then, and they are still. Too many people got hurt. I meant it when I said I didn't want you to get yourself into trouble!'

'And Bakary Ba?' Lily stirs the mixture for a final time as the rising scent of the cooked stew fills the kitchen. 'He had the vaccination, too,' she adds, 'didn't he, that's why he stammers.'

Musa nods. 'Bakary came with me afterwards to the police, but we were both arrested, accused of disrupting the peace. They put out a warning to the villagers, basically saying we'd be punished if we tried to say anything.'

Lily pours the stew into a serving dish, then sets the table: glasses and a jug of iced water, salt and pepper, rounds of fresh baguette. As an afterthought, she puts a small cubed packet of dried dates on a saucer.

'Was it you sending me the texts?' she asks mildly, laying out the cutlery, breaking open the dates, which crumble onto the saucer.

Musa shrugs. 'I had to try to stop you getting yourself in hot water.'

'And the brick?'

'Sorry, yes.' Musa shakes his head. 'That was a mistake. I wanted to scare you—'

'Indeed, you did,' Lily says. 'Why didn't you just tell me in the first place?'

Musa gives a dry laugh. 'I've kept the secret for thirty years,' he says. 'Why would I break it now?'

'So why *are* you telling me?'

'Because I realised you were right.' Musa pauses, and kisses his teeth, as if he is again overcome with emotion. Eventually he speaks, 'Aimé was a good man. There's nothing more we can do for him now than tell the truth.'

270

'Come,' says Lily softly, pushing the saucer of dates in her uncle's direction, 'break your fast with us.'

Once the girls are asleep, Lily sits on the couch watching a European gameshow involving letter and maths conundrums. The temperature is still well above twenty-nine degrees. She wears plastic flip-flops and a simple house dress of faded cotton; she drinks from a glass of iced water. When the letters are put on the board by the pretty white woman, Lily shuffles them in her mind, mutters the word under her breath. Dichotomy. Then another. Captivating. C-A-P...

She's distracting herself from the issue at hand, Lily knows. She would like to talk to Vivienne Hughes, but she is putting off the conversation, aware it is fraught with difficulties. For the umpteenth time that day, Lily runs over the facts in her mind, and it all makes sense: Vivienne's lost medical studies, an opportunity to continue as a doctor in some form with the dodgy professor, Harris Burns. In Senegal, Vivienne meets Aimé, and the two of them hatch idealistic plans to change the world.

Lily recalls their second phone call and Vivienne's passing remark, as if to herself: *I was so idealistic back then*. It is exactly as Vivienne has hinted, even if unconsciously; Lily is certain of it.

Lily scrolls through her text messages until she finds the one from Lion Savané she has been putting off reading for so long. For a moment, she stares at the old notification, biting her lip. The last thing she needs is more stress. Yet, at this moment, she needs to know for sure who Demba's mistress is, if not for revenge, then for the sake of her own emotional wellbeing. So she can move on, *inshallah*.

Lily takes a breath and clicks on the text, at which her heart turns over with a single slow, anxious thud. Déstine Fall, Legal Secretary, the text says, there in black and white, just as Lily had known it would. Out loud, she lets out a colourless laugh, shaking her head.

'*Joge fi*,' she murmurs in Wolof.

She ought to be surprised, but she is not. Pssht, it was the coral fingernails, always those tacky coral-painted fingernails. She knew, in her heart, the minute she saw them reach for her husband out of the doorway. Coral, the colour of the tropics, of Ambre Solaire and holidays, of sunshine and happiness. An unlikely colour for guilt, Lily thinks, for *adultery*. Demba must have met Déstine at that *baptême* party, or maybe they already knew each other? Had her *own husband* really pulled strings with Ida to get his girlfriend a job as a secretary at Ida's firm? The idea is preposterous. How dare he!

She ought to care more, but she finds she cares less. What does it matter now, that Demba's, what… mistress… girlfriend… soon-to-be second wife… is the new, airheaded young secretary from work? There's no getting away from the fact that, for Lily, such a revelation sets her free.

On the television, the presenter is spelling out a new word: Lily watches the three contestants in a daze as they choose vowels and consonants, Y-A-L-B-E-T-A-R, as the board flashes and spins to the tick of the countdown clock. Then the audio sting, *dada dada dadada*, indicating time up.

'Betrayal,' says Lily, out loud in the empty sitting room. She flicks off the TV, closes the text message and chucks the phone onto the floor, kicking off her flip-flops. She goes to the kitchen cupboard and fetches a cigarette, which she lights and puffs at with trembling hands.

'Fuck you, Demba,' she murmurs under her breath, curling up again into the corner of the sofa as she exhales smoke, then coughs, spluttering. In her mouth the swear word is dirty, delicious, satisfying. 'Fuck you to hell.'

CHAPTER TWENTY-THREE

Vivienne

Viv meets M at a pub near the turn-off for the A35, where a taxi is booked to collect her at noon sharp. The place is ideal for their purposes, an anonymous stop-off for drivers passing through, conveniently deserted on this cold, cloudy weekday morning. The two of them sit outside in the furthest corner of the beer garden, hidden from view to any curious punters by the overhanging branches of a towering willow. M goes inside to the bar, emerging with a tray loaded with tea things. He sits down and pours out the tea with slow, unfathomable composure.

'Chin, chin,' he says eventually with a thin smile, chinking Viv's cup, then adding sugar to his own. 'Or should I say, chin up.' He glances furtively around. 'All quiet on the Western front?'

But despite the customary banter, Viv can see M is tense and drained-looking, as though he hasn't slept for weeks. His jaw is flecked with patchy stubble. Beneath his eyes, dark bags of exhaustion. A ghost of a man, Viv thinks, sipping her drink. She sits back in her chair, hands in lap, feeling jittery and apprehensive. She entwines her fingers, worrying at a loose flap of cuticle on her left ring finger.

'M,' she says in a low tone, 'you must tell me what you know. I just need the truth.'

Her cuticle-picking draws blood. She sucks on the finger, trying to stem the bleeding, then reaches for a cylinder of sugar from the tea tray, ripping open the top. She pours a little heap of golden sugar onto the table, sculpting it nervily into tiny piles like sand dunes. 'It was something awful, wasn't it?' she adds.

'Well, no one was feeding starving African children, that's for sure.'

M's voice is hoarse, whether from the cold or emotion, Viv is unsure. For a short while, the two of them sit in silence, contemplating what he just said. His face is buried in his left palm now; he is rubbing his eyes. Viv can hear the wind through the willow branches, the distant sound of traffic. A dog barks from somewhere nearby.

Then: 'Kids were dying.'

M raises his head, his brown eyes fixed on hers, bloodshot now from all the rubbing. Viv notices that his hands are shaking.

'Tell me.' She brushes the piles of sugar onto the ground and leans forwards on the table, arms folded tightly around her chest. She is shivering. 'M,' she murmurs, 'what the hell happened?'

M gets up. 'Bloody hell, I need something stronger than tea.' He strides off and disappears inside the pub, coming back holding two crystal tumblers of whisky. 'Will you?' Viv nods and he pushes a glass across the table at her. He swigs his serving down in one.

'After the vaccinations, kids were going blind, slurring their speech. There was one who went deaf.' M's voice breaks and he clears his throat. 'The villagers were saying it was meningitis.' He taps the edge of the glass with a fingernail. 'An epidemic, that's what I heard anyway.'

Viv is shaking her head, murmuring, 'No, no, no.' She downs the drink, pushes the glass back, wishing there was a refill. 'You can't possibly know that. Nothing was ever recorded.'

'But it happened nevertheless – you can't delete the truth just by denying it.'

'So, is that what you think, that Aimé Tunkara was killed because he knew about this?'

M nods. 'Aimé knew *something*,' he says. 'After the accident, John sent me out there to negotiate with the family, pay them off. Then a few weeks later, there was another chap called Niang, whose son died. Alou. Friend of Aimé.'

'And you never found out why?'

'I could have, but—' M sighs. 'I paid the man off, didn't ask questions. I was aware that if I even sniffed at a deeper truth, my fate would be worse than just a sacking. I'd end up at the side of the road with a machete through my throat – and not from the bloody locals!'

Viv can feel the heat of the alcohol in her brain, numbing whatever emotions she is experiencing.

'John rang me after the accident, asking me to come to the embassy. You know the rest. I remember you giving me the statement, that you were driving, that the brakes failed. The police and authorities were dealt with by the FO. Christ, I mean, diplomatic immunity can get you out of anything! I paid the Tunkara family off, and the others – via the village network – and got you both out of there sharpish, off to another posting.'

'The cleaner,' she murmurs.

'Yes.'

CHAPTER TWENTY-FOUR

Vivienne

Twenty-four hours later

The small but exclusive Keur Palmier resort in Saly is virtually deserted out of season, especially during Ramadan. At the all-inclusive riad owned by a white Frenchman, Pierre, and his charming Senegalese wife, Diama, there is a large infinity pool surrounded by ornamental palms, a rattan-roofed sun terrace scattered, hippy-style, with cushions, and a beach bar with live music that opens in the evenings. There are daily Asana yoga classes, a spa, sailing lessons and art workshops, and a 'wellbeing' menu based on local ingredients featuring an abundance of freshly caught seafood. *Escape from everyday life*, reads the appealing-looking website, *return to a life well-loved, of nature and emotional freedom…*

Viv adores the place immediately, with its peace and heat and salt-scented air, its sun-baked white stone walls hot to the touch by mid-morning. There is the silvery beach with its gentle sounds of seabirds, of waves rolling back and forth over an empty shore scattered with shells. And the never-ending blueness of the sea and sky which almost makes Viv feel as if the rest of the world – the serious, non-holiday world beyond the horizon – is obliterated. Almost, but not quite.

Now as the days go by, an endless round of hourly swims, lengthy afternoon dozes and fresh food – lobster, pink crevettes, salads of fresh tomatoes, cucumber, palm hearts, catch-of-the-day with rice – Viv is aware that she should be experiencing a sense of wellbeing.

Day by day, she is growing browner and more relaxed, and there's no denying that in the heat Viv feels uncommonly healthy; her limbs are loose, her skin radiant, the slight back pain that has plagued her for some time, disappeared. She is opening up like one of those peculiar desert flowers, she thinks, which bloom with swashbuckling flamboyance every ten years or so. Yet the new slowness of this holiday existence and the constant rhythm of the sun seems to deliver not the deep sense of inner peace that Viv was expecting, but an emerging set of feelings that are not altogether pleasant, like the slow eruption of a volcano.

Half past ten, and already the barometer by the pool reads thirty degrees. A poster invites guests to an upcoming festival celebration: *Celebrate Eid with us. Gather around the flames to wish for health, prosperity, happiness, and love.* On a sun lounger, Viv applies factor fifty lotion to her face and body, and languidly eats the small saucer of peanuts left earlier by the waitress, alongside a cool drink. Perhaps she *will* gather at the bonfire, Viv thinks, given that she's here – she might as well.

And why *is* she here? Because, Viv supposes, she can't help herself. Because she is curious. Because she has something to offer Lily Tunkara, about whom she's come to, well, care about. Can that really be true? Because, let's face it, some inexorable force of the universe is pulling her back to this place, in spite of herself.

Viv finishes the peanuts and breathes in, then out, still crunching, counting the seconds between the breaths as she might do in a yoga pose. She really needs to fix the situation, and it's an easy fix, surely.

Restless, Viv swings her tanned legs over the side of the lounger and stands up, slipping on flip-flops and making her way across to the infinity pool. She discards the flip-flops and plunges in, stroking out to the deeper, cooler water, throwing her head back and coming up with hair wet and heavy down her back. Elbows on the side of the pool, Viv squints out to sea. There is no one around but a fishing boat casting its nets in the shimmering blue. In the foreground, a woman with a basket on her head and a child walk the shore, their figures silhouetted against the hard, white sun.

If she was to holiday in Senegal, it had to be Saly, Viv reflects, and not Ngor village further north, because she couldn't possibly risk being recognised, even though she can imagine the village of Ngor in her mind's eye right now. Ngor that she knows so well. Half of her feels like jumping in a car and motoring up there right now. Viv remembers that first time, the children swarming as if she were some sort of Pied Piper.

At the thought, Viv cringes; the white saviour image is too real, too awful. If only everything hadn't been so easy. Compared to England, with its countless hoops to jump through, life in Senegal in the eighties was loose and full of endless possibilities – and to a degree it still is, Viv ponders – particularly if you were white and you had cash to offer. You only had to ask. You only had to click your fingers, and it was done. That was Africa then.

Two teenage boys come into view leading a sheep on a rope tether. In the shallows, they begin to wash the animal as with violent motions it writhes out of their grip, lunging for the dry sand. The skirmish, sheep versus humans, lasts a couple of minutes before the animal goes still in submission, allowing the pair to thoroughly soap its sides, laughing and joking as they scrub at its face with a cloth, then splash and rinse down its coat.

Viv watches, mesmerised. There's no reason to be sad, yet somehow her heart melts for the helpless creature at the mercy of its child owners, oblivious to the fact that it is no doubt being washed in preparation for the Eid Muslim sacrifice. Is the festival tomorrow, Viv wonders, or the day after? The date has yet to be announced.

Viv contemplates the spruced-up sheep as it trots, pristine, up the beach, drip-drying in the sun, then breaststrokes back to the shallow end of the pool. Now she comes to think of it, those parents and their kids had never even struggled, though they were lambs to the slaughter. Viv recalls the Ngor villagers' blind faith in the white people, as if the pale colour of their skins – hers and Harris's– automatically made them *good*. Someone had told her – Viv forgets who – that *toubab* was the old word used by locals for the colonial white doctors, though these days it just meant white person, foreigner, stranger. Who would have thought it could be so apt...

Viv sighs and hauls herself out of the pool, her mind still on the sheep and its existential struggle.

'Mmm,' Viv says, flopping on the lounger, water drops sparkling on her brown skin.

If it weren't for Harris, then John, then Aimé, what would have happened to her? Would she have found another path, gone back to studying, and finished her studies like any other doctor, become the paediatric surgeon she always wanted to be?

Viv lies back and closes her eyes, letting the sun warm the inside of her eyelids. Probably. She ought to have found her own path, instead of using John. Instead, she sold her soul and married a man for money, then took a shit research job for a crooked doctor with no morals, because, frankly, she was beholden to Harris by then, desperate to do important medical work, even though she was only half-qualified. She'd let herself be used, that much is true, and in turn she herself became the user.

Viv lets out a groan and sits up, reaching for the sun cream. Maybe it's the heat, she broods, squeezing the tube onto her wet skin, or maybe a hunger for lunch, but she is restless. She can't seem to rid her mind of these intrusive thoughts of those children, thoughts of their innocent parents trustingly sending their kids to be harmed without a second thought. At the memories, suddenly sharp-focused, where before, if anything, they were a blur, Viv feels engulfed by a strange helplessness. Of all things, she wanted to help, not *harm*. Not *kill*. *Jesus Christ*.

Viv takes a deep breath. She discards the cream and stays still with head bent, arms drawn around her knees. Tears fill her eyes. She blinks them away. Is this it then, the place where she will once and for all settle her demons, here beneath the gorgeous, hellish sun? Viv feels heat flush through her body. For a minute or two, she is lost in the brightness on the back of her head, the warm wetness of her hair down her back, lost in the light as memories fill the bubble that continues to expand inside her chest, ever tighter, ever more tense. Around it, a numbness, an *absence* of feeling.

If truth be told, sometimes Viv thinks that if the bubble were to burst, she would not be able to stand it.

She gathers herself. She gets up from the lounger, ties a sarong around her waist and walks to her room, suddenly craving air-conditioning, a cold drink, cool sheets. She never meant those kids to get ill, she is thinking. *God, no*. She thought the Aspiximal trials were just a final check and the drug was pretty much approved.

We just need to get it over the line, they'd said.

Then things got out of hand with Harris, with the secondary Atlantis contract that in truth worried her at some instinctual level, with its dodgy clauses and exceptions and its lack of transparency or any formal consent procedure.

She had an inkling that Harris wasn't being honest, but by that time she'd wanted *it* so much – the research, the potential it had to change things – that she lost all negotiating power. Without work, her life was without meaning. And obviously the blasted entanglement with Harris didn't help matters…

Before Viv knew it, the wheels were turning so fast that she couldn't press reverse.

In the cool of the hotel room, Viv showers, lifting her head to the lukewarm water, soaping her sun-warm skin with the bar of rose-scented soap the staff had left on the bed. By that time, as she recalls, John had discovered what was going on; she can remember, as clear as day, their conversation in the embassy drawing room with the doors closed.

It was three months into the Dakar posting, and she'd just

broken the news about the research Harris was planning in Senegal. Heavens, John was angry at first, no doubt about that. Who wouldn't have been?

'You mean to say you've been using me this whole time?' John turned to the window, hands on hips, staring out sightlessly. 'Jesus Christ.'

'I wanted to tell you,' Viv offered in a meek voice, 'but—'

'You *wanted* to tell me?' John turned and stared with a pained look. 'Just like you *wanted* to tell me that you were actually a drop-out med student, and you *wanted* to tell me that you're involved with some dodgy medical trials run by your dodgy doctor mate.' He ran a hand through his hair. 'Bloody hell, Viv.'

'The trials aren't dodgy,' she offered, 'just secret. It's not the same thing.'

'Ha!' John shot her an incredulous look. 'Don't be bloody naïve! Why do you think people like Harris Burns and these big pharma companies carry on like this? Why do you think they're willing to use someone like you as their puppet? You haven't even got your degree! Do you actually think it's because they have good intentions? Of course they bloody well don't—'

'For heaven's sake, I'm sorry.'

John gave a deep sigh. Viv watched him stagger to the settee where he sat down, head in hands, groaning to himself. After a moment, he looked up.

'If you don't mind my asking, what do you think happens now? You don't actually expect me to keep this quiet, do you?'

But John *had* kept quiet, of course. Poor John, with his penchant for pretty village boys. How easy it was to dangle this incentive not to tell the FO, knowing that no British ambassador could afford to be caught in a scandal of that nature. It was a bargain of mutual necessity, nothing more.

And of course, when everything was said and done, John loved her as his wife, his close companion in work and politics – though it was a funny sort of love – and he'd have done anything to keep things smoothed over for both of them.

Funny how, from that moment on, their marriage became more open. John seemed relieved they no longer had to pretend to have sex. They were, she supposes, both more comfortable after admitting the sham, aware that at least they were helping each other out by keeping each other's secrets.

Viv wanders the room naked, drying off. From the drinks tray loaded with small bottles of mineral water and fresh fruit, she pours herself a glass of water, then lies down on the bed. The cotton sheet is cool and pleasant against her hot skin. She sits up on an elbow and sips the cold water, gradually cooling down. Silly to think that people in Ngor might recognise her. At the time, she was a young woman of twenty-four, a whole generation ago. Now, she's fifty-four years old. Who'd make the connection?

Still, Viv hesitates, there's no point taking chances.

If only she could turn back the clock. Now, with new medical knowledge and new research… So much could be done. Lord. At some point, it dawns on Viv, she's going to have to face the fact that, for all the harm she caused, she never achieved her ambition to be a doctor. Now here she is, an old woman, and what was it all for? Given that she's spent most of her life striving for something that never materialised, is she a failure?

Viv sighs, gulping the drink thirstily. This is not what she came here for, to unlock that part of her soul, deep, dark and ugly, where she has long buried those memories, nor to confront the threads of guilt that have lain dormant for so many years. No. She has come to relax, to rejuvenate, to *inhale joy, to exhale love*, as the Californian yoga teacher would put it.

Even so, Viv can feel something important and vaguely frightening loosening from her grasp. Demons surfacing, despite her best efforts. If she's not careful, she will lose herself.

Viv loosens the knot of the mosquito net hanging over the bed and lets the fine mesh drape over the mattress. She lies on her back, staring up. There is something protective about the hazy net enclosure with its thousands of miniscule octagons, as if, inside, Viv is shielded not just against biting insects but against her own fast encroaching demons.

A headache is beginning to throb over her left eye. Viv turns over cheek to pillow and closes her eyes. Tonight she will call Lily and ask to talk, invite Lily to come down here for a face-to-face meeting. Perhaps the lawyer will agree to come for Eid. After a minute or two, Viv dozes off, slipping into a half-nightmare in which she is running from a crowd of faceless children, hollering, reaching, grasping, until, mute and unable to shout for help, she is completely swallowed up.

CHAPTER TWENTY-FIVE

Lily

The telephone call comes at around two in the afternoon, as Lily is preparing to go out. On the other end, Vivienne Hughes explains somewhat breathlessly that she's arrived in Senegal, that she wants to meet *tout de suite.*

'I'm in Saly, you see,' says Vivienne, 'and tomorrow there will be a celebration for Eid. I wondered if you'd like to be my guest?'

'Oh,' Lily replies, at once confused and shocked. 'I mean, this is a surprise.'

'It's been booked for a while,' the other woman says in a matter-of-fact tone. 'My holiday, I mean. Didn't I mention it? God knows, I was desperate for a break! Anyway, you and your daughters could be my guests.'

'I normally spend it with family, but—' Lily hesitates, thinking the offer over in all its alluring absurdity. If Viv really had killed Aimé, isn't this her only chance to hear the truth, or so she would hope? 'Leave it with me.'

Somehow, Lily stations both her daughters with Rama Sow and family, who enthuses gaily about a festival sleepover.

'You do what you have to do, lovely,' Rama trills when Lily

drops the girls at half-past two pm in the afternoon. 'Aïda's over the moon, and they'll have a wonderful time, *inshallah*!' Rama winks. 'Go and let your hair down.'

And Lily is grateful, liking Rama suddenly for her dashing attitude and breezy brand of intelligence; she seems to be a kindred spirit – a woman after Lily's own heart.

'It's been a tough few weeks,' she blurts out without thinking. 'I'm getting divorced. My husband, he's having an affair.'

Rama's eyes grow wide, and then she smiles, reaching a slim hand emblazoned with several jewel-encrusted rings to squeeze Lily's arm.

'Oh, love, I'm so sorry.' She leans in. 'But good for you,' she adds in a low voice. 'Honestly, I do sometimes feel we can do without men completely, don't you? You'll be better off on your own. Let's meet up once you're back, just us and our girls?'

Lily laughs. 'Okay, I'd like that a lot.'

Saly is two hours south down the coast. Lily has only been there once, years ago, for a weekend with Demba, before they had children. Reached via long kilometres of flat salt plains beloved of foreign bird watchers, the beach resort is one of upmarket boutique hotels and white sand beaches that has for decades served as a go-to destination for French package holidaymakers and wealthy Senegalese city folk wanting a break from the chaos of Dakar.

Lily goes in the car, hot air blasting though the windows. She wears shorts and sunglasses, a scarf around her hair, and is reminded of an American film she saw once about two women on a road trip escaping their husbands. Their names she forgets,

Thelma and somebody. Now Lily has that exact feeling of being set free, though she has no reason to think this today more than any other day.

The bone-coloured landscape is punctuated by baobabs and flamingos in flocks, herons and weaver birds clustered in trees, the odd kite wheeling in the topaz sky. Lily passes a pair of hooded vultures hunched in the branches of a baobab. As she watches one of the birds swoops down onto a cragged area of pinkish-white salt. The other vulture remains hunched in the skeletal top branches of the tree.

Half-past four. The heat of the day is nearly over, yet the entire landscape seems to shiver with heat, the sea a dazzling sheet of light. Lily turns right at a sign saying Keur Palmier and pulls into a sandy drive, where she parks outside a cluster of low-lying huts of varying sizes with smart mud plastering and conical thatched roofs, a fashionable take on the traditional huts of Senegal's provincial villages.

On her phone is a text: *Waiting on the terrace. V x*

Lily is suddenly nervous. She climbs out of the car and makes her way past a reception desk into an outdoor restaurant area, where empty tables are laid with tablemats, but no cutlery. A smell of cooking is coming from somewhere, of spices, fish, roasting meat. Lily forces herself to hold her head high, to breathe calmly – *take deep breaths, now follow the circle* – as she walks out to the swimming pool where the light is searing, the parasols throwing skinny shadows onto the patio, looking around for Vivienne Hughes.

Yards in front on the beach, a group of men is building a bonfire, bustling to and fro between the beach bar and hotel carrying chairs and tables, trays of glasses, armfuls of firewood. In the shade of a parasol, Lily spots a slim white woman sitting with her back to her.

'Mrs Hughes?' She goes up to her. 'Viv?'

The woman turns around, gets to her feet with a smile, taller than expected. 'Lily,' she says and extends a hand.

The woman's eyes are steel blue in the shadow of the sun. Lily shakes her hand, sits down in the chair opposite.

Vivienne sits straight-backed, slender hands folded on her lap, considering her with a small smile. She is sussing me out, thinks Lily, noticing how beautiful the other woman is in the flesh: tall, sharp cheekbones, wavy ash-blonde hair contrasting with a light tan, perfect skin. Beneath a pink, peasant-checked headscarf, the waves of hair fall almost to her waist, reminding Lily of a Barbie doll.

And for a woman in her fifties, it must be said that Viv has an astonishing figure, she thinks: fine-boned and thin, but not skinny, full breasts, an enviably petite waist. She wears no make-up and a pale bikini top above a tie-dye sarong knotted at the waist. A pair of flat leather sandals are discarded by the chair.

'I'm glad you came,' says Vivienne. 'It's so nice to finally meet in person.'

'Yes.' Lily exhales, pulse hammering in her chest and forehead. She must keep her wits about her in the face of this white woman's charm, for Vivienne is quite obviously charming. 'And you,' Lily adds, 'it's nice to meet you for real.'

Now she is here, Lily finds herself overwhelmed by the sheer 3D reality of Vivienne, no longer just a face on the screen, all legs and arms and human emotion hitting her like a roar. She turns away, taking a breath. Past the pool, she can see the crouched figure of a local woman washing clothes on the flat shore. As she watches, the woman stands upright, a baby slung across her back, and makes her way back up the beach.

They order drinks, sparkling soda with a shot of lime cordial, a huge jug of ice cubes that melt almost immediately. Peanuts on a saucer that Lily declines but Vivienne scoops and pops into her mouth in a way that is somewhere between savage and ladylike, as if she hasn't eaten for weeks. Lily notes with surprise that Vivienne's long, rather elegantly-shaped fingers are bitten and raw; around several of the nails are visible ragged semi-circles of open skin, blushed with recent bleeding, where the cuticles should be.

'You didn't bring your girls?' says Vivienne.

'No, they're staying at a friend's.'

'I see.' Vivienne leans forwards with a smile accompanied by an oddly mischievous look. 'They're the apples of your eye, I expect?'

'You could say that.' Lily smiles at the idiom, the strange awkwardness of this conversation with a stranger who is not quite a stranger. 'Yes, they are.'

'I always wonder about that expression – apparently it's from Shakespeare, *A Midsummer Night's Dream*.'

'I know,' says Lily. 'The apple means the pupil.'

'Quite.' Vivienne says, and Lily notes her look of surprise.

'But I didn't come here to discuss Shakespeare,' says Lily, 'did I?'

'No. My apologies.' Vivienne looks thoughtful. 'The last thing I want to do is waste your time.' She picks the last peanut off

291

the plate and pops it into her mouth, raising an eyebrow and crunching with a wry smile that is puckish, that mischief again. 'You know, it's almost as if I couldn't stay away from this place. Part of me—' Vivienne pauses, frowning, her eyes twisting to the horizon, as if she is about to say something else. But she doesn't.

'Part of you?' prompts Lily.

'Nothing.' Vivienne takes a sip of her drink, shaking her head with a soft sigh. 'Nothing.'

The light is softening. The afternoon landscape seems to mellow and blend so that the diamond sea, the azure sky and lemon-bright sand melt into a sheer palate of blue and gold against which Lily finds she no longer has to squint. In the diminished light, Vivienne's tanned skin glows against eyes of deepest sky blue.

And as the hard, bright buzz of the noonday heat seems to relax, suddenly the women do, too, or so Lily has the impression. It is the best time of the day. Lily shifts in her chair. She finds she wants to provoke Vivienne, to push her, to find a way under her immaculately smooth skin.

'I read all the parts of your memoir you sent me,' says Lily, sipping water. 'They're very beautiful.' She leans her elbows on the table. 'I'm not trying to be difficult, but I found myself wondering if they tell the truth?'

'You may well wonder. But it's a matter of opinion, surely. Perhaps the memoir tells my truth.'

'Are you capable of the truth, Mrs Hughes?'

Vivienne laughs as if she is genuinely amused, stretching one brown, feline leg out of the shade of the parasol, then the other, so that they both catch the sun, and wiggling her toes, which in contrast to her ragged fingernails, are perfect and painted a bright shade of tomato red.

'If you're asking *that*,' she says, 'I guess I'll have to do better.'

The other woman's face is inscrutable. Vivienne reminds Lily of a cat – or rather, a big cat: beautiful and dangerous and no doubt quite willing to toy with her with its big, lethal paws.

'Look, the last thing I want to do is to talk ill of the dead,' adds Vivienne in a serious tone. With a gentle expression, she looks across at Lily, as if reluctant to embark on her next sentence. 'You see—' She sighs. 'Your big brother, Aimé, well, he was no saint. He was a great doctor, sure, and so very clever. But he can't come out of this as innocent. I have to tell you that if the community finds out what he did, your family name will be mud.'

'I see,' says Lily, taken aback. 'Can you explain?'

'Well, it was Aimé who sourced the children for me, and it was Aimé who persuaded the parents to come and see me and to sign the medical forms. That was *your* brother. Do you realise how that looks? I worry for the Tunkara name – let's face it, your brother's reputation, his memory, is currently golden, and I'm the last person who wants that to change.'

'Are you saying I should stop the case because my brother's name will be dragged through the dirt?'

'I guess I'm offering you a way out of this can of worms you've opened up. For heaven's sake, taking the case back to court will only lead to tears for you and your family, and that's the last thing both of us want. Do you really want your girls to grow up under the cloud of their uncle's bad behaviour?'

The waitress comes over. Vivienne orders more water, more ice, more peanuts. Lily excuses herself. In the loo, she douses her face with water and stands staring into the mirror. Breathe, she tells herself. Breathe.

'Are you saying it was Aimé's fault, then?' Lily says, returning to the table, sitting down again. 'All this, I mean? And not yours?'

Vivienne sighs. She leans back in her chair, picks at a cuticle on a left finger, frowns and rubs a different finger on her temple.

'Lord, Lily, it's not a question of *fault*,' she says, shaking her head. 'That's all water under the bridge, isn't it. It's about the consequences *now*, surely?'

The consequences now, what are they? That the wronged families will get compensation? That Vivienne will go to prison? That she, Lily Tunkara, will have to face up to criticism about her brother's actions? Yes, perhaps, but she's willing to go up against such things. 'Pssht.' Lily shakes her head. 'That doesn't answer my question,' she says.

'Look, I can offer you money,' says Vivienne mildly. 'Lots of it. Just like your brother. He wanted money, too, and there is no shortage of that.'

'I don't want money.' Lily draws a breath. 'I want justice.'

'Justice, justice.' The other woman shakes her head. 'You throw that word around like it can defend anything, but what does it actually mean? I must ask you, is it justice to drag your brother's memory through the mud? Forgive me, but whose justice is it, then, Lily: his or yours?'

'I don't know,' says Lily, feeling assaulted. 'It's a good question,' she adds, at a loss.

She checks her watch. Half-past six, suddenly. Where did the time go? The setting sun is a fire ball in the night-darkened sky. Everything is gold. Then darkness falls suddenly, heavily.

Around the bonfire a small crowd of tourists and hotel staff is gathering. Some of the tourists are wearing garlands made of flowers and leaves. Someone is drumming. About the place, there's a party atmosphere, but somehow it is more than that, thinks Lily, something *abandoned*. A mood of wildness and freedom that she can't quite put her finger on. Perhaps it's the fire, the drumming and the darkness, the intense heat and the remote location, like the end of the world. No rules, no limits.

How strange to be here in this place with this strangest of white women – at an impasse, by all accounts. And what now?

'Come,' says the other woman suddenly, getting to her feet. Lily watches her take off the sarong and flap it straight, then twist and tie it around her neck. 'Let's celebrate a little, shall we, and then we can talk some more?'

Do I have a choice? thinks Lily. There is something spell-binding about the other woman, something inflammatory and provocative that draws her for reasons Lily can't quite put her finger on. Together they walk down onto the sand as the flames rise and dance against the dark sea and sky. A warm salt breeze is coming off the sea. Someone puts a flower garland on Lily's head, then Vivienne's. The flowers smell sweet, musky and sensual. There is jasmine, peach-pink hibiscus, bougainvillea of pale fire.

'*Naga def*, beautiful,' the man says, grinning, and Lily smiles, thanking him with a nod.

For a few minutes, Vivienne disappears, to the loo, Lily assumes. When the white woman returns, she holds a spliff in one hand, bringing a strong scent of marijuana floating through the dark. With the garland of flowers on her head, the white woman is almost other-worldly, thinks Lily, like a fairy-tale mermaid

295

out of one of Mia's storybooks. They're always Caucasian, these mermaids, with their rippling blonde hair and silvery skins. In fact, it occurs to Lily, she's never once come across a black mermaid. Pssht, maybe it's time to write a children's book featuring characters her girls can *actually* relate to…

'You don't drink, do you?' says Vivienne.

Lily watches her extract a lighter from a small rattan handbag and relight the spliff, then puff several times and exhale smoke through her nostrils with a poise that strikes Lily as absurdly aristocratic.

'No.' Lily shakes her head. 'Never.'

'Then will you try this?' Vivienne drags on the spliff, extends it with long fingers to Lily.

Lily raises an eyebrow. 'I can't, I mean—' She trails off. 'The Muslim religion doesn't allow us.'

'You,' murmurs Vivienne, popping a smoke ring into the night sky, 'need to live a little, love.'

Lily is reminded of Lion: *You need to have a little fun, Lily Tunkara*. She gives a deep sigh. Around her, the party swirls and moves, gathering momentum. The music grows louder. She thinks of Demba, of the girl's coral-painted nails across her husband's arms and back. If he's in bed with her right now, she does not want to know. Lily swigs at her water bottle. To her mind, she is far from home here, outside her own life. Lily stares into the leaping flames of the fire, fierce now with the addition of more wood. *Fuck it*, she thinks.

'All right then,' says Lily, taking the joint from Vivienne's fingers and dragging on it once, then again. 'Thank you.'

The weed is strong, and within minutes Lily is high. She can

296

feel the smoke snaking up through her nostrils to her brain and down her body, into her limbs. From the darkness comes the frenzied beat of more drumming, louder now and accompanied by low and high talking drums, as if the instruments are calling people to the celebration. Then a loud, melodic trumpeting sound. The crowd stills. In front of the fire the handsome man who gave Lily the garland is blowing into a huge conch shell. The man wears a garland made of red hibiscus flowers around his neck. His head is thrown back, and he is huge and muscular, regal somehow in his white linen shirt against black skin. The surreal sound goes on for seconds or maybe minutes, before with one muscular arm the man holds the seashell aloft. Like some sort of surreal sea god, he stands like this, eyes glinting in the light of the flames, a herald to something.

By the firelight, Lily watches a sheep being led across the beach on a tether. More men gather. There is the silver glint of a knife raised in the air. The beast's throat is slit and Lily hears the sheep's death cry. When the crowd parts she sees the sheep on the ground, its pure white coat splashed with bright red blood. The animal's body still trembles in the final death throes. There is blood spurting from the creature's mouth, the pure life draining out. And its soul, thinks Lily, unable to tear her eyes away. Where has that gone?

Lily exhales, clenches her fists and closes her eyes, bending hands on knees to stop a rising nausea.

'You okay?' Vivienne is regarding her with concern. 'Here, have some water.'

'Thanks.' Lily raises her head, sips at the bottle. 'It's the blood, and the weed.'

'You need a strong stomach to watch.' Vivienne pats Lily on the shoulder. 'But in some ways, I find it quite cathartic.'

'I'd never thought of it like that,' says Lily.

They stand watching the dead sheep being gutted, then hoisted whole onto a spit over the fire. With another drag of the spliff, Lily feels a strange letting go, a new looseness of her limbs and senses. Nothing matters, she thinks, not Demba, not the other woman, not even the past. None of it is of any real importance. There is only her happiness, only precious Mia and Piretta. With a dazed clarity, Lily takes in the scene, the deep purple darkness slashed with orange fire, the smells of blood and burning wood, of drugs and roasting meat, and the music in her ears. The wild dancing of the partygoers who flail their arms in the air, wiggling their backsides to the beat and the fire.

After a moment, the handsome man comes up offering iced *bissap*. He has white teeth, velvet skin, laughing eyes. Lily takes the cold drink. When the stranger leans to kiss her on the lips, she returns the kiss. The man's lips are soft and cushiony; the kiss tastes of flowers. He is beautiful, Lily thinks, watching him return to the crowd, wondering at the splendour of this night, the colour of love and dreams and laughter, so beautiful it makes her want to laugh and cry all at once.

'Come on,' says Vivienne, grabbing Lily's hand. 'Dance with me.'

And Lily dances in the dark by the fire, on and on, until it is time to stop.

CHAPTER TWENTY-SIX

Vivienne

Later, after midnight. They are sitting in deckchairs by the swimming pool drinking *bissap* and mineral water from small plastic bottles. The light from the end of Viv's spliff glows in the dark, mingling with the lights of the fire on the beach below and the party still in full swing. Tendrils of music reach them through the dark, the upbeat tones of Senegalese *mblax* mixed with hip hop and R&B. Viv is smoking and staring up at the sky, pinpricked with stars.

'The stars we see have actually been dead for billions of years,' she murmurs, as if to herself. 'So we're actually looking backwards in time.' She draws on her spliff, blows out smoke that plumes upwards in feathery swirls. 'Blows your mind, really.'

Viv's feet rest outstretched on a chair, a half-consumed plastic cup of *bissap* on the ground next to her. Beside her Lily has taken off her garland and is fiddling with the decorative flowers from it, shredding petals one by one. Viv turns to the other woman, watching the petals flutter to the ground. She takes another drag of the spliff, then stubs it into the patio concrete.

She realises Lily is speaking to her. 'It's strange that you'd come here,' says Lily, and Viv can tell that her counterpart isn't stoned anymore. As for her, she is still high, though the effects of the weed are wearing off. 'Wasn't it a risk?' adds Lily. 'You could so easily be found out, not by me necessarily, but someone else. Recognised, I mean.'

'Found out?' Viv gives a small laugh. 'Yes, I suppose so.' She stares at the pool, where a mixture of moonlight and the pool lights glint on the surface. Around each light swarms a haze of tiny insects. Viv sighs. 'Perhaps it's what I wanted, sub-con-sciously I mean—'

'Really?'

'Not really. Well, I'd be an idiot, wouldn't I?' Viv takes off her own garland and begins to play with the flowers, intertwining the stalks between her fingers. 'But something draws me back here, something I can't control.'

'The court hearing's in two weeks,' Lily says, looking over at her. In Lily's dark eyes there is a troubled look, as if she is genuinely concerned. 'When it *does* come out about your involvement, there might be trouble for you here.'

'I realise that.'

'What I'm saying is, well – I'm giving you a warning, if you want to leave the country. You'll have time before they call you as a witness.'

Viv pulls a strand of lily-of-the-valley from the garland and begins to pick the flowers off one by one. The tiny white pods detach easily, releasing their rich perfume into her warm fingers. She doesn't want to think about tomorrow just yet, or what might happen when Lily goes back to Dakar. Right now she is enjoying sitting here stoned in the dark, in this magical place far away from anywhere, with the wildest of parties going on – and yes, she likes Lily's company, too. A part of her wishes they'd met in other circumstances. Certainly in another life, she and the sister of Aimé Tunkara would have been friends.

'What was he like?' Lily says then, discarding her garland to the floor. 'My brother, I mean?'

Viv smiles. 'Aimé?' She throws the rest of the pods on the ground, where they scatter around her bare feet. 'Oh, he was lovely.' She looks over at Lily. 'Beautiful, like you. But that's not why I liked him. He was clever, you see, so clever.' She pauses to flick away a mosquito pricking at the skin of her arm. 'Nothing got past Aimé. He was the brightest person I've ever met, and kind, so kind. We became friends. You remind me so much of him, love.'

'You had a connection, didn't you?' Lily frowns, as if something is dawning on her. 'I mean, you were both around the same age. Aimé must have thought you were beautiful—'

Viv lets her eyes drift over to the beach where the music has been turned off and the revellers are gradually dwindling away to bed, leaving just a few people gathered around the dying fire. One person, it might be the Frenchman, Pierre, has brought out a guitar and is strumming a song as someone else taps a drum. It is cooler now in the early hours, the witching hours, as she has always liked to think of them. A slight wind is up off the sea, and the big leaves of the banana palms near the swimming pool crackle with a dry, rustling sound that reminds her of rain in a storm.

Viv closes her eyes, listening to the leaves and the song, which is simple and folky and possibly French, letting her mind drift to Aimé and his laughing smile, the dimples in his cheeks, the way he used to pause to think about something she'd said, some random question about a medical detail, averting his eyes to concentrate before delivering some unexpected answer that she hadn't considered. How she loved his quick wit, their conversations that bounced along, horseplay turning often to something more profound as they delved together into some subject or another. The mischievous way he delighted in the peculiar quirks of other humans, always pointing out the most random and hilarious of details, sending them both into paroxysms of laughter. And the way he used to gently rib her about her whiteness, the fact she was one of *them*. The English queen, Aimé used to call her jokingly. *La reine anglaise*. Still, for her, Aimé would have done anything.

'You mean, did Aimé fancy me?' Viv opens her eyes and gives a small dismissive laugh. 'Yes, I suppose so. I fancied him back, to be quite honest. Lord, when I think—'

'What do you think?'

Lily is staring at her with an odd look. There is a long pause. Viv can almost see the machine of Lily's mind working it all out in front of her, just as Aimé used to.

How alike her brother Lily is!

'Oh, that's it, isn't it,' Lily says, eyes widening. 'You two were friends, weren't you? Maybe more? I can see it now, the two of you. Maybe it was something beautiful? Was my brother in love with you?'

But Viv stands up and pulls off her sarong. A song drifts up from the beach, one of her favourites: *Harvest Moon*, by Neil Young. With a yawn, she stretches her arms out and hums along, looking up into the sky lit with stars.

'Do you want to swim?' she says, eventually.

'No, thanks.'

Viv stands hesitating, then decides something, and speaks, 'Wait there for a minute.'

'Why?'

'You'll see.'

As the song comes to an end, Viv makes her way through the dark to the hotel room, willing herself to breathe evenly, to regulate her heartbeat and walk on past the quiet guest huts to her own room, where she takes the last, newest section of her memoir from a suitcase and stares at it for quite some while.

Presently, she is back at the pool with the printed pages in her hand. Lily is sat forward on a deckchair with an expectant look on her face. Viv registers the dark semi-circles beneath the other woman's eyes, vestiges of a sleepless night, she supposes; or perhaps a more long-term exhaustion, brought on by... what? This investigation? The break-up of her marriage? But Lily Tunkara is strong, thinks Viv with a sudden rush of warm emotion that constricts her throat; determined and focused, verging on the heroic.

Given the past, it comes as no surprise that Viv likes her, and yet, the unforeseen strength of feeling almost paralyses her.

'Is,' says Lily, 'everything okay?'

How could she possibly know, thinks Viv? How could Lily understand the fact that *of all things* she is desperate to save herself, but Aimé is her weak point, and always was. And therefore Lily, Aimé's sister, has now become her weakness, too.

Viv hands the pages to Lily, who accepts them with a look of curiosity.

303

'What are these?'

'Just read.' Viv removes her flip-flops and sits down on the side of the pool, slipping into the water with a subdued splash. 'You'll see.'

Memoir, Part Five (continued)

Ngor, Dakar, *that year*:

It's via M that I make an appointment with someone called Aimé Tunkara, who, M informs me, is a medical student from Ngor village. In his spare time, Mr Tunkara leads a British Embassy-funded youth group promoting education for young people. M suggests it would be a good idea for me to offer English lessons to the community as part of the programme, and Mr Tunkara is willing to show me around.

'Lovely chap,' comments M with customary positivity. 'You'll be in safe hands.'

I alight from the silver DS on a square patch of sand surrounded on two sides by low buildings, on the third by a sparkling blue bay, and give Lamin, my driver, instructions to pick me up at five, to leave me there, which he does with a frown, looking back through the window of the car to check I'm okay. Then he pulls away, diplomatic flags waving in the sea breeze. It must be said that I do feel a bit disconcerted. It's exceedingly hot. A couple of traders stare from behind stalls selling tie-dye sarongs and sun hats. I swear their mouths hang open at the spectacle of my arrival, and well they might. Subtle, my arrival is not.

I watch the car depart, and to my relief a man emerges from a passageway between some buildings, smiling and waving. By my estimate, he's about my own age, a big, broad-chested man in a collarless shirt, rolled up sleeves contrasting with his very black skin, loose cotton trousers and open leather sandals. I like him immediately. He's very beautiful, but that's by the by. It's like he *shines* with something, I think to myself – kindness, intelligence, *gentleness*. I remember what M said: *You'll be in good hands*, and I can see why M might have thought as much.

'Madame Hughes?' the man says with a quizzical look.

'Yes, that's me,' I say. 'You look surprised.'

'Yeah—' He hesitates, then gives a wide grin. 'I was expecting an old woman.'

'Oh?' I begin to laugh. 'Why's that?'

'Well, an ambassador's wife? I figured you'd have to be elderly.' The man shakes his head, extending a large hand and laughing. The laugh is deep and hearty, making his eyes crinkle and sparkle all at once. 'I'm Aimé Tunkara, nice to meet you.'

'And you,' I say enthusiastically, shaking his huge hand. 'Call me Viv, Vivienne.'

'Viv-ie-nne.' He repeats the word in his French-Senegalese accent, somehow making it sound as if it should belong to some fifties film star. 'Nor,' he adds with a grin, 'if you don't mind me saying, did I didn't expect you to be beautiful.'

'Oh, thanks, but hardly!'

'Well, *Vivienne*, you better come with me.'

From the get-go, we get on. Aimé is twenty-four, he tells me as we walk together through the passageways, and in his third year of medicine at Dakar University. When I ask how a village boy managed to get so far with his education, he tells me of his efforts

305

against the odds to fund his studies via diving, fishing, and other small business schemes he's pursued since he was a child, as well as various scholarships and a British bursary fund.

'So I'm a fan of the British,' says Aimé. 'My dad died in a pirogue accident two years ago, and I knew then I'd done well, because it's up to me to support the family now.' He smiles. 'I was selling *thiof* at the market when I was eight, but then I'm lucky to be a boy. My sister will probably be taken out of school when she's ten, married off, the usual. At least I've been able to wangle an education.'

In turn, I tell Aimé about my own dreams of wanting to be a doctor, of my interest in tropical diseases, and how I've had to leave my medical studies in England.

'But I'm working on research now,' I say. 'Into malaria.'

'Well, maybe we can help each other, then,' says Aimé. 'People think disease is a fact of life, here – my people like to say it's God's will. I don't believe it, though; I don't think such needless dying is necessary. That's why I want to be a doctor.'

As we walk through sand passageways children come running up, and Aimé moves easily through the crowd, shepherding me along, shushing the kids away with gentle smiles and laughter. I'm charmed by the kids in their ragged clothes, charmed by this young doctor's pleasant way with them. Appalled too, by the rates of disease that Aimé recounts in precise annual figures: sky-high annual death rates from measles, diabetes and malaria that would be a scandal in England, in Europe, if they were reported.

'It's like African lives don't matter as much,' I say. 'How can that be?'

'As I say, it's a fact of life.' Aimé turns with a smile. 'We get lots of Europeans coming here, whites like you. They want to help, all of them.'

'But that must be a good thing, no?'

'Possibly.' He shrugs. 'Forgive me, but the trouble is, you *toubabs* never stay. You do enough to make yourselves feel good, then you go flying back to your home countries, never to be seen again. And the whole thing starts again.'

Aimé's words hit hard. I decide that under no circumstances will I be like those other *toubabs*, as Aimé calls them. I'm twenty-four years old. It's 1987 and the phrase 'White Saviour' hasn't even been invented yet. It doesn't occur to me to question the cliché of myself or my good intentions. I find myself wanting to prove this dynamic young doctor wrong, and I resolve right there and then to use Harris's research project and my fortuitous role within it to change things for the better.

It will be my purpose here, I'm thinking with ardent enthusiasm; my *raison d'être*. My marriage to John and his posting in Dakar, the research job, meeting Aimé… Suddenly, things click into place. It feels to me as if the hand of fate has been mediating all along.

Aimé shows me around the village youth centre, funded by the British Embassy, and the tiny clinic established by a Western charity, where he and a team of midwives from the village vaccinate as many babies as their allocated doses will allow, and do the best they can to treat malnutrition, measles and tuberculosis.

'But there's nothing we can do about epilepsy,' Aimé tells me evenly, 'or diabetes, or malaria. We just don't have the drugs. Imagine, nearly half the world's population live in places at risk of malaria transmission, and malaria caused six-hundred thousand deaths last year, but it's not considered important enough to research a vaccine.'

'Until now,' I say.

'Yeah,' he agrees, smiling, 'until this beautiful English girl turns up pretending to be an ambassador's wife.'

We laugh. Everywhere, the children follow us.

Later on, as Aimé is walking me back to the car, I blurt out: 'What if we test the malaria treatment here in Ngor, the one that's being developed?' I ball my fists and turn to him, overtaken by passion. 'With your help, we could find the families in the village, get the trials done, and your people would be the first to get the vaccine. Wouldn't that be something? We're *doctors*, Aimé, and we could change things, you and me. Do good.'

'Nearly doctors,' Aimé corrects me with a dubious look, raising an eyebrow. 'Well, you've big dreams, Vivienne Hughes, that's for sure.' Then his face breaks into a huge smile. 'But yeah, maybe we *should* aim for the stars.'

And that's how it starts.

CHAPTER TWENTY-SEVEN

Lily

For a minute or two, Lily holds the papers in her lap, watching Vivienne swim, listening to the sound of the sea. After a couple of lengths, the other woman comes to the nearest end of the pool and rests, hanging on the concrete edge drawing sharp breaths.

'I don't know why it didn't click before,' says Lily, eyes shining. 'It's obvious now, your friendship, I mean.'

'It was a different time.' Vivienne rests her chin on an arm. Water droplets roll down her face, trickling down her neck. 'These things were taboo.'

'You could have left John.'

Vivienne makes a puffing noise with her lips. 'You make it sound so easy.' She pushes back off the edge and treads water. 'When I married John, I was trapped for life, though I didn't know it at the time.'

'And if you had – known, I mean?'

'Oh,' Viv gives a sad laugh. 'Hindsight is a wonderful thing.'

Lily watches as the Englishwoman dives down and swims flat across the bottom of the pool, kicking her legs like a single fin. Blonde hair streams along her back, again reminding Lily of a mermaid. She seems to float underwater for a long time, almost too long, so that for a moment Lily wonders if she will ever come back up.

Lily mulls over the pages she's just read, replaying in her mind the story of Vivienne Hughes and Aimé, unsure whether to smile or cry at this new introduction to her dead brother who has, in the course of a few pages, become so much more than the shadowy half-memories of her childhood. She was, what, five years old when all this happened? Even so, Aimé chooses to mention her, of all people. *My sister will probably be taken out of school when she's ten, married off, the usual.* How glad he would have been, then, and surprised, perhaps, to see her now, a lawyer and a working single mother.

Lily smiles to herself, eyes filling suddenly with tears. If Aimé hadn't died, her own destiny would indeed have turned out exactly as he predicted. How ironic it seems, and how sad! Even so, she is so grateful for the gift of her brother brought to life, once and for all. Finally, she can see Aimé in her mind - no saint, true, and quite different to how she'd pictured him in her imagination. But nevertheless, as real and gloriously flawed as any other human being, laughing, loving, grappling his way through this peculiar thing called life, just like anyone else.

Lily reaches down for the water bottle and raises it to her lips, draining the last of the lukewarm liquid. Vivienne is still swimming, that deep dive again, her easy strokes hardly rippling the water. Lily leans back in her chair, closing her eyes. She is exhausted.

CHAPTER TWENTY-EIGHT

Vivienne

The pool water is soft and warm on Viv's skin. She dives, then swims a strong crawl, banishing the final haze of weed, mind full now of memories that arrive thick and fast. As if it were yesterday, she can recall the immediate connection that existed between her and Aimé Tunkara, two baby souls drawn together by their dreams and ideals. Soulmates, though she has never thought to believe in such things. In another life, well, perhaps she and Aimé Tunkara would have been quite something: lovers, life partners, husband and wife, even. Together, they could have toured Africa, making love and curing disease. She has to admit that, even now, the idea is intoxicating. But of all things, any attraction between them was forbidden. Even a whisper of an affair between a village boy and the British ambassador's wife was unimaginable, a scandal of mind-boggling proportions.

Besides, how young she was then, and how innocent. Back then, she hadn't understood what love was. If anything, she thought love was hard, love was cruel, love was something to be endured. How could their pure and beautiful meeting of minds, of souls, be classed as love?

So they became friends, because that was the extent,

undiscussed, that they could be together. True friends. Viv dives deep again, floating underwater, holding her breath. She is unable, she realises, to cry underwater, and a good thing, too. Of all the men who ever pursued her, and there have been so many over the years, Aimé never asked her to be anything but herself. He never tried to touch her, or fuck her, or abuse her or use her, like Harris and John. No. Aimé just wanted *her*.

Viv comes up, breaching the surface and exhaling, then floating on her back, eyes closed. If Aimé Tunkara loved her, and Viv loved him back as deeply, of that she is certain. And how it hurts to think how she *used* him and failed him. For heaven's sake.

A memory, of swimming with Aimé on the island of Ngor. It must have been nearly a year since they'd met for the first time, a week, perhaps, before the accident. Down in the ravine, the sun hits the pool surface, creating a fissure of light reaching from the rocks to the turquoise depths still rippling from the impact of her body. Viv can almost see the bottom, but not quite. After the first jump, she is dripping wet, panting and laughing, adrenalin still coursing through her body.

'You should try it,' she shouts to the doctor when she gets back to the top of the cliff, still out of breath, wiping the drops from her eyes, 'it makes you feel alive!'

'I used to when I was young,' remarks Aimé, staring down dubiously. 'Young and foolish.'

'You *are* young, silly.' She laughs. 'And now?

'Now, well—' Aimé is laughing. 'What if I die? All that studying and effort, and the great African doctor dies for nothing!'

'*I* didn't die,' Viv says. 'In fact, it was amazing.' She twirls around, whooping. 'Amazing!'

Aimé begins to laugh harder.

'Come on,' says Viv. 'We'll do it together. Hold my hand.'

'God, you're cool. Why the fuck are you the British ambassador's wife? How can that possibly be?'

'John's an idiot. John's a marriage of convenience.' Viv grins. 'I should have married you.'

'Yeah.' Aimé stares at her oddly. 'Wouldn't that be something.'

'Here.' Viv takes his hand, meets his eyes. Together they walk to the edge of the cliff.

'You're crazy,' cries Aimé, half laughing. *'Tu es folle!'*

'You can do it.'

'All right, all right.'

Together they jump, hand in hand, falling and falling downwards until they hit the water's surface with an enormous splash that ricochets upwards. For a minute or two the pool fills with ripples and noisy laughter. Then Aimé is holding her with muscular arms, water drops like crystals on his skin. Wet skin, wet lips. Adrenalin amplifies the rush. For a few minutes, the two of them kiss against the rocks, losing themselves. But then Viv pushes Aimé away with a gasp.

'I can't!' she cries out, almost in tears, swimming off. 'I really can't!'

At the memory of Aimé's words, Viv finds she has goosebumps. *The great African doctor dies for nothing.* If only she'd known what was about to happen, would she have carried on kissing him? Would she have thrown caution to the wind? Would she have followed her heart, in the end?

Viv dives deep, arms straight, pulsing her legs in a strong, horizontal mermaid stroke, hovering for a few seconds at the bottom of the pool with breath held. She lets her mind wander to that kiss, that single kiss, and the memory lingers with a jolt of regret. Viv feels tears prick her eyes. Without meaning to, she let Aimé down, when all she had ever wanted in the world was to bring him happiness.

Now she feels strange, *free*, somehow. Then it dawns on her. The bubble. The bubble is gone, the bubble is burst…

Viv comes up with a splash.

'Viv?' It is Lily, standing on the edge of the pool with a concerned expression. 'You okay?'

'I'm curious, love,' Viv says, ignoring the question. With one movement, she pulls herself out of the pool then sinks into a stretch like a dancer's, right arm to left leg, then the opposite, elongating her calves with fluid movements, then the tight muscles of her back. 'Why did you start investigating the case in the first place? Was there a reason?'

'It was the thirty-year anniversary,' says Lily with a shrug, returning to her deckchair, sitting down. 'It felt, somehow, like a milestone. And, I guess with Demba leaving… I felt restless. I suppose I wanted to *change* something.'

'Just like me when I was young.' Viv emerges from the stretch, sinks to a cross-legged pose on the poolside, where she sits staring at the still rippling water, then at Lily. 'Strange, isn't it. Then, when you get to my age, you care less – or else you know you're just a tiny helpless pawn at the mercy of the great cruel universe.'

'As flies to wanton boys, are we to the gods.'

Viv smiles softly. 'Indeed. Indeed.'

On the beach the fire has gone out. Everyone has disappeared

314

to bed, but the dark is full of noises – the sound of the waves, the scratch of crickets. Also, with the early hours of the morning, a cool sea breeze.

Viv stretches out on the concrete, staring up at the unpolluted night sky. Not once, not even on a dark night at Moon Manor, has she ever seen so many thousands of twinkly stars; the constellations of Orion, Taurus, The Great Bear and Gemini, twin souls of the sky, are clear as a map. It occurs to Viv that she must be still partly stoned as she drinks in the sight of the star clusters, so far away, so out of reach, so long back in time, like ageing movie stars reliving their fiery heydays to eternity. How marvellous!

Despite herself, she lets her mind move again to the past. Of all people, Aimé was not one to believe in fate, in things pre-destined, pre-written, in the ominous pronouncements of the soothsaying marabouts of his people. He always dismissed his countryfolks' habit of putting events down to God's will. Yet, Viv thinks now, she would like to imagine that somewhere in another galaxy, another universe perhaps, the two of them were written up there in the stars.

'In your memoir, you weren't lying, were you,' Lily says then, musingly, raising Viv from her reverie. 'You just didn't mention the part about my brother. Not until the last entry. My clients do it sometimes, lying by omission.'

Viv leans up on one arm, considering the statement. 'I couldn't bring myself,' she says, 'to write about Aimé.' She stops, thinking. 'I'd blocked it all out, all that. How much I cared—'

'And it was you in that photograph I found, with my brother?'

'Yes, Aimé was teaching me how to spearfish. I couldn't even

315

hold the bloody thing properly!'

'You were both so young,' continues Lily, as if, Viv ponders, she is addressing an audience. Is this how Lily is in court, she wonders, making her closing speeches? 'You had a horrible, abusive husband, *and* this Harris guy manipulating you as well. You'd been abused by men your whole life. Oh—' Lily draws a breath. 'Then there was this beautiful African doctor, your age, your intellectual level, a fellow idealist. He must have thought you were so beautiful. There was an immediate attraction between you two, wasn't there? You clicked, an absolute *coup de foudre*! But it was forbidden, shocking – you were the British ambassador's wife, of all things, and my brother might have been a medical student, but he was still a man from the village, *and* you were married. An affair, well it would have been a scandal on so many levels.'

'Yes,' agrees Viv. 'It would. Such a thing was impossible.'

'But you two became best friends,' says Lily, 'colleagues, crusaders, I guess, in this quest to get the drug approved. You told my brother that Aspiximal would help the villagers, that you'd both be helping change their future.' Lily pauses, shaking her head. 'Pssht, you both dreamed big, but in doing so you both lost sight of the reality of the situation. Didn't you realise *you* were playing God, Viv? In the very worst way?'

'No, no,' Viv murmurs to herself, 'no, please, I can't talk about this—'

'Then the children started getting ill,' Lily insists. 'And, well, everything went wrong, didn't it?' Lily stops talking and seems to wait for Viv's reaction. 'Didn't it?' she adds in a soft voice.

Viv's face crumples. A strange, tormented noise escapes

from her throat.

'I never meant them to die.'

She can hear her voice, hoarse and cracked. She turns away from Lily, hugging her knees, burying her head, feeling her heart turn over with one slow, fearful jitter. She has spent so long burying the truth, it has ceased to be real. Now the time has come to face up to its reality. Viv lifts her face and turns to look straight into Lily's eyes.

'It wasn't your brother's fault,' she whispers. 'I was the one who persuaded him to help me organise the trials. I made him think we could change the world. I'm a bloody fool.'

Viv gets to her feet and stands hands on hips, looking out to sea. The dark sky is slashed with silvery streaks of blue black. It must be nearly dawn.

'And the baby,' says Lily, 'the pregnancy you talked about in your diary, was it Aimé's?'

Viv turns, blinking back tears. 'Oh, no.' She shakes her head. 'No, no, no, that was Harris. Believe me, Aimé and I were the picture of bloody innocence.' A pause. 'In the end, I suppose I was pushed and pulled between Aimé and Harris, between good and evil, if you like.'

'And you chose?'

'Evil. Evidently, I chose evil.' Viv flicks away an insect, staring into the middle distance. 'Oh God. Your brother's name was Loved and he *was* loved.' Her voice breaks. 'By me. I loved him.'

'Past participle.'

'Sorry?'

'Aimé's name, it's the past participle. It's always struck me as sad, as if he were always in the past tense.'

It is Lily's turn to sigh. On the chair she is leaning forward, arms on knees, observing her with a quizzical expression. What she is thinking, she does not say. But there is no point pretending anymore, Viv knows.

'What exactly happened that night?' says Lily. 'Will you tell me the truth now?'

Viv nods. She is no longer stoned, but clear cold sober. The party is over. Dawn has broken. They have been up all night.

'Come,' Viv says, collecting herself, 'let's go find some breakfast.'

CHAPTER TWENTY-NINE

Lily

The clock on the wall says six thirty-five in the morning. The air is cool, the light not yet quite up. In the restaurant, a sleepy-eyed young man in surf shorts is laying out tables. There is the chink of cutlery and a smell of brewing coffee, tiny parrots are already trilling and fluttering about in the woven rattan roof. Low from a speaker comes the chilled-out rhythm of Youssou N'Dour's *Woo Ma*.

'Oh,' says Vivienne with a small smile. 'This takes me back.'

'To then?' asks Lily, tentatively. 'I mean, to the eighties?'

'Where else.' Vivienne stands listening with a faraway look, picking at a cuticle. 'I used to love dancing down at the Tuli,' she adds in a soft voice. 'So did your brother, when I could persuade him to come. He was quite the mover.'

For a second or two, Vivienne's eyes meet Lily's, her face breaking into the most radiant smile Lily has ever seen. Suddenly Lily has a vision of the two young would-be lovers dancing there at midnight in the Tuli Club, star-crossed, hidden by the lights and the crowd and the warm darkness.

'I bet it was beautiful,' murmurs Lily, wishing she could go back and change things: stop time, perhaps.

Vivienne sighs. 'It was,' she murmurs. Then she shakes her head, appearing to gather herself. 'Heavens, love, you must be starving!' She re-knots her sarong around her waist. 'I'll see if they can bring us something out.' She strides towards the kitchen.

The song ends and Lily sits down at a table, hungry now after the *nuit blanche*, the party, and the joint. She is aware that the two of them are still dancing, too, though now it is an easy tango of minds and memories. When Vivienne returns a minute or two later, the waiter appears with a tray of coffee, warm milk in a jug, slices of fresh baguette sliced lengthways, and a saucer of butter pats wrapped in foil. There is raspberry jam, too, and European cheese.

Once they have settled in with their food, Vivienne Hughes begins to tell the last part of her story. Lily listens, sipping at her coffee.

Vivienne says:

The Tuli Club, let me help you imagine it. A vast room of chandeliers and red velvet, backed by a sweeping mirrored bar. Disco lights. Super Diomono pumping out merengue rhythms from a packed dance floor. Outside, it's pouring with rain, but there's a swimming pool surrounded by parasols, and a covered area with a plastic roof and tables dotted around a lush garden of tropical palms. I spy John sheltering from the downpour, chatting up one of the handsome young musicians from the band.

I wander over.

'Darling,' I say, raising my voice against the loud rat-a-tat of the rain pelting on the plastic roof. 'When do you want to go?'

'Go?' says John. 'The party's just getting started. I'm having a good time.' He glances at the guy, then at me. 'Anyway, isn't Harris supposed to be here?'

'Yes, he's here.'

My husband gazes at me with a half-smile, then glances at his watch.

'Let's stay an hour or two then?'

'Okay,' I agree, and leave him to it.

I check my watch. Harris is busy talking to an embassy colleague at the bar. I'm avoiding him, though I know he'll come over soon enough. I've said I'll meet Aimé outside the club at one am, and it's half-past midnight. The party's only getting wilder. More and more people keep arriving, and the place roars with music, laughter, people's chatter. It feels like the whole of Dakar's party crowd is there, and people are drunk, high, intoxicated, perhaps because the atmosphere is so hot and steamy from everyone in their soaked skin and clothes coming in from the rain. In the pool, couples are making out quite blatantly in the water; others are dive-bombing in, whooping and yelling.

There's a back entrance reached through the garden. I check to see that no one's watching and slip outside to a back street, where I stand waiting by the fence. I'm getting soaked, but for some reason I stand there enjoying the sensation of cool raindrops on my skin after the humidity of the club.

Aimé isn't here yet. There's a security guard and a couple of people snogging. No one bats an eyelid. It's the Tuli you see, and anything goes at the Tuli Club.

Then I hear the grumble of a motorbike. It's Aimé. I watch him approach, turn off the engine, kick down the stand.

'Hey,' he says, grinning. 'Sorry I'm late.'

321

'It's okay.' We fist bump, and he climbs off the bike.

I glance around, but the guard is brewing a kettle over a fire with his back turned, and the couple has disappeared. We're alone. In the lights from the club, raindrops glisten on Aimé's face. He wipes them away with a hand.

'You okay?' Aimé says.

'Sure.' I give him a smile. 'Glad you're here. Come on, let's get out of the rain.'

Together we slip back inside. Everyone's drunk or high. No one notices us sit down at a table in the corner, and if they do, they don't care. Or so I assume.

'I'm glad you came,' I say again, but then I see his face. 'What's up?'

'You know that boy you vaccinated the other day.' Aimé is frowning. 'Oumar.'

'Yes. Oumar Sy.'

'I've just got back from his place. He's not well, Vivienne. I've made him comfortable, but something's not right. Another one—'

'Oh, shit.' I frown. 'How many is that now?'

'Three kids.' Aimé shakes his head with a worried expression. 'Which means we need to stop the trial.'

Though he is perfectly calm, Aimé's disquiet manifests in the way he taps his large hand on the table, tap, tap, tap, syncing with the rhythm of the rain on the plastic roof. It's something he does when he is thinking, or stressed. I watch his square-nailed fingers collide with the shiny metal, feeling my own anxiety rise and form solid in my chest. I lean forward, keeping my voice low.

'We can't stop! We're contracted in. Harris would hit the roof!'

'I'm sorry, Vivienne, but I can't allow it. As a medical student,

322

I made a moral oath to conserve the safety of my patients. And I'm more and more convinced that this drug isn't safe.' Aimé bangs his hand on the table. 'Look at the side effects, Vivienne: vomiting, diarrhoea, and now this boy is fitting. Who knows if there'll be worse.'

'Please, Aimé, please let me sort this out—'

'No, no.' Aimé shakes his head. 'You said you'd ask Harris to stop after the first kid got ill, and he refused. I've told you and told you for weeks. Look, I—' He pauses, lowering his head with an odd expression, as if he's in pain. 'I love you, Vivienne,' he says, looking up, right into my eyes. He takes a long, deep breath. 'I love you, but I have to do the right thing. Do you see that?'

I stare back at him, taking in his words as my heart floods with misery. 'Please, don't.' I reach for his hand, but he jerks it away into his lap. 'Let me talk to Harris, if I can just persuade him—'

'No.' Aimé stands up. 'I'm sorry. I'm going to the authorities.'

Before I can stop him, Aimé is striding off towards the exit. As I watch him go, I feel a sense of rising dismay. Then a new presence by my side.

'You need to do something about that man.'

It's Harris. My stomach lurches with dread.

'Sorry?' I turn. Harris's face is dark with rage. 'It's nothing,' I stumble out, 'we, we were just having a drink.'

'Nothing? I heard what he said. He needs to be stopped. That *bloody* African, always interfering – what the hell does he know about any of this, with his tin-pot education?'

As usual, Harris's racism leaves me breathless. Before I can protest, he grabs me by my upper arm, so hard it hurts, and

323

wrenches me through to the interior of the club.

'Come with me, we need to talk to him.'

'Please!' I crane my head back, looking for my husband. 'What about John? We can't leave him here?'

'Fuck John.'

Outside Harris pushes me roughly into the passenger seat of the embassy car. He starts the engine, though I don't know how he's got hold of the key, maybe from John. The rain is hammering so hard on the roof that it fills the car with noise. I wrap my arms around myself in my thin silk dress, shivering not because I'm damp and cold, but because I'm afraid, of Harris, of what he's going to do. Harris has a wild look in his eyes, a look I recognise.

'Where are we going?' I shout.

'We're going to find that *fucking* doctor,' Harris shouts back.

My watch says twenty-five to three. I pull my seatbelt across and slot it down into the clip. On the windscreen, the car's wipers can't keep up with the torrents of water hurling themselves at the glass. As we turn onto the main road, its headlights flicker and die.

I peer out of the windscreen, but it's so dark, I can hardly see anything. Harris hits the accelerator and I know he's going fast, too fast. I grip the sides of the seat with my hands, digging my fingernails into the fabric. My heart's thumping in my chest. Then I spot the weak glow of a single headlamp. It's Aimé on the motorbike in front of us. He's just a dark figure hunched over the handlebars, but to me his broad-shouldered form is unmistakeable.

'Please, Slow down, Harris!' I'm shouting at the top of my voice. 'Slow down!'

Everything seems to happen in slow-motion. As we come alongside the bike, Harris swerves the wheel of the car as if he's trying to overtake, or worse, knock the bike off the road. He winds the window down.

'Oi!' he shouts. I see Aimé turn, eyes wide with surprise. 'We need to fucking well talk, doc!'

I see my friend's mouth form the words: 'What's happening?'

'Aimé!' I shout.

But it's too late. The car's swerving in the mud towards the bike, together, apart, together again. There's the jangling, twisting, bumping, sickening sound of metal on metal. In a daze I see Aimé's motorbike, driverless, skitter off across the road into the dark. There's a thump followed by a judder and a loud bang. Silence.

And then I'm shouting, shouting, scrambling out of the car, leaning over my friend and shaking him in the blood and mud and petrol and rain.

'Aimé, Aimé! Wake up!'

My ear's pressed to his chest and I'm crying out, sobbing and pleading, please, *s'il vous plaît*, would someone fucking call an ambulance, please, please, *help us*! I tip Aimé's chin, clear his mouth with my finger and breathe, pump, breathe, pump with all my strength against his big chest for what seems like hours, over and over, until I'm exhausted and soaking and sobbing, hair plastered to my face, rain pooling on my best friend's lifeless face as I try to breathe the life back into him.

Until someone from the gathering crowd has to drag me off kicking and screaming, *No, no, no, no!* in the face of the ambulance wail looming through the dark.

And amid the flashing and noise and the sunless half-light of breaking dawn, as I'm pulled to my feet by a group of strangers, I watch the motionless body of Aimé, my friend – my *love* – being stretchered by the paramedics into an ambulance.

And only then do I realise that Harris has disappeared, and John stands in his place, staring, just staring, without saying anything at all.

Vivienne stops talking, eyes feverishly bright. She sits very upright, tanned arms wrapped to waist, shivering slightly. When she blinks, a single tear rolls down her left cheek, then another, then another.

Lily, too, finds she is crying. She leans over the table and takes Vivienne's hand, staring at their two skin colours black and white, united in contrast. 'Hey,' she murmurs. 'It's all so utterly sad.'

Vivienne sniffs, squeezes Lily's hand back. 'I'm sorry.' She gives a watery smile. 'He was your brother. At least I got to know him, but you never got the chance.'

'I've always felt so guilty, that my success happened because he died.'

'If there's one thing I've learnt,' says Vivienne, 'it's that you can't change the past. It's what he would have wanted, love, I can tell you that as God's own truth.'

Silence. The spectre of Aimé hovers between them, real now, thinks Lily, more real than she has ever thought possible. She looks away from Vivienne through the restaurant arches to the sea and sky, like an artist's wash now it is morning – burnished with gold and pinkish blue as a tiny, semi-circular sun rises beyond the darkened line of the horizon. A single bird wings its way in silhouette, reflection doubled in the water. She can hear the gentle wash of the waves on the shore like tinkling glass. The beauty and the sadness brings a tightness in her chest. Lily balls her other fist, willing the tears away.

Eventually, Vivienne removes her hand and from somewhere produces a tissue, which she spends some time snuffling into. Then she blows her nose, rubbing her eyes, gathering herself, and pours coffee from the jug into a cup. She adds milk, stirring slowly with slow movements of her slim, ragged fingers. The British woman has stopped crying, but the tip of her nose is flushed red and her eyes are raw, giving her a vulnerable look. She seems different, thinks Lily, softer, somehow. Almost as if, from behind a veil of secrets, the real person has emerged along with the confession.

'It's strange,' Lily says. 'For the first time I feel as if my brother lives for me. I can imagine him now, where I never could before.'

'I'm glad,' Viv gives a small smile, 'there are some small mercies, then.'

In turn, Lily helps herself to coffee, adds two sugar cubes. She takes a breath, and speaks, 'What happened to Harris?' she asks.

'He fled the country,' Vivienne says with bitterness. 'Just upped and left without telling anyone. The trials were stopped immediately, of course. John hushed everything up, got M to clear up the loose ends with the police, and pay off the families.

'John and I both had something on each other you see,' continues Vivienne. 'I knew about John's philandering with the local boys, and he knew about the trials and my relationship with Harris – if you can call it that – which he tolerated, even greased the wheels of, if you ask me, because it let him off the hook in terms of our marriage.

'So it was all John's plan. I took the blame for the crash, M dealt with the media, and John and I were ushered quick sharp out of the country by the FO. No one was to mention Harris's involvement, as this pointed to the drug trials. It was a scandal, but not *as much* of a scandal as it could have been, do you see? It didn't even reach the British papers, can you imagine? Damage limitation, as M called it, though he didn't know all the ins and outs. M was always kept on a need-to-know basis.'

Lily stares into Vivienne's wide blue eyes, frank now as she gazes back, sipping the coffee, which is strong and sweet. She understands now that the Englishwoman has been fleeing these events, these memories, all her life. Lily would like to know more. If she understands most of it, still she has lingering questions.

'Do you think Harris deliberately mowed into Aimé's bike, or did he just mean to scare him?'

'I don't know.' A shadow passes across Viv's face, and she frowns. After a long pause, she says, 'But Harris was a cruel man, and impulsive, and racist. That was the question I'd have asked, if we'd ever spoken again. But I was scared of him, too.'

'And the police, they did nothing!'

Vivienne sighs. 'The one thing I learned early on about Africa is that – at least back then – death was easy. African lives were disposable. Aimé said it himself: *Death is considered God's will*. And so the whole case just got buried beneath a mountain of paperwork.'

Lily shifts in her chair, mulling Vivienne's words.

'And don't forget,' Vivienne adds, 'in those days, you know, the whites were gods.' She shakes her head with a pained expression.

'It's like we could do anything, no questions asked. We just strolled on in and demanded things, and people did it – the police, the government, whatever. It's shocking now, to think that I didn't question it – no one did.'

Lily inhales, then exhales, feeling a flush of dismay because she knows it is the truth. For so long, the Senegalese were at the whim of the white man, the French, the Dutch, the British.

'It's hard to hear,' she says, 'but you're right. It still *is* like that sometimes, to some extent.'

'Your brother was an exception; he asked questions – and look where it got him. Of course,' continues Vivienne, 'John and I lived under the shadow for all those years afterwards. John was bitter, said the whole affair had ruined his diplomatic career, and blamed me. Anyway, Harris wrote to me last year, asking to meet. I didn't go; I couldn't bring myself to face him, but John must have found the letter and gone to see him in secret, to have it out.'

'Oh?'

'Yes. When I went to Oxford a few weeks ago, to try to find Harris, they told me he'd died. Two weeks before my husband committed suicide.'

'You think John killed Harris?'

'I think Harris was dying already – his liver was screwed from a lifetime of drinking – and John eased his way out, yes.'

'Then killed himself?'

'Yes. Harris had been blackmailing him for all those years, you see. My husband had had enough – that and been living a lie, I expect, of pretending to be happily married when he was as gay as a march hare. And good riddance. Two bad men, they

329

deserved everything that came to them.'

Lily feels suddenly exhausted. She contemplates the scattered breakfast things, then the restaurant, busier now with a few other tourists, then the sea, pale pink all over.

'Lily,' Vivienne says, 'do you think you can ever forgive me?'

Lily turns her eyes to the other woman. 'Forgive you? Isn't it more whether you can ever forgive yourself?'

They get up to go, make their way through the restaurant, past the swimming pool to where a gravel pathway leads through reception to the car park. The air is already heavy with heat. Now that the sun is up, the whole place is suffused with golden light. At the front desk, a girl in a batik headscarf is turning on the computer; the sound of the machine whirrs and bleeps into life.

'What now?' says Vivienne, coming to a halt, turning to face Lily. 'Are you going to turn me in to the police?'

Lily sighs. What is Vivienne asking, exactly? Is she to call the authorities right now, drag Vivienne Hughes down to the police station, and have the British woman arrested for assisting in a decades-old crime of causing several children's deaths in corrupt drug trials? The measure seems crude, at best. As far as Lily can understand, the apportionment of blame in this case remains ambiguous. The moral implications – of intention versus action – stand at odds with any legal ones.

'They weren't your trials,' Lily says. 'You didn't knowingly damage those children. You could still be the whistleblower, you know, about the big pharma and what they did and are still doing in Africa.'

Vivienne Hughes is silent. She drops her gaze, clasping the fingers of her right hand into her left so that her hands flutter and twist. Lily watches as she lifts a thumb to her mouth, biting the cuticle with a savage movement of her teeth. A bright bloom of blood against tanned skin.

Finally, Vivienne speaks, 'Christ. You mean, actually put myself forward for punishment?' She shakes her head with an ashy laugh, sucking at her finger. 'Lord.' She lifts her face to look at Lily, forehead creased.

Lily shrugs. 'It is an option, yes. You testify in court. We get justice and compensation for those families.'

'But I burnt all the medical records of the trial, put them on the fire – they implicate me and, more importantly, Aimé, and that's the last thing I wanted—'

'Then it's probably a good thing.' Lily retains a blank expression. 'We should agree,' she says, 'to protect my brother, whatever happens. Do you agree, Mrs Hughes?'

'You mean—' The other woman stares. 'You mean, adapt my evidence?'

'Exactly.' A pause, during which Vivienne slowly nods. 'We'll have your testimony about Atlantis Pharmaceuticals,' continues Lily, 'and there'll be a paper trail of the trials somewhere; there always is. You might be punished, yes, but not for the car crash, because you weren't driving, and they can't throw you in prison for being a pawn of big pharma. The most a Senegalese judge would lay down would be a large fine. But by telling the truth, you are set free – morally, spiritually.' She fixes her eyes on Vivienne. 'I get the impression this is important to you?'

'What in heaven's name gives you that idea?' But Vivienne is smiling, frowning. The effect of the morning light is such that her eyes glow deepest blue.

'Just a hunch.' On an impulse, Lily grabs Vivienne's other hand, and squeezes. 'You can change things, even now, and we protect Aimé. His name is sacred; it will be our secret. Don't you see? *You* can orchestrate justice. It's a sacrifice, a redemption, if you like. You can still be redeemed, Vivienne.' It is the first time Lily uses her full forename.

'Your brother used to call me that. Viv-i-*enne.*'

Lily smiles. 'Aimé loved you,' she says. 'So let's do this for him.'

CHAPTER THIRTY

Lily

Six months later

It is another morning, a weekend, and the house smells of coffee and rain. In the garden, the earth pathways are still dark red from an early downpour, speckled with glistening drops from the overhanging date palm. Beyond, the sea is green-grey with cloud.

Lily is engaged in folding the clothes from the washing line. In the corner of the sofa, Mia is curled writing a story in a notebook. Lily is helped by Piretta. One after another, they take a garment each and segment the sun-hard cottons into neat rectangles on the table, first the worn wrappers that Lily wears around the house, then the girls' clothes, then tea towels, underwear, sports kit.

Finally, Lily's business clothes that she wears to the office and to court, the smart wax ensemble she wore the other day swirled with psychedelic patterns, vivid now in the half-lit room. And the girls' school uniforms. She will need to iron them before Monday, Lily reminds herself. She finds she is grateful to iron for her daughters, for simple tasks, for the easy, humdrum normality of everyday life.

She listens to the easy randomness of her daughters' conversation. Mia has stopped writing and is talking about bees, 'You know, a hive of bees can produce fifty whole jars of honey.'

'I read that there's a tiger bee,' counters Piretta, teasing her sister, 'which is an endangered species, and a lizard bee.'

'And a disguised tree bee,' adds Mia, 'whenever they fly, they're camouflaged.'

'Like an undercover bee?'

'Yeah, a spy bee.'

Their peals of laughter linger in the air.

After a while, Lily pauses the household tasks to go to the kitchen, where she brews more coffee. Outside the kitchen door, a bird shrills loudly, a sunbird, probably, or one of the tiny yellow-bibbed tinkerbirds that flit in and out of the greenery. In silence Lily checks her watch and brings the new cup into the sitting room. The time is noon exactly. She flicks on the television, over to the lunchtime news.

'The family of an Ngor man killed by a British expat have finally found justice, thirty years after the incident,' the news reader for Sene News is saying. 'Lawyer Lily Tunkara, whose brother Aimé Tunkara was run down by a car in 1987, finally saw key witness Vivienne Hughes give evidence before a judge at a court hearing in Dakar Thursday. Ms Tunkara said the case was "complex," but welcomed the final verdict of "case closed" handed out by the judge.'

Lily flicks the sound up as the screen pans to a shot of her and Vivienne Hughes emerging from the courtroom side by side. By a trick of the light, the tall, striking, linen-suited British

334

woman is momentarily flanked by two Senegalese military guards, before the men part and drift away, leaving Vivienne free. The screen flicks over to Lily's own hand holding out a photograph of Aimé. The young doctor is white-coated, smiling broadly with a stethoscope around his neck. Her big brother, ever the hero.

Lily sighs, flicking off the TV, swirling the dark liquid in the cup. She feels a jolt of sadness, but on the whole she feels good, renewed, now that it is all over. During the trial, Vivienne Hughes had stood up and testified to witnessing Dr Harris Burns, the English doctor, deliberately run Aimé's motorbike down. Vivienne's testimony included the drug trials, her own involvement and her husband's. Thanks to the revelations, the Senegalese government will, Lily has been informed, publicly request reparations from the British for its legacy of abuse – not just recognition of the harm wreaked by British doctors, but a hefty retrospective compensation package for all children and their families who were victims of the Aspiximal trials.

'Why *is* it that life can only be understood backwards?' Lily remarked to Lion the day before, over a shared slice of *mille feuille* at the Palais Patisserie. 'It's just cake!' she'd earlier pointed out to a teasing Ida, though with her formidable boss taking care of divorce proceedings, it seems she might not be a married woman much longer.

'Yeah,' Lion smiled. 'If only we were born wise, right, but I guess that's the whole point, learning, growing…'

And Lily is left with this thought, now, of life rolling backwards like a rewound film reel, backwards like a tape spool running out, clear only via the patterns formed by retrospect. How easy it is to see sense now. Back then, she was caught in the dense woods, like a blind woman.

And last night, she slept through for the first time in weeks, up there in the huge hardwood bed draped with a light cotton sheet, windows flung open to the noisy night, a deep dreamless sleep from which she woke refreshed, like a leaf unfurling after the rains.

'Oh, Mummy,' says Mia with an air of urgency. 'My wobbly tooth has come out.'

The child jumps up from the sofa, stands looking small and serious, holding up a tiny pearl of a tooth.

'Well, we must give it to the tooth mouse!' Lily reaches out her hand to take the tooth, which is jagged at the edge where it has loosened from the gum, and much tinier than it looked in the child's mouth. 'She'll bring you a beautiful new tooth.'

'No way!' Mia runs to the hallway mirror, examining the gap with excited noises. 'I still look like a pirate! Pirates have gaps in their teeth, don't they!'

'Yes,' Lily says, holding the miniscule tooth in her palm. 'Yes, they do, *ma chérie.*'

Of course, she still needs to sort out the divorce, but how far away that life seems now. Demba is gone, that much is clear, and she is glad. Lily has difficulty articulating what she feels. She knows only that now, in her beautiful home, alone with her daughters, she is happy, at long last. And the rest, well, the rest will come, *inshallah.*

Lily takes a glass from a kitchen cupboard, dropping Mia's tooth into the bottom for safe-keeping, tiny and pure, precious as a memory. Tonight, once the girls are asleep, she will bury the baby tooth in the earth, like a seed, as tradition dictates.

Lily gathers up the folded clothes in her arms, breathing in the floral citrus scent of the washing powder. After a moment, she begins to climb the stairs, one foot at a time.

EPILOGUE

It is July, mid-afternoon. Viv watches the last removal van lurch away up the rutted track. Once the vehicle has disappeared, she turns and makes her way slowly around the back of the house, then inside through the French doors.

She stands still, taking in the empty sunroom, humid now and dusty in the pooling sunlight. She wanders through to the lounge stripped of furniture and other paraphernalia, all strangely echoey and sad now – echoes full of memories that rise and come alive in the empty space. From outside comes the sound of the swans taking off, the heavy clap of wings hitting water.

Viv shivers, feeling cold despite the warm day.

Well, there we go then, she is thinking. The end of an era.

Out of the packing boxes, she has conserved tea bags, fresh milk, a mug and a kettle. *You'll always need a cuppa*, someone told her once, sharing tips about moving house, and Lord, weren't they right... People were so mundane, and yet so sensible, mostly.

At the tap, she fills the kettle, plugs it in, and waits for it to boil. She makes a mug of tea, pressing the teabag against the side with a spoon. There are no chairs left, so she goes to sit outside on the veranda step. The sky is overcast, sun just beginning to slip through a heavy sweep of cloud. In the breeze from the sea, the palms crackle and sway.

She raises the hot drink to her lips. From the silver tin – another thing kept within arm's reach – she takes out a cigarette paper, licks the edge and, for the first time in many weeks, rolls a spliff.

She lights up and takes a long puff, then another.

Later, she will drive the fifty miles south – south like a swallow – to the new cottage, to collect the keys from the estate agent. With its wisteria walls and rough stone fireplaces, its private footpath descending to the sea, its rambling garden containing hollyhocks and roses and night-scented jasmine, the place suits her down to the ground. She's sick of the empty rooms, the vastness of the space that she can never fill, and in the end Moon Manor fetched a vast amount at auction, the proceeds of which, combined with John's substantial estate comprising numerous sensible investment funds that surprised her, means she's been able to afford the cottage and a small holiday flat on Ngor island in Dakar, where she plans to spend a few months each winter.

With Lily's help, she has already put the wheels in motion to set up an education and health charity for the children of Ngor village, for which she hopes to get support from the FO and a number of international NGOs. Not an atonement, exactly, but an apology. She's not naïve enough to think that this alone can put right the mistakes of the past, but it's a start, surely?

She needs to get going if she is to collect the keys today. Still, she drags again on the spliff, taking her time, observing a stray dog-walker wander onto the footpath along the beach, a child by the looks of it, with a golden retriever on a lead. There's no right of way down here across the private land, but she doesn't have the heart to go and tell off the teenager and his dog. No, Moon Manor is not hers any longer. There are too many regrets here, and too many reminders. She probably should have moved months ago.

She thinks of Lily Tunkara, with whom she has been staying in contact via Skype. Just the other night, Lily called to check how she was doing.

'Fine thanks, love,' Viv told her. 'A new start, and all that.'

'We'll have to come to visit you,' Lily said, 'if we can get a visa.'

'Oh, that's good news.' Viv felt pleased, offering to do the necessary paperwork. 'Well, in that case,' she'd added cheerfully, 'I'll prepare the spare room.'

A shaft of bright sunlight pours suddenly from the sky. Viv lifts her face to it, closing her eyes in the warmth. With the effects of the spliff, her mind loosens and wanders from thoughts of Lily to Lily's brother and the past, these memories which loom close these days, ever-present shadows at the edges of her mind which seem to catch her at unexpected moments.

Time and time again, she sees a vision of her friend, Aimé clearly now, as if three decades is just yesterday. Sometimes he stands squarely there at the top of the ravine, joking around. Then they're in the water and he is kissing her. Sometimes in a snap, she's back to one of their conversations: his playful teasing, the shaking of his shoulders as he laughs easily, with relish, at some shared observation of theirs, uniquely funny only to the two of them.

Then comes the darkness and the pouring rain. She remembers Harris shouting, fingers clamped around her arm, shaking her. 'We're going to find that *fucking* doctor, Viv, this is *your* fucking problem.'

Then the wheels swerving in the mud and she catches sight of Aimé on his motorbike in front, lit up by the car headlights. He looks back straight into the glare, and she can see he is afraid. Their eyes meet and she mouths his name. *Aimé!*

And then with both hands she's grabbing the wheel from Harris and wrenching it sideways, left, away from her friend, and Harris is fighting, swearing; she can see the brake pedal loose beneath his right foot and the car swerves again, back and forth until finally it veers off in the wrong direction, towards the bike, towards Aimé...

No!

Her fault, then.

Knelt on the ground, as she tried so desperately to pump breath back into his body, she whispered it, in his ear, finally, 'I love you, Aimé.' But of course it was too late.

Aimé Tunkara, her equal, her best friend. The only man she ever really loved. And she killed him in the end.

'You stupid fool, Vivienne Hughes,' she exclaims out loud.

Viv stubs the spliff savagely on the concrete of the patio and downs her cup of tea to the dregs. Rising to her feet, she washes the mug in the sink, stashes it in her bag, and locks the kitchen door.

It is three o'clock. The sun has gone in again, and a wind is getting up off the sea. There is a funny, hollow feeling in her belly. She makes her way to the car, forcing herself to take deep breaths, forcing herself to not look back as, for a last time, she watches a swallow swoop and dip away towards the flat horizon.

ACKNOWLEDGEMENTS

My thanks, as ever, to my fantastic parents. Your unfailing encouragement and support mean the world to me. Individual thanks to my mum, for so faithfully reading my drafts, and always having the kettle on. And a very special mention to my dad, who's forever on hand with secateurs, jokes, wise words, and unwavering moral support (not forgetting second-to-none DIY skills). Hi Daddy! *waves*

And of course, to the rest of my wonderful fam: The Dood, Fatosh, Atlas, Maya - and Poppy and Marley, of course. I really couldn't do this without you all behind the scenes, rooting for me.

I am so grateful to my editors at different stages of this novel: Anne Hamilton, for your ever inspiring guidance and Friday afternoon pep talks; Claire Strombeck – you made me believe in the novel and myself! And Kieran Devaney, for your sharp, insightful edits. To Goran Baba Ali at Afsana Press and his partner, Aleksandra, fellow artists and literary kindred spirits, for believing in this book. To Patrick Knowles, thank you for bringing us together; to Andy Bridge, for your truly beautiful cover art, and to Ronit Lentin, for proof-reading.

Idi, merci, comme toujours, à toi et la famille. Jërëjëf.

And finally, to Bella, of course, because everything's for you, darling. Love mama x

Also by Afsana Press:

Whispering Walls

A novel by Choman Hardi

The U.S. invasion of Iraq is looming. Three siblings – two in London, one in Slemany – recall their troubled past. Stories of war, displacement, and coming to terms with the tragedies of a Kurdish family, all told from their different perspectives. *Whispering Walls* is a story of love, relationships, affection, and hope, with a cautious view of the future.

Release date: April 2023 / 304 pages

Paperback: £ 10.99 / ISBN: 9781739982454

Inner Core

Short stories by Miki Lentin

Death, anxiety, masculinity, family and children, social good and rocks. All things that touch the life of a middle-aged man. Miki Lentin goes in search of a rock with his child in Ireland, travels to Istanbul with his wife while sleep-deprived, recounts memories of working and growing up in Dublin and explores what it means to do good in society today. *Inner Core* portrays, in a minimalist tone, Lentin's life on the edge.

Release date: April 2022 / 168 pages

Paperback: £ 6.99 / ISBN: 9781739982447 – e-Book: £ 5.99 / ISBN: 9781739982430

The Glass Wall

A novel by Goran Baba Ali

The story of a teenage refugee who must re-live the pain of his past to enter a land waiting behind a glass wall. Will his story be convincing enough to guarantee his safety? A story of struggle and persecution, yet abundant in hope, *The Glass Wall* is a clear-eyed, emotionally honest account of displaced people, illustrating the true hardship that refugees experience.

Release date: November 2021 / 352 pages

Hardback: £ 14.99 / ISBN: 9781739982409